Rangoon 1941

Rangoon 1941

A Novel Based on True Events

by
S. Kella Samuels

2012

ISBN 0-9725323-3-1
ISBN 13 978-0-9725323-3-4

Publisher's Cataloging-in-Publication data

Samuels, S. Kella.
  Rangoon 1941 : a novel based on true events / by S. Kella Samuels.
  p. cm.
  ISBN 978-0-9725323-3-4
1. Burma --History --Japanese occupation, 1942-1945 --Fiction. 2.
Rangoon (Burma) --History --Fiction. 3. World War, 1939-1945 --India
--Fiction. I. Rangoon, nineteen forty-one : a novel based on true events.
II. Title.

PS3619.A485 .R3 2012
813.54 -dc23

Printed in the United States of America

Publisher Contact Information:
SKS Enterprises, Inc.,
PO Box 18696
Tucson, AZ 85731 USA
www.sksent.com

Contents

Foreword

Reports about Burma often appear in print and on TV and other media. Unfortunately, most such reports are inaccurate, in part due to Burma's censorship, lack of openness to foreign reporters, and the fact that most experts are not allowed into the country. As a matter of fact, for many years foreign reporters, writers, and multimedia organizations were kept out of the country by the government's refusal to issue a visa. In recent years, foreigners have been given visas for more than one week for tourism.

This situation spawned a number of highly incomplete and incorrect reports by incognito correspondents, whose only access to Burmese people was men who spend their time in the many tea shops that dot the cities. Correspondents do not have access to government officials. Instead, they pass on the misinformation learned in the tea shops, hotels, and from private individuals about events prior to and during the war and about post-war events. Most of their stories present the tale of how the small, ill-trained, and ill-equipped "Independence Army" (the Tatmadaw) fought the much bigger and better-equipped British and the tenacious Japanese Imperial Army to wrest independence by force from them.

Now, however, previously secret or classified British and Japanese documents have been released, allowing history to be re-written. With the release of these documents, it is time to take a look back and reassess the claims of the Tatmadaw, that it freed the country from colonialism single-handedly, protected the country from foreign designs in the post-war era, and promoted the welfare of the people. Actions by the leaders of many countries during War World II are also being re-assessed. It is in that same spirit that this book is being written. While it is written in fictional form, it is based on real events. Of course, some literary license had to be taken, to make the story interesting.

Just as this book is coming to press, interest in Burma is growing again. This is due to recent elections, changes in the government, and a new openness to the outside world. Most of the history of the battles fought in Burma and related events have been written by the victors or, at least, the

viii S. Kella Samuels

principals. Almost no literature exists in English by "natives" and others who lived through the entire war and the immediate post-war period. No numbers exist as to the number of Burmese, Indian, and other non-European people who died as a result of the war. Estimates range as high as one million. May this book help to right that wrong and mourn their loss.

PART I

The War Begins

Chapter 1
1941

The sun was setting in the west. Orange rays of the setting sun played on the brown muddy waters of the Rangoon River. The moon has just cleared the horizon in the east, glowing with a brilliant intensity and casting a magical spell on the land. The Harvest moon was so big and bright that one could read under its light. Festival lights had been lit, and people had flooded into the streets, heading for a multitude of *pwe*s [celebrations] and the night theater. It is the full moon of Thadingyut.

Thadingyut marks the end of the rainy season, the retreat of the heat and the humidity of Burma's summer monsoon. It also marks the end of Buddhist Lent and heralds mild weather. The hot days give way to cool evenings, and sometimes the morning can be refreshingly crisp. In Burma, these months of October and November are marked with Buddhist and Indian festivals. It is a time of great joy. The season is replete with celebrations, starting with Thadingyut, the festival of lights celebrated on the night of the first full moon of October. While Buddhists celebrate during the months of October and November, Christians celebrate Christmas in December. Then comes the New Year celebration—a happy time for all. The season also is a time of romance: young men's thoughts turn to girls, love, and romance.

Residents of Rangoon celebrated the relief from the monsoon season. Even amidst preparations for war—entrances to major buildings downtown were being sand-bagged, and glass windows and doors were being bricked over—residents eagerly anticipated the coming season of festivals, holiday, and *pwe*s. In the midst of all this joy, no-one in Rangoon in 1941 could imagine how swiftly life would change.

KOTA BARU, MALAYA, 2 AM, 8 DECEMBER

On a cloudy night that hid the moon, on the long sandy beach of passionate love, on the northeast east coast of Malaya, Mohamed Ahmed had spent a sleepless night, so he arose early to prepare his nets for the next day of fishing in the warm waters of the South China Sea. Even in the darkness he could make out many large objects out on the sea, close to the beach, and he wondered what they could be. Soon he heard voices, foreign voices that he could not understand, and then small boats approached the beach and landed heavily armed men. He stood in bewilderment as the men rushed past him in silence. They were part of the Southern Command of the Imperial Japanese Army, and they had come from Saigon, stealthily, to this lonely stretch of sandy white beach on the east coast of Malaya's Kelantan province.

Just behind the beach was a swamp, and beyond that the small town of Kota Baru, with swaying palm trees, dense tropical vegetation—and an airfield. The town was asleep, unaware of the peril that would descend upon it in a flash. From the pill box on the beach, manned by Indian soldiers in the British Indian Army, gunfire erupted. Soon the beach was engulfed by the staccato sounds of rifles, machine guns, Bren guns, tracer bullets, and exploding grenades. The invasion of Southeast Asia had begun.

The beach was defended by an ill-prepared, ill-armed regiment of Dogras of the 11th Indian Division of the British Indian Army. The sepoys of the regiment fought with tenacity, but they were quickly overwhelmed by the Oki detachment of the 18th Division of the Japanese Army. Almost all the defenders in the pill boxes along the beach were killed quickly. Further north, at Pattani in Siam, the Japanese made a second landing and swiftly moved south, crossing the narrow isthmus of Malay. The Japanese then headed for the British fortress at Singapore.

Just hours after Japanese forces landed on the lonely beach of Malaya, in the early morning hours of December 7th, the combined Japanese fleet attacked Pearl Harbor and savaged the American navy. In Rangoon, Burma, however, these events were far away. The city was tense, but its residents went about their daily life in the usual way. Not until 7 a.m. in Burma did

Radio Australia announce that war had broken out and Japanese troops had landed on the eastern shore of Malaya. "In the early morning hours, forces of the Imperial Japanese Army landed on the east coast of Malaya, at Kota Baru," the announcer intoned somberly. "They overwhelmed the coastal defenses and have moved north into Siam and south into Malaya." He continued, "Japanese carrier-based aircraft bombed and sank ships of the United States Navy in Pearl Harbor, Hawaii." Immediately, the station resumed with recorded music, providing no further details about this astonishing news. Word spread like wildfire among Rangoon's residents. Men gathered in small knots throughout the city. Rumors began to spread that there was a column of Japanese heading north towards Moulmein, Burma. The city's mood swiftly changed to one of high anxiety.

SAIGON, 23 DECEMBER

Supreme Commander of the Southern Japanese Army, Count (Field Marshall) Tarasaki, a member of the royal family, fervently desired to fulfil his emperor's wishes for the creation of the Greater East Asia Co-Prosperity Sphere. With the riches that these tropical lands contained—oil and minerals that the West had so imperiously denied the Japanese Empire—the emperor's armies could wage an endless war against the West and their colonies. Bangkok had given up the fight against the Imperial Japanese Army after a brief battle. On December 11th. Siam signed a treaty giving Japan a free hand in preparation for the war. Now the time had come to put the rest of the plan into action. Impatiently the Count Tarasaki awaited orders, sitting in his comfortable penthouse in Saigon's imposing Colonial Hotel.

The chief of staff to the Supreme commander awaited word from Tokyo on this great enterprise. Finally the radio came alive, and the signals officer decoded the message he received. The signals officer bowed deeply before he handed the long cable in code to the chief of staff. Normally it would simply be an order, but the Count was no ordinary military; he was a nobleman, a trusted confidante of the Japanese emperor, and the highest ranking member of Japan's army.

The cable noted that Singapore's fall was imminent, that the oil fields at Ballikpapan in Indonesia would provide the fuel for a prolonged war, and that thus it was time to implement the long-range plan to secure Southeast Asia, and deny the Burma Road to the Chinese and the Americans. Once the Burma Road was secured, the plan would be to launch an attack on Burma and India. The Indian Army, trained and led by the British, was fighting Britain's battles for her from Mesopotamia to Hong Kong. To wrest Asia from the colonial powers and secure Asia's resources for Japan, it was necessary to secure Burma and India. Therefore it was vital to take Burma soon. The cable then went on to provide the detailed plan that had been developed and to instruct that the Count implement it now. The Count nodded in the direction of his chief of Staff, then ordered, "Send the cable that I prepared, to the 15th Japanese Army in Siam."

SIAM, 23 DECEMBER

Even at this early hour, before sunrise, it was steamy at the 15th Japanese Army headquarters in Siam's city of Raheng. General Maida awaited instructions from the Imperial General Staff. He knew that the orders would be relayed through Saigon, the headquarters of the Southern Army, of which the 15th Army was a part. The bespectacled General looked confident and imposing in his formal uniform. The collar of his tan jacket bore a yellow emblem of three white stars indicating that he was a Lieutenant General of the Imperial Japanese army, and the cuff bore three red stripes and three stars. He wore jack boots freshly polished to a fine shine. His medals looked impressive. To add to—and connect with—his glorious Samurai past, an ancient gold-and-red Samurai sword hung loosely from his waist. He looked like he was going to a parade as he stood stiffly at the signals table. His favorite and sturdy horse was ready and waiting outside the building. The horse was to carry him across the border, to where the road stopped and the jungle started; the General would ride across the impenetrable Dawna mountain range, which had no motorable road. It was covered by dense jungle thick jungle of bamboo teak and tall hardwood trees and tropical vines.

The General's long wait ended. The code machine came alive. In the most secure naval code, 25 JN: the message from Southern Army Headquarters in Saigon, French Indo-China:

"MOST Secret"
NO 707
Date December-23-1941
From Saigon, Southern Army headquarters, Count Tarasaki, Field Marshall, Supreme Commander.
To Hayashi group, Headquarters 15th Army.
    33rd Division to attack from east. Cross Moei river near Kawkareik, attack Indian brigade defending Kawkareik-Moulmein sector. Principle object capture Moulmein. Stop.
    55th Division head north to Kyaityo. Capture Sittang Bridge intact. Stop.
    Retreat of British Army from Moulmein will be cut off by 55BT. Destroy 17th Indian Division with its 2 brigades east of Sittang Bridge. Reg. 212/33 will lead attack on bridge.

The British code-breakers at the signal corp on Signal Pagoda Road in Rangoon intercepted this signal, but they were so overwhelmed with signal traffic that it would take them days to decode all of the messages. As a matter fact, the Japanese delayed the messages to prevent their decoding before the Japanese could begin their action.

RANGOON, CHRISTMAS EVE

The new young Governor, a tall man of Irish-English heritage, was resplendent in his tropical white suit. His straight dark hair was parted in the middle. His wife, in a long evening gown, somehow looked uncomfortable.

She dutifully hosted the annual Christmas party at the Governor's mansion, but found the prospect of the receiving line unpleasant. She still had difficulty entertaining Burmese ministers, except for the Anglophile former Prime Minister U Po, for whom she had warm feelings, and especially his English wife.

U Po had a worried countenance. He bowed to her gently and asked to talk with her when it was convenient. She nodded. She found him engaging; he was a man who loved the country of his birth. Yet, he was an urbane Anglophile whose dress, manners, and deportment were those of a English country gentleman. While he had been Prime Minister, he had made an attempt to warn the nation about the hot-headed, young revolutionaries whose actions would unsettle the country and invite foreign power. She could trust him. He was not, however, the current Prime Minister; he had lost that position when he had lost a no-confidence vote in the Burmese Assembly. He had been replaced by—she felt—a rascal. The new Assembly was increasingly filled with Japanese sympathizers. She distrusted the new Prime Minister intensely. His diminutive stature, his broad, flat face framed with a shock of unruly black hair, his small, beady, shifty eyes, and his downward-turned mouth all hinted at a hidden cruelty. She sensed that he was unreliable; and she noted that even his admirers felt unsure of his intentions. Many Burmese politicians themselves thought that he was a scoundrel. That he was ruthless as well as ambitious was a given; she had overheard a conversation between him and the Governor over the grant of real self rule "or else."

The Governor's wife cast her eyes around the room. The women's brightly colored silk *longyi*s and thin chiffon blouses revealed more than they hid, she thought; they were rather bold, but this was the silken east. Burmese women had been liberated for as long as the kingdom had been formed. Besides, she had to admit, the bright colors of the silks added to the festive nature of the event.

Before the evening ended she sought out U Po, and they withdrew to a quiet corner, where he spoke almost in a whisper, "Your excellency, my information is that there is a plan by a group of revolutionaries to stage a revolt; they may attempt assassinations of high ranking officials as a prelude to the war. Please make sure that you take precautions, especially your family. . . ." A waiter brought drinks, interrupting the conversation.

In the old days this Christmas party had been an all European affair, but since 1937, with a grant of limited self rule, many "local" councillors, ministers, and members of the business community were in attendance. On this balmy evening before Christmas, the grounds were all lit up, despite the blackout that had been instituted in early December, after news of Japan's invasion of Malaya had been received. For the moment, the rumor of war and air raid seemed remote, and the place was lively. The Governor's mansion was a large British colonial building not far from the city center—on Ahlone Road, close to the Rangoon River. From the top floor, the river with its many ships could be seen to gleam in the tropical sun. The building was constructed of red brick, with a dome in the center and a turret at each end. The red brick front facade was Edwardian, and the center dome was taller than the ends, leading some folks to remark on its lack of character and architectural distinction. It obviously had not been designed by the great British architect Sir Edwin Lutyens, who designed so many buildings in New Delhi. The interior of the building, however, was resplendent, appointed entirely in Burma teak, the best teak in the world. It housed the giant Lion Throne of the last king of Burma. One room was the Durbar Hall where, in the past, the Prince of Wales had received local dignitaries who came bearing gifts—jewelry with the world's best rubies, sapphires, and jade. The grounds of the government house covered almost 1 square kilometer and were kept green by a retinue of Indian gardeners. The well-manicured lawn was also a tropical garden, filled with a profusion of multi-hued Burmese and southeast Asian flora.

On this Christmas Eve, glamor and festivities were the order of the day. Wars in Europe and China seemed distant. Europe had been engulfed in a bloody war for two years, and London was being bombed by the Luftwaffe, but the RAF fighter command had taken a frightful toll on the German Junkers and the Stukas. Britain alone resisted the German war machine and thwarted a cross-channel invasion. For more than five years, the Imperial Japanese Army, the "Kwangtung Army," had fought a brutal war against a poorly equipped and poorly led Chinese army. The Imperial Japanese

Army, in its quest to destroy China, had committed unspeakable horrors in Nanking, China. These events seemed distant, but contributed to an underlying sense of unease among those familiar with them. Thinking about the emergency meeting of his war council the following morning, the Governor limited himself to just one gin and tonic.

At the Club Martini—which allowed a few non-whites, the overflow crowd of revelers included the newly arrived young pilots of the American Volunteer Group (AVG). The Eurasian girls—brown-skinned girls, olive-skinned girls with names like Pinto, Calhoun, and Rawson, and a few light-skinned girls, some even with green and blue eyes—hung on to the young flyers who recently had arrived in the country to defend the Burma Road. The Americans wore brightly colored shirts. Some of the young flyers were so tipsy and raucous that they seized some of the rickshaws from the bewildered dark-skinned Indian rickshaw wallas, put the giggling girls in the rickshaws, and pulled them down the main street, drawing both frowns and bemused laughter from the people.

At the whites-only Silver Grille and the Mayfair—watering holes for the high and mighty white civil servants of Burma—the established topic of conversation was the behavior of the Americans. Some at the Grille were outraged. "What would the mothers of those young Americans from Alabama think of their young men mixing with other races?!" a rotund English matron gasped. Like the rest of the British, she was aghast at such behavior. The parties and drinking went on all night. One matron drily remarked, "I hope some of them will be sober enough to fly, should there be a air raid."

RANGOON, CHRISTMAS DAY

When the Governor arrived early at his morning conference, he sat at the end of a long shiny teak table and presided over a small group of decidedly glum men. The only attendees were his chief of staff, his aide-de-camp (ADC), and General Taylor, the general in command (GOC) of Burma, along with his Adjutant. Normally there would have a representative of the Executive Council of Burma, the Prime Minister. But the irascible Burmese

Prime Minister had been sent to Kenya, in Africa, after his arrest in Lisbon for sedition. Secretly, the Governor was relieved, as he really did not want the Burmese Prime Minister to be present while Britain's most sensitive military and security measures were being discussed.

The Governor was somber and downcast. He had a premonition that something terrible was about to happen. Dispensing with his usual formalities, he opened the meeting on a sour note, by summarizing the bad news. Looking directly at the GOC, he noted, "Since the Japanese landed at Kota Baru on December 8th, they have crossed the length of the Malay Peninsula from east to west and have rapidly advanced down the west coast of Malaya, on their way to the fortress of Singapore." Uppermost in the Governor's mind was the question of whether and when the Japanese Army would attack Burma in force and, if it did, where the attack would come from. He continued, "They now have sent patrols to Victoria Point, the southernmost town of Burma."

He turned to General Taylor and asked, "Why did the British Indian Army and Australia's crumble in Malay, allowing the defenses at Jitra to be breached and the Japanese Army to close in on the island of Penang?"

The General did not have a ready reply; he too had been surprised by the collapse of the British Indian Army. The Governor fixed his gaze on the General sitting two chairs away and told him to read the telegrams:

```
MOST SECRET
Cipher Telegram
Navel Cipher (XF)
Date 22.12 41
From: U.S. Consul Chungking
To B.A.D Washington 176
Subject: Threat to Burma.
C.C. Governor of Burma
Summary of J.I.C.


JAPANESE OBJECTS IN ATTACKING BURMA
     To  cut  military  supplies  to  China  by
cutting the Burma Road.
```

To establish bases in the Indian Ocean, for a future attack on India.

The capture of Burma will have dire consequences for China. It will deprive China of all supplies, deprive China of contact with the outside world especially America, and disrupt American supplies to China. It would deprive America of part of Burma's mining output, especially tungsten from Mergui and other metals from the Mawchi Mines.

Threat to India: it would deprive India of a third of its oil supplies through the loss of the oil fields at Yenangyaung and Chauk in central Burma. Capture of the oil fields of Burma will restore to the Japanese some oil supplies lost from Sumatra.

Possible avenues of attack:

1. From north Siam, through Kengtung in the eastern Shan States, to Meiktila on the Irrawaddy river in the center of Burma, and cut lower Burma from northern Burma.

2. From the Raheng/Tak province of Siam, across to Kawkareik in Burma, threatening Moulmein. First attack may come from Pattani in Siam, next to seize Victoria Point. Timing of the attack is uncertain--likely before Christmas--but will be part of the plan on Malaya and Singapore.

Throughout the conference, the Governor's young ADC had kept interrupting him with a steady stream of decoded intelligence messages. As the General finished reading the secret telegram, the ADC brought another newly decoded telegram: "With due respect, Sir, a cable from the Prime Minister."

The Governor read aloud:

```
MOST SECRET
Date 22-12-1941
From the Prime Minister, London.
    I have hitherto not troubled you. But I
want to tell you how much I and my colleagues
have admired your firm and robust attitude,
under conditions of increasing difficulty in
Burma. If Singapore falls, this will assured-
ly put more pressure on Burma. The defense of
Moulmein and Rangoon is of utmost importance.
    The Australian Prime Minister has refused
to divert to Burma the Australian Division
that was returning from the Middle East. You
must depend on the Indian Division and the
Tank Brigade that will arrive in February.
C.C.
C.I.G.S.
Foreign office
Colonial Secretary
V.C.N.S.
```

The Governor paused to let the enormity of the situation sink in, then turned to the General again. "General Taylor, you'd better give us the latest intelligence from the Burma border."

The General's report was not heartening. "I'm worried about the activity along the Siam–Burma border, particularly about the activities of the Bo's and other collaborators," he admitted. "Rumors are fueling panic in the civil population, and the labor situation is deteriorating, as many workers at the port of Rangoon are fleeing to India." He continued,

"Without Indian labor, the war effort and the defense of the country will suffer, and it will be nearly impossible to keep the Burma Road open."

The General got out of his chair and went to a large map at the end of the conference room. Pointing to the Siam–Burma border, he grimly noted, "Friendly Karen agents from the 'K' Force near the border report increasing enemy activity across the border in Raheng in Siam's Tak province, and in Burma itself, especially in the border towns of Kawkareik and Myawaddy," and then he admitted, "we are having difficulty finding Burmese dissidents."

The Governor responded curtly, "It is vital that we find these Thakin collaborators, because it is they who would guide the Japanese units and they who would cause havoc behind the strained British Indian defenses." To underscore the importance of the task, he added, "If the army intelligence cannot track them, Moulmein will be indefensible. And we still do not know whether the attack will come from the north at Kengtung or the south at Victoria Point."

The General replied, with some tension in his voice, "But, Sir, I do not know where the collaborators are, nor do I have further intelligence on the Japanese, . . ."

But before he could go on, the Governor interjected. "The war in Malaya is more than two weeks old, and we *still* have no idea if and when the Japanese will attack Burma? This is unacceptable." Giving the GOC no time to respond, he continued to express his dismay about military preparedness. "The news from Australia is not good either."

One of the telegrams that the ADC had been passing on to the Governor throughout the conference confirmed the Governor's fears: his request for reinforcements would be denied; the promised extra Australian Division, now onboard ships in the Indian Ocean, would not be diverted to Rangoon. Now he announced to his staff: "The Australian prime minister has refused to transfer the Australian division to the Burma front."

The Adjutant remarked hopefully that the telegram had promised one additional Indian division and a tank brigade in February and it was just a day's journey from there to Moulmein. The chief of staff, who had remained silent up to this point, interjected. "There has already been some unrest at Victoria Point and Tavoy. The Gurkha patrol defending the airstrip has encountered Japanese, and they found some boats nearby."

All heads swung in his direction. "Frankly, I think that the Japanese will attack the airstrip at Tavoy, as it is the most advanced air base and the most vulnerable. And if they do," he continued, "they may launch a seaborne attack on Moulmein." In order to soften his words, he qualified, "For what it is worth, though, my staff believes that any major attack would come from further north."

SIAM, CHRISTMAS DAY

To the north of the city of Bangkok, at Japanese 5th (Hikoshidan) air headquarters, near Phitsanalok in Siam's Tak Province, it was still early in the morning, but it was already getting hot. The dust would kick up soon, and even in December, it would heat up fast as soon as the sun rose. The cipher clerk received a telegram and decoded it immediately. He handed it to Colonel Takeda, deputy commander of the 5th Hikoshidan. It read:

```
Cipher Telegram
To 5th (Hikoshidan) Air Division.
70,30,25. Sentai Airfield, Tak Province
Break seal and follow instructions.
    With 60 Mitsubishi Ki-21, the Fighter
escort Nakajima Ki 27. Take off at 0930 local
time, assemble over Andaman Sea south of
Rangoon, cruise at 16000 feet in close V
formation. Primary Target: Destroy electric
power station, port, docks; render useless
American lend-lease supplies and storage
sheds around the port. Second wave to head
north to aerodrome and destroy Air facilities.
Render useless the Burma Road to China.
Machine gun personnel to cause panic in the
population. Stop.
```

> Destroy all RAF and AVG planes and personnel and anti air defenses. Stop.

Colonel Takeda took action quickly, giving the order to assemble for a raid. The Japanese pilots poured out of their quarters and headed for the operations room to receive final instructions. These men were battle-tested; they had sunk the unsinkable—the British battleships "Prince of Wales" and "Repulse" on 10 December. They were restive and wanted to see action again; the last time they had engaged in action had been two weeks ago. Shouting "Banzai! Banzai! Banzai!" they assembled in the operations room. The Air Division Chief went over the targets and wished his pilots good luck.

Soon the planes roared away to the west. The heavy bombers, laden with bombs, took off first and soon assembled over the Andaman Sea, south of Moulmein. The fast Nakajima fighters ascended after the bombers, also bound for the skies above Moulmein. The heavy bombers assembled in a V formation, the first a group of 4 and then groups of 3, and as they ascended they tightened their formation. Their main concern was the American P-40 Tomahawk fighters of the American Volunteer Group (AVG); their secondary concern was the RAF's slow Brewster Buffalos or aging Hurricanes.

Meanwhile, south of Mae Sot, near the Moei Rover, Colonel Sato—a tall, thin, and cruel-faced man, a battle-hardened veteran of the China theater—was in command of the 212th Regiment, part of the 33rd Division, the White Tigers. Proud of that regiment's performance in China, he now eagerly waited to add Burma to his citation and glory. His regiment would lead the main attack against the strongest British position; his regiment would cross the Belin river, head for Kyaityo, and cut off any retreat of the 17th Indian Division—a division composed of two brigades of Indians and Gurkhas that had its own pedigree as remarkable as that of Sato's own regiment. His regiment would swing into action at the moment the air raid began. Ahead of the regiment, lightly armed Burmese collaborators were in place; they would guide the regiment across the dense jungle, crossing the Dawna Range from east to west. Ahead lay Kawkareik and, further to the west, Moulmein.

RANGOON, CHRISTMAS DAY

At the British cantonment's Yorkshire Barracks, on the north side of Rangoon's Mingaladon airfield, Group Captain Phillips's family was preparing to celebrate their last Christmas in Rangoon. They were awaiting evacuation to the safety of India, but transport had been delayed. Across the road, at the airfield itself, airmen had things other than Christmas celebrations on their minds. At the Kyedaw airfield north of Rangoon, the duty pilots of the American AVG were dressed casually but were ready for a fight if it came their way. All the pilots were anxious, as they had heard about the impending Japanese attack. The airfield was home to two squadrons of the stubby, American-built Brewster Buffalos, derisively called "flying beer barrels." Rejected by the American forces as unfit for service by the U.S. Marine Corps, the Buffalos had been diverted from the Dutch air force and then passed on to the RAF. The airfield also was home to the P-40 Tomahawk fighters of the AVG.

Group Captain Philips was worried about the mismatch between the Brewster Buffalos and the few aging Hurricanes under his command and the superior aircraft the Japanese air force possessed. Very few of the squadron's aging Hurricane fighters, charged with the defense of Rangoon, could match the Zeros in speed or agility. Overall, his planes were no match for the feared Japanese Zero fighter. His plan, when the attack on Rangoon began, was to send one of his squadrons of Buffalos away from the Mingaladon airfield; the other squadron of Buffalos would, with a little bit of luck, be able to scramble early. He planned to have the planes climb high above and attack the invading bombers. The superior American P-40 fighters, directed by their American commander, would take on the Japanese bombers and the fighter escort.

At 8:30 A.M. December 25, the field telephone rang in Colonel Philips's office. The advanced spotter, on the coast of south Burma stationed in the Mergui Archipelago in the Andaman Sea, excitedly reported, "There's lots of Japanese 'Sally'-type heavy bombers with fighter escort. At least sixty bombers and more fighters, but I can't tell where they're headed."

Group Captain Phillips looked out the window at his Buffalos lined up at the south edge of the of the airfield and the few Hurricanes parked to the west end of the landing strip. He quickly hung up, ran to the Ops hut, and addressed the waiting pilots. "The moment we have been waiting for is here; the Japs are on the way. Good luck and God bless."

The pilots poured out of the hut and climbed into their planes. The Buffalos scrambled first. The handful of aging Hurricanes followed them, gaining altitude as they headed south. The faster P-40s of the AVG followed. Just as they flew over Elephant Point (a kink in the Rangoon River, a few miles south of the city's center, where the river became broader and deeper), the lead pilot saw the wave of bombers ahead. They were escorted by Nakajima "Nates" with fixed undercarriages, which were racing to meet them. Together with the P-40s, whose prows painted with shark mouths gleamed in the sun, the Hurricanes raced forward to meet the oncoming waves of the Japanese planes. From their cockpits, the Japanese could see Rangoon—the great golden pagoda and the city's many lakes and rivers.

Chapter 2
Rangoon Air Raid

Tin Oo was a stocky, broad-shouldered young Burman. He wore a crew cut to keep his unruly hair in shape. His face, for all his youth, was rough—pock marked—and it looked like he may have had small pox. He perpetually had a mild scowl on his countenance. His early schooling had been monastic, but now in his late teens, he wanted to be a doctor, so he attended a vernacular school. He lived with his widowed mother in a large two-story teak house. Since her husband's death, she had dedicated her life to bringing up her son, keeping him in line and out of trouble, and keeping him out of politics. Today she was getting ready to go to the big pagoda. She had consulted her favorite astrologer to ask about the best time to set out in the morning. Adhering scrupulously to the astrologer's advice, she had hired a *tonga* for the specified hour. Dressed in her best silk blouse and a multi-hued *longyi*, she made sure her young son was dressed as well. At the pagoda she would make offerings and prayer for her son's future; she would take offerings to the monks; and she would bathe the statues, and thereby both assure her son's future and earn merit for herself.

Jeremy Rawson, his sister CeCi, and his mother Francis were at St. Paul's Cathedral on Spark Street attending Christmas Mass. Mr. Rawson was some place between Mandalay and Rangoon, on his beloved locomotive. CeCi was about to graduate tenth standard from St. Philomena's Convent School, and her older brother Jeremy had recently graduated from St. Paul's Jesuit School. He dreamt of following in his father's footsteps, becoming a mechanical engineer and working for the railways.

At his home on the outskirts of Rangoon, Mr. Thomas got up early. He always took charge of cooking for family and friends on holidays. It took special care to prepare food to accommodate the various ethnic and religious sensibilities among his friends. Rangoon was a cosmopolitan city. He had to be careful that he offered halal meat for his Muslim friends and that he prepared vegetarian dishes properly for his Hindu friends. When he entertained at home, he had separate tables for his Buddhist and other Christian friends. With a little sigh, but with anticipation of hosting his three brothers and their families for Christmas dinner, he began his preparations. His wife and daughters enjoyed watching him work in the kitchen. His two sons, Benjamin and Peter, were readying themselves for a Christmas party downtown, port-side on the Rangoon River.

Peter was preening in the washroom. He was anticipating an exciting morning. The party that he and Benjamin were going to attend was for all non-European people in Rangoon, including Burmese, Indians, Karens, and Eurasians. In the back of his mind, though, he felt a certain unease about the Christmas party. "Why?" he asked himself. "You are neither superstitious nor do you believe in astrology." With a shake of his head he calmed himself and prepared to go to the city.

He played a little game that he had played since childhood: he would wait for the whistle of the approaching train, then dash to the train platform, arriving just as the train came to a complete stop. Although part of him, strangely, was secretly hoping that he would miss the train, he arrived in time and boarded. Dutifully, he entered the second class coach (first-class coaches were reserved for Europeans) and settled in for the fifteen-minute ride.

At the main Rangoon station he disembarked and climbed the stairs to the overhead footbridge. From the overpass he could see the busy station and the trains come and go. He descended from the overpass and reached Phayre Street, in the city center. He walked along Phayre Street towards the Port Trust building, which stood at the end of the street near the river. He clucked with both disapproval and sadness as he passed some of the dock coolies who were still lying on the pavement in front of the gritty toddy shop at the corner of Phayre and Dalhousie streets, recovering from a hangover. Like hundreds of other coolies, they were sleeping off the night before, when they had consumed large quantities of cheap foul-smelling Chinese rice liquor—toddy. This was their escape from the dirty work they engaged in. Their frail undernourished bodies carried sixty-pound gunnysacks filled with rice up the gangway to ships, then ferried all sorts of merchandise down from the ships. Away from their distant home and with no change in routine to anticipate, these poor wretches often drank their weariness away at the Chinese bar. They had come to Rangoon because the money was better than what they would earn at home, and they were able to send money home, but their lives were short. Many who came did not make it back to their ancestral home. As he considered this, Peter's sadness for his countrymen outweighed his disapproval.

Benjamin, Peter's elder brother, had gone to the Port Trust building early to await his brother. As he waited in the quadrangle, Benjamin heard the faint drone of planes. At first the noise was barely audible, but then the air raid sirens went off. He knew that he should run into a shelter, but, overcome with curiosity, he went up to the tower of the Port Trust control room. From there he could see planes in the distance: bright, small, silvery objects. As they reached overhead, people poured out of their homes to gaze at the sky. The planes came in threes. Still at a high altitude, they looked almost like toys—no more than a foot long. In the cool crisp air, they shone silvery in the bright tropical sun. Instead of taking cover like they had been told time and time again, people stood in the open and watched planes in fascination. The newspapers had been full of warnings for weeks, but when the danger finally arrived, the people in the city forgot all the warnings and instructions they had read just a few days ago. Curiosity overcame them. They streamed from their homes into the narrow streets. Crammed into alleys and streets and on rooftops, they gazed upward at the planes in the sky instead of taking cover. They did not know what to make of all the noise. They were like sheep: paralyzed, unable to move in the presence of an awesome a predator.

The Burmese collaborators, mostly communists, were in hiding from British intelligence. They had gone across the river to Twante, awaiting signs to start sabotage against the government. In the kitchen, one of the communist members agitated for immediate uprising, but Maung Aye, the senior collaborator, urged caution; a premature uprising would backfire.

The first wave of thirty Japanese "Sally" bombers was now approaching the city. They were just south of Monkey Point, with Nakajima fighters flying over to protect them. This wave was heading for the Port of Rangoon and the electric power plant. The American P-40s, RAF Hurricanes, and daring Brewster Buffalo fighters approached the oncoming Japanese planes. Even before they arrived over the city, a first huge dog fight erupted between the approaching Japanese bombers and the defending AVG and RAF fighters. Soon the fast fighters of the AVG and RAF were screaming, diving, and emitting bright orange flashes from their muzzles as they fired at the bombers and at each other. The grand and deadly main show had begun. The noise could be heard throughout Rangoon.

From his perch in the tower of the Port Trust building, Benjamin heard the scream of the AVG's P-40 fighters diving into the thick formation of the Japanese bombers. One of the heavy bombers took multiple hits, and with smoke belching from its engines, soon began to spiral down into the sea. It made a terrible noise in its dive and then exploded as it plunged into the sea. Benjamin's attention was diverted when the bombers continued to approach the city. One of the P-40s was in a dive when a Nakajima swiftly took its position behind it and fired its guns on the American fighter. The P-40 started to emit smoke, oil spewed from its engine, then it went into a dive from which it could not recover. Another P-40, with guns blazing, attacked the fighter, causing it to shed chunks of its skin, then break up. Benjamin heard a whistle, saw the fire and smoke of the fighter being hit, then heard a thunderous explosion. In a billow of smoke, the fighter fell from the sky in a spiral, like a corkscrew. "Hurrah!" thought Benjamin, "we got two of theirs, and they only got one of ours."

In spite of the valiant effort by the defenders, the waves of Japanese planes continued to head for the city. The bombers kept to their flight plan: they descended slightly, and then unleashed their bombs on their assigned targets. The whistling intensified as the bombs gathered speed and screamed earthward. Thunderous explosions followed. The electric generating plant, the oil storage tanks at Syriam, the docks which had warehouses full of American lend-lease goods bound for China—all exploded and went up in flames, spewing mud, bricks, metal, and body parts into the air.

Many civilians, instead taking cover, stood rooted to the ground. They watched even as buildings exploded and people fell bleeding. Despite the trauma around them, they continued to watch raptly as the screaming aircraft sprayed everything that moved. Other people ran helter-skelter. In their confusion, some of the poor were running towards the fires.

Just a few blocks away from the Port Trust building, Peter had taken cover behind the brick wall protecting the door to Grindlays Bank, midway between the railway station and the Port Trust building. As the first wave of bombers headed eastward, he emerged from behind the wall, keeping an eye on the fighters that lingered above the city. He watched a second wave of Japanese bombers head north to northwest, to the Gyogon railway facility and their main target at Mingaladon airfield thirteen miles north of the city center. He headed back north on Phayre Street and came upon a scene of unbelievable carnage. A bomb had fallen near where the coolies resided. Bodies were everywhere; the shrapnel had torn limbs from their bodies. One particularly horrific sight nauseated him: shrapnel had cut across a coolie's midriff, and with no restraint by the abdominal wall, the intestines spewed out. In a last desperate act, the man held his own bowels in his hands, to no avail. That is how he died. Huge black flies were covering the ugly spill. Stumbling away, Peter saw that bodies without legs and bodies without heads were grotesquely spread everywhere. Heads had been neatly severed from the torsos, he noted dispassionately. He heard a moan from a stairwell; when he went to look he found a young man crying. The man had a machine gun bullet lodged in the thigh. When Peter touched it, the bullet was still warm. He tried to remove it, but then the shrieking diving planes drew close again, and he took cover again.

There was so much destruction, but there was little he could do. Others, too, had seen shrapnel from the bombs tear into the frail bodies of their neighbors; now pulses of blood poured from the wounds while other neighbors lay dead on the street. A delayed reaction seemed to set in. Those who had the strength to run, ran to hide in whatever shelter they could find. Some aimlessly ran a short distance and then collapsed; their bodies lay grotesquely twisted, in the narrow streets, in the small filthy gutters, and along the shabby sidewalks.

At the port, mesmerized by the drama in the sky, Benjamin neglected to watch events on the ground. Plumes of white smoke enveloped the docks. Feeling unsafe up in the tower and worried about his younger brother Peter, he ran down the stairs into the street. He fell to the ground when a bomb exploded near the wharf. He was lifted off his feet and fell to the ground again with more explosions and felt a searing fire. Quickly he ran to the edge of the water and dived in. The entire wharf swayed. Some buildings collapsed. The cranes also collapsed, some left grotesquely twisted by the force of the blast. Through the fire and smoke Benjamin spotted a wood beam from one of the buildings and used it to return to land. Only then was he aware of the cries of the people, the desperate cries of the wounded.

From his position of relative safety, Peter watched the second wave of bombers head toward the Mingaladon airfield. He was startled to note how low the fighters were. He could see the red ball of the rising sun on the pilot's white bandana. Then the most frightening sight: after the planes dropped their bombs at the airfield, they set themselves on a course that looked to be straight for his own house! "Why would they bomb my home?" he wondered. Then it came to him: the huge railway marshaling yard and repair facility lay just north of his neighborhood. At exactly this same moment, he heard the whistle, saw the flash and felt the jarring explosion, and he fought back tears as his thoughts turned to his uncle's family, which lived near the rail yard.

Tin Oo and his mother were at the base of the pagoda when they first heard the drone of the planes. His mother panicked, but Tin Oo felt safe. "We are in the great Buddhist pagoda," he reminded his mother. "The pagoda will not be bombed; the Japanese are also Buddhist." Nonetheless, he took his mother to the safety of a trench near the pagoda. Then came the bombs. With loud explosions, they fell nearby. Tin Oo ran up to the next level of the pagoda, from where he could see what was happening. The bombers had not dropped bombs on the pagoda, but from his high ground, Tin Oo could see the devastation all around the city. After what seemed an eternity, the all-clear sounded, and Tin Oo and his mother hurried home.

"I want to return to my village in the country," she wailed.

"But mother," Tin Oo argued, "the Japanese are our friends. They will liberate us and help us get our Independence; they will not harm us."

At the Yorkshire battalion near Rangoon's Mingaladon airfield, the drone of planes neared. The Colonel herded his family to the shelter, but immediately left his wife and children there, to head back to his command post. Bombs had missed his headquarters, but the main barracks had been hit. He plunged into the bomb-scarred building to help with the rescue, but was increasingly overwhelmed by the damage and casualties. Fire fighters were soon fully engaged in putting out the fires, but chaos persisted well into the afternoon.

Incendiary bombs sent plumes of red and orange flames shooting heavenward from the airfield, then huge clouds of black acrid smoke spewed skyward. The aviation storage tanks were engulfed in great balls of fire, and bombs exploded along the runway. Tremendous explosions shook the ground wherever the Japanese bombs crashed. As the AVG and RAF fighters returned to the airfield to refuel, other Buffalo Brewsters took off, even though they suffered a fearful toll at the hand of the Japanese fighters. Small circular puffs of black smoke from the anti-aircraft fire hung in the air even after the enemy planes left.

The antiquated anti-aircraft guns in the city had been wide off their mark all morning but still kept firing fruitlessly. Major Abe, the fighter commander of the 40th Sentai, looked at his fuel gauge. He still had leftover ammunition and plenty of fuel, so he and his wing man peeled off from the bombers. Others in his command followed suit. Emboldened by their success and the ineffective anti-aircraft defense in the city, they now descended like a swarm of angry bees, low over the city, to kill people in the greatest numbers and instill panic in the population.

Major Abe started his strafing run. Coming in from east of the burning oil refinery, he turned northwest and shot up small craft in the harbor. At the Barr Street jetty he found the Irrawaddy Flotilla passenger sternwheeler "The Moreah"; it was belching smoke and trying to get away. He gave it a few bursts of machine gunfire and observed people jumping into the brown murky waters. He then banked to the right and followed Barr Street up to

Fitch Square, where many people were still running around in a confused manner.

Next Major Abe flew north, avoiding the Sule Pagoda, then opened fire again. As he approached the railway station, he continued his machine-gun fire at the rolling stock and engines. Past the rail station, he banked hard to the right and started to ascend. With fuel now running low, he turned to the southeast and headed to his base in Siam. In the distance he could see the silvery bridge spanning the Sittang River. As the bridge came closer into sight, he made a mental note of how it looked, then headed due east. He looked again at the fuel gauge; if he ran out of fuel, he would head for the new forward base at Nakhon Sawan, in eastern Siam. What he really wanted to do, though, was head for Don Muang airport outside Bangkok, to report on the tremendous success of the mission to his commander, General Sugi of the Fifth Hikoshidan.

When the all clear finally sounded in Rangoon, terror remained. People cowered in the gutters. Fires burned fiercely in the south at the docks, and across the river from the refinery, thick black acrid smoke billowed skyward from the burning fuel. To the north of the city, the airfield and military barracks were burning, and in the center of the city near the main railway station, the buildings were blazing.

At the Mingaladon airfield, Colonel Philips assessed the overall damage. The main runway was pock-marked with bomb craters. The twin-engine Blenheim bombers were still burning. The P-40s and Buffalos could not land at Mingaladon so had headed to the safety of Zayatkwin and Hmwabi. Pouring himself a scotch, the Colonel pondered the day's events and reviewed with bitterness his unheeded warnings about the state of defenses and readiness of the armed forces. He told his Adjutant, "Frankly, I am stunned and dismayed by the miserable performance of the antiaircraft guns. They misfired, they were inaccurate, and their range was abysmally short."

The Adjutant nodded, but added, "the guns are old, though, sir. That said, they are totally inadequate for the type of war we face."

Colonel Philips was, in fact, more angry than frightened. "But I warned the generals about the inadequacy and the poor state of the city's antiaircraft guns. Sure, they are rapid-fire guns, but Swedish Borfors guns are not suited for use against high altitude planes." Although he had promised his gunners that he would spare no effort to get more and better antiaircraft guns, in his heart he knew his efforts would fail. The whole enterprise seemed hopeless. He sighed wearily and addressed his Adjutant, "get the GOC on the phone so that I can report the horror of this day to him."

Peter was desperate to get home. He left Phayre Street, turned north, then ran along Montgomery Street, past Scot Market. Some of the storefronts were already broken; at Tejomals and Parasrams, the premier fabric stores, the iron grating was broken, and bright silks and chiffons were scattered on the ground; some already had been stolen. He passed Rangoon General Hospital, turned right, and headed toward the central jail, a large and ugly building. He skirted the grey, moldy, high wall of the forbidding structure, then headed to the north on Prome Road. Reaching the pagoda, he felt that he would be safe there. Fires were still burning profusely in the city. Behind him, he could see smoke billowing from the refinery across the river; to the north, smoke billowed from the airfield; and to the south, smoke rose from the wharves. He did not know if his brother was alive. Peter's eyes burned, and he had difficulty breathing. He was thirsty, his mouth dry and parched. He looked for a shop to buy some lime juice, but the all the shops were either shuttered or gutted; the vegetable market was empty.

A glance at his watch told Peter that it was getting late. "Soon," he thought, with a sinking feeling in his stomach, "the only people on the streets will be dacoits and criminals." He increased his pace to almost a run. As he looked to the west, the sun appeared as a dull orange disc in the sky. The thick smoke from the oil fires obscured its light, making his journey even more frightening. There were no street lights, so he could make his way only by the light of the fires arising from the burning buildings. As he got nearer to home he saw that many buildings there, too, had been bombed. All along Prome Road, bodies lay on the street; ambulances had not yet reached this section of the city. Peter suddenly felt an overwhelming need to cleanse himself of all the days horrors. "Oh, how refreshing it will be to be home, where I have a servant who can prepare a bath of hot water so that I can wash this filthy soot off my skin and erase the memory of what I have seen from my mind," he thought.

When he finally arrived home, the house was darkened. He looked all around the rear of the house but could not find his man servant Lingham. Oh, how he wanted that bath! When he could not find Lingham and discovered also that Lingham's small box in which he had kept his belongings was missing, Peter knew that he would not see him again. Totally exhausted, he walked into the house and found the family in the dark. They were so relieved to see him that they rushed around him and clung to him, each one babbling nearly incoherently about the fright they had endured. The food was still half cooked, but the coal fire had died out, so all were hungry. After darkness had set in and when there was no power and therefore no lights, the terrified family had huddled together in the darkened living room.

Peter's father remained outwardly calm. He took Peter to the front of the house away from the women. They discussed the day's events, deciding what to share with the women and what to withhold. Benjamin still had not returned, which was a grave concern. But they were hopeful that he, like Peter, would find his way home.

Peter told of the terrible death toll on the Indian coolies, the Burmese, and the Chinese. "The crowded and poor sections were the worst hit," he described. The men spoke about the destruction of the docks and cranes, but Peter thought that the biggest threat was the dock workers. "If they desert in great numbers, the city will come to a standstill, with no water, no sewage-handlers and no supplies. And the dead! Who will bury the dead?" he asked in a bit of a panic. "Buildings along Strand road are crumbled," he reported, "as is the railroad station. The biggest fire, to the south near the refinery, was still burning when I left the city."

Peter's father wondered aloud, "Should we flee the city now?"

"The roads still are clogged with burning vehicles," Peter argued, "and anyway, the military has blocked the roads." He wept as he described for his father the bodies, the mangy pariah dogs sniffing and gnawing at the dead. "When I reached the high ground of Lamadaw and looked back at the city, the smoke had nearly shut out the sun. The entire city was dark except for the glow of fires in nearly every quarter."

Mr. Thomas wanted to know of the damage to the rail head at the port, but Peter said he did not know its extent. "Although there were fires throughout the city," he said, "most of the damage was to the city center, the port and its warehouses, and the railroad." The men agreed that this was likely the result of there being so many poorly constructed homes along the river and along Pazundaung.

Uncle Reddy arrived and joined the conversation. Peter again told about the day's events. Ever since he had developed a chronic infection of his foot, Reddy had been unemployed and spent much of his time hanging around tea shops and gathering information. Mr. Thomas was becoming agitated. For weeks he had seen the India Steamship Company steamers, filled with rich Indians, set sail for India. He worried that he could not send his entire family to the safety of India; he worried that he would not be allowed to leave his government post. Wringing his hands, he turned to Reddy and asked what the family should do. Reddy shook his head in despair and shuffled home, muttering "it is not good."

The next morning, Mr. Thomas called the men together again. He asked Uncle Reddy for his opinion, especially what he had learned at the small temple nearby. Although Reddy had converted to the Christian faith, he went to the Hindu temple, and this type of syncretic fusion of two religions was not uncommon in the older generation. In the face of crisis they would invoke the help of both faiths. Uncle Reddy was not a revolutionary; he was by nature a non-violent man. His sentiments, however, had long leaned in sympathy to the cause of Freedom. Today he was thoughtful and philosophical. He mused, "we are on the wrong side of history. We are unwelcome immigrants as far as the Burmese are concerned. We have done well through hard work and mostly thrift, but to the Burmese we are usurpers. They hate us for our success." He added bitterly, "the rumors are most Hindus are terrified and that those who can afford to are leaving or planing to leave soon. The British benefitted from our presence; it was we who built the roads and rails for them, kept the streets clean, and cleaned their

Thunder boxes, but will and can they stay and fight? Or will they run, leaving us to the mercy of the collaborators?"

Peter chimed in, "Small comfort it may be, but many Anglos and other non-Burmese are in a worse plight than we are."

Mr. Thomas nodded his head. "We should consider evacuation, at least of the women and children," Reddy urged. Mr. Thomas was more conflicted in his sympathies. His job depended on the status quo, and all this talk of revolution was unsettling. He did not want to lose his job, as he had many mouths to feed.

All thoughts turned to Benjamin then, who still had not returned. One of the women brought some cold food for the men, and as they ate—more from habit than from pleasure—the door burst open and Benjamin literally fell into the house. The smiles on the men's faces showed their relief and happiness, and the hugs and cries of the women and other children showed their delight.

Benjamin finally extricated himself from the sea of arms and hugs and took Peter aside. "My best friend and classmate, Joe, and his whole family has perished," he whispered. "I ran to their house when the bombs began to fall. I thought I would be safe there. But they were all dead. None of them had any injuries, but the bomb fell so close that they died from the shock and the concussion."

Peter put his arm around Benjamin's shoulder and tried to console him. In silence, the two brothers looked out into the eerily silent street, each with his own pain and fears for the future.

The next day, Peter walked up to the narrow road beyond the small open park, to enquire after his friend Jeremy, who lived up the street. He was relieved to learn that Jeremy and his family were safe, then went to the railroad station near the house to gather the morning news. Benjamin, Peter suspected, had listened to his trusty radio last night and would share that news with the family.

When Peter returned from the station, he shooed the women inside the house so that they would not hear him. He updated his father on what he had read and what he had seen. "The air raid caused more devastation and panic than they reported yesterday," he said. "Large numbers of buildings throughout the city have been destroyed, even out here where we live. The open markets were empty, workers have fled their posts, and Petty thieves armed dacoits are operating more boldly."

Benjamin listened to the radio for any news, then gave an update from the Malaya-Singapore front: "The Japanese Army is now on the west coast of Malaya and soon will threaten the Jitra line." All the men knew that if the Jitra line was breached, the Malaya front would collapse, and Singapore would fall.

"This does not bode well for Burma and the strength of the British to defend Rangoon," Peter observed. He asked his father his thoughts. "On the night after the bombing, you suggested that we consider evacuating. Are you still thinking about that?" He added, "Many rich Indians have already left the country."

Mr. Thomas thought for a while, then spoke slowly and deliberately. "If we do that, you and your brother would have to take the family north without me," he told his two stunned sons. "I must stay at my post with the railways until the Governor releases all essential personal."

Deep in his heart, Mr. Thomas could not believe that the British could be defeated that easily. But events on the ground sure made it look possible. He felt himself to be in an impossible situation: if he and his family stayed in Rangoon, they ran the risk of being abandoned by the British, attacked by resentful collaborators, and overrun by the enemy. But if he and his family fled north, they ran the risk of being considered "rich Indians," vulnerable to attack by bandits. And, he worried, without the men it was not safe for women to travel northward into hostile country.

While the men anguished over the next move, the women gathered. Kamala, Mr. Thomas's middle daughter, began to question, "How is it we are in this predicament?" She turned to her grandmother, who had lived through the First World War, and asked her, "Why are we here?"

Indeed, how did the Thomas family get to Rangoon? Why did so many Indian families settle in Rangoon? How did the British colonize Burma? And how did this war come to Burma?

PART II

British Burma

Chapter 3
Why Are We Here?

The small grey-haired lady gathered all the girls around her, to tell them how their particular family had gotten to Burma.

"Your grandfather had died, and I moved to Hyderabad, South India, in 1918. After the Great War ended, the Indian troops returned from overseas. The demobilization that followed swelled the ranks of the unemployed. I was a young single mother without any money or family—my Hindu family disinherited me after I married your Christian grandfather. Your father's family lived nearby to me in Hyderabad. His was also a Christian family. Thomas, your father, had been born in the district outside of Hyderabad, but his father had moved his family to the big city in search of good job. His father worked for the great Peninsular and Southern Indian Railroad. The arduous backbreaking work destroyed his health. At forty he was an old man; at fifty he was dead. Before he died, he wanted to make sure that his sons received some education, so he sent them to the American Baptist Mission school. The school provided a better education than the government vernacular schools, and was also less caste-conscious. At a Christian school, moreover, Christians were not persecuted, as they often were at vernacular schools."

"Thomas was the second of four sons," Grandmother continued with a smile. "He had thick, black, curly hair and dark brown skin. He had just finished high school and obtained his matriculation, but times were difficult in India. He went looking for work, and after many disappointments found work on the same railroad that had broken his father, the great Peninsular railway that was being expanded by the Southern India railways. Although this was honest and steady work, Thomas was looking for new opportunities. He heard of the British colonial administration that was building a new railroad in the newest British colony of 'Burma.' He knew little about the new country, so in his off time he went to his old school and borrowed a geography book to learn of the country and the people. He was most struck by the fact that the people looked different. They practiced a different religion, and the country was lush and green with many golden pagodas."

Grandmother paused for a drink of water and then went on. "Thomas— your father—went looking for work. At the crowded recruiting camp, after a long wait, he got to the front of the line, finally obtained an application, filled it out, and submitted it to the jemedar, a tall northerner, who looked it over and asked him to come back the next day. The next day he had another long wait, but his name was finally called. The interview was brief. He had worried that he would not find a skilled job, but was happy to learn that it was not just the lowliest coolies who were being recruited, but also workers with some education and skills, which were needed for this difficult undertaking. Thomas was able to read English, thanks to his education at the Mission school, and he had learned how to keep a ledger. It was these skills that he used to secure work. The jemedar looked at his papers and told him to go to a roped off area and wait there until his name was called again. It was hot, and the only shaded area was under a large peepul tree. The space was already crowded, but he squeezed in and stood; there was no place to sit. Finally, as dusk was beginning to set in, his name was called. He was told that he would be employed in the coal storage department in the Rangoon Railways. The pay was going to be higher than in India, and he would get an allowance for overseas work. He was delighted."

"But before he went away on his adventures," Grandmother continued with a little smile, "his uncles and aunts set out to arrange his marriage, before he set out to a strange new country. Soon they came calling at my house to ask for your mother's hand in marriage. It was arranged, but not in the customary way; there would be no dowry, and no money changed hands. After the marriage, Thomas finalized plans to go overseas. The trip suddenly became more complex, now that he had a wife and mother-in-law to take with him."

"On the appointed day, the jemedar gathered the fortunate picks and announced that he had booked passage on a Peninsular & Oriental Steam Navigation Co. ship. None of us had ever been on a boat, much less a ship, but on the appointed day we traveled by train to the nearest port of Vizag, on the southeast coast of India. Only at that point did your mother tell your father that she was terrified of the sea," Grandmother laughed. "And he admitted that he was nervous himself, but he assured her that it would be all right." Grandmother now turned to her daughter to continue the rest of the story, and the girls' mother then narrated her story.

"Your father had to hold on to me, as I started to sway on the gangplank. From the deck we had to go down two flight of stairs, to the cargo hold which had been hastily converted so that it could hold a lot of people. We had a minimum of amenities and privacy; we slept on the rough steel decks, and there were just a few bathrooms where we could get an occasional bath of salty water. Fresh water was scarce. I had never before taken a bath in a public space, and I was terrified of the showers. Nonetheless, after a great deal of persuasion by your farther, I went to the toilet. Many of the passengers, like me, had never even seen a ship before, and most, like me, were usually too sick to eat. Our allocated area was on the lower deck. We lay out our mats and lay down to rest, but soon I became nauseous, ran to the side of the ship, and vomited. Soon after the ship set out to the Bay of Bengal, your father also felt ill, but soon recovered. He had brought some dry biscuits which he shared with me and urged me strongly that if I did not have some food I would be very ill. Again, with his encouragement I sat up and ate the biscuit. The ship rolled and rolled for three days, and finally somebody yelled 'land.' Your father rushed over to the side of the ship and, yes, he could see land. When the ship turned into the Rangoon River at Monkey Point, the ship finally stopped rocking, which was welcomed. We stopped at Monkey Point, and the harbor-master assigned a river pilot to guide the ship. This pilot came on board, and we slowly navigated the very narrow shipping channel. Soon we came upon the city, and finally stopped at the Barr Street jetty."

Mr. Thomas's wife stopped to remember her first view of the city that would be her home for so many years. She remembered how the pagoda could be seen in the distance, even though the city itself was still twenty miles away. She remembered too how thankful she was that the roll of the ship had ceased. She remembered her husband's immediate notice of how new the buildings were, how the roads ran straight up to the north. He had pointed out to her that from the top deck the small railway station could be seen.

"I started down the gangplank," she continued, "but my legs were as rubbery going off the ship as they had been going on. It took a while to get our land legs back. We both were still seasick and it would take several days before we began to feel better. Your father and I were put up in temporary housing provided by the railroad company. The house was small and cramped; it was less of a house and more like a warehouse. The roof was covered with galvanized sheets, which exaggerated the sounds of rain; the walls were flimsy woven bamboo, which provided little protection from rain but let the breeze flow through the house, to bring some fresh air inside and keep the house cool. After a couple of days, we felt mostly recovered from our seasickness. Your father finally felt well enough to attempt his in-country interview for work.

Mr. Thomas walked into the room at this very moment. With a smile, he said, "Let me tell them about my first day of work in this new land." He turned to his children and picked up the story.

"I had brought a cotton suit from India. I had never worn it before, and I had a mighty struggle with the tie I had brought, too. I went to the industrial area, close to the railway docks, where there were large warehouses filled with coal. I took a newly built trolley along Merchant Street to the interview, walking from the trolley stop to the dock side. Like most employees, I did not speak directly to the English man in charge of the dock yard, but through an assistant, who was Indian." Mr. Thomas shook his head as he continued, "Like most Englishmen, the man in charge was portly, ruddy, and not very friendly, and as the interview went on, I decided he was also a typical blimp, pedantic and pompous." The girls all giggled, as they were quite familiar with the type.

"I was handed a paper to write an essay, and when I was done I handed it to the Englishman's assistant. He was not any more friendly himself! I waited outside the office, next to the *punka walla*, and after what seemed to be a interminable wait, I was summoned back to the office. My palms were sweaty, and small beads of sweat formed on my brow, which I hurriedly wiped before I went into the office. I stopped at the desk of the assistant, who handed me an envelope. But before I could open it, he told me, curtly, that I had to be at work promptly at 8 o'clock. I was so exited that after I left the office I had to sit on a seat on the dock side before opening the envelope. My job was detailed in the letter. I was to keep a ledger of shipments of coal from India for a growing number of steam engines and an expanding railway system."

Having landed a good job, Mr. Thomas, his wife, and her mother lived in small black and red two-room railway quarters. These were small row houses built out of local wood. Their quarters had a small bedroom and front veranda; at the back of the house was the kitchen. The privy was outside; between it and the house there was a spigot, which was the only source of water. Mr. Thomas settled in and found that his work was accepted; and after a lapse of time he received his first promotion.

As the railways expanded, Mr. Thomas's work increased, and he received more promotions. He then turned his attention to his growing family. His children arrived one after another, two boys and seven girls. The oldest was Benjamin; next came Marge, Margaret and Kamala; then came the second son, Peter; and then came the younger girls. As the family grew, he had to find new quarters and find a school for his children. Soon he had saved enough money to build a house for the growing family. His quest for suitable quarters had led him to Hume road, a small new rail station. He was particularly impressed with the bucolic setting.

"I was delighted," Grandmother continued "with the prospect of buying a cow and rasing chickens and ducks, and I liked the open spaces and meadows." She reminisced, "Your father summoned up his courage and went to the realtor, a small office at the railroad station, where, much to his surprise he found a Jewish woman realtor, Mrs. Sassoon. Her father had come from British-mandated Palestine and had set up the small real-estate company. As the only daughter, she inherited the business from her father. Mrs. Sassoon showed him a lot, which he immediately liked. He made a bid for it, and after a month he met again with Mrs. Sassoon to hand the money to her, which he had borrowed from the railroad company."

"And here I built this house," Mr. Thomas said simply. "Here your mother, your grandmother, and I lived and raised our family." He reflected, "It really is an ideal setting. Grandmother can keep her milk cow in the open space behind the house, so you children have always had enough milk." The girls all agreed that Grandmother's labors had been much appreciated. She had also raised chickens and ducks. The ducks were free to graze in the meadow, the chickens roamed behind the house. Although they had always appreciated chicken on the table, they had cried bitterly whenever Grandmother had caught one of their favorites for slaughter. "Remember the time when Peter was so upset that Grandmother hid the chicken between her feet until he went off?" the eldest girls giggled.

Beyond the large meadow, the trains could be seen. The railway station was the center of the community's activities; shops, a tea shop, and an open market had sprung up around the station. The most imposing structure in the neighborhood—a great marble house—stood just across the front street, built in the Mogul style. It was on a large estate, and this magnificent building stood in the middle of the compound. It had been built by the family of the last Moghul emperor, who had been exiled from India to Burma with his many wives. The compound occupied almost a city block, and its most striking feature was the Moghul palace. Architects from New Delhi actually had been brought to Rangoon to design the buildings. Skilled marble workers had been found to lay the marble, with its beautiful inlay of semi-precious stones. A dome rose above the center of the building.

To add to its grandeur, the palace was surrounded with gardens in Moghul style. The gardens were divided into four symmetrical enclosures by walks; this pattern was said to be an embodiment of heaven. Each walk was lined with beautiful flowering ixora, and in the center of each quadrant were flowering plants and shrubs, which were trimmed carefully to add to the order and symmetry of the gardens. At night, the fragrance from the queen of the night would fill the humid air. Lovers would linger outside the palace grounds, to inhale the sweet aroma and increase the intensity of their romance. Around the edges of the grounds, Chinese hibiscus and rhododendrons grew huge, and in great profusion, along with tall mango, jackfruit, lemon, and jacaranda trees, interspersed with tamarind trees. The Moghuls loved their garden: the plants and the water fountains created a vision of Paradise on earth. All this was enclosed by a tall bamboo fence.

"Peter, when he was younger, had been most attracted by the palace and gardens," Grandmother said with a chuckle. "He used to sneak under bamboo into the gardens to gather mangos and gaze at the marble. On moonlit nights, he would slip into the grounds just to gaze at the glowing marble."

Now Peter entered the room. Hearing Grandmother talk about his youthful exploits into the Moghul garden, he sat down to reminisce himself. "You know my friend Jeremy," he said to his sisters, who solemnly nodded. "Well, he liked to come with me to steal the mangos. If I remember correctly, his family came to this neighborhood about the same time as ours."

In fact, Mr. Rawson, Jeremy's father, had come to Rangoon to work on the railroad as it was being built. His family had come from Goa, on the west coast of India, and he himself had married a Goanese Catholic woman in Rangoon who was part Indian, part Portugese, and part Irish. Their first-born had been Jeremy. He had olive skin and fine angular features, with beautiful curly black hair. He grew up to be a handsome, tall, and athletic young man. Eighteen months after Jeremy was born, their daughter, CeCi, was born. She had light skin, long dark hair, and hazel eyes; she grew up to be a stunning beauty. Her body was well proportioned. She was active in sports, especially running, and when the wind blew her cotton dress, the outline of her firm thighs turned heads. She attended St. Philomena's convent school and studied in English. If she had gone to a proper British school, her speech might have reflected proper enunciation and might have sounded perfectly British, but the sisters at the convent school she attended came from Europe, not England, so she spoke with a slight European accent. The British said that CeCi spoke "la de da," which gave away her roots. They described her as having "a bit of the tar brush."

Jeremy Rawson and his family lived on U Cho Road, in a small Anglo community just north of Peter's family home. CeCi worked at the Rangoon General Hospital, as a telephone operator, in the basement telephone room, along with other Anglo-Indians and Anglo-Burmese. There were no Burmese girls, as Burmese culture would not permit that. CeCi and her family lived in a brick house, with indoor plumbing and running water, which was unusual, even if it consisted of only one tap in the kitchen. Mr. Thomas had planned for indoor plumbing and water.

Mr. Thomas turned to Peter and said, "But you were also actually friends with Tin Oo, first. They were the first neighbors we met. Daw Khin

Nyunt, a widow, lived with her son in the same block, and it wasn't long before you and Tin Oo would become friends."

"Yes!" said Peter's mother. "And Daw Khin Nyunt one time told me the story of how she and Tin Oo came to live here. Now I can tell a story."

"You know that in 1904, the British had built the first railroad in Burma, from Rangoon to Prome. They then embarked on a more ambitious plan: to build a railway from Rangoon to Mandalay, then through the rugged mountains of the Shan Plateau eastward to China. They also wanted to expand local rail service in Rangoon, beginning with the Rangoon–Insein line. Both of these projects required another push for skilled labor, and another wave of laborers arrived in Rangoon. Some of these were again from India, some were from China, and some were villagers from upper Burma—like Tin Oo's parents."

"When I first met her," Mrs. Thomas continued, "Daw Khin Nyunt was a small, slender, middle-aged Burmese woman with waist-length, shiny black hair that she rolled up in a traditional Burmese bun on top of her head. She had been born in Singu, in the interior of the country. Her Buddhist father had been a rice farmer. You know, rice farming is hit-or-miss work; it depends on the vagaries of nature. So as soon as she came of age, her mother found her a husband, and she married him at age eighteen. She was lucky. Most men in her district followed the Burmese tradition and took up farming, but her husband had finished middle school in the new vernacular school system and had found work for the government Public Works Department (PWD). His department built roads, sewers, and other public works, and he was happy with this work. But in the 1930s, there was drought, world-wide depression, and a sudden drop in the price of rice; he was laid off and the entire extended family was devastated. The family did not have money to buy seed and take up farming, so her husband brought Daw Khin Nyunt and his young son to the new big city, to Rangoon, where he was told he would find work."

"Like your father and Mr. Rawson, Daw Khin Nyunt's husband found work for the fledgling railroad. He worked hard, saved money, and in one year he had enough money to build the typical Burmese-style two-story teak house that she and Tin Oo live in today. Daw Khin Nyunt was such a good housekeeper!"

"Yes," laughed Peter. "Did you know that she kept muslin rags at the front door, upon which she shuffled around the teak floor to keep it clean and well polished? And she did not allow anyone to enter her 'inner sanctum' upstairs, which contained the image of Buddha. All who entered this inner sanctum were required to remove their shoes."

"Her husband was not a well man, though," Peter's mother said sadly. "He could never adjust to the city life, his health deteriorated, and he soon he was dead, leaving his young wife and son to fend for themselves or return to the village." Here she stopped and wiped a tear from her eye. "It is not easy for a woman to be without a husband," she said. "I have been blessed. But Daw Khin Nyunt had to support herself and provide for her young son's education. She was clever and bright; she conducted a small money-lending business from the lower level of the house. You know that most Burmese people don't have a steady income; they depend on pawn shops and money-lenders to tide them over during lean times. Daw Khin Nyunt lent money to people she knew, taking gold and gems and jewelry as collateral. This was the only income she had to provide for her son and herself. She wanted to provide Tin Oo with good education, but she could not send him to a private school. Instead, she sent him to the monastic school, where she knew that he could get a basic Buddhist education, and some math."

Here she laughed. "What I remember so clearly about Tin Oo was his shock of wild black hair that would not yield to combing. His mother despaired of keeping it neat, so she kept it closely cropped, which gave him a rather fierce look."

"He still has that intense look," Peter observed. "The monastic school is behind the Moghul palace, so Tin Oo could walk there every day. He told me that he was taught by *pongyis* [monks] and that most of the time was spent in reciting the sacred texts. Thankfully he also learned math, and some English. But unlike the convent schools, the monastic schools taught English as a second language. He also learned Burmese history—with particular emphasis on colonialism; a bit different from the version taught in the government schools. I think that is why he, so early in life, became a committed anti-colonialist."

Chapter 4
Nineteenth-Century Burma

After the Great Mutiny in 1857 in India, the East India Company had been replaced by direct rule from London, and Victoria became Empress of India. Having "stabilized" India, the British mercantile community looked for new markets. The vast untapped landmass of China was still unexplored, and the British merchants already had business interests there. Now they found a new item to sell, the deadly opium. South China's seaports presented a challenge for the British. Chinese Mandarin rulers were not too keen to trade, considering that the British wanted to trade deadly opium. Now the English opium dealers sought information on trade routes to western China. So traders went fishing in troubled waters. They wanted a land route through Burma to Yunnan in China's west. They discovered a rarely used and unlikely route that took them, via the Irrawaddy River, to the border city of Bahmo, which was close to the border with China. From there a road led to Yunnan.

MANDALAY, 1885

It was the dry season. Inside the high walled royal city, the narrow streets were hot and dusty. Even so, the broad and high moat and the large hardwood trees kept the city inside the walls cooler than the city outside.

In the gold-gilded and mirrored throne room, the diminutive and feckless new bride sat next to the man who was her half brother and husband on the lion throne. She was almost a speck in the huge, tall, large, gold-leaf covered throne. Her husband was hapless, witless, and weak; no doubt the result of inbreeding. Unlike his wise, and competent, and benevolent father, the king was not a bright man; he was indecisive, henpecked, and vacillating. It was palace intrigue that had made him king. Nonetheless, he sat higher on the dais than his wife. But he sat on an uneasy throne. Even though he was the king, he was controlled by the powerful men and women behind the throne.

From behind the throne he heard the voice of his mother-in-law, a manipulative, ambitious, and greedy woman. To his right, on a gold-leafed stool placed at a lower level, sat the urbane, well-traveled, and wise principal advisor to the king. He had traveled to Europe and England and was well aware of the disparity in military strength, cannon, guns, and overall power between the small Southeast Asian kingdom and the larger Colonial Western powers. To the king's left sat the queen's advisor, a broad-faced surly man with small beady eyes.

The older man to the right spoke in somber tones. "If some compromise is not found, the British man of war in the Rangoon River will destroy Rangoon's defenses and then move up the Irrawaddy river to the royal city with ease."

The man to the left, of course, shook his head. Looking directly at the queen, he said, "Our mighty army and our illustrious General would easily defeat a few *Kala phyu* and the *Kala* sepoys of India."

The queen agreed with the man on the indecisive king's left. The king was torn between the two advisors. He looked weakly to his wife, who herself turned to her mother. "No," she then said firmly. Resignedly, the king nodded to the advisor on his left.

While the king allowed himself to be convinced of the indomitable strength of the Burmese army, the British government pursued its commercial interests in his country. British timber and gem traders were beside themselves over the Burmese king's receptivity to French gem traders. This rumor provided grist for more adventures. London's right-wing press questioned the "temerity" and "audacity" of the French. "They should be put in their place" was the overwhelming sentiment. Further, it was widely held to be natural that Great Britain had the first right to Burma's precious ruby mines at Mogok. The French threat and pride were enough for the government in London to declare war on the kingdom of Burma.

At high tide on the wide Rangoon River, the captain of "Man-O-War" was getting impatient. Precisely at 4 P.M., the deadline that the British had set for the Burmese king to agree to Britain's terms of trade expired. A Burmese response to the ultimatum from the British warship was not forthcoming. On the high ground northwest of the river, the Burmese governor in his stockade remained indecisive. The young, impatient, imperious British Captain ordered his gunnery officer to fire and destroy the fort. Five shells burst into the stockade, sending plumes of smoke billowing into the air. There was no return fire; the defenders had fled. "Man-O-War" turned south and took the canal to the Irrawaddy River, quickly drawing parallel to the river's main channel, easing the Army's future passage to Mandalay. The war was over even before it started. Rangoon was now another port in the expanding British empire.

After two more wars, the British annexed Burma in 1885. London, as was usual, sought someone else to pay for their exploits. So, it made Burma a province of the British Indian Empire and assigned the cost of the Anglo-Burma war to India. The Governor General of India appointed a Commissioner—a Mr. Landsdowne—to govern the new addition to the empire. He was a broad, stout, ruddy-complected man—too much tropical sun, perhaps, and too much gin. Landsdowne, continuing a family tradition, had come from England to India to serve in the Indian army. He had entered the service in the Bengal army and had an undistinguished career in the army, but he was neither a Mug nor a bounder. He retired still young. After he left the army, he joined the Indian Civil Service, where his true talents came to the fore. His meteoric rise to the top administrative position had more to do with his many non-military accomplishments, such as his ability to learn languages. He spoke Urdu and had learned Persian; and he had the ability to learn a new language and culture with little effort. Hence his appointment.

At the ornate palace in Calcutta, Landsdowne met with the Governor General of India who instructed him: "Your charge is to turn this undeveloped port of Rangoon from a tropical swamp to a modern city, with new roads, a new railroad, and make Rangoon a good port city. You will find the job challenging, but I have confidence that you will rise to the occasion."

The Governor General then handed Landsdowne a briefcase of documents to peruse. "Review these carefully," he directed. "They will provide a brief review of the recent history of Burma." Landsdowne took his leave of the Governor General.

After he settled his affairs in Calcutta, Landsdowne boarded the "Eastern Queen" of the Bombay Steam Ship Company. He went immediately to his well-appointed cabin while a retinue of dock workers brought his many pieces of luggage. Soon the ship left the muddy Hooghly River. It would be a three to four day journey to Rangoon. The ship's purser brought him a drink and announced, "Supper is at 8 PM, Sir; formal dress is customary. The Captain requests your presence, Sir."

After supper Landsdowne returned to his well-lit private cabin and poured himself a stiff peg of brandy. He opened the sealed envelope that the Governor General had given him. He sighed. It was not a brief summary; it was a lengthy report, and he had to read the entire report before disembarking in Rangoon. The report reiterated that his main concerns would be to turn Rangoon into a good deep-water port for His Majesty's ships and to find a back-door route to China. And then it turned to the details and history of Britain's new colony:

Rangoon is a steamy, tropical town, which in the monsoon turns into a malarious swamp. Burma is different from India; it is part of tropical southeast Asia and therefore its geography, topography, and people are different than those of India. In fact, Burma is geographically isolated, with mountains on three sides, and an open, littoral south. In the north, the Himalayas isolate the country from India.

Tired but interested to learn about the political situation in Burma, Landsdowne plowed on.

The Burmese king traditionally depended less on his councillors and more on his astrologers and the *poona*s and soothsayers, who nurtured the idea that the king's capital was the center of the universe, "Mount Meru." They advanced the notion that beyond the borders of Burma were the lands of the *Kalas*, the barbarians, who were inferior in every respect to the Burmese. Likewise, the king was told that his army was the strongest and was invincible.

Landsdowne had been reading for hours, and after another brandy, he went to sleep. The next day after breakfast he continued to review the papers, learning that the eighteenth century had been a turbulent time for Burma. No central Burmese power had existed, and this was, actually, a recurring historical fact: from the tenth century onward, one dynasty would arise then collapse, leading to a void and turmoil. Many times, between the rise and fall of the empires, decades of anarchy and uncertainty would result. In the mid-eighteenth century, Landsdowne read, things changed:

One man—the headman of the village of Shwebo—found the country in turmoil. It was full of dacoits, who robbed traders and rice farmers with some regularity. Rice therefore was in short supply. The headman gathered some brave men and set out to take matters into his own hands. His band of soldiers soon destroyed the robbers and thugs, thus ending the brigandage and bringing peace. A long time ago, the headman had dreamt that one day he would be king. Now, buoyed by his success, he extended his control to Ava. Then one night he had a dream in which he found himself in kingly robes and the royal sword. The next day he summoned his astrologers and seers and explained the dream to them. After consulting the charts, the alignment of the stars and planets, they professed that indeed, if certain rituals were observed, the headman would be king.

After his coronation as king, the headman consolidated his power. He swept through the rest of the country, defeating all before him. Then, with three thousand elephants and thousands of men, he invaded the Siamese kingdom at a time when it was a weak neighbor. He sacked the Siamese city of Ayutthaya and returned to Burma triumphantly in 1765. The king briefly stopped in the growing southern seaport town and declared it Dagon, meaning the end of strife. The British would later pronounce this "Rangoon." The headman had no particular affection for this swampy place. In the dry season it was habitable, but when the monsoon swept in from the southwest, it brought thunder and rain. The monsoon lasted four and one-half months. The water descended in torrents. It was relentless. Streams turned into rivers and rivers turned into huge lakes. Another reason why the king did not care for this place was because it was filled with foreigners.

The king's only satisfaction was to stop at the great pagoda where he bathed the many religious objects and gave offerings of food and robes to the monks. Once that was done, he prepared to depart, leaving a governor to handle trade and to levy duties on ships that weighed anchor and brought wares from afar. The governor would send him the monies.

After obtaining obeisance from his officials, the king left the city with much pomp and ceremony. The colorful ships proceeded up the Irrawaddy River. The king's royal barge was red and gold; gold was everywhere. The king sat on a raised dais under a royal white umbrella that he alone could use. Courtiers prostrated themselves before him, and men waved giant fans to keep the flies and mosquitoes away and keep him cool. At a lower level were sturdy men and oars, which they used to propel the royal barge against the tide, as the king returned to his palace in the north.

Landsdowne put down the papers and rubbed his eyes. He had become so engrossed in the history of Rangoon that he had not realized how many hours had passed. And now he was hungry. . . . After his meal he pushed the plates away and eagerly returned to the documents.

The city of Moulmein lies south of Rangoon, on a broad estuary of the Salween River and a short distance from the warm waters of the Andaman Sea. This ancient city had been part of the Khmer empire that stretched from the Andaman Sea to Angkor in Cambodia. In language and customs similar to the Khmers in Cambodia, the forebears of the current population had ruled this city for centuries, but then the city had endured the wrath of the Burmese kings and had been brought into the Burmese empire.

Moulmein has always been a rich trading center. Its rich teak forests in the hinterland has attracted traders, ship builders, and other adventurers over the years. The city teems with descendants of Arab seafarers and Indians, who brought their religion and culture from the subcontinent as they traded Moulmein's timber and rice, Mogok's rubies, sapphires, and jade from elsewhere in the country. In the fifteenth century, the Portugese were the first colonial power to arrive in Moulmein.

After establishing their base in Goa, Portuguese galleons sailed the warm water of the Indies in search of spices. They were in competition with the powerful Dutch. The weaker Portuguese vessels sailed the uncharted waters of the Burmese coast, where they found a safe harbor from the Dutch in Moulmein. It was a natural harbor, and had another advantage in that it had access to great timber forests that cover the Dawna Range—a range of low mountains covered with hardwoods. The Portuguese used teak from these forests to repair their ships in the city's port.

The Portuguese not only traded in Moulmein; they also established settlements there, sometimes at great cost. For example, Rabiero Pinto, a Portuguese sea captain, settled here after escaping from the Dutch and an outraged Burmese king. He escaped just in time to avoid being impaled on bamboo stakes to die most painful and prolonged death. In Moulmein, Captain Pinto built a home. He married a local woman and lived out his life. His first born was a daughter, and all of his children also married local men or women.

Landsdowne poured himself another drink and continued. Now he had reached the description of the arrival of the English.

The British arrived shortly after the Portuguese, also to harvest the teak forests. They sold the teak logs to build ships and furniture and to provide decking for the Royal Navy's great battleships. Long before Rangoon became a colonial outpost, English traders built a trading post at Moulmein. The East India Company came here to trade, but like the case of India, the small timber and rice interests took on a life of their own. Soon Rangoon was filled with mercenary Europeans—the French and British gem traders, who craved control the great Mogok ruby mines. Others came to buy the great teak logs and other forest products of Burma.

Landsdowne's reading got easier as he came to more current events. He found it interesting to see written in diplomatic language what he had heard about anecdotally from his colleagues in Calcutta. He ignored the purser's call to lunch.

The situation required a wise ruler who could keep the various foreign competing interests from gaining ground and could keep the barbarians at bay. But unfortunately, the old king died, leaving a weak and vacillating successor. This new king fell victim to the machinations of his half sister and her mother, who had been a lesser wife of the previous king. The greed of the former king's mother and half sister knew no limits, and they believed in their own grandiose scheme to battle all comers, local and foreign. Egged on by the unscrupulous soothsayers, astrologers, and court hangers-on, they were convinced of the invincibility of the Burmese army and its generals. But they were over-estimating their own history: in the twelfth century, the palaces of the Pagan dynasties had been savaged and plundered by Kubla Khan. It would be two hundred years of wilderness before, in their more recent past, they would have some military success, defeating the very small state of Manipur to the west.

But the weak young king and his wife saw only the successes and ignored the previous defeats. Believing in their invincibility and ignoring the counsel of their one wise adviser, they went to war against the British. The British, with a few British troops and Native Indian sepoy battalions, quickly and easily vanquished the inept Burmese.

"And so that is how Burma became a colony and became part of the British empire," Landsdowne muttered to himself. And with that, having now read most of the sheaf of documents that he had been given, Lansdowne retired for the day. He looked forward to arriving in Rangoon and beginning his duties there. He did not know, at the time, how his time there would change the face of Rangoon, that he would be responsible for bringing hundreds of thousands of men from India to Burma.

On the third day at sea, the Bay of Bengal become rough. Landsdowne was seasick and spent most of the day in bed, but later in the evening he turned again to the documents, reading carefully his specific charge. "You have been given the task of managing this lush but difficult land," he read. "The country has few roads, no railroad, and travel and commerce far from the rivers is non-existent." Landsdowne muttered a curse; how the hell was he to manage a vast country that didn't even have adequate roads! The Captain's purser appeared at Landsdowne's cabin at this point, to invite him to the bridge, an invitation that Landsdowne accepted with alacrity.

From high on the bridge, he could see the mouth of the river. The ship turned to port and entered the wide river. Soon the vessel stopped at a hook in the river. The Captain said, "We will stop here at Monkey Point to pick up a pilot." It was a short stop, and soon the ship was underway again. In the distance Landsdowne could see the faint outline of the golden pagoda gleaming in the bright Burmese sunshine. He returned to his cabin to ready himself for arrival.

A military committee had arranged a reception for the new Chief Commissioner, which included a band. Landsdowne went in a open carriage from the port to his quarters high on the signal hill, at the foot of the pagoda. From here he had a panoramic view of the future city. He surveyed the topography before him. This was indeed different. The lushness impressed him, and the abundance of green trees, the bright *longyi*s of the women, and the *paso*s of men added to the color. High on the hill to his left was the large pagoda. Just beyond the pagoda, the land fell steeply to the river.

The next day, wanting to survey the land to the north, he took a country boat up the river. He noted how it was subject to floods. Moreover, he could see that it was a malarious and unhealthy place. After a brief discussion with local authorities, he sent for a young Lieutenant in Calcutta who, in spite of his youth, was the best engineer in the empire. His instruction to the young man was simple: build a city on a narrow strip of land between the unpredictable Rangoon River and the pagoda on the hill. To the north the land was drier. The tide changed every twelve hours, and high tide would rise twenty feet above the low water point.

In his letter Landsdowne warned the young engineer, "the task is daunting, but I know that you have the vision and the skill to design and build the necessary roads. Come immediately." In fact, the young engineer was well known for his experience in cities bordering rivers. As he awaited the arrival of the young engineer, Landsdowne assembled as many resources as he could. He gathered old maps and assembled a survey team from the geological department.

The young military engineer of the "Calcutta Sappers" took Landsdowne at his word, booked passage immediately, and arrived in Rangoon just four days later. He spent one week studying and surveying the land and was taken aback by the primitive state of affairs. He rode his horse up the dirt road to the pagoda hill. From the high ground, he looked down to the river bank and realized that he had limited land between the river and hill. He rode in the other direction and soon arrived at the muddy creek full of fishing sampans. "What is this called?" he asked his assistant.

"Pazundaung Creek" came the reply, with a further explanation that the land to the east was a vast swamp.

"That leaves only expansion to the west," the young engineer concluded. He could extend the city seven miles to a group of small lakes, by building a small earthen dam. The next day he rode to the lakes and found the scene pleasant and bucolic. Ideas came quickly. He could enlarge the lake by blocking a stream. This would be a place good enough for the English to build homes. The railroad would be in the center of the city.

He rode rapidly back to the office to study the tides and the effect of the monsoon. He concluded that he would have to build an embankment, to prevent the waters of the river from overflowing its banks. And he knew he would have to drain the malarious swamps. He realized that the task he had been given was more than he had anticipated, but he also recognized that he had been given a free hand to design a city from scratch. What a challenge! It took him six weeks to devise a plan. Rather than allow haphazard growth with narrow winding streets, his main streets would be broad. Long streets would run from east to west, short cross streets from the river's edge to the pagoda hill, in the middle of the city.

He had one more problem: a small pagoda in the middle of the city. Then he hit on a brilliant idea: he would build an open space and have a square of green grass and small park that he would name Fitch Square (Fitch had been the first English visitor to Burma). The square would divide the city into four quadrants, with the square as the center. The young engineer worked many days and nights by oil lamp and candle light. He finally had the plans, he would meet the deadline. He stopped at the Commissioner's office, "I am ready," he announced to the Commissioner's secretary.

At the appointed hour he went before the Committee. They were all middle aged, which made him feel uneasy. He unrolled the thick rolls of blueprints and painstakingly explained his ambitious plan. He could tell that the Committee was impressed, but the only verbal response was from the financial secretary, who wondered aloud about the cost. The committee meeting broke up awkwardly.

A week later the Committee summoned him back. This time the lieutenant governor was there. They drank many cups of tea brought by the *chaprasi* bearers. The *punka*s moved some air, but the long hours made the room stuffy. This time the Committee had many questions and suggestions for alterations, but his plan finally was accepted.

Construction started immediately, but soon the anticipated recruitment for labor ran into difficulty. The Commissioner sent the lieutenant back to Calcutta to raise money from prospective investors, both British and Indian, especially the Maharajahs. But before he left for Calcutta, the Commissioner told the young engineer, "Tell them that the Burmese never forgave the British for annexing the country, the war and the humiliation of their king. There is no labor to be found here—either skilled or unskilled." He further advised the engineer to recruit labor in India where workers were plentiful. "India, especially south India, and Bihar, will be prime recruiting grounds; transport would not be a problem. I know," he interrupted the lieutenant's attempted response, "transport is not a simple task, but some of the ships can be refitted for a large number of passengers."

The young engineer, eager to build what he was beginning to think of as "his" city, went about organizing the effort to recruit good labor for the project.

Chapter 5
Cosmopolitan Rangoon

By 1941, Rangoon, had fewer Burmese than Indians, Chinese, and European residents. The city had become increasingly cosmopolitan, with roads, trains, and even a aerodrome and a busy port. It was the most modern city in the British empire east of India. The city was called, variously, the Pearl of the Orient and Paris of the East.

In the early twentieth century, the waterfront, which had earlier been lined with wooden huts, now presented a vista of glistening new colonial buildings, such as the red-bricked Customs House, the Irrawaddy Flotilla building, and others. The new Strand Hotel was among them, overlooking the Rangoon River. It was one of the great hotels of the colonial era. While it did not have the storied long bar of Singapore's Raffles Hotel, it had been built by the same Sarkies brothers. It had its own glamor, with its floor of finest Burmese teakwood, its high ceilings with fans, and its wood and cane furniture. The bar was crafted from solid teak, carved in a semi circle. The Strand was the quintessential refuge from the heat and clamor of a busy city, and it was where the colonial society assembled. All the great colonial writers stopped here; lounging in the bulky wicker furniture and soothed by the overhead fans. Somerset Maugham and Noel Coward wrote of the romance of the tropics during sojourns at the Strand. White society partied here. It was noted for pink gins for breakfast, English gin parties, and grand balls. At night, bathed with light, it actually glowed. The colonials assembled here dressed for dinner, a black tie for the men and long dresses for the pale-faced English women. They drank cocktails and wine, listened to the gramophone, and danced all night. If the walls of the rooms could speak, they would speak volumes about the assignations, affairs, and peccadillos of the British.

The doors of the hotel rarely were darkened by brown-skinned natives, even though the hotel was built not with British money but by an Armenian family. Natives were permitted only through the back door, the servants' door, in the narrow dark alley that ran north of the hotel. At the main entrance was a small notice, "no dogs or natives allowed." Before electricity, dark-skinned Indian men sat outside the club and repeatedly pulled a *coir* [coconut] rope to keep the memsahibs and sahibs cool in the steamy tropical heat as they sipped their whiskey. The gin and tonic had been born when Englishmen, in remote places of the empire, added bitter-tasting quinine (to ward off malaria) and some sugar to their gin.

Each ethnic group tended to cluster in its own enclave within the city. The Burmese were concentrated around Kemmendine. The Chinese and Indians lived in their own enclaves, and most of the Anglos lived in a small Eurasian quarter east of 41st Street. The English lived in enclaves along the banks of the Inya lake, in Golden Valley, and in Kokine. They lived in comfortable surroundings, with many servants: first cook, second cook, bearers (all, surprisingly, single males), gardeners, *punka wallas.*

The British military cantonments were built in the best locations. Other than the coolies, the cooks, the gardeners, the bearers, and other natives who kept the place going, the cantonments were built only for the pleasure and ease of the British. Like at the Strand, there were signs that clearly stated "No Dogs, Indians, or Natives Allowed."

The well-manicured green lawns were kept short by legions of Indian men who, with machetes, cut the grass with precision. The colonial buildings, Tudor-style buildings, and Scottish buildings were regularly painted to keep the mold and moss off the walls. Inside, the floors were made of the finest woods of Burma: teak, rosewood, and padauk. Hardwoods covered the walls as well as the floors. At the Gymkhana Club, near the Governor's Mansion and considered the best in the colonies, young red-faced British men practiced their polo while young women, wearing filmy tropical dresses and multi-hued hats to protect their complexions from the Burma sun, sipped cool drinks and engaged in gossip. Some also spent their time looking for husbands. They sat on a raised dais and surveyed the young unattached men. They assessed the way the men handled their horses, hoping to find a hint of derring-do; then in the evening they would sip "Luke's" warm India pale ale, Empire beer, or gin and tonic, and they would party and dance late into the night. And when the opportunity presented itself, they slept with the young man of their choice.

At the Silver Grille, Indian cooks prepared Coronation Chicken, steak and kidney pie, and Yorkshire pudding. Behind the bar, big Indian men from north India served the best single-malt Scottish whiskeys, English gin,

European wines, and Empire beer to Americans and non-British Europeans. Bar patrons drank and brawled till late, and some danced into the night.

The military watering holes were different. They were the top tier clubs in the Indian empire, open only to the upper military and upper-class British. Families of the military and the civil servants all lived by the cool lakeside, in homes boasting colonial verandas and spectacular gardens.

The locals sweltered in the hot tea shops on Mg Talay street. On Frasier Street they ate biriyani, the rich dish of Indian long-grained rice with pungent spices. For the Burmese, mohinga was the most popular: thin rice noodles in a fish-sauce broth. It was ubiquitous on street corners and in tea shops. The aromas of curried chicken, mutton and fish curry, kebabs, and keema parathas pervaded the center of the city.

The Club Martini was one of the better restaurants that served Western food. Well-dressed Eurasians were admitted, and it was where Anglo girls hung out. Natives were also admitted if they were dressed in Western clothes. Young footloose Brits looking for a easy lay frequented the Club Martini, as did other Europeans; and a rare American might also come looking for easy sex and a one-night stand. Especially as the war loomed, some Anglo girls would sleep with any white man if he could get her to Europe.

A Scottish company ran the Irrawaddy Flotilla Company, whose flat-bottomed paddle boats and stern wheelers plied the great Irrawaddy River. First-class berth was reserved for Europeans only. The Flotilla Company's shallow-draft boats carried most of the foreign goods and people north. The Company was housed in a building at the end of Phayre Street and was a local landmark. In the front were tall Corinthian columns opening to the foyer, which was spacious and decorated with wood. Other companies, such as Steel Brothers and the Bombay Burmah Trading Company, also put up grand colonial buildings. Most businesses in the city were foreign owned. Traders from the province of Sindh in India owned the first tram and electric trolley car, and other transportation companies as well.

British business controlled the large companies, such as the railroad, and charged exorbitant prices, but it was the coolies who kept the city in a sanitary condition. They cleaned the "thunder boxes" of the sahibs, the toilets of the high and the mighty of the colonial establishment. In the homes of the British, sweepers kept the floors spotless. Coolies who unloaded all the goods that came into the port of Rangoon were the grease that oiled the wheels of commerce. These poor men carried sixty-pound rice bags on their frail bodies from the ships to shore and delivered from the ships all the luxuries that the Europeans in Rangoon enjoyed. They had come to Burma to earn a few more annas than they could earn in the villages of Bihar and the Madras presidency. These wretches were held in low esteem by most inhabitants of the city, including the upper-class Indians. Their life spans were short, but the money they sent back to their families made it all worthwhile. Their children, they dreamed, would not have to work for a pittance in a foreign land.

In Colonial Burma, like in India, there was a social pecking order. It was called the "Warrant of Precedence" and set the arcane rules as to who could sit next to whom. Society was rigid, with all the brutality of the British caste system. The British military sat on top of the pecking order; they were a caste unto themselves. Then came the British civil servants, the "teak wallas" and other sundry merchants; next came other white Europeans; then came the Anglo-Burmese and Anglo-Indians; then the various races of the Asian continent. It was not fashionable to be Indian in Burma, so the "Indian" was dropped and persons of mixed Indian and European descent called themselves, simply, "Anglo." Of course the Burmese did not accept this; they saw themselves at the top of the pecking order—temporarily dethroned but soon to be restored to their rightful position.

Peter had seen this pecking order firsthand. All of the Thomas children had gone to the American Baptist Mission school on Spark Street and Dalhousie Street. Every morning they would take the train for a five-mile ride to downtown Rangoon, crossing the overhead bridge to Phayre Street, then walking four blocks to the school. The building was a colonial building, but rather austere. The five-storied building was painted the usual yellow. Along with English, Math, and other subjects, the education was also religious. Teachers belonging to the Baptist mission instilled "good" Baptist values, and deplored some of the local practices.

One episode bothered Peter in particular. One day on the train, his sister tried to sit next to a Hindu lady, only to be shooed away. The lady was a high-caste Brahmin woman who feared that a touch from—or even the shadow of—a lower-caste person would pollute her. "Ashund, ashund," she had said, shooing Peter's sister away from the empty seat. The Burmese—who disliked Brahmins in general—nearby were angry at the woman's haughtiness, and one woman among them took umbrage, took her slipper off her foot, approached the Brahmin woman, and started to curse and beat the Brahmin woman. After she bloodied the woman, the other passengers intervened to prevent further beating. But the Burmese women shouted, "go get purified!" Ever since that incident, Peter had been keenly aware of the undercurrents of racism and nationalism that ran through Burmese society.

There also was a small Japanese community in the city: traders employed by the rice, sugar, and timber trading companies; also many Japanese dentists and doctors, who over the years had built extensive practices and connections, which would play a role in the coming war. The Japan-Burma Society was on the corner at 37th and Merchant streets. Since the Russo-Japan War in 1904, the Burmese who aspired to become independent had developed an admiration for the Japanese, who had been the first to defeat a European nation. When the Japan-Burma Society first was established, in the early twentieth century, many Burmese visited the office to read Japanese English-language newspapers and learn more of Japan. The Society had been founded to promote better relationships between the people of the two countries, and also to foster Japanese business. However, after the mid-thirties, many trading companies had became fronts for spying and for clandestine operations. Tokyo in the mid-thirties had little or no information about Southeast Asia and Burma. In 1937, the Japanese Imperial Army clashed with the Chinese in Manchuria. This incident added some urgency to know more about the southern lands, as Japan realized that she may have to seek the resources of Southeast Asia if the Americans cut off supplies. If need be, Japan knew that she would have to go to war.

In the late 1930s, Rangoon's Japan-Burma Society office was quite small. The secretary was a young woman whose father worked for a Japanese sugar manufacturing company and whose mother was Burmese. She spoke English, Burmese, and Japanese well. At the office, she dressed in Western clothes, and dressed and speaking English, she could go to places frequented by Europeans, places where ordinary Burmese were not welcome. At the same time, she could easily change into Burmese clothes and mingle with the Burmese. So, on weekends she spent her time visiting the pagodas as well as the railways and docks. When she came back to her apartment, she carefully made notes of the information she gathered. The Rangoon police and the CID kept a close watch on the Society. They watched the Japanese traders, but failed to monitor the young secretary as closely. They only commented on her budding romance with a trader for a nearby sugar manufacturing company. The tall, thin Japanese man would visit the Society office frequently and hover around the secretary. The Rangoon police and CID secretly made fun of his timid appearance, but unbeknownst to them, he regularly carried away information that the secretary had accumulated.

The secretary's boss was friendly with a Japanese dentist who had his practice in a large compound in Lamadaw, near the central jail. The dentist's clients included some high-ranking British civilians. In reality, the dentist was Colonel Suzuki. He held the rank of Lieutenant-Colonel in the clandestine branch, Minami Kikan, of the Imperial Japanese Army. His assignment was to gather information about the roads and railways, and any other information that the Imperial High Command needed. He would take long holidays in the countryside dressed Burmese style. One of his favorite places was Lashio, on the Burma-China border. It was difficult to keep track of him, as he would go disguised as a Burmese. But the special branch of the police knew that something amiss, so they kept a watch on him. Nonetheless, they could never find enough evidence to arrest him.

By 1941, Mr. Thomas's two sons were young men. Benjamin had attended university and was in the final stages of his medical studies. Peter had finished high school and now faced an important choice: work or college. Many in the family tried to talk him out of going to college. "Work," Uncle Reddy urged. Peter was a slender young man with bright sparkling eyes and an easy smile. Work would bring him some satisfaction and money, but he had a inner drive. He was intensely inquisitive and curious, and he was determined to go to college and get ahead in life.

On Sundays, the whole family went to church. It was an occasion to dress up and take the train to the city, to Fitch Square, where Immanuel Baptist Church was located. Services went on almost all day: early morning in Burmese, midday in Telegu, and the late service at 4 PM in English. The Thomases went to the midday service. After church, at home, the young people would play sports in the meadow behind the house.

Peter' friendship with Tin Oo had remained firm as they grew up. When he had reached adolescence, Tin Oo had to go through the traditional Buddhist coming-of-age ritual, called the *shinbyu* ceremony. It is the obligation of both the parents and the boy to go through this ceremony, to earn merit. Peter had been excited to have been invited to Tin Oo's *shinbyu* ceremony. On the appointed day, the elaborate ceremony was held at Tin Oo's house, in the presence all his relative and friends, who had journeyed from outlying villages for this special occasion. He sat in the middle of the pavilion, dressed in bright silk like a prince, with his face painted. With the clash of cymbals and the beating of drums, he climbed aboard a lorry, which took him around the city. Aboard the lorry was not only Tin Oo but also his friends and family and a musical troupe. The lorry made the rounds of the monastery to offer food and clothing to the monks, then, blaring loud music, visited Tin Oo's favorite places in town, where fellow Buddhists would come out to throw money at him and pray for him. Only then did the lorry return home. There he went through the religious ceremony. His makeup was removed, his head was shaved, and he donned the yellow robe. He was now initiated. His family paid their respects, his mother brimming with much pride and with tears in her eyes. Tin Oo offered his respects to her by kneeling in front of her and bringing his palms together. That done, he left for the monastery with only his begging bowl. He would stay there for two weeks. That day, Peter had returned home with much to tell his family about the interesting events.

At the monastery, Tin Oo went through rigorous training. He got up early in the morning, before sunrise, to pray. Then, taking his lacquer begging bowl, he joined the rest of the young novices and older monks in a single-file line. They set off to collect the day's alms, stopping at each home, where the devout would stand with bowls of rice, curry, and other food. On their return to the monastery, he would offer prayers and eat the only meal for the day. The rest of the day was devoted to prayers and reading the scriptures. After hours and before sunset Tin Oo joined the rest of the boys to kick the football in front of the monastery. He spent two weeks on this routine. He learned to recite the scriptures in Pali, and he was taught Burmese history by the older monks who collectively were known as the *sanga*. He was to discover how unhappy the *sanga* were, and he began to harbor a resentment toward the British and all the foreigners.

Despite their differences, Peter, Tin Oo, and Jeremy remained firm friends. The three young men would go to the tea shop in the late afternoon after school. Most of the time, tea-shop talk would turn to girls. Jeremy talked about Noreen, whom he admired from a distance. For Tin Oo, marriage would be arranged, so he instead liked to talk about *pwe*, the Burmese night theater, to which he was nearly addicted. But he always went first to the pagoda to pray and make offerings.

Peter and Jeremy enjoyed long walks in the evenings. In October, just before harvest, the paddy fields would be golden yellow. The evening tide would swell the river. They often went to downtown Rangoon, to the cinema: the New Excelsior and the Odeon were their favorites. The pictures were Hollywood westerns, with an occasional non-western picture. After cinema they would stop at the Orient restaurant for ice cream, faluda (an Arabic ice cream), or French pastries . . . or Peter's favorite, German black forest cake.

Tin Oo was always self-conscious about his English and his poor English grammar. Part of this was due to his dislike of the British, whom he disliked for many reasons. He was not alone. For example, even as the British talked about limited local rule, there was a rebellion led by a *Saya*, a learned man. The *Saya* was captured, tried in British court, and sentenced to death—a sentence the Burmese considered far too extreme. At the tea shop, Tin Oo had read to Peter and Jeremy from a crumpled news clip, "the life of a person who wages war against the king-emperor is forfeit to the state, and upon conviction he is liable to receive the sentence of death." Tin Oo spat out, "They hung him, and I will never forgive the British." He had heard his father's outrage at stories of British soldiers walking with their boots on in sacred places, and also deposing the king—not that the Burmese liked the king—and bringing Indians and other foreigners to Burma. As he left the tea shop that day, Tin Oo warned, "I tell you, as a friend, that soon there will be difficult times. . . ." His voice trailed off. Tin Oo was anxious to leave the tea shop, as a *pwe* was being held at the marketplace. He knew he had offended Jeremy and Peter, so waved goodbye more vigorously than usual.

As Jeremy and Peter walked home, they wondered what Tin Oo's warning was all about.

Chapter 6
Train to Lashio

MID SUMMER, 1941

The heat of the summer impelled the annual exodus of European women and children to the cool hill stations in the north of Burma. The Governor and all his administration soon followed. Local residents did not have that luxury. Mr. Thomas was one of the few lucky railway workers to receive a pass to go north. It was a reward for long faithful service to the railways. He chose not to go to the hill stations in the north, however, but to the border town of Lashio, to the northeast, in the Shan Plateau near the China border. Mr. Thomas jumped at this chance, wanting to seize this opportunity in view of the ominous future. He had heard rumors of the "Burma Road" and about possible war in the future." He waited until he had his pass for two second-class coaches in hand before he told his family that they were in for a vacation. When he told them, there was much excitement.

On the scheduled day of departure, the family arrived by taxi at the large open entry to the railway station. This new station had just been built in 1937. From the outside, its three spires were typical Burmese design, but the inside was well appointed in the British colonial style and was far superior to the previous station. The first-class lounge was furnished with furniture crafted from leather, wicker, and Burma's fine woods. The old *punka*s had been replaced with fans whose blades were made of polished teak. It was cool and well lit. The lounge was located on the north end of the long Platform One and was reserved for Europeans only. There, English women and their children could wait for the trains in relative comfort. The second-class waiting room was clean but spartan. Reserved for middle-class Burmese, Indian, and Eurasian travelers, it was a recent innovation. Third-class passengers stood outdoors on the sweaty, crowded platform awaiting the evening mail train to Mandalay.

Mr. Thomas left his wife and young children in the second-class lounge, then went with his sons out to the platform. Crowds of people were milling about while the train was being cleaned on a siding. The crowd was getting impatient and began to buzz with excitement as a shunting engine finally backed the long train in front of Platform One. Mr. Thomas and his sons were swept up in the excitement. After the shunting engine pulled away, the engine that would pull the mail train on its journey was coupled to the long string of cars with a mighty bang. "What a beautiful piece of machinery," Mr. Thomas murmured to his sons, with obvious pride. The long green and gold locomotive was a Y series. Big and powerful and new, it had been built in Scotland and had entered into service only a year before. It had three large traction wheels on each side, a long coal tender at the back, and two pistons on either side.

Fascinated as he was by the engine itself, Peter was interested also in the train's crew. In the past, the engine driver would have been British, but recent changes allowed locally born men to be engine drivers. This engine driver was a ruddy-complected Anglo-Indian. The first fireman was also Anglo Indian, but the second fireman was Burmese. He eventually would be number one fireman. The engine driver had trouble keeping admiring people away from the engine. He alighted from his perch with a wad of cotton wool in his sweaty left hand and an oil can in his right hand. He examined the wheels and other gears. Steam hissed from the cylinders in large, soft billows. Having satisfied himself that all was well, he climbed back to the engine cab and awaited the signal to get underway.

By then the rush had begun, as the passengers realized that boarding and departure were imminent. "Go fetch your mother and sisters," Mr. Thomas directed Benjamin. The third-class section at the south end of the platform already was teeming with people shouting and running, looking for their carriages. With difficulty, the station staff managed to herd the third-class passengers into their carriages. Then the second-class passengers were asked to board, which was more orderly. Peter looked for their assigned coaches, then helped the women and children enter the carriage. His older sisters took charge of the younger children, who clambered aboard fighting for the window seats. Benjamin and Peter hoisted the luggage and stored it before settling in for the long journey.

"I've time to buy a newspaper," Peter announced. He left his window seat and ran out to the platform. Lingering there, he watched with interest as the first-class passengers now boarded. Indian coolies carried the memsahibs' steamer trunks precariously balanced on their heads and loaded them into the carriages Only then did the memsahibs themselves saunter slowly to the train and enter their first-class carriage at the front of the train. Bringing up the rear of the train was a carriage of fully armed Gurkha soldiers. Their English sub-lieutenant traveled separately in a carriage reserved for officials, both civil and military. At the scheduled hour, the engine driver blew the whistle three times and looked back to the conductor for clearance. The conductor unfurled his green flag and waved it. Peter clambered aboard.

Mr. Thomas looked at his watch "It is exactly 4:30 P.M. Right on time," he announced with pride and satisfaction. The distinctive whistle of the steam engine sounded three long blasts and three short ones. The engine belched a dark billowing cloud of smoke out of its smoke stack, hot steam hissed from its cylinders. The third fireman had been stoking the fire furiously just for this moment. "That's the signal!" explained Mr. Thomas. The great wheels chugged several times before they caught the rail. Slowly the train stretched out like a concertina, then pulled out of the station.

Inside their second-class coach, the family settled in. The green leather seats seated four, and were soft and comfortable. Two small fans whirred overhead to bring some welcome relief from the heat. As the train progressed, it first picked up its speed then shortly reached full speed. It seemed to literally race past small stations. "But watch carefully," Mr. Thomas admonished. Sure enough, the children were able to see how the train picked up a mail pouch at these small stations. Fascinated by this act, the younger children clustered by the window whenever the train approached a small station.

The narrow-gauge carriages swayed from side to side rhythmically as the train sped onward. Peter settled in. He opened and read the paper, to find that the news was not all that positive. In fact, the news had been reflected in the crowd at the train station. Even though the boarding had been orderly, there had been tension in the multi-cultural crowd. The newspaper underscored this tension, with stories about sporadic attacks and fiery speeches. It was time for reflection. Peter wondered why Hindus, Muslims, and Buddhists had so much difficulty getting along. He had friends from all religious groups, and Anglos as well. As the evening shadows lengthened, he closed the newspaper. The swaying of the carriage and fatigue made him drowsy.

The first stop would be Pegu, the old capital of the Mon kings, and next, in the early morning hours, would be Mandalay, the major rail junction. It was here that the rail lines split, the main line going northward to Myitkyina. At Mandalay, those headed to the British hill station of Maymyo would get off and take the road to their destination. A separate line went northeast from Mandalay to Lashio. The coaches to Lashio were decoupled and shunted off to a different track. Only a few carriages were going to Lashio, so it was a much smaller train. Before long, a different, older, D-type engine was coupled to the carriages. Soon it left the rail junction and set out to the east. It would leave the plains of Burma now and head for the hills.

Roused from his slumber, Peter had watched the shunting and coupling with interest. Now he looked ahead and, in the gentle light of dawn, noticed a row of low hills and mountains, blue in the soft morning sun. The dusty plains gave way to hills. The topography changed rapidly. Ahead he could see the mountains. As it approached the mountains and began the long climb, the train slowed. The scenery gradually changed. The Shan plateau had been uplifted eons ago by tectonic events that had occurred when the Asian plates collided, and the uplift had caused an endless ranges of mountains. As the train ascended, the air cooled.

The engine strained to keep the speed as the train climbed the hills. The engineer had his fireman stoke the fire. The man, sweating profusely, still kept taking the coal from the tender to the huge furnace of the engine. The steam pressure built up for the effort. The grade become steeper. The large hard clumps of bamboo disappeared, the trees became shorter, and even an occasional pine and evergreen tree appeared. The railroad had cut through deep gorges, and for a while ran parallel to the Salween River. A few hours later it diverged from the river and then slowed; it was coming up to the Goitek gorge, the deepest gorge in all of Asia. The Salween River had created this gorge in its rush to the sea when it abruptly changed course in the past. The bridge over the gorge had been built by an American company, the Maryland and Pennsylvania Bridge Construction Co. The gorge was more than 3000 feet deep. At the bottom, wild animals, including Burmese tigers, roamed freely. In a rare bonus to the passengers, the engine driver slowed the train to a crawl, so that they could view the great scenery. They hung out of their carriages; some stood on the meager footing of the carriage and clung to the handrails. Faces were pressed to every window. Soon the gorge came into view. The narrow bridge gleamed in the late afternoon sun. A collective intake of breath could be heard as the passengers marveled. The engine made a sharp turn to the right, then the sound of the wheels intensified as the train rumbled gently over the bridge. Peter hung on to the handles and peered down onto the gorge. The bottom was barely visible. Once it passed the gorge, the train sped up, and soon darkness set in once again.

The train did not arrive at Lashio until midnight. Peter was awakened when he heard the two carriages being removed and shunted to a siding. Peter heeded the conductor's earlier warning not to leave the carriage at night, as tigers were occasionally seen near the small station. At night, the roar of the animals could be heard. It was dark, so Peter could not see any of the animals or determine how close they might be, so presently he went back to sleep.

In the morning he was first to arise. As he alighted the carriage, he noticed how cool the air was, and how refreshing. The station was small, with just two platforms and a station office in the middle of the longer platform. At the end of Platform 2 was the water tank, and some distance away was the coal shed. Because the station was built on high ground, Peter could see in the distance a river in a valley. The tops of the mountains were covered by low clouds that hung over the peaks, and mist obscured the valley. Lashio's strategic value to the Chinese and Americans quickly became obvious. It was a busy transit point for lend-lease supplies from the U.S. to China.

The platform soon filled with hawkers, who walked up and down the platform announcing their wares. Some sold fruit, others offered sweets, and still others dispensed the traditional breakfast soup Mohinga. It didn't take Peter long to smell fresh coffee brewing. He ordered a coffee, gulped it down with relish, and decided to take a walk before the rest of the family arose. He took a gharry to the city, just a short distance from the sation. He found it a strange town, with nearly half of the population Chinese. And, unlike in lower Burma, this border city was full of hill people in their colorful dress, decorated with many silver ornaments. Leaving the gharry, he walked over the wooden bridge and soon came upon a large *basha*. Intrigued, he took a peep inside. He saw rows of bamboo beds on which men reclined. Some were asleep, some smoked small pipes. He wondered what it was, but continued to walk. As he approached the main road, he saw that it was being rebuilt. He dodged several fully loaded lorries as he ran across the street, heading to a tea shop.

Seated in a small chair at the teashop, he watched the traffic roar up and down the busy road. He could see the road curving far to the east, where it would eventually continue across the border into China. Soon a waiter wearing loose pants and a vest brought him a pot of coffee. He was neither Burmese nor Chinese; he was a "Panthay Muslim," a people different from the ethnic Chinese. His people came from far away to the west on the Silk Road. The teapot was darkened with soot, as though it had not been washed for weeks, but as the waiter poured the deep brown liquid into the mug, Peter nodded with appreciation.

The waiter lingered, so Peter asked "what is in the large *basha* down the road across the street?"

The man frowned. "That place is an opium den, where men go to smoke opium." Looking at Peter carefully, the waiter concluded, "The dens are owned by Chinese criminal gangs, but all the opium is supplied by the British since last century." Reverting to his role as waiter, he inquired, "do you want clotted milk in your coffee?" When Peter shook his head, the man left.

Peter's attention was focused on the traffic, which was heavy on the Burma road. Olive green trucks with American markings and covered with tarpaulins lumbered past the tea shop. Next to him he noted a light complected young man, probably Japanese, who was watching the trucks go by even more intently than Peter. He seemed to be mesmerized by the trucks, and appeared to be quietly counting the number of lorries that were passing by. But he made no effort to move his lips; just occasionally he would put his hand in his pocket to fetch a pad and make some notes on the cover. Peter, ever the student of human behavior, found this intriguing. He poured another cup of coffee and continued his own observations.

Presently the waiter returned; he seemed to have taken a liking to Peter. Peter laid down a tip of an anna and pointed to the trucks. The waiter smiled. He had a small goatee and began to speak in Urdu, rather than the more widely spoken Burmese. "You want to know where they are going?" Peter nodded. "Wanting. In China. They are carrying arms to help the Chinese fight the Japanese. You know?" Peter nodded, and the waiter continued. "There is bad news out of China. Reports of the war expanding. Radio reports of serious fighting in central China. Nanking fell to the Japanese. You know about Nanking, the Chinese city?"

Peter said "I heard of rumors but have not read anything."

The waiter's eyes turned misty as he said, "Bad things are happening. The Japanese captured Nanking two years ago. It was a terrible tragedy. They committed unspeakable horrors and crimes against civilians. They murdered thousands of men and women and children. They gang-raped the women. Then they killed them."

Peter muttered, "Yes, the 'Greater East Asia Co-Prosperity Sphere'."

"Hah!" the waiter snorted. "The Chinese government tired to reassure the public. But they kept retreating and retreating, to the West. To Chung-king. Closer to Burma." He went on, sadly. "My sisters were killed by the Japanese. They completely destroyed the homes. They killed all the men. The women, even young girls, were abducted." His voice trailed off.

Peter didn't know what to say, so just patted the waiter's hand in sympathy. As though he had given the man strength, the waiter asserted, "We cannot fight them with knives and spears; we need guns, planes, and training. The Chinese government could not stop them. Now the Japanese have turned south to the interior of the country, and they will soon be at the Burma border."

Shocked, Peter asked, "Surely the British can stop them at the border, can't they?"

The waiter shook his head sadly. "I don't know. The Japanese are strong. Where will I take my family if they come here?" he worried.

Peter finished his coffee, left the waiter another anna, walked over the wooden bridge spanning little a creek, and approached the main road. He headed back to the train station with his mind racing.

The rest of the family had finally assembled and eaten a morning meal, and Peter joined them for a tour of the city. "It is full of gambling dens and opium shops!" decried his mother. The younger children were fascinated by the colorful hill people, and Benjamin and Mr. Thomas, like Peter, were intrigued by the variety of lorries plying the main road, as well as the amount of traffic that lumbered through the city.

Peter determined to visit the same tea shop again the next morning, to get further information from the Panthay waiter. "He seems quite well-informed for a waiter," Peter mused. "I wonder if he is a spy and, if so, who he is spying for—Chinese? Maybe communists?" This thought made the idea of returning to the tea shop even more alluring.

The next day he returned to the tea shop and ordered tea. Again he watched the heavy traffic. Every so often convoys would pass; now he saw personnel carriers. The waiter had been pleased to see him return and seemed even more eager to talk. Glancing around at the empty tables on the sidewalk, he sat down himself and drew his stool close to Peter's.

"The Chinese are desperate for help. This is where the Americans come in. If China falls to the Japanese, then the Japanese will create a big army in the Pacific against the Americans." He then gave some details. "I have seen two Americans in Mufti. From the Chungking Embassy. Yes, I knew that they were military men by their bearing."

He paused to look around, then drew a folded piece of paper from his pocket. "This city is full of spies," he said, as he surreptitiously passed the paper to Peter."I never can tell who is spying on whom. Every day there is a new rumor."

He paused to look around again and continued. "The two Americans were here to make sure that the American and Chinese take control of the Burma Road. The British cantonment and border control, is up on the hill." He nodded his head in a northerly direction. "The British Special Branch knows the Americans were here to prepare to take over the Burma Road if Japan invaded Burma. Even American airplanes have flown over the city. Some landed at the airstrip. Unmarked planes," he whispered. "I have heard that the Americans passed a 'Lend-Lease' act. That is why now the lorries, full of arms, move up the road to Mandalay and then on to Lashio. The road is narrow and rutted on the Chinese side. Drivers, newly trained, frequently run off the road. Only half the stores that leave the Rangoon docks arrive at Wanting." He chuckled. "Most are lost or stolen." So saying, he left.

Seeing that he was still alone on the sidewalk, Peter turned to the paper the waiter had given him. It was a clip from what looked like a position paper. It said "the American President will forward $100 million for the control of the Burma Road, from Kunming to Chungking and control of traffic on the road." It went on to explain that "the road was only 50 per cent efficient. The British will control the road from Kunming to the Rangoon dockyard. Such a policy will strengthen the U.S. policy of opposition to Japanese expansion, but Japan may launch a preemptive attack on Burma. Such an attack would come through China or through French Indo-China and Siam." Peter noted that the paper conveyed more urgency and fear of war than was visible in Rangoon.

On the long ride back to Rangoon, Peter thought about all that he had seen and learned in Lashio. He found the hill-country different, the scenery fascinating, but remote and forbidding. Passing through on a train, he found the mountains and rivers were beautiful and breathtaking, but he knew that it would be perilous here if war came. He turned to look one more time at the mountains. After the harsh white rays of the midday sun, by late afternoon the hills had changed color from blue to purple; the valleys were lush and green; and the mountainside was a riot of color from the various brilliant tropical flowers. As they left the mountains behind, Peter could see some clusters of houses and huts. "What do they do for a living?" he wondered.

Soon the sun was at the horizon, coloring the sky in various shades of orange. He was absorbed in watching the sun set when his mother brought him some rice and curry and tea. She sat down next to him. "You have been very quiet and secretive these past few days," she said. "More than usual," she said with a smile." Are you feeling well?"

Peter smiled back at her. "Thank you, mother," he said. You always worry about me. I'm just trying to process everything I saw and heard in Lashio. You know, these are troubled times."

She nodded. "I know. I don't know the details, but I can see the worry in your father's eyes."

Peter reassured her. "I'll be okay. But I think I'll stay in my seat for the night rather than retire to the sleeping carriage."

Soon after the rest of the family had retired for the night, he felt the train speed up. The hills were behind him now, and the land was once again flat with rice fields and irrigation ditches. The train pulled into Thazi station for a long stop. Here the engine left the train, and a new engine would be attached for the next run to Rangoon. The shunting engine now coupled the train with a bright green and yellow engine. Again, by the distinctive engine, Peter could tell that it was the mail train. The train set out into the darkness. The next stop would be Toungoo.

At the Toungoo stop, Peter got out to stretch his legs. He was surprised to see many European men on the platform. As he approached them, he could tell by the accent that they were American. "Another piece of the puzzle," he thought. "I wonder what they are doing here in this remote part of the country. Obviously, something to do with the war." He spied an Anglo-Indian railway staff, and he asked "why are there so many European men here?"

The man hesitated at first, then replied, "they are building a aerodrome a short distance from the city. Its name is Kyedaw."

Peter thanked him. "This must be where the AVG are headquartered," he concluded.

Back on the train, he dozed for a while, but could not sleep because his mind was racing. He looked out the window to see shadows. He always felt a little nervous at seeing such shadows. Some childhood fear no doubt. He tried to put together all the things he had seen, and he wondered if there was a false sense peace, if war was closer than Rangoon would admit. Restless, he slept fitfully for the remainder of the journey.

Chapter 7
Undercurrents of Discontent

Political change came to the British Indian empire in the 1930s. In India, Gandhi and Nehru agitated for home rule. These changes in British India had inspired the Burmese to form their own movement for home rule. The movement was comprised of seasoned people who were well educated and even held high position in the civil government. But the most vociferous were young rebellious men who leaned toward socialism and communism. These young Turks were impulsive, angry, and demanded change immediately, and they would not listen to their tested leaders.

In the mid-1930s, strikes by students at the University of Rangoon had paralyzed the educational system in the country. Then came the usual riots between ethnic groups. Even with the separation of Burma from India in 1937, Burma's economy was still closely tied to that of India. There was not even a Central Bank of Burma; money was printed in India, stamped "valid only in Burma."

The new Governor of Burma found that his task had grown increasingly difficult. He called his principal advisors, political and military, to discuss current events in the country. A middle-aged man whose previous job had been in intelligence opened the comments. "There are a plethora of political parties, some with only a few hundred members; some larger, with thousands; some looking for arms and even looking overseas for support. The good thing is," he continued, "typically a party forms, then in a short time it divides into two, and then divides again, and then in some instances it disappears."

He paused. The Governor interjected, "Yes, that's good, but there are now some communist movements also. They come in all sorts, from Stalinists at one end to Fabian socialists at the other, and with all stripes in between."

The Governor then asked his political adviser, a civil servant with many years of experience in the colony, to continue.

"The group that is potentially most dangerous is the Bo's," he reported. "They have attempted to contact the Chinese government in Chungking, to seek their help in acquiring arms and other help." He took a sip of water and continued, "Our sources tell us they have not been successful. . . ."

The General interrupted, "We have been following a number of those young men, and we have reason to believe that they have or will contact the Japanese. This group indeed represents the greatest threat to security." All three men nodded in unison.

"Thank you for your good work," the Governor said, then addressed his intelligence chief. "But you have to get names of these rebels soon. We then have to cut them off from their overseas contacts and arrest them. We know of at least one Japanese dentist whom we think is a spy, and there are undoubtedly others whom we need to identify and neutralize."

After the meeting broke up, the Governor reflected on the current situation. While the committee had discussed the most pressing problems, events outside Burma were making his job even more difficult. Japan had seized Korea and Manchuria and had been conducting an expansionary war in China. It had brutally occupied China's capital, Nanking, and had committed unspeakable atrocities against that city's population. The Chinese capital had moved inland to Chungking. All of the country's seaports were occupied by the Japanese and closed to others. China was completely isolated. The United States was intent on helping the Chinese repel the Japanese, and in order to supply the Chinese armies it wanted to use the port of Rangoon and the road through northern Burma to China. The Americans were pressing him to keep open the road to China. The Japanese were exerting their own pressure on him to close the road. Burma had no army to defend itself, so the Governor was compelled to close the road in 1939. He also refused the U.S. request to use the port of Rangoon.

Given the threat from Japan, the Governor called in his military generals. "Raise some local battalions," he advised them. Before they could object, the Governor went on, "You know that Britain has always depended on the Indian Army to control Burma's borders, ever since we added Burma to the British-Indian empire very late in the nineteenth century." He continued, patiently arguing his case, "The British empire now stretches from Iraq through the Middle East, to Singapore and East Africa. For years we have played The Great Game with Russia, 'keeping peace' in Asia Minor. We saw no threat from the East." He paused for effect. "We have traditionally had only two British battalions in Burma. This is no longer sufficient. Now Burma is on her own. The country has had no army of its own since the collapse of the Burmese Kingdom in 1885. But with the war in China and changes in French Indo-China, our defense forces are woefully short of manpower for any future war. We have no significant native units. This must change."

His generals stalled. "Sir, the Burmese are not like the Indians and Africans," they objected. "After their defeat last century, the Burmese have been in no mood to serve a colonial master. Professional soldiers are rare, and mercenary armies are nonexistent. We can only get conscripts." A lone voice piped up, "We can enlist the Karen's and the Kachins."

"I don't care how you do it," the Governor retorted, "but you must do it if we are to retain this country in our empire." The generals knew he was right, and upon leaving his office began to plan to raise native troops.

But the generals were correct to be worried. Unlike India, where the war-like "martial races" joined the British-Indian Army regularly, some with a long family history of service to the empire, Burma had no such tradition. Over a period of years, the Indian regiments had acquitted themselves well in the Middle East and Europe, serving the British empire with pride and distinction. Because no such historical relationship existed between the Burmese and the British, the Burmans in the south of the country were unlikely to join an army whose purpose was to defend the British empire. So, the generals recruited in the frontier areas. The ethnic peoples who lived there had been long abused by the more powerful Burmans. The Karen, for example, in the past had been enslaved by the Burmese king and were eager to serve and to protect themselves from Burman chauvinism. The Karen joined the new units, as did the Kachins and Chins. They made up the bulk of the new regiments.

But as the British recruited men from the ethnic peoples of Burma, so also did the Japanese recruit young, disaffected Burmese men.

PART III

On the Eve of War

Chapter 8
The Future Revolutionary

Away from Rangoon, in the country, village life was not much changed from earlier years. Rice-growing on a small scale was the lifeblood of the economy. One typical town was the small town of Henzada; here Kyaw Khin grew up. In towns such as this, revolution was always in the air. Kyaw Khin's father—part Burmese and part Chinese—was a mill worker. Feeling a need to prove himself a "true" Burmese, Kyaw Khin would listen to Burmese patriots talk of revolution and freedom. At school he had much difficulty with math and science, due both to his inadequacies and also the fact that he was consumed by politics. He told his father "I will join the revolt against the British." But his father mandated, "only after you finish your education."

1933 was a bad year for Burmese rice farmers, particularly in Henzada. The rice mill broke down, and because its owner could not find the foreign exchange to buy the parts necessary to refurbish it, he simply closed it. Kyaw Khin's father lost his job. The Burmese farmers felt betrayed. With no income, Kyaw Khin's father knew that he could not feed the family. "There is no future here for us," he told his wife. "We must move to find work." He had a brother in Kemmendine, Rangoon, who told him that jobs were plentiful in Rangoon, so he and his family planned to go there. "We will live with my brother only until I can find work," he promised his wife and son. He gathered the last of his money to buy the rail tickets.

For Kyaw Khin the journey would be a dream come true; it would be his first train ride. He was particularly intrigued by the sound of the steam engine. As the train approached the station, he ran to the edge of the platform. His mother ran after him, grabbed him, and pulled him back to the safety of the mid-platform. When the boarding began, he followed his father and rushed to find a seat. These were no more than benches secured to the floor boards. He poked his head out of the window to see the conductor wave the green flag, the trains wheels chugged, then caught the rails, then began to move, ever so slowly at first, and then pick up speed. As the train reached its full speed, the carriage rocked from side to side. It passed a small station, and Kyaw Khin asked "why didn't we stop?" This is a mail train," his father explained. "It does not stop at small stations. But if you look carefully the next time, you will see that the train slows and the mail is picked up." Kyaw Khin focused carefully at the next small town, and sure enough, at the back of the train, he noted a hook that picked up a mail bag effortlessly.

The train stopped at a big station with many tracks going in different directions. This was going to be a long stop, so he could get up and stretch his legs. He noticed men and women along the platform calling out announcing their wares. He jumped off the train and paid one anna for some sweets and a lemonade. Three minutes later the whistle blew, he jumped back on the train, the conductor waved his green flag, and the train got under way again. It picked up steam and started to rock again, and soon the landscape changed. The green rice fields were replaced with built-up areas with houses on both sides of the track.

Late in the evening, the train pulled into the Rangoon station. Kyaw Khin's father took him by the hand. "Stay here until I fetch your mother and his sister." Kyaw Khin looked around with interest. The long platform had many shops. The third class passengers' tea shop was outside of the main platform. He did look at some restaurants, but they were for the upper classes, and he knew enough not to go there. After the family assembled and gathered all their belongings, they went outside to a large covered room. "The last train to Kemmendine left earlier," Kyaw Khin's father explained wearily. "We'll spend the night here and take tomorrow's train." Kyaw Khin walked out to the open maidan at the back of the station. From here he could see the big buildings and many lights. There were more lights than he could ever have imagined.

The next morning, the family traveled uneventfully to Kyaw Khin's uncle's house in Kemmendine. His family was warmly welcomed, and it wasn't long before they felt at home in Rangoon. The most difficult adjustment was at school. Kyaw Khin did not like being with the *Kalas* and other non-Burmese, because they did not speak Burmese and he had difficulty speaking English. When the time came to sit for the matriculation examination, which was conducted in English, his father tried to help him, but to no avail. He failed the first time, and felt very bitter about it. "I know I could pass it if it were conducted in Burmese," he insisted. The next year he memorized most of the answers, and still barely passed the exam.

With tutoring from his mother, Kyaw Khin finally finished high school and proceeded to the university. At the new Rangoon University campus, all brick colonial buildings were painted a pale yellow. The campus was set next to the lakes, in a leafy suburb, and dotted with tall peepul, mango, hibiscus, and jacaranda trees. Beneath the leafy surroundings and well-maintained gardens there was tension. The source of this tension was external; it had little to do with education. Almost daily there were political demonstrations. Negotiations for dominion status under the British were not going favorably, in part because the British were pre-occupied with preparations against the threats of war from Japan. The Governor promised home rule for Burma if the Burmese would help the British, but the Burmese wanted guarantees before any promise of assistance. There were discussion groups at the student union building on University Avenue.

Here Kyaw Khin fell under the spell of student leaders. Their theme was that the British imperialist education only served the masters. Kyaw Khin went to lectures on socialism, where he heard of a new party, the Communist party. He found the speeches given by their charismatic speakers on how to throw off the yoke of imperialist rule very compelling. He found the rhetoric of speakers who advised their audience to look East to Japan and Russia for the liberation of workers very appealing. He told his family that he had classes daily, but in fact he did not attend classes. Instead, he spent more and more time at the student union hall, where he now found a new cause.

He was particularly impressed by one young student leader, whose speeches were full of anger and agony. This fiery orator dwelled on the "plight of the Burmese farmer." He ranted, "The farmer toils in the fields, in hot and humid weather, knee deep in water. He spends months tending to the young rice saplings, transplanting each one at the proper time and buttressing the walls so that the water will not be drained out and his crop dry up. This is necessary after each hard rain, as the heavy sheets of monsoon rain wash away the retaining walls." The speaker's eyes widened, and the veins in his neck engorged. They stood out prominently, while beads of sweat formed on his forehead and ran down his face. "It is a constant struggle," he continued, "but after the harvest the farmer can sell his harvest to the rice mill. But if his harvest fails, he will not be able to pay his debt to the money lender. Or, in a moment of weakness he might gamble and loose; then he loses his land to a money lender." His voice rose several decibels and he shouted, "all foreigners, especially the Chetty Indians, are raping the farmer! The only way to change this unfair situation is to overthrow the tyrants, even if we resort to violence!" The speaker's rage soon enveloped Kyaw Khin. "I will join a group that will provide me with weapons to overthrow the colonial rule, even if it means killing neighbors," he promised himself.

Swayed by fiery rhetoric, he considered joining the Communist party, but he suspected that the communists were fighting for an international order. It might free the workers, but such a rule would subordinate the country to outside rule. The social ideals of the Communist party would have to wait for a while, he decided. Soon he fell under the spell of another young speaker, who ridiculed the idea of Gradualism. "All the elders such as U Po are British lackeys; all they do is talk. They have never won anything for the Burmese. Their way will never win Independence," he harangued his listeners. "For that," he stated boldly, "we need the help of the Japanese."

One middle-aged man rose to ask him about the Japanese intentions, noting that the Japanese were hardly liberators in other countries such as Korea. The speaker waved the man aside. "If the Japanese do not honor their promises, we will throw them out," he vowed.

"How?" the man asked.

The speaker continued, "they will provide us with arms; we will use them against the Japanese if we must."

With that, the meeting ended. Kyaw Khin was so impressed that he immediately sought to join the speaker's movement. "Finally!" he thought, "I have found a party that promises to equip me for the coming struggle."

Kyaw Khin joined the "Patriotic Student Alliance," which had connections to the Bo's. The Bo's soon identified Kyaw Khin as a young man of potential to their cause, and they promised arms, money, and military training to him if he would help with the organization of rallies. He did not know or care where the money came from and plunged into his new activities with a passion. He rarely went home, and when he did, he told his mother that his studies kept him busy. At the two-storied colonial Student Union building, he spent all evenings until the buildings closed at 11 P.M. Then he went to one of the dormitories and slept on the floor. He was mesmerized by the student leader who talked about going abroad to obtain military training. He was doing badly at school and saw going abroad as a way to avoid acknowledging his academic failure. He wanted desperately to leave the university, telling his friends, "at the university I am only getting a colonial education, learning to be a cog in the wheel of the British. It would be better to go away to be armed and to fight."

One day he heard that there was going to be a important meeting that night, and he eagerly joined a few other young men at the meeting, held at a vernacular school on the outskirts of the city. Two men entered the small room at the back of the school, one a Burmese and the second a foreigner. Kyaw Khin could not tell where the second man was from but soon learned that he was Keiji, a Japanese who had spent many years in Burma. Secretly he had come to Burma to spy on the movements of ships and the traffic on the Burma road. He could speak Burmese, and now addressed the crowd.

"Victorious Japanese armies in China are advancing towards Burma and Indochina," he explained. "War in the rest of Asia will break out any moment. The Japanese will have to stop American supplies to China, which is a puppet of the imperialist powers bent on enslaving Asian people." Now he had warmed to his topic. "Only Japan can liberate the people of Asia," he shouted, "and help you throw off the yoke of colonialism!"

The crowed became excited, more speeches were made, and then the man who accompanied Keiji rose to his feet. "It is time for action," he said simply. He asked for volunteers.

Kyaw Khin was the first to step forward, followed by a handful of other men. Keiji dismissed all the others. Then he turned to the volunteers. He made them take an oath, assigned each to a small, secret cell of other like-minded men. To seal their bond, the young men performed the traditional

Burmese ceremony of *thwe thauk*, in which each man made a small slit in his arm or finger and let the blood drip into a large bowl where it commingled with the blood of his comrades; then each man sipped from the large bowl, sealing their fealty to one another.

Keiji then proceeded to lay out the plan to help the Burmese overthrow the hated British overlords. "The Japanese army needs patriotic Burmese to help the Japanese army and navy," he explained. "Volunteers will trained, in Formosa or the San-Ya camp in a island in the South China Sea. The best will be selected to go to the island of Hainan, where they will be further trained in the use of weapons, motors, radio communications, and they will also be taught Japanese."

Without as much as saying goodbye to his parents, Kyaw Khin set out on this new adventure. His slight build and overall frail appearance belied his strength and endurance. He was taken from one secret hideout to another, part of his training in how to avoid the British Special Branch and Criminal Investigations department. He was taught not only how to avoid the police but also how to shake off British spies. After qualifying, he was told that he and five other volunteers were to go to Twante, south of Rangoon, for military training. "After your military training," he was told, "you will receive special training. You may even be sent to Japan so that you can lead the fight against British and free Burma from the yoke of colonialism."

At the Rangoon jetty, he met the other five men for the first time. They boarded sampans in twos. The man rowing the sampan was also a member of the group; their eyes met, but no words were exchanged. The sampan left the dock. The man rowed hard, as he was fighting the current, and soon they entered a narrow creek with high banks. Kyaw Khin knew the high banks were man-made; he had read in his history book many years ago that it had been a small creek that connected the Rangoon River to the Irrawaddy River. In the last century, the British had dredged the canal to deepen it and provide a direct route from Rangoon to the Irrawaddy River. The sampan rocked from side to side in the middle of the channel as the many launches criss-crossed the river. The wake of the motor launches made the rocking worse, and Kyaw Khin began to feel sick. He closed his eyes and his comrade pushed his head down between his legs. Soon the rocking stopped, and the sampan entered the canal. The man rested from time to time, letting the current carry the boat forward. Living in the city, it had been rare to see the sunset. It was evening now, and the sun turned into A orange ball. It was a sight he relished. It was getting dark, and soon he could see lights. At last the rower spoke for the first time. "This is Twante," he said. He stopped the sampan in a shallow area and beached the boat. "Walk down one block and turn right. Look for a man in a red *longyi*," he pointed. Then he whispered the password.

The young men jumped out of the boat. Kyaw Khin landed in a puddle. He cursed as he lost his flip flops, and he had to dig in the mud to find them. The man in the red *longyi* silently led them to an old two-storied house at the edge of town, where he and his comrades were given a meal. Soon a middle-aged man ordered the small group to assemble in the upstairs room. There he was given a number of pamphlets, including one describing the roots of the revolution. That night Kyaw Khin slept fitfully, but he got up in the morning, for the traditional breakfast of mohinga. The middle-aged man, accompanied by a non-Burman, took the group out to the countryside, where in a deserted marsh they were instructed in small-arms training. After a dinner of rice and Burmese curry, they all assembled again in the upstairs room to hear indoctrinating speeches, both political and military. This training went on for two weeks.

Each night, Kyaw Khin would go to sleep on a mat on the floor, totally exhausted. After two weeks, at last the non-Burman spoke haltingly. "Two of you will be selected to be smuggled to Japan and its territories to receive advanced training."

"Let it be me," Kyaw Khin thought to himself.

The next morning the young men assembled. All were hopeful that they would be chosen. Instead, they were taken by the leader to the Lamadaw section of Rangoon, to a well-tended dental clinic. The young men slipped in the back door and entered a small room behind the main office. There the non-Burman, who by now was recognized as a Japanese, announced that Kyaw Khin's comrade Ba Sein was chosen to go to Japan, and that Kyaw Khin was second choice. The two friends were ecstatic and proud. They were spirited to a monastery on the outskirts of Rangoon to spend the night.

The next morning the two young men were introduced to a man named "Shozo," who gave them their final instructions. "You will pretend to be Chinese," they were told, "and will dress as seamen." They were quickly taught a few words of Chinese. "You will proceed to Bassein and will board the Shunteen Maru and stow away."

On the "Shunteen Maru," Kyaw Khin went through another period of seasickness, but finally arrived at the island of Hainan. He and Ba Sein were taken to a camp run by the Burma section of the Imperial Army and named the "San-Ya Training Center." It was fifty miles from civilization, deep in the jungle.

Kyaw Khin was assigned to the officer's course. He found the physical training from the Japanese officers to be arduous and intense; he would arrive home every evening and collapse on his bunk. He barely survived, but he hung on, fueled by his desire to assist in driving the British out of his country. He survived the rigorous basic course and passed; next he underwent training with live ammunition. He had not expected the training to be so harsh. He had much difficulty keeping up. The Japanese sergeant would shout at him, "How do you think you'll drive out the British in this war!"; "how can you get independence if your spirits are so weak!" The training was vigorous, and Kyaw Khin was afraid that he would fail, but one day Colonel Kawamura announced, "you have now completed your training, and you are amongst the graduates." Kyaw Khin was elated, but was too tired to celebrate.

A week later at a meeting, the commandant Captain Kawamura told the assembled young men, "You are being sent to Saigon, then overland by train to Bangkok. From there you will be transported to the border town of Mae Sot, Siam, where you will be attached to forward units of the Imperial Army, to await the invasion of Burma. There you will get your specific assignments."

Chapter 9
Rumors of War

The war in Europe was one and a half years old; and Britain had been at war almost alone against Hitler. Late in the fall of 1940, France had fallen, and the French colonies in Southeast Asia were now part of Vichy France. Britain stood alone. The Battle of Britain and its pilots were the only good news on the horizon. In the East, Japan was waging a cruel war against the enfeebled Chinese. The advance guard of the Japanese 11th Army was slowly creeping toward Burma, but most of the British residents there had little conception what lay ahead, and they made no plans. Instead, they believed the governor of Singapore, who had proclaimed, "should the Japanese attack our great Fortress Singapore, it will be no problem to chase the little yellow men away."

Churchill's broadcasts were prominently played over the Rangoon radio. "If Britain falls," he promised, "I will continue the war from Canada." The armies of the Crown, he promised, would sail with him. The Executive Council of Burma issued a proclamation that, should war come to Burma, the Burmese would not help to defend Burma unless the British promised home rule. To this Mr. Churchill responded, "I have not become the First minister of the Crown in order to preside over the liquidation of the British empire." Soon, in tea shops throughout Rangoon, rumors were rife about the presence of a Japanese fifth column and an underground national movement.

Peter and Jeremy were both now eighteen, and both young men now approached a major crossroad of their lives. Tin Oo was one year older, still filled with a passion to free his county and still loyal to his childhood mates. Peter had filled out from being a skinny adolescent. He was tall, had curly black hair, and intense dark eyes. He had passed his matriculation and had completed his first semester at university. Jeremy was a little taller, a handsome man with olive skin and straight hair that he parted in the middle, and hazel eyes. He was attending technical school. Tin Oo was already at university, studying politics. Tin Oo knew what he wanted to become; "I will enter politics and will engage in whatever it takes to free Burma from colonialism," he declared with typical passion. Jeremy and Peter were less sure of their future plans.

At the Orient restaurant one day, Peter and Jeremy talked about plans for the future. "Do you want to follow Benjamin into medicine?" Jeremy asked Peter.

"I'm not sure. I want to finish my intermediate studies before I decide what profession to follow," Peter offered. "But I am inclined towards to medicine."

Jeremy nodded. "I'm not surprised. I will go to technical school for the present, and will decide later on the future. If I can apprentice at the Union auto dealership on York Road," he continued hopefully, "I will have enough experience to get a good job with the railroads. Like my father."

But for both young men, the war loomed large in the background. They did not want to face that grim reality, so the meeting ended.

Before going home, Peter stopped at the book shop Smart and Mookerdum, where he bought the *Rangoon Gazette*, and the weekend *Illustrated Weekly of Calcutta*. Ever since Peter had begun studies at the university, he had developed a intense and all-consuming passion for learning. One of his most pleasurable activities was reading—great books and current events. It was like something deeply buried within him had been brought to the surface. He devoured books and spent most of his pocket money on books of every description: English literature, science, evolution, physics, and adventure. His favorites were Voltaire and Zola. His study of physics and biology raised questions in his mind about religion and the world. This brought him into conflict with his mentors, as he started to question some of the extreme views of his religious teachers, especially the American Baptist missionaries, who taught at the university. One of his professors, however, noting his keen interest in reading, pulled him aside and advised him to expand his intellectual horizons. He recommended that Peter read Darwin and the great English classics, as well as a number of other diverse titles. It took a while, but after much introspection Peter started to move away from the parochialism and extremism of his strict Baptist upbringing. His mind opened to new ideas.

Peter's broad outlook led to underlying tensions in the family home. Others in his family were intolerant of non-Christians, while Peter gave no thought to a person's religion. He knew many Buddhists and Hindus who were good people; some were also mentors to him. His elder sister would sing "Onward Christian Soldiers" at inappropriate times, which alienated non-Christians neighbors and embarrassed Peter. For the most part, Peter ignored her extreme views and behavior, especially her negative view of other cultures. But he questioned his sister's glorying in her proselytizing, and he questioned the use of religion to justify colonialism. He himself took every opportunity to go to temples and pagodas; there he observed and took an interest in the various practices and beliefs. He did this to be able to get along with his peers in school.

Reading the daily newspapers had also became an obsession for Peter. All the newspapers were full of stories of the war, usually news from London. In the *Illustrated Weekly* there were many pictures of bomb devastation and stories about the Luftwaffe's day and night bombing of England. Peter was pleased to learn that the RAF had taken such a toll that the Germans changed course. He read also about the massive attack on Russia. The British papers carried far less news about China, and Japanese intentions and actions nearer to home.

Peter's immediate concern was what was happening in Southeast Asia. by November Japanese armies had moved into Indo-China without a shot being fired. When the rains ended, preparations for the war began in Rangoon. Warnings about spies were common, and along the streets the walls were covered with bills warning about fires. "Rangoon shall not burn," one said. And then there were the air raid drills. But the authorities continued to assure that there would be no war.

Peter heard rumors, some accurate others wild. "The Japanese have always coveted Burma's oil and its mineral resources," the Burmese told one another. "They will come to seize our wealth." Others focused on control of sea communications. "Japan and Siam are in negotiations to give Japan bases from which they can attack Malaya and Burma," these rumors revealed. "Britain was busy defending the islands," others declared hopefully, "and it is defending itself in Europe, North Africa, and the Middle East. Britain will not abandon us." "But there are shortages of search lights and guns," others argued; "the British have just two fighter squadrons, one made up of the American-made Brewster Buffalos and the containing RAF Hurricanes, and a few bombers." "Soon there will be disturbances," worried residents of Rangoon whispered. "Riots will break out."

Peter's father was tense. "As Indians, we may be caught in the middle," he fretted aloud. "I hear rumors that the Burmese will attack all foreigners,"

Peter confirmed his father's fears. "I, too, have heard that the Burmese will turn their wrath on the foreigners who came with the British, took their jobs, and now are buying up the land."

"But the British have guns," his father said, trying to reassure himself and his son. Nonetheless, there was a lingering fear that was to endure.

At the university, the emphasis was on recruiting and volunteering for the war effort. One morning Peter called at Jeremy's home. CeCi met him at the door; as usual, he thought, she looked stunning.

"Jeremy, you have a guest," she called.

Presently Jeremy appeared. "What's up, Peter?" he inquired.

"Could we meet at the tea shop at the railway station? I have something to tell you," Peter responded.

Railway stations were the center of life in Rangoon. At the east side of this station was a cluster of shops. One was a savory shop, run by a one-legged man, a former solider who had lost the leg in Iraq during World War I. He made the best samosas, lentil patties, and other chick pea savories and lentil soup. Across from this shop was a Burmese shop that offered fried noodles and mohinga. Shops on the west side of the station sold dry goods and a variety of rice, including the rich starchy Za Be Na, the best that Burma's rice basket produced; there was also a small pharmacy and other shops.

The tea shop was in a shed-like structure. It was not fancy but was clean and always busy. The tea was made in smoky pots. On the table were sugar and always milk—condensed milk. For an extra anna, patrons could obtain clotted milk—rich milk made from boiling milk with concentrated fat, which greatly improved the taste of the tea. But clotted milk was for the well-off men. Most of the men who hung around the tea shop's small tables and low chairs were unemployed men or working men who stopped after work to have a cup of tea and buy some savories to take home.

The tea shop was also a meeting point where men shared information about the grim news of impending war; where rumors were generated and sometimes embellished; and where good and bad news alike was share. The educated might buy a newspaper, but most hangers-on relied on the stories circulated at the shop; for some of them, it was their only source of news. Here there were spies, police informers, and saboteurs. But here also the young men would meet to go over the day's events. Here they met to discuss the rumor that all schools and the university would be closed.

After they had ordered a pot of tea, Peter said, "Jeremy, there is much talk of war, you know; at the university they talk about it all the time." Jeremy nodded. Peter continued, "If war comes to Burma, we will have to contribute to the defense of our land and homes. I really want to finish my studies first, but if that is not possible, I need to think about what to do. I am thinking about joining the frontier force."

Just then the pot of tea arrived. It was strong and hot, as the young men preferred. Jeremy slowly poured the tea into the cup, added a teaspoon of sugar and added a dash from the small container of warm clotted milk. After taking a sip of the steaming hot tea he responded.

"Yes, I suspect we will be at war soon. Mother and CeCi are terrified. In fact" he laughed, "CeCi made a grand and hysterical pronouncement last night. She said, 'I will walk all the way to India if I have to; I do not want to live in a country run by the little barbarians.'" But Jeremy turned serious. "I'm not going to run; I've too made up my mind to join the frontier force and fight to defend my home if war comes to Burma! Maybe the newly formed Burma Rifles."

Peter interjected, "Let us join the same unit; at least we will be able to help each other."

"Great idea," Jeremy responded. Then he continued, with a pang of sadness, "I guess Tin Oo will not join the war effort."

"He will probably join the Bo's," Peter whispered, with a hint of humor mixed with sadness. "Yes, he will probably join the other side. I trust we will not have to fight him; that would be most unfortunate." On that note, they left the tea shop and returned to their families.

Chapter 10
Rangoon on the Eve of the Invasion

As 1941 wore on, Benjamin was still working at the Port Trust, which was increasingly busy. On his way home one day in early December, he picked up a copy of the *Rangoon Gazette*. There he read that, because Siam feared a British attack and annexation, the Siamese had signed the Japan-Siam treaty. Now, he read, a railroad between French Indo-China Saigon and Bangkok had been completed. The *Gazette* further speculated that if Japanese troops could move by rail to Bangkok, they could move quite swiftly to the Burma-Siam border, making an offensive from Siam possible. Such assessments frightened Benjamin, but he was mystified by the reassurances from the British Army leaders. "Even if the Japanese attack," the leaders pronounced, "they will be easily repulsed by our superior troops." Once again Benjamin read the familiar refrain that the Japanese soldiers were near-sighted and were poor shots; that myopic Japanese pilots could not see well enough to threaten RAF pilots.

Benjamin muttered to himself, "this is such a familiar refrain! But I am not convinced." He remembered reading in history class that the same had been said before the Battle of the Tsushima Straits in 1904.

Like others in Rangoon, Benjamin listened to the BBC and Radio Australia, which had strong signals in Rangoon. The newscasts were considered sources of the most reliable news, and most of the news was about the European front. Benjamin recognized how badly the war was going in Europe. He saw that the Allies had underestimated the resolve and abilities of the Germans, and he worried that the British and Australians were, likewise, underestimating the resolve and strength of the Japanese.

Benjamin had been hearing his mother lament for weeks now, "Many shops are closing. Prices are rising rapidly and, worse, supplies are getting scarce. No doubt people are hoarding." Benjamin had responded, "Lots of supplies are coming into the port, but they are not reaching the markets; they are going directly to the military. And the military is also buying provisions in the local stores." His father had added, "Tension is rising throughout the city. Medicine is becoming scarce also. We need to set aside monies to stockpile rice, oil, and other staples." Just recently, Mr. Thomas had purchased several sixty-pound bags of rice and other staples. "At an exorbitant price!" he had complained.

The news was not all doom and gloom, however; there was some relief. The American ship "City of Tulsa" had arrived in port, with its hold full of fighter planes. The planes had been assembled and then flew over the city, but they soon left upcountry for Toungoo, which was to be their base. The sight of them cheered the anxious residents of Rangoon. "See," the city's residents told one another, "the British and the Americans will protect us."

One week before Christmas, an AVG (American Volunteer group) squadron (P 40s) arrived in the city from their base at Kyedaw airdrome in Toungoo, in central Burma. They would bolster the air defenses of Rangoon and protect the Burma Road. Two days after they arrived, some of the pilots and crew came into the city for R&R and took the city by storm. Their antics brought smiles to the street crowd, but what most amused the people was the fact that, unlike the British who always kept their distance from the natives, the Americans did strange things. For example, one day Benjamin was standing at the corner of Sule Pagoda road and Montgomery Street, in front of the New Excelsior cinema. A crowd had gathered, and he wondered what was going on. Then he saw white men, AVG pilots, pulling rickshaws with the rickshaw men as passengers. This amused some of the locals, but some of the conservative Burmese were not amused. "What will happen to our Buddhist country if antics such as these become commonplace?" they asked quietly among themselves.

In the British clubs too, the behavior of the Americans caused considerable consternation. They were loud and boisterous and frequently drunk. Worse, after leaving the clubs they frequently picked up and spent the night with Anglo or even native women. The governor tried to discourage this behavior, saying "such behavior will cause the white man to lose face and prestige." But given the desperate military situation, he could not formally object to the AVG command. The pilots were essential to the defense of Rangoon and Southeast Asia. All the governor could do was assure members of the British clubs that this novelty would soon fade and encourage them to look the other way at the proclivities of the Americans.

The city was indeed tense, and the city's residents were always mindful of the looming crisis, and any help was welcome. There were occasional air-raid drills, and blackout precautions were in effect. Nonetheless, people went about their business.

By late December, pre-Christmas parties were at full swing, and one night Jeremy and CeCi went to the Anglo-Indian Club where Anglos congregated. The Club typically played the latest western music, mostly American and mostly gramophone music, but today they had a band of sorts: the members were all amateurs, and they missed a beat every now and then, but it was good to listen to live music. The band played a number of Irish ballads, some joyful and some somber. The favorite of the crowd was Molly Malone, "Cockles and Mussels, alive, alive O!" Jeremy walked over to ask the pretty dark-haired girl a table away if he could have the next dance. He didn't know Noreen well, but he had seen her at the Club many times before and had a crush on her. This evening he mustered his courage and asked her to dance. As they danced, they talked, and Jeremy was surprised to learn that she lived near his own home. They danced several dances and then Jeremy bought her a cold drink. He had rum and lemon. At a break in the music he and Noreen overheard a conservation between two crusty old men who had fought in the first World War.

Talking about current events in Southeast Asia, the men expressed angst about the future. The older of the two wondered, "If we go to war now, will Japan have the upper hand? I'm not sure that the British have the strength to fight another war."

His companion expressed another concern, "Will we Eurasians be considered as stooges of the British? If the British ever retreat from Burma, will Eurasians be given a chance to retreat with them?"

"You're right to worry," replied the elder veteran, "any of us left behind would suffer a terrible fate if the Japanese win and occupy the country."

CeCi joined Jeremy and Noreen near the end of the break. She was happy to be with so many of her friends, and especially happy that Jeremy had borrowed a car this night. They could stay later than usual. As the evening wore on, however, the talk increasingly turned to the war and to what would happen to them, Burma's Eurasians or Anglos. CeCi began to detect fear in the eyes of the party-goers. They shared a common worry about what would happen if war came. With both the *Prince of Wales* and the *Repulse* sunk, there was nothing to stop the Japanese navy from launching a sea-borne landing and invasion of Rangoon. "But the British will put up a good fight," they consoled themselves. The party finally ended with the band playing "Just Before the Battle," "'Til the Lights of London Shine Again," and "'Til We Meet Again." A female singer joined the band as they played Gracie Fields' signature song, "Wish me luck as you wave me goodbye; cheerio, here I go, on my way." This brought all talk to halt. It helped them overcome their fear and gave them the sense that they were not alone in the war. Finally they all joined in singing "God Save the King." A shiver ran down CeCi's spine; she knew that this bonhomie would not last.

Chapter 11
Duty Calls

After returning from Lashio with his family, Peter had thought constantly about what he had seen and learned. One day he approached his all-knowing Uncle Reddy and told him of the facts that he had gathered. Over cups of tea he told of his experiences. "Why," he asked, "can a small country like Japan savage a large ancient country like China, which gave the world paper, paper currency, and gun powder?"

Reddy, eager for such a conversation, replied, "It's a long story. Weak leaders and disunity led to the decline and breakup of the Han Empire. Then, at the turn of this century, the communists and Marxists entered the fray, further weakening the central government. All of this made China vulnerable to the ambitious new Imperial power of Japan." Reddy warmed to his theme. "At the turn of the twentieth century, Japan and Russia went to war, and when the Russian fleet was defeated by the Japanese fleet, commanded by Admiral Togo in the battle of the Tushima straits, Japan started its drive to be the dominant power in East Asia." He paused. "Eventually the Marxists will win, and China will be united again. In the meantime, Japan will try to fulfill its ambition to conquer all of Asia. That's what we have to worry about. If Japan expands her war to Burma, we must think of a plan to leave." He paused, then continued "Actually, it is not a question of 'if 'but of 'when' and 'how soon'."

Although Peter, from his reading, was not as sure as his uncle that the family would need to leave Rangoon if the Japanese started a war, he better understood the danger that Japan presented to all of Southeast Asia. In the *Rangoon Gazette*, information about the war was not front page news but was buried on the second and third pages. Nonetheless, it did present a grim picture of the war in China. Spirits were high in Rangoon, but the men at the border had been more sober. Events were moving faster than anyone thought possible. Peter was convinced that war would, as his uncle had predicted, come to Burma. But he wanted first to finish his studies.

At the tea shop, he had told his friends about what he had seen and learned in Lashio. "It is like a different country there," he said.

Tin Oo knew little of the frontier areas and was alternately interested and bored. Peter explained. "Our governor, under pressure from the Japanese, closed the road to China, but then London pressured him to open it again. You see, the American president wants to keep the Chinese in the war, so he wants us to keep the road open, a difficult task. Japan's armies are closer to the Burma border than you might imagine. They could attack any time. British defenses are weak; they do not have the troops to stop the Japanese. So, our governor finally announced the reopening of the road."

Tin Oo cut in, "it is not just the road; the Japanese want Burmese resources, especially the Tungsten mines at Mawchi and the oil at the Chauk fields. The Japanese are winning and soon will be at the border."

Jeremy blanched at Tin Oo's assessment, but Peter confirmed it. "Today I went to the university to register for next semester's classes, and learned that it has closed—'delayed opening,' the sign reads. But it may not open again for years. Flyers urge students to join the war effort. I feel as though I should join that effort, to defend my home. But I'm not sure what to do."

"There are reports of territorial units being formed," Jeremy offered. "And a new jungle unit has been created, set in the hills near Maymyo, to train for jungle warfare. In fact, I think preparations for war are occurring secretly throughout Rangoon."

"You and I once talked about joining the new frontier force, Jeremy. I think I'm ready to do that," said Peter.

"Yes," said Jeremy. "I've even told my parents and CeCi. They are worried, but with a father so dedicated to this country's railways, how could I not dedicate myself to defending it?"

"You two may join the British colonialists," Tin Oo inserted, "but I have no intention of fighting for the British." He rose from his chair and abruptly left the tea shop.

The next day Peter told his mother about his decision. She cried and was worried, but Peter was firm. "What will he face?" she asked her husband that night. Mr. Thomas simply said, "Our options are limited. We have to defend our home."

Peter and Jeremy soon entered a program of six weeks of intensive training, including jungle warfare and small arms training. At the end of the six weeks, if they were successful, they would be inducted into one of the recently formed Burma Rifle units. Indeed, they were successful, and their induction ceremony was held outdoors, in front of the chancellery building on the university campus. The bands played. Then the Colonel, in his cap with a red band and epaulets, addressed the class:

Soon you will swear allegiance to the King, Country and Empire. You have been given the privilege of being a member of a great and glorious army. You will soon join the ranks of a proud regiment. You will uphold the true fighting sprit of the army; will display honesty and integrity. Hope will be your guiding spirit; and you will uphold these values to the best of your ability. You will soon be engaged in battle against a brutal, ferocious enemy, and you will be expected to fight with honor. Some of you will show uncommon valor. You will at all times obey your superior.

It was an impressive ceremony. The pipes and the bands brought the ceremony to an end.

Life soon would change for Peter and Jeremy. Both were both assigned to the same new BurRif battalion, one of the better trained units. When they arrived at the barracks, they were greeted by the man who, in keeping with tradition, would be the most important man in their lives after their commander: Subedar Major Saw Dunn. The subedar was a stout man. Because of his short stature and stern demeanor he looked fearsome, although he was a cheerful man. The lingua franca in the unit was Urdu, as it was throughout the British Indian Army. The Burmese spoke little Urdu or English; the only English the Gurkhas knew was "Tek Hi Johnny" [don't shoot Johnny], but somehow over time they forged a cohesive unit and fought well.

Jeremy and Peter spent their days in marches, drills, arms training, and classes in tactics; and two new Burmese battalions were formed in Rangoon. But elsewhere the war seemed far away. At Fort Dufferin in Mandalay, club life was unchanged. The officers quaffed Pink Gin, Empire beer, and drank late into the hot dusty evenings. The Supreme commander in Singapore and Burma issued his yearly statement that "military preparation are adequate. The Japanese army would not be much of a match for the great British Army."

In the city, Japanese, spies, saboteurs, and various collaborators were increasingly active and knew otherwise. American lend-lease supplies started to arrive by sea in Rangoon. Ships were arriving regularly. The first had been the "Jaersfontien," flying the Dutch flag. Next came the "City of Tulsa." At the Rangoon port, Benjamin had looked at the manifests of the arriving ships. That for the "Jaersfontien" showed a number large crates, but more interesting was the fact that when he checked the passenger manifest, he noted that there was an unusually large number of Americans, young men in their twenties and thirties. He wondered about that, but his wonder was short lived.

That evening as he was leaving work, a familiar car was parked in front of the Port Trust building. As usual, the Japanese dentist was there. He offered Benjamin a cigarette out of his gold case. "My friend," he said, "I notice that there are some large crates. Did you see what they contain?"

"I do not know what is in the crates," Benjamin replied, "but I did note that there were a number of young Americans on board."

This piqued the interest of the Japanese. The two men exchanged more information before Benjamin headed home. The dentist thanked him but stayed on. He wrote in a notebook and lingered a while, intensely observing the scene. The stevedores unloaded the crates onto American lorries, and then the lorries headed north to the aerodrome at Mingaladon.

Benjamin took the train home. In the second-class coach he entered, there was one Burmese, and a number of Anglos headed to Gyogon, the Anglo community about a mile north of Insein. He overheard a conversation between two elderly Anglos. The news he heard was rapidly becoming commonplace, but this time the source was impeccable. The Anglo girls who hung around the Silver Grille got snippets of information about the Americans. And Andreas the Greek, head chef at the Grille, apparently had confirmed that the Americans were pilots. "Something big is about to happen," the two elderly Anglos concurred. "The cooks at the Grille are being told to sharpen their skills in barbecue, and hot dogs." They continued, "the Chinese also need fighter aircraft to keep the Japanese air power from overpowering the Chinese armies. So the Americans are headed to China." Benjamin found it interesting how supposedly secret information and events were so rapidly disseminated throughout the city.

Chapter 12
Emergency Measures

At the Governor's mansion, the chaprasi-bearers had brought breakfast—toast, eggs, bacon, jams, and marmalades—to the large table. The men sat around the table, with charts, maps, and cables in front of them. They awaited the arrival of the Governor, who was late. He had spent a sleepless night, and when he finally arrived, the ADC told the bearers "go, go; *chalo*." Given the highly secret nature of the meeting, he knew that the help could not be present. He did not want to offend them, but did not want them to be present when secret matters were being discussed.

The Governor sat down and motioned for the rest of the men to take their places. "Pour me a cup of black coffee," he instructed the ADC. After his first sip he said, "Gentleman, you may have breakfast. I do not have much of an appetite." He ignored all the food on the table because, as a matter of fact, he felt a little queasy in the stomach. "Let's proceed."

With an anxious countenance he looked squarely at the GOC and asked, "have you reviewed all the Intelligence and CID reports?"

"Yes, Sir," came the General's reply.

Gravely the Governor noted, "I am particularly concerned about reports of increased enemy activity along the Siam-Burma border. It is only a question of time as to when the attack from there will come."

The men around the table sputtered and assured the Governor that they could hold the Japanese at bay, but the Governor waved them into silence. His own intuition was that he faced a grave crisis. He turned to each of his political advisors in turn and questioned them, "What measures must we take to be able to repel an attack?"

The first to arise was his civil administrator, who said, "I wonder if your measures are too harsh, Governor. There are many voices of dissent."

The Governor retorted, "I'm the one who has the unpleasant task of formulating these harsh measures. And I'm sorry, but I will have to overrule your objections. I will promulgate laws for the defense of this country and will prepare for the invasion that is sure to come."

He then asked his chief political officer to read the new measures aloud, listening intently. "Rangoon General Hospital will discharge all non-critical patients. All surgeons will be kept on standby. All non-essential vehicles will be commandeered. Criminals and known dacoits will be incarcerated. All suspected spies will be held until the emergency is over. . . ." The list continued. "Voluntary fire brigades will be directed to fight important defense-related fires, as they occur."

The chief civil surgeon interrupted. "We cannot prevent some of the senior surgeons from leaving, as many of them are not gazetted in Burma; they are on loan from the Indian Medical Service. If they leave in large numbers, there will be a critical shortage of doctors." He continued. "Then there is the matter of the Karen nurses; they also will flee the city, and then we will have a very critical problem."

The Governor intervened. "Every government servant must stay at their post till I release them," he announced firmly. "I will declare martial law if necessary. Every ward must have a cadre of air-raid wardens (ARWs), a fire brigade, and rescue squads. All long-distance trains will be reserved for our troop deployment and emergency use. Police patrols will be placed on a 24-hour alert, and these orders will go into effect immediately."

There was silence in the room. Then his civil affairs adviser protested. "Sir, some of these measures are draconian."

The Governor nodded his head. "I know. But these are difficult times." With that, he adjourned the meeting but asked the GOC to stay to discuss security matters.

Rangoon was electric with tension. Rumors swirled frantically: "All the senior doctors, especially the Indians, have left Rangoon General Hospital! The majority of the nurses have also left or will soon do so! All essential government servants will be ordered to remain at their stations!" No one knew what to believe, and all of the rumors carried bad news for Rangoon's populace.

One day, Benjamin was driving the family car, a blue-grey Wolseley, down Ahlone Road when he was stopped by a police road block. A light-skinned Anglo-Burmese policeman ordered Benjamin out of the car and demanded the car registration. He took it to the senior police officer, then he returned and informed Benjamin, "the car is being seized in the name of the Defense of the country. It will be returned at the end of the war."

Astonished and angry, Benjamin tried to reason with the policeman. "My entire family relies on this car, to get us to work!"

But the policeman became irritated and began to read a proclamation by the governor, which curtly said: "All private cars should be commandeered for the war effort." Benjamin was shooed away, and the police drove the car away, leaving Benjamin to trudge home on foot.

When he arrived home, he was despondent and shaken. "I can't believe they are seizing our means of transportation to work," he lamented. "Don't they depend on us to keep the ships and trains running? The streets clean?"

When he heard the news, Mr. Thomas was openly worried. He had hid his fears until this point, but now the ring was closing. He was approaching his sixth decade, and as the oldest living brother, he carried the extra burden of the responsibility for the entire extended family. He regularly held meetings with his younger brother and nephews, and now he called an emergency council.

Mr. Thomas began the meeting with his own observations. "All of the most powerful steam locomotives have been sent north of Pegu and held there," he reported. "But more ominous is the fact that rail carriages, mostly first and second class coaches, are being shunted just to the north. Rumor has it that these coaches are being set aside to make a run to Rangoon to evacuate British women and children."

Reddy interrupted. "And what provisions have been made for non-Europeans?"

"None that I know of," admitted Mr. Thomas. "That said, Mr. Churchill has always vowed that the British would not abandon Burma. I, too, will not abandon Burma." Now his face showed fear and anguish, but he tried to hide this in the presence of the family. "If war comes to Rangoon," he declared, "I will stay."

Reddy listened quietly, but his leanings were to the political left, and he sympathized with the Independence movements in India and Burma. He interjected, "war *is* coming, he announced with certainty." Fire brigades have been placed under the control of the military. Air raid precautions have begun, including digging of shelters. We have a lights-out at 7 P.M. order, and the military governor will soon issue more restrictions." Reddy disliked the British and harsher aspects of British rule. "I think that, when war comes, the women and children should be evacuated."

A somber Thomas asked Reddy, "but if there are no ships or trains, how would they escape, now that the car has been confiscated?"

Grimly, Reddy replied, "we will join the exodus and walk out—by bullock cart and on foot."

No consensus was reached by the men, but Reddy's opinion was gaining urgency.

LATE NOVEMBER, 1941

At work, Mr. Thomas received his notification. He knew what was in the note and dreaded the message, but opened the note anyway. That evening when he returned home he found Reddy awaiting him. He too had heard about the new stern measures. Mr. Thomas sat down next to Reddy. His wife brought him cold lemonade, which she had just made. Thomas was sweating, not only from the heat but also from the unpleasant news he was about to break to his family. He sipped the cold lemonade, then turned to his wife. "My job has been declared essential," he announced gravely. "That means that, as long as the edict remains in effect, I cannot leave the city. He paused. "I think you should leave the room and let Reddy and me discuss this further."

After she left the room, he turned to the man next to him, his kinsman with whom he had shared so many challenges and so many joys. "Reddy," he said, "I cannot leave, but I don't want the family to stay. I realize that breaking up the family is dangerous, and joining the refugee exodus already in progress is difficult and dangerous. What should we do?"

Reddy replied, "I'll look into the possibility of sending the children and women by train to Mandalay with a male escort, but this will not be easy; all the trains are being used by the military. Yet it is worth a try, because the idea of walking to India from here is terrifying; there is no road, no access to food, the local population may be a threat, and the whole journey would be perilous indeed."

The two men sat in silence a few minutes, contemplating their options. Then Mr. Thomas called his family together. He glanced around at the many faces of his beloved family. The elder children were worried; the younger children in their innocence were curious but unafraid. He told the gathering of the measures the government had announced and would now enforce. "We will have to be prepared for air raids. I will go to the shop and buy the regulation long green conical lamp shades. Once they are in place, our night life will change. Dinner will have to be completed before dark, then the lights will have to be turned off." He saw the worried looks spread around the room "You will get used to the dark, do not be afraid."

"What about homework," Kamala asked?

Mr. Thomas smiled at her. "You can study before dark, of course." Then he said, "I rather think, however, that schools will be closed." He returned to the theme of preparations. "Next, we need to build a shelter and stockpile food. Reddy and I will begin those tasks tomorrow. For tonight, go about your business as usual. Tomorrow will begin our new life."

The next evening, Reddy joined Mr. Thomas and Benjamin as they began work on an air-raid shelter. Regulations called for shelters to be six feet deep. But when the men had dug only four feet, water began to seep into the shelter. Secretly, Mr. Thomas worried about snakes, but he kept his fears to himself. After the digging was completed, a roof of wood and bamboo matting was laid atop the trench and covered with dirt. Two days later, Mr. Thomas's worst fears were realized: a cobra was found in the shelter. The men quickly dispatched it with their shovels and buried it where the women and children would not discover it.

In the meantime, Peter had received his orders to report to the 4th Burma Rifles barracks. He had five days to gather his equipment and attend to his personal affairs. Peter got up early and, while drinking his coffee, turned on the radio. He had just tuned in to Rangoon Radio when the announcer in somber tones announced that the Japanese were going to Saigon. The announcer explained, "the Burmese frontier, however, is quite safe." In the bazaars and the tea shops, however, rumors were rife. Many friends and neighbors were leaving or had left. At evening family gatherings, the discussion invariably turned to who had left and whether the family should flee the city. This led Peter to question whether the Burmese frontier was, in fact, so safe.

Peter knew the reality that he would be sent to the front and that he could die, but he took comfort in the words of the Commander of all British forces in Southeast Asia and his battalion commander that "the Japs are not a match against a western army. The British Army is superior to all others, especially the Japanese, even if they did beat the Russians in 1905."

But still, Peter had doubts. He asked Uncle Reddy about the past history, and Reddy, always happy to hold forth, told him, "there is a chance that the Japanese will 'liberate' Burma, and then, once Burma is secure, India would be freed." Clearly, Reddy was a nationalist at heart. "I think," he said, "that the rumors of Japanese atrocities in China were exaggerated."

But Peter questioned Reddy's assumptions, and his doubts remained unresolved. He remembered a quote from the poet Kipling from his schoolbook:

"Far called, our navies melt

On dunes and headlights sinks the fire

lo, all our pomp of yesterday

Is one with Nineveh and Tyre."

Before Peter left for the barracks, his grandmother insisted on a familiar Indian ritual. In spite of her Christian beliefs, she still went through the Hindu ritual of placing red chiles on hot coals and offerings mantras to protect him from evil. Peter had no faith in any such rituals, but he stood still to assuage his grandmother's concerns. As soon as he was out of sight of the house, he pulled out a letter that he had carried around for two days. He had not wanted to open it at home. But now he took out the letter he had received from Amy days ago. He looked at it for a long time before he opened it and read it with great anticipation. It was in her neat handwriting.

My Dear Peter,

I left Rangoon for my home in the hills. I am now at Mawchi and am working at the small hospital here. If you are going to leave Rangoon, I would like to see you before you leave. I work the late shift, with a break at 6 AM. Please meet me on the east wing of the general ward. There is a wide veranda and a quiet spot. It is so difficult for me here; it is quiet and lonely. I miss you so much.

Love Amy

Peter had met Amy at the Rangoon Hospital, in the company of CeCi. In her thin white *aingyi* and red *longyi*, she looked fragile; she was a guileless, beautiful girl. She had high cheekbones, round eyes, was light skinned, and had shiny, silky, long black hair. For the most part she was a Karen, but her beauty was enhanced by non-Karen ancestors. She had just passed her exams and was a junior nurse. It had been mutual attraction, and with the passage of time they got to know one another better. It turned serious. Being seen together was not acceptable, so they had met surreptitiously. Peter sighed as he remembered their last meeting. He had made arrangements to meet her at the Rangoon Zoological gardens, not far from the city. There they just met and pretended to talk. The gardens were appropriately called; the zoo housed some of the most ferocious Burmese tigers but also was landscaped with great flora. The shrubs and flowers brought a great number of birds—greatly plumed, multi-hued birds. Of these, the Burmese Peacock was the most exotic bird, and well-loved as well; it was the emblem on the Burmese flag. The showy male displayed every color of the spectrum, but it was bird's iridescence that caught Amy's eyes, "It's beautiful, just like you," she blushed. Late in the afternoon, they walked to the end of the west gate. She pulled him gently by his hand behind a bush. "I have something important to tell you. You know the situation. My parents want me to come back home to the safety of the hills. They worry that Rangoon will be unsafe for me. I will go to work in a small hospital in Bowlake, set on a hilltop overlooking the town. It is quite pretty. If you go away to the front, I want to see you before you go." Now, with Amy's letter in hand, Peter resolved to see Amy once more before he was sent off to the front.

Peter and Jeremy reported to their barracks in Rangoon together. Their daily routine was not onerous, as recruits were arriving each day. Peter asked permission to leave the barracks for two days, to attend to personal affairs. Without even telling Jeremy of his plans, he hired a car and went to Mawchi to see Amy. It took two to three hours to get to Toungoo, and from there the road to Bowlake was slow going. The narrow winding road with switch backs made driving difficult. By the time he arrived in the small mining town, it was late in the evening, so he looked for a place to stay. There were no hotels anywhere, but finally he found a small guest house. The room was tiny and Spartan. He got up early in the morning, surprised at how cool it was. Mist hung low over the hills, and the top tip of the disc of the sun was just above the horizon. He climbed the narrow road to the hospital. It was built on a hillside, on a spur, and consisted of three small low buildings, all painted colonial yellow with red roofs. In the semi-darkness he walked past the operating theater and the small lab.

He found Amy in the ward, a traditional long room, with a row of beds along each side. At one end of the long room was a kitchen and the nursing station. She was attending to a patient at the far end of the room, and looked tired after having worked a long night. But her eyes widened and a little smile crossed her face; then she circumspectly turned her attention back to her patient. To avoid suspicion, he pretended he was looking for a patient, walking right past her to the veranda. Presently she came walking out of the open ward, towards the broad veranda. He approached her and smiled at her; she whispered "walk to the end of the veranda, where there is a small watchman's room. He will have left. I will meet you there in ten minutes." Peter nodded his head and took leave of her. He walked to the tiny room, and she had been right: the watchman had already left.

While he waited, he noted that the hills were still draped with low clouds—wispy, thin, cottony clouds that shrouded the mountain peaks—and that the sun was just peeking over the horizon. Soon the rays of the sun filtered through the thick foliage. In the distance he could see the silvery river. "That must be the Salween," he thought. Suddenly the great disc of the sun rose swiftly over horizon; orange and yellow rays of light broke through the clouds in giant streaks, and the light scattered the mist, making the scene literally glow. Flocks of tropical birds flitted from tree to tree.

Engrossed by the sights and sounds, Peter did not hear her footsteps. She surprised him as she came around the corner. "Hello," she whispered; then they embraced tightly. "I missed you very much, Peter. I have been terribly worried. Where are you going and when?" He remained quiet for a while, then said, "I will be going to Moulmein in three days." She remained silent for a while, then sobbed quietly. He held her face in his hands and whispered, "I will come back when this madness is over." She shook her head. "I don't think it's going to be that easy. We have many enemies. If we can resist the Japanese onslaught, it could be over in a short time, and we could be together again. But I don't know, I don't think it will be easy; please be careful," she pleaded. "I want see you again . . . soon." The sun was rising rapidly, and the night staff were leaving. "You better go," she said. She let him go reluctantly, after kissing him on the cheek, then quickly turned and walked to the Quarters behind the hospital. He stayed till she disappeared behind the building. He lingered there for a while, wondering whether he would see her again. With great sadness he returned to his hired car and rode pensively back to Rangoon.

PART IV

Battles at Moulmein
and the Sittang Bridge

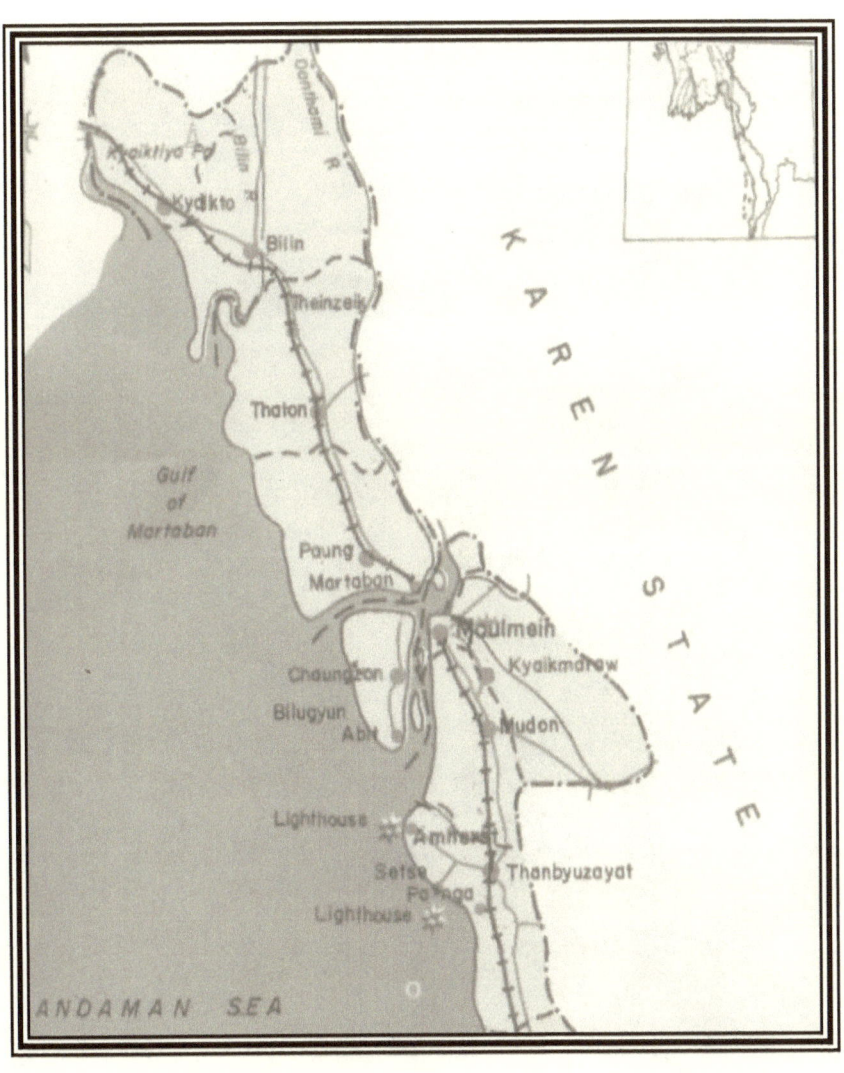

Chapter 13
To Moulmein with the Burma Rifles

The young men received orders to proceed to Moulmein. They went to the railway station in the morning, taking comfort in the fact that they were embarking on this adventure together. At Platform One, they boarded the long military train that would take them to Moulmein. It took time for the commanders and bearers to get all the personnel and their equipment on the train. It was now fully loaded, and ready to depart. Smoke billowed from the engine's smokestack, and steam hissed from its huge pistons. The conductor shooed the last stragglers onto the train, then waved his green flag. The engine whistled three times and then it slowly chugged. It took a few minutes to leave the main platform, but soon the maze of rails and the marshaling yard gave way to two tracks, and the train rapidly left the city to head north to Pegu.

On either side of the tracks were green paddy fields, but in a few minutes the landscape changed. The paddy fields gave way to marshland, and the train passed through the bog, high above the marsh on an embankment. Peter settled in. He could see the road that paralleled the railway, and noted that it was full of military traffic—long convoys of lorries and military cars and jeeps all heading in the same direction: north. The wetlands were criss-crossed with *chaung*s (small creeks), and eventually the main river came into view. "That would be the Pegu," Jeremy said.

The train slowed, blew its whistle several times, and then stopped. The station sign read Pegu, which would be a short stop. When the train left the Pegu station, it turned sharply to the east, following a spur line. The main line headed north to Mandalay. Fatigue overcame Peter, and he dozed off. About an hour later, the slowing train awakened him, and as he peered out the window, he saw houses, streets, and buildings. The station sign said Waw. Once a sleepy village, Waw was now a divisional headquarters, and the platform was filled with soldiers and ordnance. The train stopped. The engine decoupled and headed to the large water tank to replenish its water. Peter got out to stretch, and walked up and down the platform. The wagons were cramped with guns, ordnance, and armored cars. When he saw the engine come back, Peter knew it was time to re-board the train. He ran to his coach just as the train got underway. After a brief talk with Jeremy, Peter fell into a deep sleep.

Jeremy too closed his eyes for a while, but slept lightly. The slowing of the train wakened him, and after peering out the window he shook Peter awake. "We're approaching the Sittang Bridge," he said. "I thought you would want to see it."

"Thanks," responded Peter with a laugh. "You know me well!" By the time he got to the window and his eyes adjusted to the darkness, he could just make out the silvery bridge. It was dimly lit. The clickity-clack changed to the hollow sound of the train going over the long iron bridge. The bridge seemed suspended over a high gorge, at the far end were three hills. The railroad cutting was through these hills, and far below it was the fast flowing Sittang River. Peter counted eleven spans.

Peter was not the only one impressed by the long-span bridge over the deep gorge. Jeremy's nose was pressed to the window as well. About halfway across the bridge, he looked back at where they had come and gave a little shiver. "I have a strange premonition," he said to Peter. Expecting a jocular story from his friend, Peter turned expectantly. But Jeremy was pensive. "That we will see this place again." The bridge would, in fact, play a major role in both men's lives.

As the train reached the east bank of the Sittang River, Peter spotted two hills directly ahead, to the east. On top of the highest hill was a pagoda. He saw another hill to the south. After crossing the bridge, the train turned south and proceeded along a high embankment that was cut through the hillside. Descending the embankment slowly, the track reached the flat land, then turned away from the river. The train sped up and then passed small stations, slowing only when the Thaton station came into view. But the train did not stop.

Once the seat of the Mon kingdom and an important big city, Thaton had been a great trading center; ships had come from afar for timber and gemstones, and it was fabled for the great ruby owned by its king. Now, however, it was a decaying city. Fifteen minutes beyond Thaton, the train slowed again and finally came to a stop at a marshaling yard. The station sign read Martaban, the end of the line. Just beyond the marshaling yard lay a large body of water, the estuary of the Salween River.

The tired men rushed to the doors, but disembarked in a orderly manner. Once on the platform, the Company Commander assembled his company and ordered them to bivouac beyond the station and rest for the night.

Early the next morning, the men fell in and marched to the Martaban ferry crossing. The jetty was packed with traffic: ferries, launches, gunboats, flat boats, and country boats all crowded along the river's edge. The men packed onto a ferry that was already fully loaded with vehicles of all descriptions. The ferry soon left the dock and crossed the three mile wide estuary of the Salween river. By noon they had arrived at the busy Moulmein port. The port jutted out into an estuary of the Salween river, and the ferry pulled into one of its many docks, the Mission Street jetty. The men disembarked and assembled on the jetty, waiting for orders from their CO. After an interminable time, he ordered the company to proceed to the St. Patrick school, which had been converted to a military barracks. The men duly marched to the school, and by the time they arrived and were assigned to quarters it was late; they were happy to unload their haversacks and, exhausted, quickly fall to sleep.

The next morning at breakfast, Peter and Jeremy sat together. Peter had read the booklet on Moulmein that his CO had given to him. Moulmein was described as the capital of Burma's Tenassarim district. It had a rich trading history, stretching back to the time of the Mon kingdom. Portugese, Dutch, and British traders had arrived in the seventeenth century. Teak was plentiful in the hinterlands, and it was this that drew the British to Moulmein in 1824. Here they refitted His Majesty's warships and trading galleons. The British built a colonial outpost at Moulmein, apart from the city. Clubs for the British flourished: the Flotilla Club, the Marine Club, and the Gymkhana Club.

"Moulmein is a much smaller city than Rangoon," Peter informed Jeremy. "It is actually surrounded by the Salween River on three sides and a high ridge on the east side. Through the Salween River, it is connected to the Andaman sea and the Indian Ocean."

They turned to the little booklet together and read, "to the north of Moulmein, beyond the Salween River, are the Karen hills, home to the Karens, an ethnic group distinct from the majority Burmese. To the south of Moulmein is the long narrow Kra Isthmus that Burma shares with Siam; further south are Malaya and the island of Singapore."

"So," Jeremy said, "We are not far from the Siam-Burma border."

Peter commented, "You have had some signals training. Have you any knowledge of signals traffic from across the border, from Siam?

Jeremy responded, "I'm not privy to the latest traffic, but I sense that the traffic has increased five-fold. The scuttlebutt is that there is a heavy concentration of enemy forces just across the border."

"Given what I saw at the China-Burma border," Peter shared, "I do not think that the China Expeditionary Force (Japanese) is near there." He continued. "I think we will bear the brunt of the invasion."

Jeremy remained silent, then added. "You are probably right. It is merely a question of whether the attack will come from the east, from Raheng, or from the south, from Tavoy."

Peter wondered aloud, "What if the attack comes from both directions?"

"Then we are sunk," Jeremy summed up.

Peter and Jeremy settled down to drills, marching, and live ammo practice. All of this was in preparation for future action. One evening Peter remarked, "it is so quiet and peaceful here."

"Now it is," Jeremy responded, "but I wonder how long will it last." The routine of preparations continued. Both of them were assigned to the C company of the 4th Burma Rifles. In their free time, the men explored the city. Moulmein was, in its own way, a cosmopolitan if small city. The seaside was where all the action was. It was noted for its seafood, but also the broad promenade that attracted young men and women, who surreptitiously eyed one another as they watched the Salon fisherman bring in their great catch: foot-long lobster and tiger prawn as big as cold-water lobsters. Peter and Jeremy quickly found a favorite restaurant, a large, open-air seafood restaurant at one end of the promenade that served the best grilled lobster.

One night, Peter and Jeremy noticed a beautiful Eurasian woman sitting alone at the table next to theirs. The three fell into conversation with one another. Jeremy asked her how her family had come to live in Moulmein. "It's a long story," she laughed, "but since my date has not yet arrived, I'll tell you." "My great grandfather, a Portuguese sea captain named Pinto, brought his man-of-war to the shores of Moulmein. He found himself here not by choice but by accident, captain of a crippled ship. He settled here after escaping from the outraged Burmese king just in the nick of time to avoid torture and death. Not having a way back to Portugal, he beached his ship and built a home. He lived out his life and married a local woman. Two generations later, his grandson, my father, married a woman who was herself of mixed blood, and I am their firstborn. I have a younger brother, Carl. My father built a house just below the ridge overlooking the city, where sea breezes from the Andaman sea make the heat bearable."

Peter was listening intently and noted that Pearl was, in fact, a stunning beauty. "I'll bet she really turns heads," he thought. In fact, on weekends when Pearl walked on the beach, she did turn heads and invite stares, even from some British men. But generally, she did not impress the rest of the English for, despite her great beauty, she was but a half caste, a "blackey-white." To the Burmese she was a *kabya*, a half caste, lowest in the Burmese pecking order. Only the Karens were below her type. To the Hindus she was a "Chi Chi"girl. "Do you work here in Moulmein?" he asked. "Yes, for the Bombay Burmah Trading Company, known here as the BBTC," Pearl replied.

Just then Pearl's date arrived and whisked her off. Like Pearl, he was employed by the Bombay Burmah Trading Company. Many young men in their twenties came from England and Ireland to work for the BBTC. They lived alone in the teak forests, supervising men, elephants, and the "ozzies"—the men who trained and handled them. It was a lonely job, and to while away the evenings and nights, they drank gin and whiskey. Some of them became alcoholics even before they turned thirty. Those who survived were promoted and brought back to civilization. Pearl's date was such a man. He was Celtic in appearance, with a shock of red hair and fair skin that burnt easily. He was slightly portly, and not particularly good looking. He had been promoted to Assistant Manager of the Timber Mill in Moulmein, and Pearl was his mistress.

Pearl was not desperately in love with her date—she had a local boy who appealed to her—but she was tired of being a second-class citizen of the empire. She hoped that her date would marry her and take her away from her unhappy station in life to merry old England. She could not go to the British clubs, so the young man drove his mistress in his MG roadster with the top down, to a small seaside town named Amherst, named after a Viceroy of India. It was a small resort where those who liked the sun and sea came to rest and get away from the busy city. There were many small coves at the edge of town where lovers could enjoy the sun and the sea. After relaxing and enjoying a fantastic seafood supper, Pearl and her date would set out back to Moulmein. On the way back was a small isolated cove, where they would make love at the water's edge.

On this particular night, Pearl's date had drank one too many gins and thus had some difficulty with sex. He finished prematurely, leaving her unfulfilled. She lay on the sand saying nothing while he smoked his cigarette. Finally she sat up naked and looked into his eyes. "Will you join the territorial unit to defend the country? Or will you leave?" He inhaled deeply and blew out the smoke. Instead of answering, he dressed and walked to the car muttering, "they are all the f.... same" and abruptly left.

Chapter 14
District Commissioner Forrester

Presiding over the city of Moulmein and the Tenassarim district was Commissioner Forrester. He was a stout, broad-shouldered man with a round face. His thinning salt-and-pepper hair was combed from side to side to cover his bald spot. He sported a thick moustache, which had a streak of grey. It added character to his face. He looked fierce, but he was a careful and soft-spoken man. His charge included the courts, the collection of revenue, the administration of justice, and much more. Three generations of his family had served in India; his grandfather had been educated at the Company's Haileybury College and subsequently had joined the Indian Civil Service. His father had the privilege of going to Oxford and then served under the Viceroy of India. Forrester himself followed in their footsteps, having gone to college and studied Farsi, and Urdu, the lingua franca of the Indian empire. He was the civil-service version of the British ruling class: while he relished the prospect of a gin and tonic before dinner, he was not the boorish gin-swilling empire builder. Instead, he was among a number of high-minded members of the British raj who set out to rule, firmly but fairly, and to improve the living conditions of the natives by maintaining high and fair standards, all the while maintaining their own integrity. While he believed in the Imperial enterprise, there were moments when he had his doubts. He was partial to the writer Edmund Burke, whom he quoted often. His favorite quote was "I dread our own power and our ambition, and I dread our being too much dreaded. It is ridiculous to say that we are not men, and that, as men, we shall never wish to aggrandize ourselves." Of course, Burke's words were usually considered applicable only to European peoples, not to "savages" in the colonies. Forrester had studied history and remembered the brutality of the Irish war for independence. He was less sanguine than officials in Rangoon about the coming war. He understood from events in nearby China the ambition and determination of Imperial Japan to expand its empire, and he intended to protect the British empire; he would pursue all of his tasks with vigor.

As new Commissioner, Forrester was charged to inquire into the progress of an investigation of the murder of a British district officer. He summoned the police commissioner and asked him to summarize progress on the investigation.

"The Investigation is progressing slowly because the local people are reluctant to talk to the police." His brow was crinkled and he was worried. "The old man had many enemies, and not only political; it appears that there is a woman involved." He went on. "The old man came from the old school. He subscribed to the old imperialist line, treating the locals like children. 'Even though they may be physically mature,' he would tell me, 'their minds are childlike.' He believed that the locals needed to be guided because they were not capable of ruling themselves." The police commissioner paused to see how Forrester was taking this. Seeing Forrester's impassive face, he continued. "He used to say that unlike Englishmen, the Burmese and Indians were childlike, that all non-white races retained juvenile traits. He even had a name for this condition, I think it was 'neotony'? He was convinced that the locals would never become fully adult and thus would never be capable of self rule." Forrester listened glumly and was relieved to dismiss the policeman, telling him to leave the report. Forrester wondered about the police commissioner's truthfulness, as there were some questions he had about him. But he appreciated the detail in the investigative report and the man's new insights into the reasons for the murder.

Forrester believed in the superiority of the British and the obligation to carry the white man's burden, but he also believed that if given time and nurturing, at some future date the Burmese could be trusted to rule themselves with guidance from the British. He kept that in mind in the administration of his district, especially with the looming threat of war.

Forrester knew that the king's empire in Asia was beset with problems and wanted to administer his district in a more benign way, a way that would ultimately lead those being administered to respect and want to emulate the British. But he was even more concerned with war, rumors of war, and preparations for war.

He had recently returned from a meeting in Rangoon, where the Governor and the GOC had advised him that the most probable route of attack would be across the Tenassarim, whose largest city was Moulmein, so that the first attack would likely fall on Moulmein. They had shown him a cable from the U.S. consul in Chungking, describing the possible invasion. The GOC had directed him to "gain access to the attitudes of the Burmese, as the success of the defense of Moulmein will depend on the support of the people. The General had said "We hear that Moulmein is teeming with spies and Japanese-trained collaborators."

Forrester had tried to explain. "The police have tried to keep a close watch on the comings and goings on, but with little success. This is not easy, as there are many Japanese ships berthed in the port, and Japanese sailors wander freely around the city, many incognito."

"What I fear most," the General had admitted, "is sabotage, especially of the port and telephone lines, by Japanese agents and spies and returning collaborators. And I am concerned about the reputedly sizable fifth column at the Siam-Burma border." Looking Forrester directly in the eye he had said, "your task is to know at all times what is going on in your district."

When he had returned from Rangoon, after meeting with the Governor, Forrester knew that he had to cultivate the help of a trusted highly placed local Burman. Happily he had one in mind, and it would also serve his other purpose, namely, to widen the membership in the Moulmein Club. His plan would have been unthinkable a few years ago, but now, five years into Diarchy (five years after Burma was split administratively from India), with many Burmese elite in high government positions and the unease of the war hanging like a pall over everyone's life, things were different. He would seek a competent Burmese who would be invited to join the Moulmein Club. Then, he—Forrester—would milk that member for information. Forrester agreed with George Orwell about the failures of colonialism and the need to have the Burmese friendly to them.

The Moulmein Club overlooked the waterfront and the esplanade from high ground away from the noise and the dust of the city. The setting was pastoral: the front gate was draped with multi-hued bougainvillea and a well-manicured lawn. Tropical flowers and decorative shrubs grew in great profusion. Before 1935, no man of color had been permitted to darken its front gate; they had entered through the back door. The servants' quarters were in the back of compound.

Forrester had already approached the management with the suggestion to open membership to elite non-whites immediately, but he had encountered stiff opposition, especially from the older entrenched members. Many in the club agreed with the management and club secretary that under no circumstances should non-whites be allowed into the club. In frustration, after one of his late-night binges, Forrester stole the sign outside the club that he found so offensive: "Indians and dogs not allowed."

He knew that he needed an intelligence office to ferret out the mood of the Burmese. He already knew that the Japanese had an extensive spy network, that they were recruiting high Burmese officials and students; the Japanese would whisk the recruits to Japan to train them as spies, planning to then bring them back to Burma as "freedom fighters" in the coming war. In this process they could brainwash the recruits to join the Greater East Asia Co-Prosperity Sphere. He would counter this with his plan to find "suitable Burmese" to come to the Club as guests, so that he could create a "liaison" with the civilian population. Now, though, it was important that he find and cultivate a "suitable" Burmese source who could provide him with the intelligence he needed. But where to find such an intelligence officer? And how to browbeat the Club into accepting him? He mulled over this for a while. Soon he had a brain wave, a smile played across his face, and he set his plan in action.

He called a meeting with the President and Secretary of the Club to discuss the issue. It was hot, even with the fans running. The Club president was an old blimp of an Englishman and a old-line conservative imperialist, to the core. Forrester felt sweat dripping down his neck. He spoke slowly and firmly. "We all know that there is little trust between the British and the Burmese. This has actually worked to the advantage of Japan. In order to stop Japan," he said patiently, "Britain requires help from the Burmese. If we invite a prominent Burman to join the Club, he can help keep us informed. He can help keep in touch with the local community," he explained. "In fact, the military commanders in Rangoon are concerned about Britain's lack of intelligence, especially about conditions along the frontier." Before the president could respond, he continued, "so I suggest that Mr. Mya Maung, a prominent Burman lawyer, be invited to join the Club."

The Secretary had already had too many drinks, and he became furious at the idea of non-white members in the Club. He was a tall imposing man, overweight. He wore a permanent scowl. He was loud and had no fear of expressing himself. Now he turned red and expostulated, "I'm no bleeding-heart liberal!" He ranted, "The Asian races are decaying; the British are noble and virile men; and no native is civilized enough to join this Club." He jabbed his finger at the plaque hanging on the wall; it contained a quote from Kipling, written in support of the American effort to suppress the Filipino insurgency at the turn of the century. But the British had embraced Kipling's words to justify their own colonial enterprise. "Let me remind you of Kipling's eloquent words," the Secretary thundered as he pointed:

> Take up the white Man's Burden,
> send forth the best ye breed,
> Go bind your sons to exile
> To serve your captives' need:
> To wait in heavy harness
> On fluttered folk and wild.
> Your new-caught sullen peoples,
> half-devil and half-child.

Without missing a beat, the Secretary moved on to quote the Governor of Singapore, whose misplaced assessment of the Japanese would later lead to the sack of Singapore: "the British army should be able to chase off the little yellow men if they attack us." He paused for effect then continued. "Really! It is preposterous to think that savages could defeat the great British Army. Absolutely no native is civilized enough to join this Club," he repeated. He raised his voice literally to a shout, "I will oppose this betrayal with every fiber of my being. It is as if the land of hope and glory were being violated. In fact," he charged, "I think that our Commissioner is using the war as a sinister plot to mongrelize the club." He snorted, "You,

Commissioner, are a do-gooder. You are using your position to bring Niggers and Wogs into the Club. If you get your way," he warned, "those natives who have long lusted after our women will have a license to leer and lust after our women."

As the Secretary paused to catch his breath, the president quickly interjected, "Facts in the world, in Europe and in Asia, are changing, of course; perhaps it is time to take a new approach."

"Harrumph!" said the Secretary as he strode from the room.

Forrester remained undeterred. He was encouraged by the fact that not all club members shared the views of the Secretary and that the president seemed open to his suggestion.

At the next meeting of full Club membership, Forrester put forth his proposal again, first stressing "the importance and gravity of the situation that his administration faced." There was much heat and anger by some members, but finally the president called for a vote to change the membership rule. Swayed by Forrester's considerable power as the chief officer of the crown in the district, and his considerable persuasive skills, the membership agreed to accept the motion to invite a native to be a member "for political purposes."

One of the members asked "do you have anyone in mind, Sir?" and Forrester immediately submitted the name of Mya Maung. After more discussion and bluster from the Secretary, Forrester was able to prevail. He was finally given permission to offer a temporary membership to Mya Maung, but Mr. Maung was to be excluded from the swimming pool and the dining room. He would be limited to the bar, where he could only be served drinks when accompanied by a member in good standing.

Chapter 15
Mya Maung, Reluctant Spy

Mya Maung was a small man with a broad face, small eyes, and jet black hair. He was well educated. He had studied in England and therefore held a high position in the civil service; in fact, he was one of the first native civil servants in his native Moulmein. He and his family enjoyed certain privileges that came from his position, and he was a leader in the Burmese community. But he was also interested to help free his country from colonial rule. So he was a conflicted man, caught between his strong sense of patriotism and the comfortable life of privilege he had created for himself and his family.

Recently, Japanese collaborators had approached him to solicit his support for the "free Burma movement." They had insisted that "the Japanese will free Burma, then grant Burma her independence from the hated British." Mya Maung, however, had deep misgivings about this promise and feared it was an empty one. He had read about Manchuria, which the Japanese "freed" from the Russians and then brutalized. He knew that he had to make the decision soon about whether or not to collaborate.

Forrester brought Mya Maung to the Club as his guest, making sure that they sat at a table away from the more boisterous members. At this first visit, Mya Maung not only had to overcome the hostility of the British but also had to endure hostility from the contingent of Punjabi bartenders. The Englishman ordered drinks, "Burra peg for me; is ko chota peg." The Punjabi bartender made sure that the number of drinks served to the new member was limited. He knew that Burmese could not hold their liquor!

After the two men settled down at their table with their drinks, Forrester spoke. In hushed tones he asked, "how do you think the Burmese would react in the case of war? Japanese propaganda says that Asia is for Asians, that they will liberate Burma from the yoke of colonial brutality." He paused for his words to sink in. "But look how brutal the Japanese have been to their fellow Asians in China. The British have not treated anybody that badly. All this Japanese propaganda is a ruse. When the Japanese take over Burma, they will do the same here as they are doing in China."

Mya Maung was slow to respond. Finally he said, "to most Burmese, this is not their war. They just wish all foreigners would go away and leave the Burmese alone to tend their paddy fields. You know," he continued, "we once ruled ourselves quite well. We have a strong religion and culture. But to answer your question more pointedly," he said, "most Mons would be neutral or be helpful; Karens, without hesitation, would side with the British; so would the many Indians and the Anglos, but not the Burmese. In fact, some Burmese political parties are already helping the Japanese." He paused and fell back on an excuse that he always used when he had difficulty finding the correct word. "May I smoke?" The Englishman nodded. Mya Maung lit a cigarette, inhaled deeply, then exhaled slowly. He took a deep breath and said, "I would like to help, but the British have been very stingy with granting rights to the Burmese. Frankly, the political climate is not conducive for the Burmese to help you." He listed some items that the British needed to do, and do soon. "The main issue," he observed, "is the granting of self rule." He continued, "I myself, and others like me, am well disposed to the British. But in the poor sections of the country, spies have great sway over the people."

Forrester now came to the substance of his quest. He called for another drink, took a sip, and looked into the eyes of the Burmese and asked, "What do you know about the Burmese so-called Bo's—the collaborators?" He did not want to inflame Mya Maung's feelings so continued carefully. "British intelligence and the Criminal Investigation Division (CID) know about the surreptitious escape of conspirators from Burma to the Japanese island of Hainan, to train and come back to fight against the government of Burma."

Mya Maung looked surprised but soon recovered. "I do not know all the details, but there are rumors in the Burmese community about many young men who have gone underground and about some who went overseas and some who are living along the border with Siam."

After his third drink, Mya Maung became flushed. The good whiskey was more potent than the foul Triple X Rum that he was used to drinking. Forrester's timing was impeccable. He asked Mya Maung, "How many young people have gone underground? How do they leave the country? Do they have help from people here in Moulmein?"

Mya Maung responded carefully. "Some dress as sailors and coolies and leave the country aboard Japanese and Chinese freighters." He paused.

"I think some of them went to Tokyo, and from there to a jungle training school on the island of Hainan."

"Do you know any of their names?" Forrester inquired casually. "I'm really interested in a young man by the name of Kyaw Khin, wondering where he might be."

Mya Maung hesitated at first, then said, "I do not know where he is. But I have heard of the name. And that he is involved with a clandestine Japanese spy organization called the Minami Kikan. In general, the country to the east of the Belin river is where the spies are." He waved his hand vaguely, "Maybe he is on the Siam border opposite Myawaddy."

Forrester was excited now and wanted details. He lowered his voice. "Exactly where might he be? And how many Bo's are with him?"

"That I do not know," admitted Mya Maung.

Forrester abruptly changed the topic. "What do you think the Burmese would do if the Japanese attacked Burma next week? What is happening at the Siam-Burma border?"

"This I know," said Mya Maung. "The Japanese General Yamashita is half way down the Malay peninsula." His tongue had been loosened by the fine whiskey, and he was eager to please the Englishman. "There are Japanese army units opposite Kawkareik and at a small hamlet closer to the Burma-Siam border, and probably elsewhere."

Forrester was blunt. "Will you fight with the British? We know that the Indians will fight, but will the Burmese help in the defense of their own country? Or will they help the Japanese?"

Mya Maung looked uneasy. "Indians will run away at the first sign of trouble," he offered. He repeated what he had said earlier. "Most Burmese are very angry not just because the British deposed their king but also because the British desecrated the royal palace and the religious institutions of the Burmese by wearing shoes." Maung Mya repeated himself. "You know, the Burmese will not derive any benefit from the war. It is not their war. The only reason the Americans are here is because they want to keep the Burma Road open, to supply China, so that China can stay in the war to tie down a large portion of the Japanese army in China."

Mya Maung was left a little breathless after this speech, so lit up another cigarette to gain a few moments. Just then the inebriated Club secretary came over to their table. Pointing his finger at Mya Maung, he accused him of being a bloody traitor. "You and your like are all spies. All the monks are subversive; they should all be thrown in jail or shot." Mya Maung felt rage rise in him, but held back. He quickly but diplomatically headed for the door. Before he could leave the Club, he was accosted by another drunken Englishman, who blocked his way. Mya Maung felt the man's gaze and looked into his fierce grey eyes but kept on walking to the door.

He left the Club as quickly as he could. He glanced at his watch. It was getting late, but he did not return home immediately. He went to the promenade to clear his mind. The moon was rising, and he watched the moonbeams play on the silvery waves. He had an agonizing decision to make. He was patriotic but also liked the life that he and his family enjoyed, and he wanted the very best for his two daughters. He thought mostly of the benefits that his family enjoyed. His life was well ordered. He lived in a cozy cottage, high on the ridge. He had a BSA motorcycle, a rarity in Burma. His two daughters were at the convent school, a privilege that few Burmese enjoyed. With a good convent education, they could go to the university and then to England; if they worked hard and did well in school, they, too, might be even someday be called to the Bar. All of these conflicting emotions ran through Mya Maung's mind as he slowly made his way home.

Mya Maung called on the Commissioner two days later. He placed a manila folder on Forrester's desk. "Spies have crossed over to the Burmese side of the border from Siam. They will provide the invaders with information about trails and routes and will act as guides." He nodded toward the folder. "Here are names of men and routes, jungle trails that they could use, and other details about where the attack is likely to come from." He paused and Forrester was silent. "The main problem will be that, simultaneously with the attack, some of the Burmese will rise up and help the enemy; I do not know who or where." With that he asked to be excused. He was very nervous. He rushed out of the office, even before the Commissioner could thank him.

Forrester read Mya Maung's report, then sent the information by dispatcher to the Army commander of Moulmein. It landed on the desk of the brigade Adjutant, who then passed it on to the Brigadier, who in turn would take it to the conference he had with the Governor the next day.

Chapter 16
Troops Amass at Moulmein

Public morale in Rangoon was at its lowest in weeks. To boost morale, the Governor announced the arrival of fresh troops from India. Benjamin joined the crowd that was waiting in great anticipation for the arrival of the troops. To the worried people of Rangoon, the arrival of additional Allied troops in Rangoon was a boost to their sagging morale and an antidote to their fear of the Japanese.

Dressed in their desert uniforms of khaki and bush hats, led by pipers and drummers and covered with exotic leopard skins and plumed hats, the British and Indian soldiers marched past the docks to the tunes of "British Grenadier" and "Scotland the Brave." The people of Rangoon, although only a sprinkling of Burmese, cheered wildly. Their spirits seemed to rise, and many smiled for the first time in a long time.

The brigade commander, Jonah, ordered the offloading of the men's equipment, and soon the troops boarded transport and took to the road leading north, out of the city, toward Moulmein. Brigadier Jonah climbed into his staff car to lead the convoy. Captain Shaw of the Dogras regiment boarded the first lorry and led the convoy out of Rangoon. Again the people waved to them and cheered them. The soldiers took in the scene of the city with pride and gratitude. As they left the city, the road took a turn to the right and led directly in front of the big jail building. The lorries lumbered past the jail and up Prome Road. They passed the leafy university campus and then the Inya Lake. Beyond the lake, the road narrowed, the city faded, and the Burmese countryside was everywhere to be seen. Beyond the aerodrome there was nothing but paddy fields, water buffaloes, and the usual pariah dogs.

After an hour the convoy came upon another city, Pegu, the city of the reclining Buddha. The lorries rumbled across the bridge over the Pegu River, and at the railway station, the long convey halted. Captain Shaw alighted and walked to the pagoda to see the reclining Buddha that he had heard so much about. In front of the maidan the troops had tea, then headed out east, to the Sittang River and the city of Moulmein.

As rumors of war and an imminent attack flew around Moulmein, the city and barracks had filled with troops. These included not only sepoys of the British Indian Army but now also Gurkhas, Karens, Kachins, domiciled Europeans, Sikhs, Dogras, Madrasis, and local Indians and Anglos. All had been brought here hastily to train as a cohesive force. They spoke many diverse languages, and communications were complex. Gurkhas did not speak English or Burmese; Indians could not speak Burmese; and the Burmese knew just a few English words. Nonetheless, the British had formed cohesive fighting units, with Urdu as the lingua franca.

Among this collection of men from diverse cultures were Peter and Jeremy. They shuddered at the confusion in languages, but were glad that they were fluent in English and capable in Urdu and Burmese. "How do commands get communicated?" Jeremy asked his superior officer.

The tall Indian man laughed and said in Urdu, "In battle, all are one. You will understand commands."

"I sure hope so," muttered Jeremy in a worried tone.

"He's right," Peter said. "The British have been at this for decades; they know what they are doing. And besides, that's what training is all about."

As their training period came to an end, the men were reassigned. Peter was detached from the company and assigned to the 8th Burma Rifles, who were to defend the southern approaches to Moulmein. Jeremy was sent to Sukli Point, near the Siam-Burma border, joining with a unit of the Frontier Rifles to defend Burma's eastern border. The two men took leave of one another with sorrow and promised to stay in touch with one another as best they could.

After settling in Moulmein, Brigadier Jonah flew back to Rangoon for an intelligence update. The GOC greeted him with a sobering picture. "Your brigade, part of the 17th Indian (Black Cats) Division, is presently under-strength. The other two are still in India. We will expedite their departure.

They will embark for Burma soon." Brigadier Jonah blanched, and the GOC continued. "They will arrive in two weeks."

Brigadier Jonah interrupted. "You mean that I have only the notoriously unreliable and poorly trained BurRif battalions to defend against the best battle-hardened Japanese divisions across the border?"

The GOC reassured him. "The Burma battalions will be organized into a new unit, the First Burma Brigade, and they will be seconded to your brigade."

On paper this might have been impressive, Brigadier Jonah knew, but in reality it was a sham. "Even combined," he argued, "we will be woefully lacking in motor transport and heavy guns. Our main defense will be light arms of the Indian brigades, till the heavy equipment arrive. They are well trained and experienced."

The Governor interrupted, "That army is stretched thin. We have been promised that a division from the western desert of the Middle East will diverted to defend Burma, but like the troops from India, it will not arrive any time soon." Suddenly the GOC looked tired, and Brigadier Jonah knew that he himself was unhappy with the current troop levels and composition in Burma. The GOC promised, "I will appeal to the Prime Minister for verification that it is we, not Singapore, who will defend Burma and will urge the diversion of more troops here. In the meantime, we will work with what we have."

Brigadier Jonah did not find the conference very comforting. Plans for the defense of Moulmein and Rangoon were virtually non-existent, and there was confusion as to the command structure. He did not have confidence in the GOC's promises. But now, it was getting late, and he wanted to return to Moulmein. He boarded the Blenheim bomber that was waiting for him at the aerodrome, with engines running. Already, most of the seats were taken, so he took the navigator's seat. "I'll get a bird's-eye view," he consoled himself. As the bomber approached Moulmein, he craned his neck to look at the city from his perch. What he saw of the topography led him to become even more worried about the defensibility of his position.

The next day he set out with his Adjutant to reconnoiter the defenses in person. They surveyed the geography and determined that it was unsuitable for defense with the forces available. Brigadier Jonah was filled with angst. "From the top of the Moulmein ridge to the seashore, the land is narrow, just a few miles wide. The eastern ridge is vital," he declared aloud. "If it falls, our options are limited. And if we fail to defend the city, escape by sea to Rangoon will be difficult, if not impossible." He turned to his Adjutant. "What sort of water craft are available?"

"Sir," the Adjutant answered, "we have a few launches, and then there are the native boats. But if the monsoon comes early, exit by launch and native boats would be impossible."

"Examine and tally the ships available," Brigadier Jonah ordered. He then turned his attention to the south, to the aerodrome at Tavoy. "The Japanese could overrun it in a couple of days! There are no allied forces there whatsoever!" He knew instinctively that it would be bad. It was not so much that the city was indefensible, but that the "plan" for the city's defense was really no plan at all. Untrained troops, not enough equipment or transport, and no leadership from professional army troops.

Shaking off his worry, Brigadier Jonah took a few moments to form an appreciation of the area. Moulmein was set amid lush greenery. Its golden temple on the hill to the east of the city glistened in the morning sun, and to the west, the sea was calm. He found the place to be strangely peaceful, even with war looming. It was different from what he was used to in the northwest province of India. He paused to reflect. It was here, he recalled, at the very spot on the parapet of Kyaikthanlan Pagoda, that the colonial writer and poet Rudyard Kipling would write of England's newest conquest:

> The Temple bells are calling, an'
> it's there that I would be—
> by the Old Moulmein Pagoda
> Looking Lazy at the Sea.

Brigadier Jonah wrenched himself back into the present. Moulmein may be a romantic setting, but it was a defensive nightmare. Worse, its defense was his responsibility. "Time to go back to the barracks," he told his Adjutant.

Back at camp, in his headquarters tent, Brigadier Jonah began to record his observations. On three sides, the city was surrounded by water. To the east of the city, the pagoda stood on a ridge. A road ran the length of the ridge, and from that ridge road, crossroads ran downhill to the west, ending at the wharf. It was on these crossroads, below the ridge, that the locals lived. Here were the city's churches, mosques, and pagodas. Immediately beyond the pagoda on the ridge, the land took a deep plunge and faded into dense forest. Beyond the forest rose the mountains of the Dawna Range, an uncharted range of mountains that separated Burma from the Raheng province of Siam. The land between the two countries was rugged, with fearsome jungle and many predators.

The Salween River, a wild, tempestuous, non-navigable river flowed on the north and west sides of the city. Due west of the city lay a low-lying, uninhabited mud bank, at the river's mouth to the Andaman Sea. The river and the mud bank would be barriers to quick retreat if war came. Then, just north of the city was the gulf of Martaban, where the railroad ended. The only way over the Salween at this point was by ferry or other water craft.

Brigadier Jonah put down his pen. Now that he understood the topography of the land, he knew that he had to reorient his thinking. He had to prepare for jungle war, not the desert war for which he had trained.

The next morning, Brigadier Jonah called a conference with his chief of staff, Adjutant, and the intelligence officer. He summarized yesterday's "military appreciation" from Rangoon, and without any thought at all, his chief of staff blurted out, "This a nightmare! We need at least a full division to defend the city!" He had verbalized the Brigadier's innermost thoughts.

"But," Jonah admitted, "I am not sure I can impress upon Rangoon the peril we face. The GOC acts as though we can wait weeks for additional troops, and he does not seem to appreciate the challenge that the defense of Moulmein poses. He seems over-confident."

His chief of staff spoke up. "The fighting ability and reliability of the locally raised rifle battalions, especially the Burmese units, is suspect. They have only rifles, few heavy weapons; and even if they had such weapons, they would be unreliable in the hands of these new men." He continued in some detail. "The BurRif battalions are of poor quality, except for the 4th, which is composed mostly of non-Burmans. They simply are not trained, let alone well-equipped, and they will be facing the best and battle-hardened Japanese divisions who have years of combat training in China."

Brigadier Jonah agreed with his chief of staff, although he felt sanguine about his own troops. "Yes," he said, "the problem is that most of the units include only a few ethnic Burmese, with large numbers of hill peoples—Karens, Chins—and locals, along with Indians, Gurkhas, Anglo-Indians, and Anglo-Burmese. And these peoples traditionally are not overly fond of one another." He continued, "And another question is whether or not they will obey their commanding officers."

Brigadier Jonah remained silent for a while. He then said decisively, "We need to stiffen the under-strength and untrained Burmese battalions with some well-trained Indian men. That way, each battalion will be composed of some experienced Indian troops and some inexperienced new recruits. If we re-jigger some of the units, we may be able to cobble together enough units that have good leadership. Then we'll have to hope for the best."

The Adjutant nodded. "I'll get to work on it immediately, Sir," he said and left the room.

Depressed and despondent, Brigadier Jonah and his intelligence officer made their way to the signals room to review the cables that had come in the night before. The captain in charge summarized. "Signal traffic to the east from Siam was heavy, indicating that something is going to happen. The first signal was really unsettling: 'contact with Victoria Point lost'."

Brigadier Jonah asked quickly, "Do you think that it was sabotage?"

The captain shook his head. "The point is indefensible anyway. It has just a small contingent of the 8th BurRif. But its importance is its airfield, which the Japanese covet and from which they could keep up a sustained attack on Rangoon."

"Of course," Brigadier Jonah observed, "its airstrip would first be used against our position at Moulmein and then against Rangoon. I am certain that the first attack on us will come from the east rather from the south."

The intelligence officer agreed. "There has been increased patrol activity by the enemy all over," he acknowledged. "But I believe that the massive attack will come from across the Moei River, which forms the border between Burma and Siam."

The intelligence officer turned to Brigadier Jonah and pleaded, "It is important that you point out to the Division GOC the grave situation before us."

That night, Brigadier Jonah's chief of staff paid a visit to the Brigadier's tent. The two men sat outside in the dark and discussed the problem of the weakness of the locally recruited units. The chief of staff said, "Happily, the problems of distrust that led to the Indian Mutiny are, for the most part, behind us. But, in spite of the changes that the army has made in integrating the officers' mess and the desire to improve relations between the English and the Indians, the news coming out of Malaya is not encouraging."

Brigadier Jonah agreed. "I was really disturbed by reports about the egregious behavior of the British plantation owners and their wives, by their ugly racial attitudes and their treatment of Indian commissioned officers, especially by their seizure of railway carriages for their use over the needs of the military. If that were repeated here, the consequences would be dire, as I fear we have a more dissatisfied populace."

The chief of staff noted, "I think we can depend on our troops putting up a good fight. And I do not think that the politicians in India will do anything to impair the military effort. Our troops have performed well."

"You're probably right," said Brigadier Jonah. "Come into my tent for a moment." The two men ducked into his tent. "Let me read you this Whitehall report," Brigadier Jonah said.

Brigadier Jonah read aloud, "[We] rejoice [s] to place on record the deep sense of gratitude and pride in the heroic conduct of Indian troops whose deeds of valor and conspicuous humanity and chivalry in the Great War of 1914 are winning the respect of civilized mankind." After his valet brought him another whiskey and water, he continued to read. "The Indian Army fought with distinction at Neuve Chapelle and La Bassee in France. These men from the warm tropics withstood the bitter cold, the dampness, and the water-logged trenches. In India they had been only partly trained units; but when they faced the German Army, which was armed with high explosive guns, howitzers, heavy motors, and machine guns, they fought like heroes, enough that the men won citations. King George V said, 'You have shown Europe that the sons of India have lost none of their ancient martial instincts. . . . You fought side by side with the British and our gallant French allies. You fought for your King Emperor, and history will record the doings of India's sons. Your children will proudly tell of the deeds of their fathers'." The two men sipped their drinks while their minds traveled to years past.

Chapter 17
In the Civil Lines

The city of Moulmein remained calm, at least outwardly. But in fact, there was deep apprehension among the population about the unfolding events.

Carl Pinto, Pearl's brother, had finished school in June. He weighed his options and concluded that, given the political situation, he should join the newly formed Burma Rifles. Like Peter and Jeremy, he underwent military training following his enlistment and was assigned to the 4th Burma Rifles. This battalion was formed specifically to guard the Burma-Siam border. Before being dispatched to the border, Carl was given leave to visit his family, and now he was assailed by doubts. At the family gathering he openly discussed his apprehensions.

After dinner, the talk turned, as it invariably did these days, to the crisis building in the east. "If war comes," Carl observed, "Moulmein will be the first major city to be invaded." Pearl expressed her anxiety, saying "There are large numbers of military men in the streets. There are shelters everywhere. The streetlights no longer illuminate the streets at night." Pearl left the veranda, leaving Carl and his father alone.

"I actually feel ambiguous about the whole thing," Carl confessed. "Why should I go off to fight? What would I be fighting for?" His father looked puzzled, and Carl explained. "I would not be fighting for the Burmese; they despise me, and the feeling is mutual." He smiled. "But am I fighting for the British? I can't go to their clubs. They treat me like a dog, or worse. And if the British are defeated, would they allow us to retreat with them?" He asked his father pointedly, "would they allow Pearl to board the train with the English families?" Lighting a cigarette, he concluded bitterly, "there are already plans to evacuate the white people, so what are we fighting for?"

His father admonished him, "we are fighting for our home, our humble home where you were born. It is true that this is not our land; we live here amidst people who have come from many different places. But this is our home. If we do not defend our home, where would we go?"

"You're right," Carl said. "Our forebears, the Portuguese have long since left. Some of us cling to the notion that we could some day go 'home' to England, but the English laugh at us for such a silly notion."

"So," Carl's father continued, "this is where we will fight and die, even though this is not our country. Do you see, son, there is really no home? Only where we live in the present is home. The future is not in our hands; it will be controlled by events that are bigger than us. In part, it will depend on what the British do. That is why I made no effort to stop your enlistment; there is no other choice." He looked Carl in the eye and said, "You will go and do the best you can. And may the Lord help you and have mercy on us."

The next morning, Carl returned to his barracks and headed off with his company to Sukli Point, the observation post near the Burma-Siam border.

Chapter 18
Imminent Attack

Brigadier Jonah had not slept for days. His intelligence and signal corps were suggesting that an attack was imminent. He told his chief of staff, "I will make one last effort to tell the division commander about our near hopeless situation, but I am not hopeful." This time Brigadier Jonah went by car, to the division headquarters in the town of Waw, just west of the Sittang River. Throughout the drive he kept his eyes open to make a mental image of the topography. As the car climbed the narrow and steep rail escarpment, he thought, "if the enemy has the high ground, it would be disastrous to retreat through the gauntlet, and impossible to defend the eastern approaches to the bridge." He crossed the bridge to the west bank of the Sittang River, and discovered there the small village of Abya. "This place is no place to mount a defense. If the enemy controls the heights across the river, there are no natural barriers to stop them." By the time he arrived at the General's forward headquarters at Waw, Brigadier Jonah was more determined than ever that changes to the battle plan had to be made.

As his car stopped in front of the General's headquarters, Brigadier Jonah sprung out of his staff car and announced to the sentry "I am here to see General Burnett. Brigadier Jonah from Moulmein. It is urgent that I see him immediately." After a brief disappearance into the headquarters building, the guard re-emerged. "This way, Sir." Brigadier Jonah found the General already seated at the conference table, with his chief of staff and his intelligence officer. On the table was a large map of Southeast Asia. As soon as formalities were complete, Brigadier Jonah began.

"My chief of staff and signals officers are certain that the enemy's goal is to simultaneously capture Moulmein and the bridge across the Sittang River. Intelligence suggests that it will be a two-pronged attack: the White Tigers (the Japanese 33rd Division) will attack Moulmein while another division (the 55th) will attack the bridge. Their next move will be to capture Pegu." He paused and then said pointedly, "They will come through Waw on their way to Pegu. If that happens, it would trap the British army and destroy it. Pegu will seal the fate of Rangoon and all of Burma."

General Burnett turned to his intelligence officer, "Give us an update on enemy strength and position," he ordered.

The officer pointed out on the map the suspected enemy positions. "The main enemy division is the dreaded White Tigers. In addition, we have new information that an Imperial Guards division from Pitsanalouk (Siam) has arrived in Mae Sot (Siam), just opposite Myawaddy (Burma). The White Tigers would likely lead any attack on Moulmein, and the Imperial Guard might then attack Pa-An and the bridge."

Bolstered by this support, Brigadier Jonah continued to press. "Sir, forces to defend the area are inadequate. The two brigades we have are not at full strength. We must bring more Burma battalions here, and other frontier units as well, for example, more Burma Rifles. Furthermore, we have no experienced NCOs and no young commissioned officers. If we had them, we would have a fighting chance."

"Respectfully, Sir," he continued, "the new young subalterns have no combat experience. In good times, most of the officers would be seconded from the Indian Army, but its ranks are being stretched thin." Taking a deep breath, he continued. "Frankly, I am distressed about the constant command changes between Singapore and Delhi. I have tried to impress on you the danger we face." Now Brigadier Jonah came to his most important point. With great reluctance but with resolve he said, "I would like to have permission to retreat from Moulmein across the Salween estuary to Martaban, and then further northeast to a more defensible position across from the Belin River. Belin's topography would provide a natural barrier and shorten our lines of communication to the bridge."

General Burnett became visibly upset. He shook his head and waxed philosophical. "Every thirty years or so the British Army comes face to face with a crisis . . . and we overcame the crisis every time. We can succeed in the defense of Moulmein if we show resolve."

Brigadier Jonah was incredulous. "I am reminded of a another time, Sir. I remember another general of the British expeditionary army, a portly, irascible, and hypersensitive leader who sat on his hands while his front collapsed at Gallipoli. We now have another portly, short-sighted general sitting in his headquarters in faraway Java, who has no idea of the situation here on a remote front."

The Adjutant of the Division, Colonel Cochrane, a big man, joined the conversation. He had been in Burma for two years and was well aware of the local situation. Brigadier Jonah turned to him and asked bluntly, "what do you think of the native troops?"

Colonel Cochrane did not hesitate. "The ethnic Karen will be loyal; they can be trusted to fight. Unlike the Burmese, they are good soldiers. But I am not sure that there are enough of them, or that we have enough time to train them."

"Can they withstand the ferocity of the Japanese?" Brigadier Jonah asked.

Cochrane replied honestly, "They could delay the advance of the Japanese but not stop them."

"The promised tank brigade would help," Jonah observed, "but it is not scheduled to arrive for weeks. What about the promised Chinese aid?"

Colonel Cochrane glanced at General Burnett quickly before answering. "Frankly," he confided, "The Chinese and the American command have problems. Besides, the Chinese have a poor record against the Japanese, even in their own country."

Brigadier Jonah remained silent for a while, allowing the dreadful news to sink in. Nonetheless, he asked the General a second time to allow him to evacuate Moulmein so that he could make a stand at Belin and the bridge. "We could do a better job and hold off the enemy far longer," he pleaded.

General Burnett responded, "That is out of the question. The Prime Minister in London is not in favor of losing another city. The evacuation of Moulmein is not possible. Such an action would be a blow to British prestige and to the morale of the fighting units. Your request is rejected." He arose abruptly and left the room.

Brigadier Jonah locked eyes with Colonel Cochrane. Both men knew the coming battle would be devastating. "British prestige!" muttered Colonel Cochrane. "Good luck, Brigadier," he said, rising. "You'll need all you can muster."

Brigadier Jonah returned to Moulmein and immediately briefed his command. "We have to prepare for the worst and do the best job we can with what we have. I don't know how much time we have."

Chapter 19
The Japanese Advance

Lieutenant Colonel Sato was of medium height, stocky, and held himself so erect that he appeared taller than he really was. He had a small, closely cropped mustache and seemed always to clench his teeth. His eyes were small, mere slits, and he seemed to have permanent scowl, which gave him a cruel countenance. He suffered fools poorly; subordinates trembled in his presence. He had been in Manchuria, where he had been involved in the "China Incident." He was one of the officers who had fabricated an attack on his own unit and blamed the Chinese Army for instigating an attack on the Japanese. With utter indifference, he had then ordered the execution of innocent Chinese in retaliation. He himself had supervised the beheadings and seemed to actually take pleasure in watching the heads roll. His ruthlessness and efficiency at vanquishing the enemy had earned him a promotion to full Colonel and a transfer to Formosa.

Now, in the Fall of 1941, his regiment had trained intensely in jungle warfare. His new orders called for him to fly from Formosa to Saigon, where he joined his new unit. From Saigon, the unit took the train to Bangkok. Next they headed to the Siam-Burma border in a convoy. As his staff car, at the head of the troop convoy, passed Bangkok's Don Muang airstrip, it was stopped by a crowd of dissident Siamese who not only stopped the car but then attempted to overturn it. Colonel Sato alighted from the car, unsheathed his Samurai sword, and stated to swing at the crowd. Soon the frightened people fled, and the convoy got back underway.

Away from Bangkok, the road was a mere track, so the journey was a rocky one. When Sato came to Pitsanalouk, he called on his old friend, now the commander of a fighter squadron (Senti) that would provide air support for his unit. Colonel Takeda of the (Senti) 5th Air Division was happy to see him, and the two men discussed the forthcoming operations. At the end of the meeting they drank sake and said goodbye. Sato climbed back into his staff car and told the driver "make up the lost time and get to the border before the convoy." The driver pushed the staff car to its limits and raced passed the lorries of the convoy, bearing Colonel Sato to the border ahead of his troops. As the lorries lumbered into the camp, Sato took time to dress up. He wanted to do this for the last time before the battle. He stood resplendent in his tropical uniform: a khaki jacket and slacks, with a white shirt and polished jack boots; his sword hung loosely at his waist. He greeted the troops with a speech. The troops gave a chorus of "banzai!" before Sato dismissed them to their quarters.

After a day's rest, Sato called his staff to headquarters to discuss details of the battle plan. The assembled staff stood up stiffly when he entered the room. Looking straight ahead, he strode to the seat at the head of the table and sat down. Only then did his officers take their seats and remove the covers over the maps: of the South China Sea and Southeast Asia. "With the arrival of my troops," he announced, "the White Tigers have been brought to full strength. We have been battle hardened in Manchuria and Formosa. We are now ready to capture the East Indies and the other Pacific islands, where we will gain access to oil fields and mines for our Emperor. Our unit will capture Burma and, moving through that country, will strike the British in India." Sato licked his lips with anticipation and satisfaction. In a rather jocular mood, he turned to his chief of staff and said, "The British supreme commander does not think much of the Japanese; he says we are myopic and cannot shoot straight enough to hit the side of a barn." He laughed harshly. "We will show them how wrong they are; you know what we did to the Russians." Then he reminisced about the Chinese. "I still remember the severed heads of the Chinese bandits. I will enjoy doing that to the British and their lackeys, the submissive Indians." He narrowed his eyes and turned to his intelligence office. "For the present, I will say nothing about the Burmese, but one false move on their part, and we will treat them worse than we did the Chinese. Nothing will stand in the way of the Greater East Asia Co-Prosperity Sphere! The Master race will rule over these backward peoples!"

His staff shouted their support, and then Sato turned to the details of the plan, questioning each officer in turn. He tapped the maps as he explained:

After cover of darkness, we will move northward before crossing the Moei River into Burma. There are few roads, and we will not use them. We will use footpaths and trails pointed out to us by our Burmese friends. After crossing the river we will move westward across the Dawna Range, and will surprise the defenders at Sukli Point. We will demolish the British outpost there. They will flee in disarray. Then we will move from village to village, taking Kawkareik in Burma, and then moving onward to Moulmein. There, the 55th Japanese division will position itself north of the Sittang Bridge. The White Tigers will attack Moulmein from the east/southeast, encircling and destroying the city, and then join up with the 55th. The terrain favors this plan. Burma's jungle is a harsh place, with tropical diseases, mosquitoes, leeches, wild animals, and other dangers. But we are sons of Japan! We will prevail!

Sato asked for confirmation from his signals officer, provisions officer, and intelligence officer in turn that they were ready for battle. "Yes, yes, yes," they chorused. "Our surprise will be complete and will assure capture of Churchill's supplies."

"Will the weather be in our favor?" he asked his intelligence officer.

"Yes, Sir. The skies are clear for our air support. At the same time, there is just a sliver of a new moon, so the night will be dark. Also, the seas are calm, so the waterways will be navigable."

"Are our supplies in place?"

"Yes, Sir. Food, drink, and ammunition are sufficient. We will have mules and even some elephants to carry food for our forward troops."

"Have your collaborators found suitable paths for us to take?"

"Yes, Sir. The young man Kyaw Khin is invaluable. He has gathered much information from various and sundry sources, and has drawn excellent maps."

Sato asked his chief of staff, "So, then, are we ready to move out?"

"Yes, Sir," the chief replied.

"Excellent," Sato responded. "We should get word from Tokyo within a few hours; then we move. You are dismissed."

The staff bowed to Sato as they left the room. Each man returned to his own section headquarters to review readiness before the action began. Sato's batman had warmed the sake and brought him a full bottle. He poured the sake for his commander but apologized that he could find no suitable woman in this remote jungle.

Sato sipped his sake and reviewed the information that he had received over the past few days. He was most pleased with the assessment he had received from the Count, Supreme Commander of the Imperial Southern Japanese Army: "the British-trained and led Indian army that fought from Mesopotamia to Hongkong has lost its nerve." Sato mused, "We can achieve our goal." His cruel lips curved into a smile. His new adventure would be in the most exciting front. Burma would be the last victorious battle for the conquest of Southeast Asia. French Indochina had been won without a battle; Siam had given up virtually without a fight; Singapore would fall in just a few days; now only Burma remained. Then the Emperor's desire to create the Greater East Asia Co-Prosperity Sphere, with the riches that these lands held, would be fulfilled. The oil and minerals that the western nations had so imperiously denied to the Japanese empire would be seized forcefully. With them, the Emperor's armies could wage an endless war against the West and their colonial exploitation.

The next morning, Colonel Sato sought out Colonel Koga of the Minami Kikan, the clandestine organization comprised of Japanese and Burmese collaborators. "Muster your men for action," he directed, "and have them bring you the latest intelligence." Colonel Koga left and went to his tent. He summoned his loyal field commander, Kyaw Khin. "Bring me information on enemy positions and foot trails," Koga instructed, "and identify where we can get help from villagers." Kyaw Khin nodded and slipped silently from Koga's tent. At dusk he returned with the requested information. Koga praised him. "We are now ready to move," he said in broken Burmese. "Come with me to headquarters." The two men took the maps and village names to General Maida's 15th Army headquarters, and as soon as Colonel Sato arrived, the four men disappeared into the inner sanctum.

After their meeting with the General and Colonel Sato, Colonel Koga and Kyaw Khin returned to their camp. Kyaw Khin called his collaborators around him and produced a silver bowl. "We will perform the ancient ceremony of *thwe thauk*, or the drinking of blood." Into the silver bowl he poured copious amounts of cheap liquor and then encouraged each man to slit his finger and let the blood drip into the bowl. Kyaw Khin mixed it well, then the men dipped their cups into the bowl and drank the blood-stained liquor, swearing solemnly that they were bound together by blood and would fight the enemy to the bitter end.

Colonel Koga then spoke. "We now set out on a perilous journey."

Kyaw Khin took up the theme. "Soon we will be on the precious soil of Burma again, but as free men, not subject to British colonial masters."

The men cheered before returning to their quarters. Koga took Kyaw Khin aside. "I have good news for you. You are promoted to Major." Both men smiled, and Koga said, "now you are Bo Kyaw Kin.

Kyaw Khin nodded his appreciation of Koga's use of the Burmese honorific "Bo." "Thank you, Sir," he said earnestly, "for the promotion and for your efforts on behalf of my people."

Kyaw Khin and his fellow Burmese had provided an astonishing amount of information. They had visited local tea shops that the Burmese and Mons frequented and had gathered information about trails across the mountain range. They had learned where mule tracks were, but had been cautioned that travel was hazardous for the uninitiated. Aside from the thick bamboo forests there was a series of razor-like precipices that the troops would have to traverse once they entered Burma. "The bamboo grows so profusely here that the sun's rays cannot get to the ground," the men in the tea shop warned. "The ground is moist and literally teems with biting insects. At times it is one step at a time, and one misstep can mean death to mule and man."

Kyaw Khin had relayed this information to Colonel Koga dispassionately, but subconsciously harbored an additional fear. The mountains were known as the abode of ogres and Nats, who inhabit the dark forest at night. Like most Burmese, Kyaw Khin was extremely superstitious and rarely ventured or embarked on anything important without consulting his astrological charts and his numbers (numerology). Right now, he was actually more concerned about these ogres and Nats that resided in the trees and rocks than he was about his numbers. These Nats were said to be humans who had met a violent death and whose spirits now roamed the jungle. Kyaw Khin remembered the tales he had heard at home about how Nats took strange forms, how decapitated heads could turn into raging fireballs and roll down the mountainside with a frightful noise. He knew that he would be armed and in the company of other armed men, but he also had heard that ogres could mimic soldiers. They could also transform themselves into beautiful women who seduced the innocent and turned them into ghosts and ogres. Superstition aside, the mountains of the Dawna Range were also the home of the very real and very fierce Burmese tigers, which were known to like human flesh.

Kyaw Khin sat in the dark and looked out at the Moei River. He looked longingly to the other bank, to his homeland. He had awaited this moment for the last year. He had trained under the Japanese in the jungles of Hainan and at the Japanese base at San-Ya. Some mornings he had hated getting up. Every day had begun with homage to the flag and the Emperor, to be followed by training in the hot fetid jungle full of mosquitoes and insects. The creeks had been full of leeches. Some days, he and his fellow Burmese had thought their training was done when orders would come for a session of night fighting. Through it all, Kyaw Khin had kept his faith, and as he looked across the river, he knew the effort would be worth all his hardships.

Sato's instructions had been clear. The Japanese would break camp in the dark and sneak northward along the river. After crossing the shallow Moei they would first take out the British observation post at Sukli Point, then march to Moulmein, taking that city before joining with the 55th Division to take the bridge over the Sittang River. The signal came to assemble, and Kyaw Khin took his men to the assembly point.

By the time the troops all arrived at the river Moei, it was low tide and the banks were muddy. At their crossing point the river was less than 200 yards across. By the time Sato and his troops arrived, Kyaw Khin's men had assembled all the rafts. Sato looked carefully at Colonel Koga's collaborators for the first time and noticed that they all wore *longyi*s. This surprised him, for all the Siamese men wore pants. He shrugged. His unit was to be the forward unit, and they would be guided by Koga's Burmese collaborators. Burmese porters would bring up the rear, with the unit's equipment. "They can wear anything they want," Sato thought to himself, "as long as they lead me to my goal and bring me my equipment."

Once across the river, the foothills gave way to the steep slopes of the mountains. The jungle closed in on the columns. Even though he had trained at the jungle base, the city-bred Kyaw Khin was not prepared for the dense Burmese jungle. Each step involved cutting through the underbrush. Vines clung to the men's feet like serpents. The men cut their way through the jungle, being careful to maintain silence. They constantly had to fight off mosquitoes, yet as soon as they loosened their shirts in an effort to cool themselves, the mosquitoes swarmed around them and bit them relentlessly. As they climbed higher, they encountered bamboo of every size, even the great bamboo reaching a foot in diameter. The bamboo stalks were thick and rose to the sky, extending acre upon acre. Cutting through this obstacle would be nearly impossible, but the collaborators had learned of the trails that had been used by smugglers. As quietly as they could, the men trudged upward on the narrow trails, arriving soon among tall, broad-leafed teak trees that grew to the sky. Now the men became anxious, for in this thick bush lurked the most feared predator. Sure enough, without warning, the men heard a blood-curdling roar of a Burmese tiger, more in fear of the men than in search of food. It did attack a soldier without warning and tried to carry away its victim, but the wild firing by the terrified men made it free the victim and disappear. It took a while for the column to recover, but the officers soon restored order. The trails now narrowed, became much steeper, and hugged deep chasms. The men could only march single file, and they climbed slowly, hanging on to the vines and creepers. Kyaw Khin heard a piercing cry, a rustle, then silence. In the chasm below he could see a pack mule that had slipped off the trail and tumbled down into the ravine. Quietly the column passed onward. Soon they stopped climbing and knew that they were approaching their first objective: Sukli Point, the British defensive bunker, sited high on the ridge, overlooking the Siam-Burma border.

Sukli Point was manned by a squad of Company C of the 4th Burma Rifles, with some men just recently attached from the BurRifs in Moulmein. Company C had no battle experience, so in order to stiffen its resolve, a Baluchi noncommissioned officer (NCO) of the 1/5 Baluchi Battalion had been assigned to the squad. He was a tall, fierce-looking man, with a great hooked nose. In spite of his looks, however, he was an amiable man, and the men respected him. In addition to regulation arms he carried a large dagger in his belt. He only spoke Urdu. The other man on whom the men depended was Subedar Dunn, a Karen who had some experience in the border wars. The young men of the company looked to these two veterans for guidance. They themselves were equipped only with antiquated Enfield rifles and a few carbines. All were tense, for they had been charged with the tasks of keeping watch for potential infiltrators from Siam and, if necessary, blocking any such initial attack. The British commander had directed the men to dig bunkers. With large axes they had cut down teak logs, which they had used to cover the bunker top, then they covered the logs with thick layers of dirt. The weapons pit was at the far end of the bunker. Now the men watched and waited.

Jeremy wished he had not been seconded from his unit to this new position. He had always depended on his friend Peter for support, and Peter had been ordered to remain in Moulmein with the defenders of that city. "I'm going to stick by Subedar Dunn," Jeremy vowed.

The Japanese column, using the jungle trails, had climbed the mountain range undetected. They had bypassed Sukli Point and now doubled back from the west to outflank the British defensive positions. As the Japanese readied themselves, their sergeant gave one bullet to each of his men. "After the first bullet is fired," he told his men, "fix bayonet and then charge to kill, kill, kill. Hand to hand fighting. Kill everybody. No prisoners," he ordered.

Subedar Dunn heard a bullet whizz past his left ear. He turned his head to the left, when he heard screams and the clash of cymbals. He heard a Japanese officer yell "Tusokome! Tusokome!" With fixed bayonets and screaming, the Japanese charged the defensive position with overwhelming force. Lance Corporal (Niak) Limbu unsheathed his *kukri* and ran to the top of the bunker. Slashing at the Japanese, he turned to his comrades and yelled to them to run. He killed the first Japanese, but soon three others charged and bayoneted him to death. "Retreat!" cried Dunn. "Retreat!" He told his outnumbered men, "jump into the dry creek behind the post and run to the west."

In their hurried retreat, the defenders left behind their gear except for their personal weapons, climbed out of the bunker, and ran toward the rear, but they were quickly surrounded by the enemy. A daring bayonet charge killed the enemy, and then they ran as fast as they could. When Jeremy and the other retreating defenders got to the dry creek, Dunn gathered his men. As he kept firing, he ordered the men "Retreat to the village!" Jeremy and the other men ran until they could not hear the enemy. They crossed a small river and headed to a small village called Kawkareik.

Kawkareik was the sub-divisional headquarters and was held by another company of Burma Rifles. Breathless after having been on the run for hours, they arrived at Kawkareik only to discover—to their dismay—that the company defending the sub-divisional headquarters had already come under attack and had abandoned the village. Once again Jeremy and the remnants of his company retreated. Haggard and hungry, they took to the jungle trails, but much to their surprise, the trails also were under attack from Japanese patrols. "How did the enemy get so deep into the country?" Jeremy wondered.

The exhausted men wanted to rest until daylight, but Subedar Dunn urged them onward. "The forward positions are all overrun. We need to head toward Moulmein." The retreat was sounded again, and once again the company took to the jungle trails. They were headed to a *chaung* that fed into the Gyiang River, and again to their surprise, they were fired upon by a Japanese patrol. "The Japanese are getting ahead of us," the men cried in fear. "As soon as we arrive anywhere, the Japanese attack us!"

The company continually fought desperately to remove the Japanese blockades as the retreat became ever more chaotic. Jeremy did not know how many of the men from Sukli Point were left. All he knew was that their number seemed to be continually decreasing. It was still dark as the men headed for the nearest village, hoping to find motor transport. Finally they arrived at a mixed Muslim and Mon village but found it quite empty; the people had fled for their own safety. They had left in such a hurry that there was still warm food in the kitchens. Subedar Dunn stopped for a moment. "The Japanese seem to be at every village ahead of us. Let us avoid the trails and follow the *chaung*."

The men followed his advice and waded through the knee-high muddy water. As they progressed, the water became deeper. Their process was slow and onerous, but at daybreak they arrived at the junction with a larger river and found the army motor pool nearby. "Thank God we have Dunn with us," Jeremy murmured with gratitude. "Without him, there would be even fewer of us left." He looked around at the survivors of his unit. There were just a dozen or more men, all tired and muddy, many with torn uniforms and bleeding cuts on their exposed skin.

The men found that the motor pool was also on the move. Just one lorry remained. Again it was Subedar Dunn who assembled the remnants of the unit, commandeered a lorry, and hustled the men onto the lorry. "Hurry!" he urged, "hurry!" The driver drove like he had seen a ghost. Twisting and careening they headed inland on the dusty and rutted roads. The men shouted to the driver to keep driving till they reached safety. Suddenly they heard planes. Two Nakajima "Nates" came in low over the lorry, and the first fired its machine guns. The lorry took a few hits but miraculously was not disabled, nor were any men injured. The driver stopped with a lurch and the men piled out of the lorry, unloading the stores that they had found packed into the lorry when they had commandeered it. They headed for cover under the trees. The second "Nate" came in for its sortie, and this time the lorry took a direct hit. "Break up into small groups and take to the trails again, men," Subedar Dunn shouted. "Head for Kyondo and then Moulmein. We'll join up with the main army there."

Jeremy stuck close to Dunn, as did Carl Pinto. The two young men had met in Moulmein and, in whispered conversations, forged a friendship at Sukli Point. Both were Anglos, both new recruits, both frightened, and both utterly dependent on Subedar Dunn for their survival. Carl was bitter. "Didn't army intelligence know that the Japanese were poised to attack Sukli Point? Once they knew, why didn't they send reinforcements? It is probably because we are the Burma Rifles, and we are expendable."

"Surely that is not the case," argued Jeremy. "These things happen in war, and we are in the midst of it."

Subedar Dunn was silent.

Eventually the men arrived at the outskirts of Kyondo village. It was just to the east of Moulmein, and on a large *chaung*. "We could get to Moulmein by sampan if we could find one," Carl whispered. "I grew up in Moulmein and know that this *chaung* feeds into a still larger river near the city."

Subedar Dunn's eyes glinted. "Let's take a look, boys," he said.

Jeremy waded a few hundred yards downstream and found a small sampan. He whistled. Subedar Dunn and Carl materialized from the jungle and the three men clambered aboard, nearly swamping it. They rowed a few miles and were quite pleased with themselves, when suddenly they came under attack from the north bank. They abandoned the leaking sampan and once again took to the jungle.

"This is getting old," Carl whined, but kept running.

After walking several more miles through the jungle they finally arrived at the top of a ridge, where they saw a bunker. "This is the eastern defense of Moulmein," Carl whispered. "We have finally arrived at our destination."

The three men warily approached the bunker with guns pointed. Suddenly they heard "Stop. Identify yourself." And they heard the cock of a rifle.

"Remnants of 4th BurRifs, retreating from Sukli Point," Subedar Dunn said. "Dunn, Rawson, and Pinto here."

A turbaned head poked out of the bunker and peered at them. "Ok. Come," said the guard. At that the three men flung themselves into the bunker, grateful to have arrived safely.

But their safety was short lived, and Carl and Jeremy's hopes of finding something for breakfast were dashed. By mid-morning they could see the Japanese advance and could hear the Japanese guns. Despite a plucky defense, the men in the bunkers were outnumbered and realized that they would have to fall back. "Retreat!" yelled the Subedar over the din of the gunfire. Carl got to the top of the foxhole, then felt a searing pain in his right thigh. A bullet had torn through his entire thigh, entering on the right and exiting medially.

"Stretcher!" cried Jeremy, who was right behind him. Miraculously, stretcher-bearers materialized and helped Jeremy roll Carl onto the stretcher.

Carl was moaning in pain and clutching his leg, pressing his hand over the exit wound. The men ran to the river, making Carl's pain even worse. But finally they reached the river and loaded themselves onto a boat. They headed north. "I suppose the Japs will be there, too," Jeremy thought grimly.

To the south of Moulmein city, looking to Mudon, Peter was in his bunker near the Mudon aerodrome. The Japanese attack on the aerodrome started with mortar bombs all around, and Peter could feel the shocks of the bombs that landed nearby. Then Japanese infantry troops came screaming out of the jungle, with cries of "banzai!" With fixed bayonets they charged into the ranks of the defenders. By forenoon, the enemy had broken through the aerodrome's outer wire defenses. Peter kept shooting his old bolt-action rifle at the enemy, but they were too many. Even if he hit one every time he squeezed the trigger, he could not slow them down. The defenders were forced to the perimeter of the outer limits of the city. The unit was in disorder; the company commander had already fled. As the men ran, the Japanese came out of the jungle and put up a block behind them. Peter could hear the cries of the stragglers as the Japanese bayoneted them; then silence again, the fight was over.

The second in command of the company now gathered his dispirited remnants and headed towards to the perimeter of Moulmein, but the Japanese had brought with them hundreds of bicycles, which they used to head the defenders off. The men took cover in an abandoned farm building on the city's outskirts, and the second in command whispered, "We must hold the line at all cost." But intense enfilading gunfire erupted, and it seemed that nothing could stop the Japanese. Within minutes, the second in command was killed, and casualties were heavy. With the loss of their commanding officer and his second in command, the men were demoralized. Peter joined a small group of men led by Havildar Saw Travis, an ethnic Karen, and the stragglers put up a stiff fight as they retreated. Hungry, tired, and exhausted they continued to retreat, hoping to reach the city center and join up with men from other units.

But the enemy had attacked not only from the south but also from the east, shrinking the defensive perimeter of the city to just two miles. The enemy had swarmed over the pagoda ridge east of the city and were heading to the city center. The brigade headquarters in the city was already under fire. The chief of staff cried out, "The Japanese have landed by sea to the northwest of the city! If they seize the jetties there will be chaos! They will have surrounded us on three sides, leaving the north and Martaban as our only avenue of escape!"

If the military were in chaos, the civil lines were even more so. The fire of old Enfield rifles, the staccato fire of machine guns, and the "whoosh" of bombs created a terrifying din. The people who had remained in the city had never heard anything like this before. They cowered in any hole they could find. The Burmese fifth column had set the bazaar on fire on the north side of the city, and now fires were also burning in the south and east. The smoke hung low over the city, increasing the confusion.

Peter and his comrades had retreated from the aerodrome south of the city, through the city center, and had arrived at the jetties west of the city which were also under attack. Peter was struck with dismay, but his morale was bolstered by an extraordinary act of valor: The Japanese had launched an attack against the Dogras gunners defending the jetties and were almost upon them when the gunners fired with open sights. But soon the defenders were overwhelmed, and their guns fell silent. Suddenly the Indian lieutenant in charge of the defending gunners led a charge against the Japanese and re-seized two guns. He quickly loaded them and began firing, but his attempt was, in the end, futile. He was wounded and captured. Peter shuddered. "I don't want to think about what will happen to him," he thought.

Just then Peter heard a whistling sound, and then a thunderous explosion destroyed the post office. "Let's get out of here!" Peter cried to Saw Travis. "We have to get to the waterfront and hope to find a boat to leave this lost city."

The fighting was confused, positions kept constantly changing, and mortar bombs fell on the jetties. Peter and Saw Travis dodged the explosions, aided by the Jat gunners who kept firing 25-pound guns from their position near the north jetty. This at least helped to slow the Japanese advance, although the enemy soon overtook the gun emplacements.

At the Mission Street jetty, the fuel storage tanks and munitions dumps were on fire, and their explosions added to the frenzy and fear in the city. Smoke billowed skyward. At the Mission Street jetty, there was a see-saw battle. Peter and Saw Travis spotted the battalion's Major shouting in an agitated state, "Retreat to board whatever seaworthy craft you can find. Cross the Salween estuary!" The Japanese were rapidly closing in from all sides. There was a mad scramble to get to the boats. Some of them were full of wounded. Another group of Indian gunners continued to fire point-blank, to give the retreating forces time to get to the boats.

But the retreating soldiers had to vie with the civilian population to seize launches. The gulf was filling with all manner of boats: paddle-wheelers, shallow draft launches, and local boats, many full of screaming civilians. Terrorized people, in fright and despair, some with only the clothes on their backs, were desperately trying to flee from the Japanese positions to the north bank of the Salween river, and thence to the rail head of Martaban. Through the smoke that hung low, from burning buildings and munitions in the city, came the shouts of men giving orders, the fearful cries of children, and the soulful weeping of women who had in the blink of an eye lost nearly everything of value in their lives.

Mr. Pinto, his wife, and his daughter Pearl had run to the river with other civilians. They had been lucky to hop onto a open country boat. Now they cowered in the bottom of that boat, terrified. They watched the fight for the jetties unfold. They saw the fanatical banzai charge by the Japanese and saw them capture the 25-pounder guns. They saw the Indian captain of the Jats gunners counter-charge with his men to retrieve the guns. In the counter-charge, the young Captain took a direct hit. Clutching his abdomen, he continued to lead his men and order them to fire, which gave covering fire to protect the loading of more launches, boats, and sampans. The Captain ignored his own wounds, but eventually his position became untenable. With the collapse of the 25th went the last hope of escape from the city. The Captain's men destroyed the guns and carried him onto one of the overloaded boats.

The boats now headed to the north. Some had already reached the jetty at the Martaban railhead, others were still in the middle of the estuary. Suddenly, Pearl cried out, "I hear planes!" Four Japanese planes appeared overhead. Two planes peeled off from the main body and descended to attack targets of opportunity on the wide estuary. Skimming the water, they opened fire on the boats. There was unbelievable carnage. The motley collection of boats carrying civilians and troops was caught in the open water, presenting an easy target. Those who did not swim drowned. Casualties were tremendous. The air attacks continued with the arrival of more Nakajima fighters, which continued the attack. The earlier planes had focused on the smaller launches; these Nakajimas now focused on the larger boats and ferries. Commissioner Forrester and the other last British civilians were on a large ferry, halfway to the safety of Martaban. In the Japanese attack, the ferry took a direct hit. Forrester, on the upper deck, could see the Japanese fighter come over the front of the ferry with guns blazing. He clutched his chest, let out a cry, keeled over the rail, and fell overboard into the gulf of Martaban. The fighters circled around for another attack, and soon the ferry began to list and slowly sink. The smaller sampan, with the Pinto family in it, took a direct hit and sank quickly, taking the family to the bottom of the estuary.

Over and over again the same scene played out. Japanese planes dove low to strafe the terrified populace of Moulmein, who had fled their homes in the futile hope of escaping death. Soon their work was done, and the Japanese fighter planes moved on. A silence fell over the estuary. Jeremy jumped into the water and swam to the north shore. Only an occasional thrashing of a survivor in the water could be heard, or the wretched sobs of a woman who had lost everything except her tenuous hold on life itself.

Chapter 20
Retreat from Moulmein

Peter and Saw Travis had been among the lucky. As they had approached the north bank, they had jumped out of their boat and swam the last few feet to the jetty on the opposite side of the estuary. "The gods must be smiling on us," Saw Travis remarked. "For now at least," Peter responded wearily. The two men walked warily to the rail junction a hundred yards to the north and spotted the goods train. Joining the ranks of exhausted and dispirited troops, they boarded the train. The engine driver waited till darkness before he pulled the train out of the marshaling yard and headed north for Thaton, a town that lay to the south of the Sittang Bridge. But soon the train was stopped by a blockade across the tracks. Intense firing could be heard ahead. Mortar bombs exploded nearby but missed hitting the train. The weary soldiers got out and joined in the fight; eventually, they pushed the enemy back and cleared the tracks. Silently the men re-boarded the train and headed north again towards Thaton.

Brigadier Jonah and his headquarters company had crossed the estuary ahead of the main body of the brigade and thus had escaped the carnage. The brigadier swiftly established a new headquarters at the village of Mokpalin, south and east of the Sittang Bridge. "This is the new assembly point," he announced to his chief of staff. "The rear guard will assemble at the rubber plantation further north, near Kyaityo. Direct the rest of the troops here, to Mokpalin."

Through the night, the train carried Peter and Saw Travis until, just before dawn, the driver held the train in a siding and the order was given to evacuate. They alighted and were ordered to the Boyagyi rubber plantation. The plantation was vast, with carefully planted rows of rubber trees. They arrived weary and footsore. It was easy to get lost in the vastness of the plantation, and while it provided shelter, it lacked ground cover; it was not easily defensible. Nonetheless, the men were grateful to have arrived at what seemed to be a secure location.

"All I want right now," Peter whispered to Saw Travis as they plodded through the darkness, "is to lie down and sleep . . . and forget what I saw today."

"My friend," Saw Travis said, his eyes glistening in the moonlight, "I'm afraid this is just the beginning."

While Peter and Saw Travis had made their way to the rubber plantation, Jeremy's battered Company B had headed to the Belin River, the last defensive outpost east of the Sittang Bridge. The company's retreat from Sukli Point had been wildly chaotic. For a while, Jeremy had become separated from the company when he took cover but eventually rejoined them. Neither he nor his fellow soldiers had eaten any food for two days. They were hungry and exhausted. Moreover, Jeremy had been immensely saddened that the company had left his friend Carl behind. Carl's wounds were more serious than had been initially thought, and he was unable to walk. Carrying him on a stretcher would have risked the lives of three men, not just one, so the company commander had made a difficult decision. Jeremy could not bear to look back at Carl lying on his stretcher and clutching his gun. "When the Japs get to him, they will not treat him tenderly," Jeremy sighed.

At Mokpalin, north of Moulmein and just north of the Belin River but still about fifty miles southeast of the Sittang Bridge, Brigadier Jonah called an early morning meeting with his senior officers. The reports on the precarious state of affairs dismayed him. "Contact the division commander," he ordered his signals captain.

The agitated captain responded, "many of our radios and code books were lost in the air raids. I need to repair one of the radios or need to contact the division commander in the clear."

"Get to it, then, in the clear," snapped the Brigadier.

Jonah paced nervously while the signals captain bent low over the radio. Suddenly it crackled to life.

Brigadier Jonah rushed across the room and shouted into the microphone, "Can you read?"

The response from headquarters came swiftly, "Yes." Brigadier Jonah demanded, "I cannot get to bridge in scheduled time. Need support. Request Yorkshire battalion to move north to help Gurkhas hold bridge till all allied troops are evacuated."

The voice from divisional headquarters responded immediately. "Yorkshires will remain in their current position. You must get to the bridge and hold it until all troops have safely crossed."

Jonah replied angrily, "Understand. Over and out." He turned to his chief of staff in disgust. "This is absolutely outrageous. We have a disaster on our hands."

His signals captain looked confused. "I'm sure we will do what we have to do, Sir, but I cannot see their logic."

Jonah sighed. "You are dismissed. I'll confer with my chief of staff."

Jonah knew that the Gurkhas holding the east side of the Sittang Bridge had almost a century of distinguished service. But now they had been badly mauled by the enemy, and he worried about the unit's cohesion. Its officer ranks—all British—were decimated.

"The Gurkhas are dependable," he told his chief of staff, "but I am not sure that they can hold. Their position, on the hills overlooking the approach to the bridge, is precarious."

The chief of staff concurred. "The Gurkha is deadly in close combat; their skill with that damned curved knife of theirs, the *kukri*, is renowned. But he is not a particularly accurate marksman."

Brigadier Jonah summed things up. "But what choice do we have? We must do our best with the resources we have."

Jemedar Lal Bahudar led the company of Gurkhas holding the Buddha hilltop which overlooked the Sittang Bridge from the east. He was a small, experienced, and determined man. He came from Gorakphu, as did all of his men. Their community had a long history of great soldiering. He came from a family of great soldiers: his father had won the Victoria Cross, and, like his father, Lal Bahudar was a good and dependable soldier. He recalled his father's place of honor in the regiment with pride and hoped that he, too, could conduct himself with distinction.

Jemedar Bahudar summoned Lance Corporal (Naik) Motilal, who had been recruited from Gorakphu with him. "Look at this pagoda. Doesn't it remind you of home?"

His companion smiled. "Yes. And it brings to mind our recruitment."

Recruitment time in the Gurkha villages was an annual ritual of testing for the recruits, as there typically were more applicants than the regiment needed. Competition was fierce.

"When that recruiter came to our village, though, we were ready, weren't we?" asked Motilal.

Bahadur had known that his entry into the Gurkha regiment of his father would be difficult, but his father had nurtured his son well, as had Motilal's. "We were the best!" Bahadur said truthfully, with no boastfulness. "I think it was our shooting ability that made us stand out from the others."

Gunfire in the distance interrupted the men's reminiscence and put them on high alert. They jumped into their foxholes and waited tensely the impending attack.

BATTLE AT THE BELIN RIVER

Colonel Sato's regiment was full of pride and bravado. Colonel Sato could not contain his glee at the success of his regiment. They had rapidly swept through the jungle to the west of the Moei River and had sent the defenders of Sukli Point running into the jungle. The presence of collaborator guides had been essential in finding the jungle trails; allowing the regiment—on foot, bicycle, and mule—to skirt all the roads. Sato was eager to get to the east bank of the Belin River. If he could cross the river, he could capture the Sittang Bridge, which would block any British reinforcement from Rangoon to help hold the bridge.

From the village of Kyondo, Sato's regiment advanced rapidly. He drove his men mercilessly. Leaving his motor transport, he proceeded on horseback. He exhorted his men to advance quickly and stealthily through the jungle, aiming to reach Duyinzeik, a small village north of the bridge that spanned the Belin River. But he knew that before he could get to Duyinzeik, his regiment would have to overcome the defenders at Danyingon and Kuzeike. He was not worried, though. He captured one village after the next and had no doubt in his mind that victory was within his grasp. The few troops of the Burma Rifles—Jeremy's battalion—had already been decimated, so he expected no opposition.

From his headquarters at Mokpalin, Brigadier Jonah had ordered the reorganization of three Indian units: the Dogras, the Baluchis, and the Jats. Stragglers from the BurRifs, survivors from Sukli Point, were to be attached to the Baluchi unit. As dusk approached, the British colonel commanding the reorganized units held a conference at his new headquarters in Kuzeike to go over the defense. Kuzeike, a small village lying just to the east of the Belin River, would be the main site of defense.

"Brigade headquarters directs us to hold their position, to the last man last round. Failure will endanger the Sittang Bridge and the road that is the lifeline to Rangoon," reported the colonel.

The commanders of the battered units looked glumly at each other. There was no plan for the defense; there was no barbed wire; no bunkers; and no time to build a perimeter. Now, in the dry season, the river was not deep and could easily be forded by the enemy. It was a position that under the best of circumstances would be difficult to defend, and these were not the best of circumstances.

The villagers of Kuzeike, of mixed Burmese and Karen ethnicity, had already fled, leaving all their belongings. They had even left their cooking fires still burning. Late in the evening, the Baluchi unit to which Jeremy had been attached began defensive preparations. They dug foxholes as best they could, given the terrain. The effort was difficult, however, as water soon filled the trenches. The men spent the evening in the wet trenches. Despite their uncomfortable surroundings, and despite their worries, the weary men dozed on and off through the night.

Sato waited for his artillery gunners to arrive, who were some distance from the river. At midnight, the mountain gunners were ready. They unleashed intense fire at the defenders of Kuzeike. The ground shook as artillery shells exploded all around. Sato detached one of his battalions to head six miles to the north. With help of the Burmese collaborators, the battalion crossed the river and got behind the Baluchis. There was a cacophony of Bren guns, rifles, and Japanese light machine guns. It was a terrifying din. Mortar bombs fell among the Indians, then they came under a banzai charge. The company commander held his flare gun high over his head and fired it; the flare soon bathed the sky in light, and Jeremy saw the Japanese running towards them. They were so close! As he fixed his bayonet, he heard the towering Baluchi jemedar in the next foxhole curse in his native tongue that nobody could understand.

Jeremy jumped out of his shallow foxhole and joined in the charge. The noise, the confusion, the cries of pain, and the screams in the heat of the battle disoriented him. He stumbled and fell. He saw the bayonet glint, rolled over quickly, and heard a sharp rifle shot. He leapt to his feet and, holding his rifle firmly in his hand, slowly backed away from the dead and the screams, the Baluchi jemedar and his smoking rifle at his side.

Bodies were everywhere, and losses were heavy. In spite of an intense defense by the Baluchi battalion, the screaming Japanese swarmed over the defenses and simply overwhelmed and overran their position. One brave Baluchi led a bayonet charge against the enemy, killing three of them before he was cut down by a machine gun hidden behind a low mound. To Jeremy's amazement, despite being mortally wounded, the Baluchi continued his charge until he fell. Then the last charge fizzled out, their position was swarming with Japanese, and mortar bombs continued to fall to their rear.

One of the bombs hit the command tent. The British colonel of the Baluchi Battalion lay mortally wounded. He had sustained a shrapnel wound to his right jaw; the hot razor-sharp metal had entered the angle of his jaw and exited posteriorly on the right side of his neck. But he was still alive. The blood was gushing from the severed facial artery, and the side of his face was a bloody mess. Around him all was chaos and confusion; there was no longer a front line. Suddenly the flaps of the command tent opened and a Japanese sergeant pointed his pistol at the colonel. With great effort, the colonel signaled to the sergeant to shoot him. The Japanese was taken aback at the courage of the wounded man and paused a moment before shooting him. He then ran out of the tent toward the river bank.

The Jat battalion holding the left flank came under intense fire, but soon they were outflanked. As they began a retreat, the left flank of the Baluchi center defense began also to falter. Along the right flank, the redoubtable

Dogras charged, buying a little time for their comrades to reach the city of Belin, which spanned both sides of the Belin River. But the Japanese charged forward relentlessly, and soon the Dogras themselves retreated. The beleaguered troops now fled in total disarray, hoping to find safety on the west side of the river. The enemy pursued the desperate troops into the river.

Jeremy joined the exodus. Once again he was on the run. Splashing and swimming with desperation, Jeremy and the other survivors from his unit reached the west bank of the Belin River in the early morning hours. He wondered where Peter was and did not know whether or not his friend was safe. All he knew was that his exhausted and decimated Burmese battalion was no longer a fighting force.

In the early morning hours, much to their surprise, the retreating men found the western part of the city of Belin in chaos, with Japanese troops closing in. "How could they get behind us with such facility?" Jeremy wondered.

He fell in with a large body of men, all retreating westward. The only officer of rank was a major, who collected the rabble and advised them in clipped and anxious tones, "head to Kyaityo."

Kyaityo, a holy city, was the site of a famous Buddhist pagoda, built precariously on a large boulder. Pilgrims flocked to the pagoda throughout the year, but now the place was deserted. The road from Belin to Kyaityo was dusty and narrow, not an all-weather road. The men trudged in a forced march to the north. Driven by the rapid advance of the enemy, the men took only short rests by the roadside, at the edge of the dense jungle. They had no food and little water. As the sun rose, it beat down on them mercilessly. The heat and dust compounded the men's misery. "*Pani, pani*" [water, water], the Indians shouted. But the water-bearers had no water left.

Jeremy took his own water bottle and tipped it up. "Not a drop." he muttered.

From the west the sound of planes could be heard. The men looked up. Their spirits soared as they identified the markings on the planes as clearly friendly. "RAF Hurricanes!" the men cheered.

"And AVG planes too!" Jeremy cried. He recognized the shark's teeth painted on the prow. Jeremy and his comrades waved at the low-flying planes, but to their horror, the planes dove towards them! The men screamed and scattered as the planes began to strafe them. Again and again, the planes strafed the beleaguered men.

"Get the air force!" shouted the major who was nominally in charge of this assortment of dispirited men.

"Our radios are destroyed, Sir," came the reply. "Besides, where exactly are we?"

Casualties were high. The men had been hit by the Japanese, the Burmese, and now their own aircraft. They were demoralized and enraged. They shook their fists at the air and cursed the pilots. "They could see that we are not enemy; they must know we are allied soldiers," the men wailed.

Jeremy complained, to no one in particular, that "this is the straw that broke the camel's back." He wondered aloud, "Does anyone care?" He just could not believe that such a mistake could occur. The irony of being destroyed by friendly fire! How could such a blunder occur?!

The major gathered the battered men and warned them, "Be vigilant. Keep moving." He ordered them to march to a large rubber plantation near Kyaityo where they would rest for the night. "From the plantation, we will proceed to Mokpalin, the last village on the east side of the Sittang Bridge. And from there we will cross the Sittang River." The young major assured his men, "After we cross the Sittang, we will have some breathing space."

The march resumed, with the column keeping a careful watch on the sky as well as the jungle. "We could be attacked from all sides," Jeremy moaned. Only the hope of crossing the Sittang River to safety kept hope alive and the men marching.

Without enough radios, the British General at Waw had no way of maintaining contact with his retreating units. Knowing how desperate it was, he ordered the signal man to go in the clear. He knew that the Japanese were rapidly advancing toward the Sittang Bridge, and he knew that his own troops were retreating to the bridge as well, from Moulmein and the rubber plantation and from Belin. "We cannot allow the Japs to get the bridge," he declared to his chief of staff. "If they do that, they'll have a clear shot at Rangoon."

Chapter 21
Battle at the Sittang

Having captured Belin, Sato ordered his chief to "race forward to reach the commanding heights overlooking the Sittang Bridge. There is a motorable road to Sittang, but you will take the jungle trails." Sato spelled out the details of his plan. "The Gurkhas have a post atop Pagoda Hill. We will attack them, but first we will have to occupy Buddha Hill, which is a bit southeast from Pagoda Hill. After you are dug in at Buddha Hill, have your gunners concentrate fire onto Pagoda Hill." With glee, Sato continued, "You will turn the British retreat from Moulmein into a rout." As usual, Sato licked his lips with satisfaction.

Colonel Koga's spies had gathered information and intelligence about the construction of the Sittang Bridge, its weaknesses, and its strengths. Sato leaned back in his chair and expounded, "The Sittang Bridge was built early in the century and consists of eleven spans supporting a narrow-gauge rail. It is the only rail connection to Rangoon." Anticipating the question, he continued, "Yes, it is a narrow railway bridge but can be converted into use by motor transport by placing planks between the rails. But because it is narrow, it can bear only one lane of traffic."

"Just as well," Sato's chief of staff responded with a smile. "We don't intend to re-cross the bridge back to the east, after we chase the British westward."

Both men chuckled, then Sato rose. "May you achieve success," he said as he bade his chief of staff good-bye.

Sato's chief of staff had placed great reliance on the intelligence provided by Kyaw Khin and ordered him to proceed ahead of the column. Kyaw Khin followed a narrow trail north for a quarter of a mile on the high ground, to confer with the village headman. The headman confirmed that there was indeed a trail from the village to the bridge, which would lead them upward to the top of Buddha Hill. "When I was a young man," the headman said, "I used to run down there to watch the Rangoon–Moulmein mail train." He looked carefully at Kyaw Khin, trying to assess his ability to run up the hill. "It is an uphill climb," the headman warned. "And the trail is covered with thick bamboo."

Kyaw Khin assured the headman that running uphill would be no problem and that the thick bamboo would provide good cover. He went back to Sato and reported, "We can get to the hill before sundown."

The chief of staff called his trusted regimental sergeant major (RSM). "You will command a patrol in strength," he directed. "Kyaw Khin here will guide you to the bridge."

The RSM ordered his men to follow him. The trail wound around the Burmese village and headed up the hill. With Kyaw Khin in the lead, the patrol climbed with difficulty, and although breathless, it arrived at the top of Buddha Hill late in the afternoon. The RSM nodded his appreciation to Kyaw Khin.

For Kyaw Khin, it was the first time he ever saw the silvery bridge. Silently, the men crept around the crest of the hill, looking for cover. The hilltop had few shrubs, and soon the NCO set his men to building a bunker. "Keep silence and work swiftly. Gather boulders and build a small bunker to hide the machine gun, which will be brought up and assembled by nightfall."

Indeed, by dusk the patrol had set up the light machine gun. Kyaw Khin crawled next to it and looked intently at the bridge upon which it was trained. At any other time it would be a beautiful setting and a breathtaking view: the rays of the sun made the silvery bridge glow a bright orange. Far below the bridge was the river. On the far side was a small fishing village, Abya. Kyaw Khin's thoughts were not of the serenity of the scene, however, but how to get beyond it. The bridge was the last obstacle standing between him and Rangoon, where he looked forward to meeting his family and his comrades again.

THE SITTANG BRIDGE

Brigadier Jonah had transferred his headquarters from Mokpalin to the top of Bungalow Hill, which lay due south of Buddha Hill. From here he could see the bridge to the northwest and could also stay apprised of the progress of the 2nd Brigade, which was retreating toward the bridge from the southeast. The Sittang Bridge sat high over the river, and the approaches to it were built on high embankments. It was painted silver, making it glow in the sunlight. "Easy to identify from the air," Brigadier Jonah thought grimly. A few gunshots rang out, and Jonah realized the peril that he and his men faced. "If only the division General would listen to me!" he cried. His intelligence chief entered the room and cleared his throat. "Sir."

"Go on," Jonah directed.

"The enemy has done the impossible," the intelligence chief reported. "They used jungle trails, and on foot, by bullock cart, and by bicycle have bypassed the Thaton road and overnight have arrived at the top of Buddha Hill, overlooking the bridge. They made their first attack on Pagoda Hill but were repulsed by the Gurkhas. But the Gurkhas hold their position tenuously. I am not certain how long they can hold."

Brigadier Jonah summoned his signals officer. "Call the Division," he ordered with an urgent tone to his voice. Once General Burnett came on line, the signaler gave the phone to the Brigadier. He said, "Jonah One to Alice One. Jonah One to Alice One." When he got a response, the Brigadier said coldly, his words very precise and clipped, "My ability to hold the bridge till morning is in doubt. The Japs are already on Buddha Hill. I have no reserves. My position is becoming untenable." Jonah continued, his voice beginning to shake with anger, "I beg you to move the Yorkshires whom you are holding in reserve; move them to the north to defend the bridge, and place them under my command. I must hold the bridge till mid-morning tomorrow in order to give the 2nd Brigade coming from Kyaitio time to cross."

There was a pause, and Jonah waited for a response. The General spoke, "Jonah One, your appreciation is understood, but I cannot let you have the Yorkshires. You must counter-attack with the forces you have at hand. And you must hold the bridge till mid-morning tomorrow." The General's voice became more stressed. "The bridge must not fall into enemy hands. If the counter-attacks cannot dislodge the Japs, blow the bridge before dawn. Good luck. Out."

The brigadier had held his anger during the conversation, but when he hung up, he screamed, "the bleeding General doesn't know what the hell he is talking about!" He paused for a while to gather himself, then ordered the Gurkha company atop Pagoda Hill to be reinforced. He said sadly, "I am not sure that this can end well."

On Buddha Hill, in their small bunker, the Japanese gunners sat ready with their machine gun. In front of them, a line of troops lay hidden in brush. Sato was some distance away from the hill but was in radio contact with the machine-gun unit. They were waiting for more infantry support before firing on the column of retreating British Indian forces who were now heading for the bridge. "Take a small contingent of infantry," Sato ordered, "and move against the Gurkha unit holding Pagoda Hill. Our infantry reinforcements are nearly there and will join the assault."

A forward element of the Japanese infantry crept up Pagoda Hill and surprised the Gurkha defenders, who momentarily fell back. Then Jemedar Bahadur regrouped his men. The Jemedar, however, looked worried about his ability to withstand a subsequent attack. "We have very little ammunition, and there is no time for resupply," he noted. He did not fool himself that reinforcements would arrive. Jemedar Lal Bahadur gathered his men around him and addressed them gravely in their native tongue. "I took my oath to fight to the end. Our orders are to defend this position to the last round last man. That we will do." He added, "We can expect no support." He shook hands with each of his men in turn. They said nothing, but their determination was written in their faces. They knew it would be the last battle, but to them it was their calling.

"When the ammo runs out, we will fight to end with our knives!" they vowed. Jemedar Bahadur unsheathed his *kukri* and cleaned it, then ran the blade over his left elbow to draw blood before he re-sheathed it. To put it away without drawing blood would break with tradition. He wondered how many times he would use it.

It was not long before the Jemedar heard rustling in the bamboo grove downslope of his unit's position. The first shot passed to the left of his head. He pointed his rifle and fired in the direction of the footsteps. The enemy then came swiftly, and soon he could not tell who was friend and who was foe. His ammunition expended, he threw his rifle away and unsheathed his *kukri*. A shot hit him in the thigh. But with a precision honed by daily practice in the past, he wielded his deadly knife with a "whoosh." As the screaming enemy came racing toward him, the blade of his *kukri* flashed in the sunlight and the severed head of the enemy fell to the ground. Jemedar Bahadur retrieved his weapon and made two more slashes at the rushing enemy before he felt the sharp point of a bayonet between his shoulder blades. He swung around and, with his blood draining from his back, he slashed again; another Japanese fell at his feet. He felt the sting of another bayonet. They were coming from every direction! He uttered a prayer to his god Shiva. He heard a grunt of "Kura! Kura!" and the long knife penetrated his heart. He fell dead in a pool of blood.

Pagoda Hill was now in Japanese hands. Silence fell over the dreadful scene. Even the Japanese soldiers were awed by the fighting ability, courage, and tenacity of the Gurkha defenders.

As soon as he realized what had happened at Pagoda Hill, Brigadier Jonah directed his signals officer to call divisional headquarters at Waw one more time. Radio communications were poor at best. In desperation, the call was placed in the clear. "Hello Alice," he called.

After a while the General answered, "I read you. Go ahead. Over."

Brigadier Jonah reported, "the Gurkhas put up a last man last round defense. They are all dead. They have been wiped out. It is grim news." There was silence. He continued. "Japanese machine gunners hold both Pagoda and Buddha Hills. I have very few men to order a counter-attack." He stopped. There was nothing more to say.

"Understood," said General Burnett.

There was another long pause, then Brigadier Jonah pled. "Sir, I need more time to get the brigades across. Request to not blow bridge."

The news that the Japanese now dominated the commanding heights made it excruciatingly painful. General Burnett knew that if the bridge were blown, many men and much equipment would be trapped on the east of the Sittang River. But if the Japanese captured the bridge, a fast column could race to Waw and then on to Pegu. His intelligence had told him that Burmese collaborators had already commandeered fast boats and had taken them over the creek that ran parallel to the road to Pegu. "If the Japs get to Pegu, all hell is going to break loose," he said aloud. "I will carry this decision to my grave, but the order stands. Blow the bridge at dawn," he said emphatically.

"Understood and out," came Jonah's terse reply.

The General's chief of staff and intelligence officer sat listening to the grim conversation. General Burnett turned to his advisers and remarked, "It's going to be bloody, a bloody mess. I feel for the beggars on the wrong side of the river."

Brigadier Johan slammed down the receiver. He realized the General's many troubles: he was a sick man, in pain from his many infirmities. In fact, it was well known that he was recovering from recent surgery. Nonetheless, the order to blow the bridge seemed reckless. Brigadier Johan turned to his chief of staff and reported sadly, "The order to blow the bridge stands."

BLOW THE BRIDGE

At midnight, Brigadier Jonah called Major White, who commanded the Bengal Sappers and Miners, which was camped on the west side of the bridge. "I have been in touch with the General at Waw," Brigadier Jonah explained, "and Division has ordered that the bridge be blown."

The Major was aghast (even though he had suspected this). He blurted out, "Does the bloody old fool know what the bloody hell is going to happen? Why, we will have to leave our men to the mercy of the jungle, the river, and the bloody Japs and their collaborators!"

Brigadier Jonah put his head in his hands, then responded sadly. "There is no alternative. But you can rest assured," he continued, "that history will absolve you of any blame for what is to come."

The Major summoned his trusted Lieutenant Ahmed, a sturdy Bengali with a broad face and thick, curly black hair. Lieutenant Ahmed was skilled with explosives, and he would do the dirty deed. The Lieutenant's heart sank when he received the summons. He knew something terrible was about to happen. The grim-faced Major said, "I am afraid that the General wants the bridge blown, to prevent the Japs from capturing it intact." Lieutenant

Ahmed blinked but otherwise betrayed no emotion. "Place explosive charges in the middle spans of the bridge," directed the Major.

There was a period of pained silence, then the lieutenant quietly demurred. "It has never been the practice to question a direct order, Sir," he said, "but if I may be permitted, Sir, I would like to ask why we are demolishing the bridge when so many of our soldiers are on the other side."

The Major looked pale and shivered in the warm air. He nodded gravely. "I too have questioned the Brigadier, but the General at Waw insists that we cannot let the bridge fall to the Japanese," he said unconvincingly. "If the Japanese control the bridge, they can race on to Pegu and, then, Rangoon." The Major was angry and sympathized with the young Indian lieutenant, but he knew that he would obey his orders. "We must blow the bridge at dawn," he repeated, then terminated the conversation and dismissed the lieutenant.

Lieutenant Ahmed was stunned and saddened. But he, too, knew that soldiers were expected to execute the orders they were given. From the tent at the west end of the bridge, he walked high over the bridge. There was a gentle sea breeze from the south. He was accompanied by three of his best miners; two carried rolls of wire, and the third carried the charges and battery pack. The two men with the wire stopped at the 6th span. One of them climbed under the bridge bed and then signaled that he was ready for the charges to be handed over to him. He was worried that the charges were so heavy that he might lose control of them, so moved with great deliberation. He first placed the charges into the dynamite, then secured them at the panel points with tape and rope. His partner on the bridge passed him the wires and the splicers so that he could splice the wire and connect it firmly in the charges and the sticks of dynamite. He then passed the wires and climbed back up to the top of the bridge.

Lieutenant Ahmed felt great guilt and anxiety about what he was to do. In spite of the breeze from the Andaman Sea, he felt hot and sweaty. He trembled. "If this were May," he thought, "the swirling winds from the southwest would knock me off the bridge! Happily, the weather at this time of year is quite reasonable."

Dodging the heavy traffic on the bridge, he climbed down under the bridge to inspect the men's work and to make sure that all the charges were well placed. All was well. Climbing back up to the roadway, he nodded to the men and they walked back in silence. As they walked, they unfurled the rolls of wire along the girders of the bridge. All the time the men worked, lorries and jeeps drove over the bridge in a continual flow.

The narrow railway bridge had not been built to handle heavy motor traffic, but for this emergency evacuation, heavy wood planking had been placed in the middle and along the sides, providing a surface on which the vehicles could drive. It was now well past 1:30 A.M.

20 FEBRUARY 1942

Nervous drivers continued to drive cars and lorries over the bridge in a continuous stream. As Lieutenant Ahmed looked across the bridge, he saw a line of vehicles that extended far into the embankment, as far south as Bungalow Hill. Lieutenant Ahmed hurried back to camp and notified his Major, "all charges are in place. All explosives and the detonator are in place." The Major nodded at Lieutenant Ahmed. The Major looked at his watch and walked to his tent.

From his vantage point on the west side of the bridge, Lieutenant Ahmed could see the eastern approach to the bridge. Sporadic gunfire from Japanese positions had begun to spray the retreating convoy. The Japanese were on the heels of the retreating men and were getting closer. The retreating soldiers were dispirited and frightened. A young Indian driver had just reached the top of the bridge in his American lend-lease lorry when he took a quick look down at the fast-moving river. At the same time a blast of gunfire ripped the air. Scared stiff, he panicked, ran his lorry off the wooden planks, and jammed it into the bridge girders. Utter confusion and wild yelling followed. "Get that lorry back on the motorway," the men shouted. "It is holding up the line!" The other drivers and soldiers on the bridge quickly got out to get the lorry back on the wooden planks so that the rest of the retreat could go as planned.

Lieutenant Ahmed watched, entranced. "If they do not get the lorry back onto the planking, I will have to delay the whole mission," he thought with mixed emotions. He knew that the Second Indian Brigade and the Burma Rifles were still miles from the eastern approach to the bridge. He worried about the dramatic drop to the river. He knew that many Indian soldiers could not swim. "My only comfort is that the agonizing decision will be made by the General commanding the Division," he told himself. But after what seemed to be an interminable time, the lorry was pushed back onto the planks. The driver was so unnerved by the experience that he refused to drive, and one of the other men took over the wheel.

At 4 A.M., the inky blackness of the night began to give way to a faint glow from the east. From high on Pagoda Hill came muzzle flashes from the Japanese machine guns. Traffic came to a halt on the eastern terminus of the bridge. Lieutenant Ahmed held his breath, wishing he could avoid the next few minutes. But his field telephone rang, and the Major's voice came on line, "Are the charges in place? Are you ready?"

"Yes, yes, Sir," Ahmed replied in a quavering voice. He said a prayer to Allah.

"Good," came the Major's less-than-sincere reply. "You have ten minutes to push the plunger,"

Again in a quivering voice Lieutenant Ahmed replied "Yes, Sir." He took a deep breath and cursed softly. "If I survive this war, I will have to live with this act for the rest of my life. But what alternative do I have?" With all his might he raised his right shoulder and pushed the plunger in. Instantly there was a flash, a thunderous explosion, and the two center spans of the bridge rose as in agony high into the air. There they hung momentarily, then collapsed and crashed into the muddy waters of the river. The debris and the planks, the girders and splinters of steel, the stone foundations rose into the balmy morning air and in eerie slow-motion then fell into the river. Lieutenant Ahmed could not see the splashes in the river because of the smoke and dust, but he could hear the metal hit the water. When the wind cleared the air, the center of the bridge was gone. At his end, the bridge girders were twisted grotesquely. Lieutenant Ahmed wiped the sweat from his forehead. The firing ceased. Even the Japanese gunners could not believe their eyes. As he slowly walked back to headquarters, Lieutenant Ahmed passed small groups of men—Indian, Burman, Karen, and British—who stood in awe and astonishment at what they saw. In front of the Sappers and Miners headquarters, the Major heard a voice from behind, "May God have mercy on their souls."

DESPERATE RETREAT

There was chaos on the east side of the bridge. Darkness was just giving way to dawn, and panic gripped the desperate men who now realized that they were stranded. Each minute, more soldiers arrived at the bridgehead, and soon there was a chaotic pileup of men and lorries, all facing an incredibly steep drop down to a fast-flowing river that now had no bridge across it. The desperate men arrived at the bridgehead and stood in stunned silence, then terror set in, especially amongst the men from the Himalayan mountains, most of whom could not swim. Brave men broke down and cried; company commanders desperately tried to rally their troops. They advised their men, "for those of you who cannot swim, there is a ferry up north." Few took that option, however, not knowing what they would face or whether the Japanese were already there.

Peter and Saw Travis had just reached the approach to the bridge when it had blown. Now Peter reflected on his good fortune to have learned how to swim and float on water at the Inya Lake. He joined the other officers who organized the strong swimmers. "Abandon all equipment except for your jungle knife," they told the men, "and swim to the west bank." Just then the Japanese machine gun on the hill started to fire again, adding to the misery that engulfed the British-Indian troops. Some of the men slipped down the muddy slope to the river and plunged in, never to be seen again. Others bobbed in the fast current, and were carried out of sight. Men waved their hands frantically and screamed for help, but to no avail. To add to the confusion, mules took to the river and tried to swim. Some men climbed onto the animals, causing the wretched mules to drown and take the men with them. The "lucky" men who reached the west bank were greeted with a muddy bank to scale. Even mules got stuck in the oozy muck, with no hope of getting out. A few more experienced muleteers were able to guide their animals across and up the bank, although many drowned.

The men still standing on the east bank watched the horror unfold with consternation and fear. Some went to a nearby fishing village where they hoped to buy or confiscate fishing boats. Brigade Colonel Ashcroft led a group of men north to the ferry. They took to the jungle and headed upstream through hostile territory. They got turned around, then ran into some Burmese who promised to help. But soon the Burmese turned on them, overwhelmed them, and killed or captured many in the party. Only a few exhausted men finally arrived at the ferry. But the Japanese had arrived ahead of them. The collaborators shot every solider except Colonel Ashcroft. Kyaw Khin grasped his new sword and, his face contorted with anger and rage, personally beheaded the Colonel.

Back at the site of the devastated bridge, it was a free-for-all. Vehicles were abandoned willy-nilly. Men continued to jump into the river in hopes of swimming across. A few men stood rooted in fear. Saw Travis and Peter hastily chopped down bamboo from the nearby jungle to make a raft. "It doesn't have to be a big raft," Saw Travis said. "Just big enough to keep your upper body afloat."

Jeremy and Subedar Dunn had left the protection of the rubber plantation at Mokpalin just before dawn. Out in the open, the heat soon became unbearable. The water they had brought with them was consumed all too soon. Even the water pots that the Burmese traditionally set out at the side of the roads were soon empty. Subedar Dunn saw his troops flagging and scolded them, "be vigilant." The words were hardly out of his mouth when sniping came from the edge of the jungle. They returned fire but kept moving. Then they heard the drone of planes. After their last experience, the men ran for cover. They did not wait to see if the planes were RAF, American, or Japanese. After the planes passed, the men resumed their march and finally arrived at the river. They had been shot at by the enemy, strafed by the British, American, and Japanese, and they were thirsty, hungry, and exhausted. Now they joined a chaotic mass of desperate men on the river's east bank, all seeking a way to cross the river to safety.

Subedar Dunn sized up the situation in a flash. He pulled Jeremy toward the jungle. "Here. Cut bamboo like this." He wielded his bayonet deftly. "We will split some stalks and lash them together to make a raft." As Jeremy hacked bamboo, Subedar Dunn gathered a few other men from his unit and set them to work beside Jeremy. Soon they had a small raft ready. Meanwhile, some of the men in the forward area, closest to the river, had launched a feeble counter-attack against the Japanese position on Pagoda Hill. Using the cover of this diversion, Subedar Dunn led his men in a mad scramble down the river's bank. He was a strong man and a good swimmer; he stood on the bank holding the raft while the terrified non-swimmers clambered on. Just as he and Jeremy were ready to jump onto the raft and push off, another small, flimsy raft came sliding down the muddy bank, followed by two dirty men. Jeremy started. "Peter!" he cried. They hugged but said little, being dirty, hungry, and beyond exhaustion.

"Help me," shouted Peter's companion, Saw Travis.

Peter's eyes met Jeremy's and he smiled. Subedar Dunn called out "Get on the raft!" He pushed the large raft into the current and joined Jeremy to help hoist Peter onto the smaller raft. The two rafts plunged into the current and were quickly pushed to the south of the bridge by the current. That with the remnants of Jeremy's battalion swirled in the center of the river, while the raft carrying Jeremy, Peter, Subedar Dunn, and Saw Travis drew closer to the river bank. After what seemed an interminable time, the raft reached the bank, and the men collapsed on the wet muddy embankment. Jeremy and Peter lay side by side. "How many men just collapsed and died will never be known," Peter said sadly. "Believe it or not, we are the lucky ones."

With the brown gooey river mud stuck on to them up to the waist, the four men who had fought through the jungle and had crossed the tumultuous river now lay exhausted on the west bank "Now what?" asked Jeremy. They heard voices, in Urdu, and Subedar Dun said "Friends!" The Indian soldiers helped the four survivors and urged them to make haste to the nearest friendly village, Abya. There they had a cup of warm tea and some biscuits. Gunfire continued to come not only from Pagoda Hill on the opposite bank of the river but also from closer, from the edge of the river. The men knew that they had to leave and find their units or it would be over for them. The thought of being captured by the bestial Japanese made them shudder. They realized that the retreat from Abya to Waw had already begun. They summoned what residual strength they could muster and joined the retreat down the already-crowded Pegu road. They knew they had little time; the Japanese would themselves be crossing the river soon and would cut them off again.

As they stumbled along the narrow road, a canvas-topped 1500-pound lorry appeared. They waved down the lorry and climbed in. The men sat facing each other and recognized a few familiar faces: men from their units who, like themselves, had been lucky to survive the Japanese gunfire and the raging river. The driver wanted to get to Waw in a hurry. For a while there was silence, then Jeremy spoke." We have to find what remains of our unit." Peter, Saw Travis, and Subedar Dunn nodded. They were looking forward to rejoining their units, but doubted if the units had survived the retreat and the disaster at the bridge.

At the end of the afternoon they arrived at Waw, which was still in friendly hands. The lorry dropped its passengers at the far east of Waw, near the fire station. Here they found an open mess—rice and Burmese curry. It would be their first warm meal in days, and it tasted delicious. At a temporary bivouac behind the fire station, under a large peepul tree, they would rest. Waw was in chaos. The civilians had fled. The fire engines stood silent in the building, even though there were fires burning. The firefighters had all fled. The weary men fell asleep. "Who would have thought I would be grateful to sleep in the dirt under the stars?" thought Peter as he drifted off.

In the morning Dunn announced, "I am going to seek my battalion commander or another authority. I do not wish to desert, but I must defend my family against the barbarous Japanese and their collaborators. I can join the Allied secret K-Force and can collect intelligence." Saw Travis looked at Peter, with whom he had endured so much hardship. "I, too, must search for and protect my family." So saying, he left. After receiving reluctant permission from their respective battalion commanders to return to their villages, Dunn and Travis took their rifles and disappeared into the jungle.

Peter and Jeremy made their way to division headquarters, which was a large house on a back street. In front of the house was a large open space, where there were tables set. General Burnett was nowhere in sight, but the staff was busy organizing the remnants of various units. Gunfire continued from the east, and when it subsided, the drone of planes could be heard. It was the Nakajima "Nates" again. Everyone ducked for cover and trembled until the planes headed further east. Jeremy and Peter learned from the General's staff that there was no transport available for the retreating men except for a few civilian cars. Most motor transport had either already left for Pegu or had been abandoned on the east side of the Sittang River. The medical unit had set up tents to treat the worst injured and was trying to get the less severely wounded to Pegu before the Japanese closed the road. Jeremy and Peter searched through the clumps of dispirited men and found a few old faces, but the old battalion had very few men left. They joined up with some Gurkhas and hurried westward toward Pegu.

Tall tamarind trees lined the road. Beyond, the land was flat and featureless, dusty and yellow, and covered with thick scrub. Only a few trucks carrying the wounded passed the men as they made their way to Pegu. All the while, the men remained on the lookout for enemy planes. In their exhausted condition, the men could not make it to Pegu before nightfall, and they knew that it would be dangerous to continue in the dark. They paused for the night. "Maybe the trucks will return from Pegu to pick up the remnants of the battalion," Jeremy remarked hopefully. He wondered about what had happened to Carl. He knew Carl had been badly wounded. He did not want to think about what the Japanese had done to him, if they had captured him. Did he die quickly, or was he tortured? He hoped not.

In the night, Peter and Jeremy were awakened by gunfire quite close by, coming from the west. They grabbed their rifles and crept stealthily toward the source of the gunfire. Just as they arrived at the edge of a clearing, the shooting stopped, and they heard two Gurkha soldiers talking in their native language. After identifying themselves, Peter and Jeremy joined the two men in the clearing, where the bodies of several Japanese soldiers lay sprawled. Peter searched the bodies and found in one sergeant's pockets a map and some papers. He scanned them quickly. "We've got to get this information to the commander in Pegu!" he said excitedly. "It reveals the Japanese battle plan!" Even though it was still night, the four men moved slowly toward Pegu, rifles at ready. They knew that they had important information that could affect the outcome of the war.

The perimeter guard around Pegu challenged the four men. "We're from the Burma Rifles. "Teik Hi Johnny," Jeremy called out, fear evident in his voice. "We've retreated from Moulmein and Sittang. We found maps and papers that your commander must see."

The guards shone their flashlights over the four dirty men, and their leader grunted. Gesturing with his rifle, he said, "this way to headquarters." He roused the battalion commander and returned to his post.

Peter handed the maps and papers to the commander and explained how he and Jeremy had joined up with the two Gurkhas and how the Gurkhas had killed the Japanese soldiers. As the battalion commander perused the papers, his eyes widened. He shook off any residual drowsiness and summoned his intelligence captain. "I want you to read these papers and hear you confirm what I think they reveal," he told the captain.

The captain read the papers and blanched. He, like the commander, came to the frightening conclusion that something big was about to happen: the Japanese were going to cut off and encircle the city. "They plan to bypass Pegu by going west of the city and then splitting into two columns: one turning south toward Rangoon and the second turning north toward Diak Yu!" he exclaimed. "If they are successful," he continued, "it will be devastating to the British defensive forces."

The commander turned to the four weary men who had brought this information. "You have rendered immeasurable service to our military," he said. We must reassess our own strategy and implement it rapidly. Until we are sure of our plans, why don't you men have something to eat and then rest?"

Peter, Jeremy, and their two Gurkha companions needed no further urging. They saluted and withdrew, running to the mess tent that the commander had pointed out. After satisfying their deep hunger, they ambled to a secluded area under a tree and immediately fell asleep.

The commander summoned his advisors immediately. He explained the new situation. "We can draw some comfort from the fact that this intelligence indicates that it is a patrol of the White Tigers 212 regiment, not the main body of the Japanese, which is to head to Diak Yu." He continued. "I pray that the main body is still east of Waw. But we cannot rest on that prayer; we have to make a run for it now. We cannot let the Japanese trap us here." He turned to his advisors. "Destroy all equipment. Move out as soon as possible, on the double."

PART V

The Evacuation of Rangoon

Chapter 22
Evacuation by Cart and Rail

At Aunty Nyunt's house, Tin Oo told his mother, "I have made arrangements to have you evacuated to your native village near Singu." Aunty Nyunt did not like leaving the house, and she feared that gangs would strip the house and ruin all that she built over the years, but she knew she would be safer in the village. So, after some persuasion and a promise that she could take a bullock cart full of her possessions, she consented. Tin Oo hired a car to go a short distance to the bullock cart trail. He loaded the cart and paid the owner of the cart. His mother sat next to the driver. It would take them two days and nights before they arrived at the village. Tin Oo returned to the home to guard it and welcome the Japanese. He looked forward to liberation by the Japanese. He had no fear. In fact, he was looking forward to the revolution, no matter how fierce the fighting. He would join the new freedom block and help Burma regain her freedom. Tin Oo was not representative of all Burmese, however; there was a range of perspectives on the Greater East Asia Co-Prosperity Sphere, from embrace to skepticism to fear.

The tension in the Railways office was palpable. Mr. Thomas wrung his hands. Regular supplies of coal had not arrived from India, complicating his work immensely. As he leafed through the morning's orders, he came upon a very disturbing document. It noted all the trains departing daily out of Rangoon and announced that the last train to leave Rangoon would depart tomorrow. "If the Europeans and military are planning to leave the city," Mr. Thomas surmised, "the British will abandon Rangoon." He reassured himself, "surely all my long years of service to the railways will enable me to get my family onto the last train out of Rangoon."

That night, in spite of his fear of being separated from his wife and children, he told Reddy, "Take the family to board the last train tomorrow."

He broke the news to his stunned family. His wife cried, worried about how she could manage without him. "Reddy will go with you," Mr. Thomas explained. "All he has to do is give my name to the guards, and the railway officials will let you board. Benjamin and I will withdraw with the troops, on a military train," he consoled her.

Rumors had already spread throughout the city that the last train would depart soon. The next day, crowds arrived at the railway station early in the morning. They arrived in gharries, *tongas*, rickshaws, and on foot, carrying pitifully small bundles of their possessions. Desperate people, "essential personnel," who now realized that the British themselves were evacuating and who did not want to be left behind. They had worked closely with the British and could only imagine how they would be punished by the Japanese for their loyalty. The gharry, *tonga*, and rickshaw drivers were doing a brisk business. No sooner did they unload one group of passengers than they plied the streets to quickly find new passengers.

In front of the tall wrought-iron gates of the Railways, the would-be passengers waited. This was a large outdoor anteroom where passengers gathered before they bought their tickets. Guards let only European women and children through. After the European women had purchased their tickets and moved on to the platform, the non-Europeans jostled closer to the gates, waiting their turn. Then suddenly, the Gurkhas closed the gates, barring all non-Europeans. A roar went up from the crowd. "Do not leave us!" they cried. Some tempted the guards with gold, "Here, take this!" they pleaded. "Just let me slip through." Other entreated the Gurkhas, "We are brothers; let us through, please!" But the Gurkhas stood firm, obeying their orders. Only Europeans were to board the train.

Bereft of all their usual decorum, British women clutching their children rushed toward the trains and formed a line to start boarding. In spite of the chaos, the train soon was fully loaded with Europeans. Just a few stragglers were coming through the gates, and the soldiers were focused on keeping the growing and increasingly angry crowds of Indians, Burmese, and Anglos at bay.

The train blew its whistle and pulled slowly from the station. White faces stared out of the windows at the dark mass of humanity outside the station gates. Reddy and the Thomases returned home completely demoralized. The family was somber and tearful, and nothing Reddy tried worked to calm the family or staunch the tears.

When Mr. Thomas arrived home and discovered his family still there, he turned ashen. Reddy related the day's events. "The British only care for themselves," he spat. "To them we are nothing. All your years of service; I couldn't even get close to the gates to plead our case."

Soon Benjamin returned home and the story was told again. He, in turn, updated his father and Reddy of news from the front. He had read the papers until the *Rangoon Gazette* had stopped publication, and listened to the radio every chance he got. Through his co-workers at the docks also, he knew what was happening in Rangoon. "The Japanese routed the British at Moulmein and are now racing to Pegu." he said to his father. "If they capture that city, they will be in Rangoon within a week."

"Have you any news of Peter and his unit?" Mr Thomas asked.

"None," Benjamin said sadly. "Also ominous for us is the fact that two sentai of the Japanese air force are now operating from Moulmein."

Mr. Thomas exhaled sharply, with a little gasp of dismay.

"And there is more," Benjamin went on. "I have heard more news of losses of the RAF and AVG. They were leaving the city for the safety of the inland airports. An early morning surprise raid caught them on the ground and destroyed many planes. The remaining allied planes took off the next morning and headed north; there now are no air defenses for Rangoon. The city is defenseless."

Mr. Thomas shook his head. "We cannot use lights or cooking fires at night; and we'll have to cook between air raids. Tell your mother."

That evening after dusk, the dreaded night raids began. The siren heralded an air raid when the planes were already overhead. The younger members of the family huddled together. Grandmother and mother told stories to soothe the children. Soon the sound of a heavily laden bomber could be heard nearby. The engines roared, then almost fell silent, then roared again and sounded even more ominous. The changing pitch from low to high, from the unsynchronized engines, caused the windows to rattle and added to the family's terror. The sound intensified as the bomber started its dive. Mother hugged the children tightly, wedging them between and behind big rice bags that had been stored. It was too dangerous to go to the shelter. Kamala, defying her grandmother, went to the window to see what was happening. The bright beams of searchlights desperately pierced the vast inky sky, seeking the offending deliverer of death. Suddenly they locked onto the plane. The anti-aircraft gun tracers went up to the plane but didn't quite reach it; the ground shook with a thunderous explosion. Then, much to her surprise, she saw a small fighter on the tail of the Japanese bomber. Tracers raced toward the enemy plane and hit it; the bomber spun and started to spiral towards the house. Kamala ran to her mother in terror. "Don't worry," mother said, "the noise is terrifying, but it is not headed to our house." Indeed, the family heard the explosion and shortly even felt a gush of heat, then heard secondary explosions. The glass in the front window splintered, scattering glass in every direction. The men looked at one another. "That was too close," Benjamin said. Soon the night took on a eerie silence. When they felt the bombing run was over, they tried to sleep, but did so fitfully. Their sleep was shattered by a second wave of bombers, which carried on until late.

Meanwhile, CeCi had continued to work at the hospital, despite all the rumors. The evenings were frantic in the basement telephone room of the hospital. The hospital was full to capacity, so she was busy. In the course of her job, she overheard conversations that were not meant for her ears. For example, she overheard the superintendent of the hospital asking the head of railways for a carriage for his family, the pet dog, and the nanny.

The day she overheard that conversation, CeCi took the evening train home. At the station, all the streets were dark because of the blackout restrictions. Her mother had kept food warm for her. For the second evening, her father was absent. She discussed the information she gathered at the hospital with her mother. Her mother was worried, but CeCi could not quite put her finger on one particular thing that was bothering her. She had not heard from Jeremy at the front, and she knew that war was approaching Pegu. Finally CeCi asked her mother, "Where is father?"

"He is assembling a train to go north," explained her mother, without providing any more details."

CeCi accepted the explanation. She had seen for herself what was happening, even though most civilians were left in the dark. She knew that the British clubs were all closed and padlocked, and knew from the snippets of conversations she overheard at work that the British women and children were getting ready to leave. There had been rumor of a special train set aside for the last British evacuees.

At the rail yard, Mr. Rawson prepared the long, powerful, green and gold locomotive. All the third-class carriages that typically carried the native people had been removed. The head of the Rangoon station had personally taken charge of preparing the train. He had sent out orders to assemble all the first-class and second-class coaches and have them cleaned and provisioned—all with great secrecy. He feared that if it became widely known that the British were fleeing the city, there would be widespread public panic; worse, he feared that thousands of desperate people would rush the train and destroy it. Mr. Rawson had told his wife that he had to work at night due to the constant air raids; he did not reveal the real reason. But he was bothered by the fact that this train he was preparing was for Europeans only. He wanted to know if the children of those faithful Anglos who ran the trains would be excluded, left to fend for themselves against the Japanese and their collaborators.

One morning, over coffee, toast, and jam, Mr. Rawson laid his hands on the table. "CeCi, you have heard rumors about the evacuation of Rangoon, I'm sure. I have an opportunity to take you away from the city. Your brother is already at the front, and we have not heard from him recently; your mother and I could not bear to lose you, too. You must go to India. I can get you evacuated. You must come to work with me today."

CeCi was stunned. Yes, she had heard the rumors, but rumors were notably unreliable. Then she remembered the call she had routed yesterday, from the head of the hospital. She realized suddenly that soon even the hospital would close. "Father, I know you are right," she said. "But surely we will all evacuate together, won't we?"

Mr. Rawson glanced at his wife. "Your mother will stay here for Jeremy. I will go with you. But this is an opportunity we cannot miss. Pack a little bag and come with me."

Despite the secrecy desired by the head of the railway station, the rumor about the evacuation of the British on a special train—the last train from Rangoon—began and spread quickly through the city. By the time CeCi and her father arrived, the large open area in front of the railway station was jammed with an assortment of vehicles. Cars brought the European women and children; tongas, taxis, rickshaws, and handcarts brought hundreds of Indians, Anglos, ethnic Karens, and Burmese. The tall gates to the station were closed and guarded by soldiers, but they let Mr. Rawson and CeCi pass. From the windows of her father's office, CeCi could see the crowds growing larger. All day long she agonized about whether she was making the right decision, how she would cope on her own, and what life would be like in India.

Finally the train was ready for boarding. There was a great rush of evacuees from the interior and main platforms to board the train. British woman clutching little suitcases and juggling babies and small children. All norms of civil behavior were set aside; the rush was on. The crowd of Anglos, Indians, and Burmese in the outside anteroom stormed the gates, but they were restrained by bayonet-wielding soldiers.

"Now," said Mr. Rawson to CeCi. The two walked briskly to the line of stragglers. The guards recognized Mr. Rawson and allowed him to proceed. Mr. Rawson pushed CeCi into the midst of the cluster of British women boarding the train. A last squeeze of her hand and she was on the train. Mr. Rawson boarded the engine to resume his work.

Finally the whistle blew. A wail arose from the pitiful crowd of non-whites outside of the station as they realized they would not be allowed on the train, even if there was room. The conductor flashed his green lantern and the great engine—the largest in Burma—blew its long whistle three times and the train pulled away from Platform One. Only police and troops were left on the platform. No families waving handkerchiefs, no lovers blowing kisses; only, behind the police and troops, the stunned and angry faces of the non-whites left behind. The train gathered speed and was soon was out of sight.

The vast crowd of brown faces outside the railway gates, in despair and with downcast eyes, slowly started to leave. It would be midnight before they would reach home, terrified even as they pondered their future.

In the cab of the engine was a British Major of the Yorkshire Regiment. He sat on the spare seat, clutching his leather briefcase. He had it secured to his hand by a chain, and in the briefcase were his instructions. Before he had boarded the train, he had called the GOC's office to make sure Pegu was still in British hands. "Yes sir," had come the answer. Now he ordered the driver, "Make haste. I have important business. I must make sure that all these passengers arrive safely in Myitkyina." Once the train got underway, it would travel at a higher speed. The Major opened the briefcase and pulled a file marked "top secret." His instructions made it clear that the safety of the women and children on the train came first, no exceptions. The other papers contained instructions for when the train it reached its destination at Myitkyina.

It was late as the train approached Pegu. As the train slowed, CeCi leaned out of the window. In the distance she heard gunfire; she pulled back quickly to the corner of the carriage and prayed quietly. Normally the train would stop at Pegu to take on water and coal, but this night it only slowed; it did not stop. The Major had instructed the engine driver to not stop, because of the great risk that the fifth column might be operating here. The signals were still working, and the signal light was yellow. The engine driver looked at the Major, who nodded to proceed. After crossing the bridge over the river, the train picked up speed again. It would be midnight before they would reach Toungoo, which was still held by Chinese troops. They would protect the train as it halted for the night.

The next morning, CeCi found it curious that the train did not continue. She soon learned that Japanese aircraft were active, and there were rumors that the Japanese had launched a new offensive that posed a threat to the railway. There were many Chinese troops milling about the train. The emblem they wore indicated that they were part of the Chinese 5th Army. The passengers were relieved that the Chinese troops were there, but CeCi thought that some of them seemed as confused and panic-stricken as the passengers themselves. Nonetheless, it was reassuring to see soldiers with guns drawn guarding the train. CeCi took the opportunity to get out of the train to stretch her legs. She was careful to avoid the British women; she did not want to be pointed out as an Anglo, on the train against orders. For the first time in her life, she saw British women carrying their own luggage and water, as there were no Indian porters available.

The engine detached and took on coal and water. The Major consulted with the Railway military command. He came back from the station master's office and told Mr. Rawson to get the train ready for a long run. "There will be no more long stops, and you must make the best speed to ensure the security of this train." Unsure of how much he should say, he paused. "You may as well know. The military front is collapsing. The Chinese divisions are retreating in confusion up north. We have to cross the Sagaing Bridge, the lone bridge across the Irrawaddy River, before air attacks damage it." While they were en route, the Japanese 56th Division, newly arrived from Singapore, had a launched a attack from Lashio in the north and were headed to Myitkyina, to bisect the country in two.

The words were barely out of the Major's mouth when the air raid siren sounded. There was a mad scramble to get off the train, as it would be a target. The passengers and train personnel alike hid under the golden Mohur trees and in the trenches under the trees. CeCi watched the sky nervously and wondered where her father was. The last she had seen him, he had been with the British Major, in the engine. She heard the planes, but they were to the north. The all-clear signal sounded, the passengers ran for the train, and the train hastily left the station.

The train swayed from side to side, and soon the rocking of the train lulled her into a light sleep that did not totally obliterate her thoughts and fears. Other than her father, she did not know anyone on the train. She was alone. True, her father was also on the train, but she knew that he was committed to stay with the railways. She knew that Myitkyina, the northernmost large city held by the British, had a major airfield, from which the British women and children would be flown out to the safety of western India. She wondered how her father planned to get her on board any of the flights. She was light-skinned, but not white like the British women. And she would be alone, with no sister or friend or child.

At about midnight, CeCi heard the train go over a bridge, and she awoke. She knew intuitively that they were passing over a major river, probably the Irrawaddy. She was relieved to find that the bridge had not been damaged. Then the train picked up speed again, and she fell asleep again, this time into a deep sleep. She awoke at dawn to see that the topography had changed. In the distance she could see mountains. Soon the train slowed and wound its way along the side of the river. The tracks turned due north, where the dry plains gave way to low undulating mountains. She noted that the green paddy fields were sparse. Normally there would be a stop at Ye, but for this train, there would be no stops. On and on it went till the next morning, when the train slowed as it approached another river.

Mr. Rawson informed the Major, "We will be coming up on Mogaung." At Mogaung was the last railway bridge before Myitkyina. Soon the bridge came into sight. CeCi could see the river on the right side. The passengers craned their necks to look ahead to their destination, and presently the train slowed. The passengers could see the station in the distance. It was not much of a station; just a single platform with tracks on both sides.

The tired passengers were herded off the train. Armed troops were everywhere. Beyond the station CeCi could see a row of lend-lease lorries, cars, and buses, all guarded by troops. "To take the British women," she thought. Indeed, the British citizens were guided to the transport and helped onto the vehicles. They rushed off, "to the aerodrome, no doubt," thought CeCi. She glanced beyond the railway road and saw there a mass of civilians, mostly Kachins, Burmese, and a few Indians. They stood silently, gazing at the train and at the British as they hastened from the train to the vehicles.

CeCi's father walked towards her. He hugged her tightly and held her. She had tears in her eyes and was frightened. Her father reassured her. "You know, you have some relatives in Myitkyina. They are waiting for you over there." He gestured to the small station house set back from the tracks. "I will return to Rangoon to take care of your mother. Besides, I have been ordered to return immediately to Rangoon."

"Father," said CeCi in fear and exasperation, "why didn't you and Mother come with me? How can I do this myself? The British Railways can get along without you; look at them: they are running away and leaving you behind!"

"Hush," he said. "You are safe here."

They hugged again, tears streaming down from CeCi's big eyes. "Please be careful. The Japanese planes seem to have filled the skies, and you know how they like trains."

Her father smiled and patted her on her back. He was fighting back tears himself. His whole family was being torn from him. He did not know where his son was, he had left his wife in a deserted and dangerous city, and now he was going to leave his daughter alone to start new life in a strange country. He turned to her extended family at the station house, waved, gave CeCi a little shove in their direction, and whispered, more to himself than to anyone in particular, "take good care of my little girl."

CeCi carried her small suitcase to the little house. Like all railway quarters, it was painted black. Her aunt was waiting solemnly on the veranda. Aunty kissed her on the cheek and said, "Oh, you look so beautiful!" She then hugged CeCi tightly. "It has been such a long time since I've seen you!" She guided CeCi to the tiny living room, where the rest of the extended family had gathered. A steady stream of distant relatives arrived at the tiny house, and after dinner they sat down to talk about the war and plans for evacuation. CeCi marveled that all of her relatives, despite their own concerns for their own safety, accepted her as one of them. "We have a friend with a car," her aunt told her. "Tomorrow morning we will drive to the airport when the evacuation begins."

After a night of fitful sleep, crammed into one of the small rooms with the extended family, CeCi awoke with a knot in her stomach. The family stuffed themselves into the friend's car and headed to the aerodrome. The rumors were that the British set up a shuttle of Dakotas to transport the refugees from Myitkyina to Calcutta.

When they arrived at the air port, CeCi saw that the airfield was heavily guarded by British and Gurkha troops. It was Rangoon all over again. The local police were on the perimeter to prevent any rush of the planes by the local refugees. The last British civilians from towns in north Burma arrived with their children in military vehicles and were swiftly escorted to the tarmac. CeCi now started to worry about her chances of getting aboard a plane. "This is just like the train," she thought bitterly. "British first."

After a short time they heard the drone of a plane, and everyone looked skyward. Soon the plane came into view and landed. It taxied to the apron and left its engines running. The British police tried to keep all non-Europeans away. There was much pushing and crying as the British women and children crowded onto the plane, and when the plane started to taxi away, the local people broke through the police barriers to chase the plane, in a desperate attempt to throw themselves on it. "Well," thought CeCi, "that is just the first plane. They have a shuttle going."

She pushed with her family closer to the police lines. But as the day wore on and planes came and went, she realized that she had no chance to get anywhere near any plane. She said to her aunt wearily, "The sun will set soon. This is probably the last plane of the day. It will leave, and we will still be standing here in dumb hope." Then something happened that terrified her. In the distance, she heard the sound of a fighter plane, and then the plane that had just taken off, fully loaded with women and children, was attacked. It burst into flames and plunged to the ground. Trembling, CeCi said a little prayer for the victims and thanked the forces that had spared her a terrible fate. She remembered her mother's words, "be careful what you wish for; you might get it."

As dusk set in, the last hope of escape by plane was over for the day. "There are still a few white faces left," one of CeCi's distant cousins grumbled; "so there will be another plane tomorrow." But the next day, the same procedures were followed. All the British were boarded, leaving the brown and dark faces. Soon the soldiers guarding the airfield began to shoo the locals away, and close the gates to the airfield. CeCi and her family followed the crowd back to the city. The road was filled with cars of all descriptions, and overloaded lorries heading west out of the city. She asked her aunt, "is there a land route out of Myitkyina?" She knew the answer, but asked anyway.

"There are only two routes: one south, from here to the Indaw Lake beyond the Chindwin River; and a second, more arduous, from here north, through the Pangsu pass to Ledo. Beyond the Burma border, there are no roads, only trails through the thick jungle." Her aunt fell silent, then added, "we must have a family council tonight."

CeCi was hungry and was happy to return to her aunt's small railway quarters. The family ate some cold food by candle light. The rumors were that the Japanese were just south of the railway station and that all roads, including the river route, were either closed or would soon close. CeCi's family discussed their options. It was Hobson's choice: was the danger of staying greater than the danger of fleeing the advancing Japanese?

The people of the city were fleeing Myitkyina. They had no idea of what sort of terrain they would have to traverse to get to the safety of India. Both the southern and the northern route led through remote, wild, and dangerous places. Even the intrepid British had not ventured to survey this wild land. The Burmese who lived in Myitkyina did not know that the land lying between them and India had once been a shallow sea before the India plate had slammed against the Asia plate sixty-five million years ago. But they knew that it was rife with mountain ranges and large valleys. They had heard rumors about the Kumon range and the Hukawng valley. They had heard that the monsoon in that area dumped relentless torrents of rain. They also had heard that the heat was intense, and that these hot and rainy conditions spawned a dangerous steamy jungle that contained some of the world's deadliest insects, venomous reptiles, and largest predators. They would use ancient trails but were not aware of the peril they faced.

The refugees who would leave Myitkyina would have to trek through a dense jungle covered with a canopy of large, broad-leafed trees: Tamarind, peepul, teak, padauk, sisal, pine, and other trees. Beautiful birds of paradise towered over the valley floor, and wild banana (plantain) trees grew densely closer to the ground. Every millimeter of the valley floor was covered with vegetation: some friendly and some poisonous. Living amidst this was a staggering array of stingers, bitters, and stabbers. The vicious Bengal leeches grew to be six inches long. They attached themselves to the skin and secreted a poison to bleed the host. Smaller leeches caused intractable "Naga sores," which ate the flesh down to the bone. Insects, especially mosquitoes, lay dormant in the cold but turned deadly as the temperatures rose; the most deadly kind caused black water fever. Mites carried an agent that caused the dreaded and debilitating Scrub Typhus. And snakes! Spitting cobras, king cobras, pit vipers, and spitting Russell vipers all roamed the valley. Then there were the large predators, such as the Bengal Tiger and leopards, which feasted on Gaur, Sambar, and sometimes a human. These conditions made any journey through this land perilous even in the best of times.

Most of CeCi's extended family decided against the trek. "It is too dangerous," they pronounced. "Surely the Japanese will not hurt us; they are just after the British."

"Do we have to worry the collaborators?" CeCi's aunt asked. "They see Indians and Anglos as collaborators with the British."

"We will depend on our neighbors!" the cousins cried. "They are not our enemies. Besides," they said, "some of us have Burmese spouses, we have children; this is our home."

CeCi's aunt looked at her and shook her head. "I don't know," she said slowly. "I've been watching how the British treat us at the aerodrome, and also watching how the Burmese look at us. I'm not sure I want to take my chances with them." She turned to the extended family. "You are all grown and have your lives here. I am old and have no children living here. In fact, my son is working in India in the shipyards, and I don't know where the railways have sent my husband. I haven't heard from him in months. He has family in India as well. I think I should try to get there."

CeCi agreed. "My father sent me here because he worried about me and wanted me to leave Burma. Here in Myitkyina you may think you know your neighbors and that they will not harm you. But in Rangoon, I could already see the social rules breaking down. When there are no more police and no more British military, the chaos will increase." She turned to her aunt. "Aunty, if you go, I go. We will help one another."

The family sat in silence for a long time. Slowly the extended family came over to CeCi and her aunt. "We love you and wish you the best, Aunty," they said. "We will pray for you." And then they slipped out of the room and bedded down for the night. Tomorrow they would return to their homes. They had given up the idea of escape by air and had reconciled themselves to making the best of things in a changing city.

Chapter 23
Evacuation by Plane and Convoy

MARCH 1942

When news of the debacle at the Sittang Bridge reached Rangoon, panic set in. Looting began that very evening. Shops and fashionable stores were broken into. Many of the low-level police fled their posts. Others joined in the looting and were seen carrying away loot from the ransacked stores. The emergency administrator now ordered military police to fire on looters, even if they were police. It took the arrival of the commissioner of police, who summoned his best men and officers, mostly Anglo-Burmese and Anglo-Indian, to stop the riots and bring order to the chaotic streets of Rangoon.

The once-vibrant restaurants and clubs were mostly closed, and those that were open had only a sprinkling of customers. The dancing halls were empty. Food and medicine were becoming scarce. The *Rangoon Gazette* had stopped publication, and Rangoon Radio had taken a hit during the air raids so no longer broadcast. In the absence of newspapers and reliable news, rumors took on a life of their own among the remaining population. Adding to the woes, enemy planes were overhead almost all the time.

Most of the civil population had already left, except for the "last ditchers," people who could not leave, by government edict. The last days of free Rangoon were coming to a end. Fifth columnists and dacoits were making their presence felt; fresh food supplies from the hinterland were not arriving into the city; and the people were becoming increasingly hungry.

General Taylor and his chief of staff arrived at the government house late, although still before sunrise. "The battle for the Sittang Bridge is over, and the fight for Pegu is increasingly uncertain," General Taylor informed the Governor. "The Japanese are closing all escape routes. The city is on the verge of being isolated."

The Governor's eyes blinked and fear laced his voice as he asked, "is there a plane available?"

"Yes, Sir," the chief of staff answered. "We have a Blenheim bomber waiting for you at Mingaladon airfield."

The Governor rummaged through his drawers and pushed a few items into a satchel that sat next to his desk. "I've been worried about this for some time now," he said. He nodded his head at the satchel. "And I've been preparing for this moment. Nonetheless, it is not easy, and I fear for the city." He stood up and announced, "General, I hereby turn control of the city over to you. It is now a military zone." Then he shook hands with General Taylor and his chief of staff and headed to the airfield.

"God speed," whispered General Taylor.

The Governor had sent his family by air to Maymyo a week ago. Now it was his turn. Some of the seats of the bomber had been removed to make room for baggage. To avoid enemy aircraft, the bomber left even before the sun rose. After a short flight it arrived in the cool hills of Maymyo.

As soon as the Governor's plane left the tarmac, General Taylor declared martial law throughout the city of Rangoon, with orders to shoot criminals and dacoits. Then he turned to his chief of staff. "If the Japanese advance captures Pegu and advances to Hmawbi, they will have cut both of our escape routes, to Mandalay and to Prome, and we and our whole garrison will be trapped. We will be annihilated. This is unacceptable. And that is precisely what General Maida is determined to do."

"What about the newly arrived British tank brigade and field regiment?" asked the chief of staff hopefully. "And the 5th Tank regiment should arrive any day now. Surely this will strengthen our garrison."

"Even the additional tank brigades and field regiment cannot stem the Japanese tide," the General mused. "This is all simply too late." General Taylor chewed his lips before issuing the order. "We must evacuate all troops now," he told his chief of staff. "See to it." He added, "And leave instructions for the 5th Tank regiment to follow us out of Rangoon north-ward to Pegu, as soon as they disembark."

"Yes, Sir," the chief of staff nodded. "I will inform all commanders of your order."

Within a matter of hours, the tank brigade that had arrived so jauntily in the city just two days earlier led the British retreat northward out of the city. It was followed by a long column of jeeps, lorries, and cars of every description. The convoy soon passed the leafy campus of the university. The lake houses were empty, the doors thrown wide open by robbers who had emptied the contents. Then it passed the aerodrome, where buildings were still smoldering. There were wrecks everywhere, and the main airstrip was pockmarked with bomb craters. Burnt-out vehicles littered the roadside, some still smoking and emanating an acrid smoke that made breathing difficult.

The rear guard of the retreating forces followed General Taylor's orders to destroy everything that might be used by the Japanese. The sappers and miners started their demolition of all ordnance, military stores, and ammunition dumps. They rendered bicycles inoperable, remembering how effectively the Japanese had used bicycles in Malaya. It pained the General to destroy so much equipment, but he knew that the lightly armed Japanese depended on capturing allied supplies; they called these "Churchill's gifts."

The city's zoo keepers, knowing that there soon would be no food for the animals, opened the gates; the released tigers, leopards, and elephants were let out to fend for themselves, and soon some animals could be seen in the city, feeding on carcasses. To add to the fear, there was gunfire. It had a terrifying effect, causing people to panic and run senselessly for non-existent cover. Rumors abounded that Japanese spies were shooting people to cause panic. The general public was defenseless; the only people with arms were the rebels and criminals.

With each passing minute, it seemed, the roads leading out of Rangoon became ever more chaotic. Rangoon's rumor mill had sprung into high gear, and desperate civilians, fearing what the Japanese might do to them, clogged the roads with cars, tongas, bullock carts, and on foot. The sick were left behind to fend for themselves. The rear guard tried valiantly to control the situation, but with little success.

Just beyond the aerodrome, which was at milepost 13, the military convey slowed to a crawl. Gunfire could be hear ahead. At milepost 16, at Taukkyan, the main road out of Rangoon forks. One road leads north, to

Pegu, and the other west, to Prome. The lead column had just passed the fork when it came under attack. Unbeknownst to the British, a Japanese battalion had been waiting in the surrounding jungle, with orders to cross over the Rangoon–Prome Road from east to west and attack Rangoon from the west, in effect completely surrounding the city. The men in the rear of the convoy could hear big booming explosions, indicating that the tanks were engaged in battle. "We are going to have to fight our way out of this," they said grimly as they checked their rifles and ammunition.

Luckily, the Japanese battalion commander lost radio contact with his divisional commander at Pegu. Misinterpreting the General's orders, the battalion commander led his troops away from the road, into the jungle west of the city. Had he stayed to block the road, the war would have ended right there, because the Rangoon garrison had no other escape route. It would have been surrounded and annihilated.

Chapter 24
Evacuation by Road and River

The day the military began to abandon the city, the Thomas family awakened shaken, sleepless, hungry, and terrified. Daytime air raids kept them indoors and huddled behind their rice bags for cover. Benjamin observed, "They are trying to demoralize us. If this keeps up, there will be no food or water for us. The river route and sea route to escape are now closed off. But we really must escape. Our only route out of the city is northward, to Prome, the same route that the military convoy is taking."

"Not yet," Mr. Thomas said, "I must go to the Railways office and tell them I am leaving. But you are right; we must escape."

Mr. Thomas gave thanks that during the past week he had converted his paper money to gold, gold coins, and small portable jewelry items that could be hidden and sold. He had gone to Coombe's Jewellery store and purchased rubies, sapphires, and some British sovereign gold coins, as well as some gold bullion with his paper money. Today he hailed a gharry to take him to the Railways office. Unwisely, as it turned out, he dismissed the gharry. He found the office almost empty, and a notice posted on the door. It was the Governor's emergency decree, declaring the closing of all government officers and advising that the police had orders to shoot dacoits and looters on sight. "Well, at least I am officially released and will not be abandoning my post," Mr. Thomas consoled himself.

The old *durwan* [caretaker], whom Mr. Thomas knew well, emerged from the empty building. He waved in the direction of the road and said "English have *chaila gaya* [gone]. English say you are free to leave now."

Just then a young subaltern of the Bengal Sappers came out of the building and told Mr. Thomas to leave. "Demolition charges have been put in place and we are just waiting for orders to blow up the whole installation."

Mr. Thomas hastened to his desk, collected his papers and personal belongings, and left in a hurry. As he left, he told the *durwan*, "you should leave too, quickly."

"This is it," Mr. Thomas thought as he hurried to the bus station, keeping an eye out for a free gharry as he walked briskly down the street. "Where will we go?" he wondered. "There are no trains, no busses, no planes. We have no car. It is impossible!" The more agitated he became the faster he walked. He dreaded the thought of walking out of Rangoon, but knew also that it was imperative that the family leave. "We will just have to walk back to India," he told himself resignedly. At the produce market he spotted a gharry. Running to it he threw a few rupees to the driver; in good times the ride would only have cost two annas, but prices of every-thing had risen dramatically each day.

The roads were still clogged with people. Some carried only what they could throw over their shoulder; others were in cars; some had managed to acquire bullock carts; and others fled on foot with push-carts. Like him, they were "last ditchers," forced to stay until the very last moment, to render vital services to the city. They had served faithfully, and now they were bitter, very bitter, that the government had abandoned them.

Meanwhile, Benjamin took a gharry to the dockyard and sought out his Karen friend Saw Lu. "Hurry. This way," he urged Saw Lu. They ran to a storage area where the lend-lease supplies, including lorries, were stored. The sappers were already laying explosives under the docks, to destroy all stores that the Japanese might be able to use. They would soon move to the storage area. Saw Lu knew where the keys were stored and knew which keys matched the best lorries. Wordlessly he an Benjamin looked at each other and shrugged. Saw Lu grabbed two keys and raced toward the trucks, with Benjamin close behind. Saw Lu pointed at a lorry and tossed the key to Benjamin; he climbed into another lorry himself. Swiftly the two young men maneuvered their vehicles out of the storage area and roared out of the dockyard. In the commotion, they were not noticed. As they pulled away from the dockyard, they heard explosions go off. Later they would learn that the American officer in charge of lend-lease supplies had ordered his Chinese subordinates to destroy all stores. One thousand American lend-lease lorries, jeeps, and other vehicles went up in a giant fireball.

Saw Lu and Benjamin had discussed this operation earlier. They drove to Saw Lu's home in Insein, which was set back from the road in a grove of trees. There the lorries would be safe from prying eyes. After dark, he and his brother would drive the lorries to Benjamin's house, and the family would evacuate. At Saw Lu's, Benjamin asked once again, "are you sure you and your family do not want to come with us? We can all go together."

Saw Lu smiled and shook his head. "We will be safe here. We are Karen. Besides, my mother will never leave her home. I am just happy to help you and your family get through this difficult time."

Benjamin clapped his hand on Saw Lu's shoulder and said, "I am lucky to have a friend like you." Then he slowly made his way back home, down Insein Road.

The gharry let Mr. Thomas off at the end of his street, refusing to go down the narrow lane. As Mr. Thomas walked quickly down the lane, he saw men armed with *dah*s at the end of a side street. He moved quickly and soon arrived home, frightened and tired. Benjamin was on the verandah and leapt up when hey saw him.

"Father," said Benjamin, "I have found two American Dodge lend-lease lorries. We can use them to escape, but we have to leave, without delay. The lorries are fueled and ready to go; my friends will bring them by tonight before sunrise. And we must keep this quiet; if others find out, they will jump on the transport and destroy our only chance of escape. There are collaborators, spies, and saboteurs everywhere," he ended bitterly. "I heard that the British are going to blow up the city, and if they do, the city will have no security until the Japanese arrive." Mr. Thomas, remembering the Bengal Sapper Adjutant he had met at the office and the men armed with *dah*s on the side street near home, simply nodded wearily, sending Benjamin first to collect Reddy.

As soon as it was dark, Saw Lu and his brother brought the lorries. The entire family clambered aboard the olive green lorries, the children needing a footstool. Each member of the family carried only what he or she could carry, in a small bag. The women and children huddled in the beds of the lorries and covered themselves with blankets; there were no canvas covers to keep the sun out. Benjamin drove one lorry and Reddy the other. "Are you sure you do not want to come with us?" Benjamin asked Saw Lu again. "Please."

Saw Lu smiled again. "Don't worry about us. We will be fine." He waved in the dark as the lorries drove slowly down the lane to the main road.

As the lorries headed north along Prome Road, the family could hear detonations and explosions all around them. Smoke rose furiously skyward—thick black smoke from the oil storage tanks to the south obscured the city and made breathing difficult. The nearby railway marshaling yards at Insein were also burning. Even Reddy showed concern and fear.

The roads were filled with the last stragglers leaving Rangoon. Indians, Burmese, and Chinese all took to the road on foot, with only what they could carry. They had wrapped their meager belongings in blankets and slung the blankets over their shoulders as they started their perilous journey into the unknown. They scurried in the shadows, fearful of dacoits, Japanese, collaborators . . . and their own shadows.

The Thomases whispered a prayer of thanks to Saw Lu as they crawled past the pedestrians. They passed Inya Lake and its beautiful colonnaded homes. The homes were now deserted, stripped of all their beauty. Even the commodes and kitchen sinks had been ripped out. As their little convoy moved northward, it passed burning vehicles at the side of the road. At the aerodrome, they saw the damage caused by weeks of pounding from the Japanese air force. The airstrip was pockmarked with bomb craters. Off to the side of the runway were the hulks of Japanese, British, and American aircraft. Sappers had set charges to destroy all remaining equipment and buildings. The control tower, the hangers, the crew quarters, all were demolished. The regimental quarters of the Yorkshire battalion was leveled.

Past the aerodrome, the road took a turn to the left and ran parallel to the river, then hooked right again. At the crook in the road, Benjamin spotted green spoked wheels on an abandoned and burnt-out car. He recognized the MG; knew who owned the car. The young Englishman who owned the car had always driven with the car's top down. The car had turned many a young man's head and attracted many a young woman as well. The owner typically had an Englishwoman at his side as he drove through town. Benjamin would have liked to have driven an MG, but such cars were beyond his reach. He sighed. He was sad to see the green leather burned. "Even in its ruined state, the car is gorgeous," he thought.

Just when they reached milepost 14, they heard gunfire from ahead of them. A Japanese aircraft flew low overhead and began to strafe the road ahead. Bofors anti-aircraft fire added to the din. Benjamin's heart thumped in his chest and he waved to Reddy, behind him, to slow. Suddenly an armed soldier blocked the road. He looked at the two lorries suspiciously. "Friend!" Benjamin called out in English. "What is happening ahead?"

After peering into the cabs of both lorries and peeking at the frightened women and children in the lorry beds, the soldier relented. "Intelligence is that the Japanese have set up a road block. Japanese fighters have attacked as well. We are trying to break through."

Ahead, vehicles had come to a stop. Soon the lorries were stalled, and the fighting seemed to be drawing closer. The slower refugees from Rangoon began to pile up behind the lorries, stopped also by the soldier and his comrades. Panic set in. The refugees cried and wailed, running around in a panic. They did not know what to do, where to go. Even the soldiers seemed to be running in every direction, taking up positions and abandoning them in quick succession.

Benjamin and Reddy conferred. "This is getting dangerous," Benjamin observed. "The situation may soon get out of control."

Reddy agreed. "I'm sort of familiar with this area. Let me scout around a bit."

Benjamin was reluctant to let Reddy out of his sight, but realized that there was no other way to get information. Mr. Thomas climbed into Reddy's place in the driver's seat, after having told the family to stay low and quiet. He wanted to be ready to escape quickly, even abandon the lorries, if necessary. When Reddy returned, he brought a villager with him. The villager whispered, "advance units of the army were already at the road junction, but they ran into a Japanese roadblock." He continued. "Earlier I saw an Englishman with a red cap, accompanied by other high-ranking British officers."

Benjamin surmised that this had been General Taylor. "Where was he heading?" he asked.

"I don't know," the villager responded honestly. "The Japanese battalion, I think, has crossed from Pegu to the west and has infiltrated the jungle. They are attacking the tank column from behind." He offered his assessment of the situation. "The Japanese are getting intelligence from Burmese agents, and they are likely to trap the British and capture the commanding general."

Reddy interrupted, "My friend, what can we do?"

The villager offered his advice. "The only chance to escape is to leave the road. There is a bullock cart track to the west. Deep in the countryside, you will find a large rubber plantation. You can hide there. If the Japanese have not already reached there, it will be safe." He added, "I have some bullock carts. For a fee, I can take you to the plantation. From there, when it is safe, you can take the river north to safety."

Mr. Thomas had climbed out of his lorry and joined the three men. Listening to the villager describe the safety of the rubber plantation, he was torn. "Can we trust this man?" he whispered to Benjamin. Just then another loud boom of explosive rent the air, and a shell hit just north of where the lorries were idling. The men could hear the drone of planes in the west, heading toward the convoy that was stalled ahead of the lorries.

"I don't think we have a choice," Benjamin whispered back to his father. "If we don't take the man up on his offer, the fighting will soon overwhelm us."

Mr. Thomas went to the cab of the lorry and rummaged through his bag. He came up with a shiny gold coin, handed it to the villager, and said, "Get the carts. We accept your offer gratefully." As the villager disappeared into the night, Mr. Thomas muttered to Reddy, "I hope he and his gold coin don't disappear!"

But the villager soon returned and gestured to the family. They quickly abandoned the lorries. The young had to be helped down, sobbing and crying. "Take only what you can carry," Benjamin admonished them. They followed the villager back to the house where the bullock cart was parked. They were city folk; they had never been on a bullock cart before. Instructed by the driver, they clambered onto the cart. "La, la, la!" the driver called out; "hurry!" Mr. Thomas was the last to board, taking a last glance at the lorries that had seemed so promising. The driver sat at the yoke, in the front of the cart. A lantern sat next to him; it would help in the dark. The two big Brahma bulls walked briskly, and soon the sound of gunfire and explosions faded.

The jungle rapidly began to close in on them, and the city dwellers came face to face with the Burmese jungle for the first time. All varieties of bamboo grew here, some thin as reed and some as big as small tree trunks. They grew in great clusters, some so high that they hid the sun. Elephant grass covered the ground, vines grew from the giant trees and covered the ground, and the trees were covered with climbing plants and vines that grew with abandon, some thread-like and some as big as a rope. It was easy to get entangled in the vines, making walking through in the best of times difficult. The ox-cart, no matter how uncomfortable, was far better than walking.

The thunderous sound of bombs receded, and the family fell into a fitful sleep. As urbanites, they were not used to this mode of travel, and they were discomforted by the bouncing. In the wee hours of the morning the bullock cart came to a halt. The driver explained to Benjamin that they would stop for a short while to rest and feed the bulls. After they set out again, the trail wound deeper into the jungle, where the bamboo grew thick as a young woman's waist. Mosquitoes and other biting insects filled the air, and Benjamin, walking behind the bullock cart, swatted at them incessantly until his hands were red and swollen.

The dim light of the lantern barely shed enough light to see what was on the ground. Soon the family could feel the ground dropping as they entered a deep ravine and heard the sound of water flowing. To the east the sound of bombs exploding could be heard, but thankfully only faintly. The driver stopped the cart a second time, got out of the cart, walked to the edge of the water, then waded across. He then returned and told Benjamin that he could indeed drive the cart safely across. But the climb up the bank on the far side proved harder. Benjamin helped push the cart up the muddy bank. Not long thereafter, he realized that his legs itched. He rolled up his pant legs and even in the dim light could see a black squiggly object. He instantly knew that it was a leech, and he immediately grasped the slithering thing, pulling it off. A raw bleeding area was left in its place, but there was nothing he could do; until the anti-coagulant wore off, the area would bleed. Benjamin had little time to worry about infection at this point; he told himself that he would attend to it in the morning.

They walked for what seemed an eternity. Benjamin could see the faint glow of the rising sun behind him and could see how the dew hung like a humid curtain. As the sun rose in the sky, he began to perspire profusely until his shirt was dripping wet. There was no breeze this early in the morning. Mynah birds stirred at daybreak, and soon there was a cacophony of noise.

Ahead in the distance Benjamin could see row upon row of tall trees about ten feet apart and in straight lines. He could see the ground beneath the trees; there was no underbrush visible. He knew that, finally, they had reached the rubber plantation. There was quite a buzz of insects and chirping of the birds, but otherwise it was quiet. The bullock cart entered the plantation, passed many rows of trees, and presently came upon a set of low buildings. The family alighted—battered, sleepy, and half starved. To them the trees all looked alike, but Benjamin realized that they had arrived at the center of the rubber plantation. The bullock cart driver busied himself with resting the bulls and resting himself before heading back to his village. The family was left on its own.

Benjamin looked around. It was so quiet! Normally at this time the workers would be collecting rubber milk, making fresh cuts into the tree trunks, and re-positioning the collection cans. Instead, Benjamin saw that the cans were overflowing with the thick, viscous white milk. The place seemed deserted; there seemed to be no workers anywhere. "Something must have scared the workers away," he whispered to Reddy.

A closer look, however, revealed smoke emanating from a small hut behind the buildings. Reddy walked up to the building and tried to open the door. It was not locked, and it creaked a little as he entered. He noticed some food on the dining table, but thought the place was empty. Suddenly a small, bent, old man arose from his chair in the corner of the room and, before Reddy could say a word, he spoke. "They are all gone," he said in Burmese. "They went away last night in a hurry, not long after the Japanese with their Burmese allies came. They did not stay. They left in a hurry, going to the south and east." The old man continued, "But the Japanese could be back any time."

"Do you have any food we can buy?" Reddy asked. The old man took sympathy on Reddy and brought some tins of food from the storehouse. Paying the man a few annas, and thanking him, Reddy hurried out with the food. The children grabbed it with delight.

"We still face danger," Reddy explained as he related to Mr. Thomas and Benjamin what the old man had told him. "We can stay here until the situation clears, but the presence of the enemy so close by adds to our risk. We need to be extra careful before we make a run for the river."

Just then they heard noises, and the old man ran out of the building. He led them deeper north into the plantation, and hid them in a little hollow surrounded by small trees. Here they would be safe for awhile. Mr. Thomas tried to calm his jittery family.

Meanwhile Benjamin took off alone into the bush to watch the happenings. He stayed low and crawled to the edge of the plantation. The first thing he noticed was the railroads tracks and a small railroad station. "This must be the Rangoon to Prome railroad, the only escape route to the west for the British," he decided. He spotted movement to the south, next to the escarpment. He could make out only the heads of people, but from the peculiar caps they wore and the long Arisaka rifles they carried, he could tell that they were Japanese. In the middle of the column was a Japanese officer, a Lieutenant Colonel, who was different from the rest. He wore a tan jacket that sported a row of ribbons on the left side of his chest. On the left side of his waist there hung loosely a gold-plated sword. "This must be the high-ranking officer," Benjamin thought. He watched the officer closely, and realized that the Japanese seemed to be in a hurry. They were still in the gully but were approaching the plantation, so Benjamin bent down to crawl under the plentiful underbrush. He peered out again. The Japanese seemed to be straining to hear a noise to the east. "The train!" Benjamin realized. Then it dawned on him: the enemy was getting ready to set up an ambush, and he and his family were in the thick of the battle again.

From his hiding place, Benjamin heard the train as it approached the station. It had almost reached the place where the Japanese were hiding in the gully when he saw the enemy rise up and throw a grenade at the engine. It landed in the cab, and the explosion caused steam to hiss from its many pipes. Gurkha soldiers alighted from the carriages, and he saw their *kukri*s flash as they hit the ground. They attacked the Japanese at close quarters and killed many of the enemy. The Japanese called off the attack, broke contact, and retreated from the embankment. The British Colonel commanding the Gurkha troops now jumped out of the carriage and led the soldiers in a retreat away from the smoking train. As soon as the British were out of sight, the Japanese returned to plunder the train, then they too left the scene. Within an hour, it was quiet again. Benjamin left his hiding place and returned to his family. He told his father and Reddy what he had seen.

Again it was Reddy who said, "There must be a village nearby. I will go there to seek help in getting to the river. I fear it is not safe here on the plantation; it is in the thick of the battle." He peeked out of the family's hollow before leaving quickly. He walked to the deserted train station, and from there spotted a bullock-cart trail. "This must lead to a village," he thought. He carefully and quietly followed the trail and came to a village. He sought out the headman to inquire about hiring a boat. The headman agreed. They agreed on payment and arranged how the family would get to the boat.

Reddy hurriedly returned to the family and informed them, "The headman of the village has a boat and agreed to provide a crew with it to transport us northward to Prome. We agreed on the price with rupees and some small gold jewelry. We must get to the river now. We will have to run to the village undetected, and board another bullock cart there. The cart will take us to the river where the boat is anchored."

In small groups, the family set out. Mr. Thomas ran with his younger daughters. Benjamin ran with his older sisters. Reddy and the oldest women brought up the rear. They crossed the railroad tracks and headed south. They ran from tree to tree and paused in the shrubbery around the village to foil detection. On the outskirts of the village the headman waited with his bullock cart. Reddy offered him a small gold chain, and his eyes lit up. He gestured to the family to climb onto the bullock cart and, as soon as the last person had clambered aboard, slapped the bulls and took off at a rapid pace toward the river, the boat, and the next leg of their journey to safety.

It was a large country boat that plied the Irrawaddy, carrying paddy, dried fish, and other cargo. It was fifty feet long and made entirely of teak. To the rear was the rudder man, who sat high off the water, his hand on the steering column, smoking a cheroot. The captain's cabin came next; forward was the crew quarters and a small cook house, from which steps led down to the cargo hold. The boat had a single large sail. The captain was a middle-aged man who appeared friendly "I am Soe Naing," he said as he pointed them to the boat.

A flimsy gangplank led from the river bank to the boat. Mr. Thomas's wife was afraid to cross, and he had to encourage her. "Just like me, when

I came to Burma from India," remarked Grandmother with a laugh. This broke the tension and the girls crossed the gangplank quickly. The captain guided them to a small ladder which led into the cargo hold. The space was cramped, and water sloshed around on the floor. There were bamboo mats on the floor, but they were hardly dry. It was a far cry from their comfortable home in Rangoon, but they hurriedly settled in, as they were anxious to get underway. In these cramped and damp quarters, the Thomases would spend their days on the river.

Two men with twelve-foot oars pushed the boat to the mid-stream. The tide was going in the right direction, and soon they were underway. Soe Naing clambered down the ladder below decks and told the family to stay down beneath the deck, not to appear on the deck during the day. "There are many villagers," he explained, "who are unfriendly. The villages are infiltrated with spies and saboteurs, and they are armed; they would think nothing of attacking the boat if they knew *kala* [foreigners] were on it."

That was enough for the family to stay in the hold, although Grandmother took offense. "I have lived here for many years, and all of you children were born here. We are not foreigners!"

"Just do as he says," warned Mr. Thomas. Events of the past day, the cramped space, and the dampness made everyone uncomfortable and claustrophobic. They sat down where they could in fear and silence.

Benjamin could not contain himself and sneaked up to the deck of the boat. Whenever the boat passed a village, the captain kept the boat mid-stream. From the unfriendly villages Benjamin could hear shouts, "Are there any *kala* onboard?"

Soe Naing would wave and shout back, "No, there are none here."

During the daylight, aircraft flew overhead. Sometimes they were headed north, but every now and again they flew low over the river and buzzed the boats that plied the river, terrorizing the people in the boats. This went on for three days. Sporadic gunfire could heard, and the constant drone of planes began to wear on everyone's nerves. "How long must we continue this odyssey, and when will we be able to land and walk around?" Mother asked her husband.

Even in the dark, as the boat passed villages, calls would come, "Are there any enemies on board?" And each time Soe Naing would call back

"No, there are none. We have only cargo." But he had taken on supplies for only two days, and soon could no longer delay buying food. He approached a village that he knew was friendly and persuaded the villagers to sell him more rice and drinking water. The villagers asked no questions. Soe Naing also asked the headman for news from Rangoon.

On the fourth night, gunfire could be heard ahead. Soe Naing knew that a hostile village lay ahead and warned Mr. Thomas and Reddy, "It is getting dangerous to proceed upriver."

Early the next morning, Soe Naing heard fast gunboats, away to the east. Then he spotted three gunboats, still far away. Soon the drone of motors could be heard, and Soe Naing steered the boat to the shore. He ran down to the hold and told Mr. Thomas, "I am sorry, but I cannot go any further. Those are Japanese gunboats, and they will overtake us."

"Where will we be safe?" Mr. Thomas asked in somewhat of a panic.

"There is a friendly village ahead, called Zakagyi. I will arrange with the headman to find you refuge there."

Mr. Thomas was despondent. He realized that the family's escape to safety was at an end. He hid his fear and feelings from the family, assuring them that they would keep trying. But in his heart, he was losing faith. "What sort of husband and father am I," he chastised himself, "who cannot protect his family?" And a bitterness arose in him as well. "All those years of working for the British, and where do they leave me?" he mused.

Soe Naing cautiously took the boat to Zakagyi, where he went ashore and found the village headman. This riverside village was a mixed village and, for the most part, friendly. They negotiated a price. Under cover of darkness, the family disembarked and walked to the village. Mr. Thomas paid the headman, who accepted the money with a smile. He called one of the villagers to escort the family to a hut. It was serendipity that the man called was an old railways hand and recognized Mr. Thomas. Mr. Thomas felt as though a large weight was lifted from his shoulders. "We should be safe here," he whispered to Reddy.

The family was directed to a *basha*, in essence a large hut with a thatched roof and open side. It was traditionally used to store paddy. Its sides were covered with mats woven from four-inch strips of bamboo. One corner of the floor was covered with metal, for drying the paddy, but could also be used to cook upon. The floor was raised, made of giant bamboo cut and opened and flattened. A small wooden stairway led up to the floor, which creaked whenever people walked on it.

As soon as the family was all accounted for, Mr. Thomas disappeared down the stairs. He crawled under the *basha* and dug a shallow hole in which he hid the gold and money. Meanwhile the family hung blankets from the bamboo to create rooms—one for Reddy and Benjamin; one for Mr. Thomas and his wife; and one for Grandmother and the girls.

The youngsters reveled in the closeness, peeking through the blankets and squealing with laughter. They were delighted to be away from school and able to play new games. But Grandmother kept them inside. The headman had warned the family that they should not be seen on the streets. Sure enough, by nightfall the familiar sound of gunshots could be heard. The Japanese were nearby, and a rumor raced through the village that a man with a burp gun was leading a group of bandits to raid the village. The villagers scrambled to hide their valuables and their young girls. The fear was evident. The Thomases huddled in their *basha*, more fearful, perhaps, than the local villagers.

The roar from the river indicated that the gunboats were near, then a burst of gunfire erupted. It came from a cannon on board the lead gunboat. Three Japanese gunboats had arrived in the village. These were fast boats, painted grey. Each had a small cannon on the foredeck, and a Bofors gun on the after deck. The lead boat weighed anchor. All its guns were trained on the village. The two other boats were further downstream. The small jetty was built of large logs sunk into the mud of the river. At high tide, the water reached the top of the jetty, but the tide was not full yet. The villagers cowered together and looked aghast at the scene that greeted them. Some sailors took water from the river for bathing, and some of them were stark naked. This offended the modest Burmese. The village men shooed their womenfolk away.

Small boats appeared, carrying many fully armed men from the gunboats. This was the first time Mr. Thomas had seen a Japanese soldier. "They are not very tall," he thought as he peered between the bamboo slats of the *basha*. He was particularly struck by the peaked caps that the soldiers wore, some of them with cloth hanging from sides as a protection from the sun. They all carried long rifles with fixed bayonets. The commander was stocky and wore an open shirt, with red bands on the collar and a single gold braid on the shoulder. His sword was very long, but he carried no rifle.

The soldiers and sailors fanned out and secured the perimeter of the village. There was no resistance. The villagers were unarmed and untrained. The two officers walked to the headman's house, where they stopped and summoned the headman. The old and frail man was made to stand in the open sunshine while the Japanese commander asked if there were British or Indian troops nearby. They kept repeating the same question over and over, and the old man kept repeating over and over that he had not seen any for many days. It was getting ridiculous. Then an officer stepped up and whispered in the old man's ear, "If you lie, you and the whole village will be severely punished." The old man turned to his assistant and told him to accompany the Japanese as they looked for suspects.

Three soldiers accompanied the young man to search the village for British or Indian troops. A group of sailors had requested a table and chairs and set them up under a large tree. The commander then told the headman to bring all the village men before him. They had no choice but to gather Reddy, Benjamin, and Mr. Thomas as well. If they had not done so, the soldiers searching the village would find them and punish the entire village.

The men formed an untidy line in front of the table. Suddenly an officer grabbed the shirts of some men and pulled them to the head of the line. Mr. Thomas was one of them. He stood erect as the Japanese officer asked him, "What is your name?"

"Mr. Thomas," came the reply.

The officer's face contorted with rage. He was angry. "You are not a Hindu," he asked, with narrowed eyes.

"No."

"Where do you work?"

"For the railways."

"Aha!" the officer then screamed. "You work for the enemy!"

"No. I work to feed my family."

The officer changed tactics. "How many trains left the Rangoon station in the last day?"

Mr, Thomas said, "I am sorry, I do not know. I did not go to work for a week,"

The officer slapped Mr. Thomas. Mr. Thomas's first reaction was one of outrage; he had never been insulted before, even by the white Englishmen. The officer yelled at him and threatened, "Unless you cooperate, your treatment will be most harsh."

Mr. Thomas had tears in his eyes as he finally said, "I think the last train left for Prome three days ago. I do not know who was on the train."

Not getting anywhere, the officer stopped questioning Mr. Thomas. He turned to some soldiers and spoke to them rapidly in Japanese. As the officer walked down the line of villagers he pointed to some men who looked suspicious and ordered the soldiers to take them to the jetty. Mr. Thomas was herded along with the other suspicious men. The men were tied to a large tree. The sun was still high, and it was hot and humid. There the men stood until dusk, with no food or water. Mr. Thomas felt nausea and faintness overtake him, and he passed out. He had been warned about his blood sugar, and now he was sick.

From the second gunboat, more Japanese officers appeared. They were kempeitai, Japanese military police. The chief kempeitai officer threw water at Mr. Thomas and, when he had revived, took him to the village for further questioning. Mr. Thomas tried to tell the kempeitai that he a held a unimportant job at the railways. "All I did was keep track of the coal supplies!" he explained. But the kempeitai officer was undaunted.

"Surely you must know where the British hid the coal and railways supplies."

Again Mr. Thomas tried to explain that he knew nothing, whereupon the Japanese corporal standing next to the kempeitai officer slapped him across the face. This time a trickle of blood dripped out of his mouth, and Mr. Thomas's knees buckled. He fell to the floor. Another Japanese joined the corporal and picked up Mr. Thomas for more beating. Again Mr. Thomas passed out.

The commander rested his sword on the chair. The procedure of gathering the men was not going fast, nor was any helpful information being gleaned. He barked some orders to his men, which frighted the villagers. Apparently he had ordered his men to abandon their questioning in the village and move on to another village. By nightfall the Japanese had released most of the men, although one gunboat remained behind and its soldiers kept some men under guard for another two days.

Mr. Thomas was lucky in that he was released and returned to the family. Benjamin attended to his father's bruises and wounds, with Mother and Grandmother fussing and clucking and crying about. With Mr. Thomas recovering from his ordeal, it fell to Benjamin to take charge. He and Reddy would have to make all the decisions for a while.

That night the two men sat in the dark just outside the door to the *basha*. "We will never escape now," Benjamin said simply. "We waited too long."

Reddy's hopes, too, were dashed. "We cannot stay here. I had hoped we would find safety here, away from the city and the roads, but the Japanese are everywhere!."

"I think," said Benjamin slowly, "we should take the family back home. You must come to stay with us so we are all together. There is safety in numbers."

Reddy agreed. "At least there, we have solid walls and a roof over our heads." He gave a little laugh. "Well, I'll go out again to find a boat large enough to take us back down the river to the old home."

Within a week, Reddy was successful. The family bid farewell to the headman and the villagers who had taken them in and who had suffered along with them. It took the family many days to return. The river was full of gunboats and paddle-wheelers carrying Japanese troops. Benjamin and Reddy, dressed in Burmese *longyi*s, sat on the deck of the boat they had hired and watched the river traffic. "No doubt those boats are captured Irrawaddy Flotilla Company boats," Benjamin observed.

"Hummphff." Reddy expelled his breath. "So much for your British." But he was not angry, just sad and worried. "What will await the family back in Rangoon?" he wondered.

Chapter 25
Evacuation by Foot

The day after her aunt and she had decided to trek from Myitkyina to India, CeCi awoke early. She was dreading the day but felt relief that she was finally making progress on her father's goal to get her to India. She packed a small bundle of necessities: money, gold, medicines, soap, rags, water, dried fish, and biscuits. There was no room for luxuries. She packed a change of clothing but abandoned her fancy shoes and wore only sandals. She knew there would no shops or facilities along the road. Then she and her aunt joined the group of diverse people headed out of the city. They were taking the southern route to Indaw. "Japanese patrols have reached the outskirts of city!" came the cry, up and down the line of refugees. "Gunboats are active in Mogaung River! There is no time to waste! Head north!"

There was pandemonium as the motley group switched direction. With the southern route in Japanese hands, CeCi and her aunt had no choice but to take the longer northern route. Again CeCi did not know exactly the route she would follow. She heard that the path would lead to Fort Hertz in the Kachin state and kept hearing of Ledo, but she knew little about either place. There were Kachins, Burmese, and Indians all fleeing the Japanese, all now jockeying for position along the road that led north from Myitkyina. Among the civilians were also some troops, mostly Gurkhas. The noise of clanging pots and braying oxen mixed with the fearful voices and crying children.

By midday the temperatures started to rise. The refugees stopped under the trees, fanning themselves and sipping their meager water supplies. Had they been in the lowlands, their thirst might have been slaked by the ancient Burmese custom of leaving pots of water for travelers. But this was the Kachin high land, and there would be no such pots of water. The man sprawled in the shade next to her told CeCi that he had been a school-teacher. "Do you know why there are no direct roads to India?" he asked. Without waiting for her reply, he spat out, "the imperious Viceroy of India at the turn of the century saw to it that there would be no direct roads."

CeCi's thoughts turned to the pompous Viceroy. "I wonder what he would think now if he could see the plight of these desperate people," she mused.

They had no map; all they could do was follow the people ahead of them. They walked on the hot metaled road, and as the temperature rose, so also did the heat from the metaled road. CeCi tried to cool the soles of her feet by walking on the shoulder, but it was too rough and rutted. Her feet began to hurt, but she got back on the metaled road. Trees and vegetation that had been cut and well-maintained closer to the city soon gave way to jungle. By evening, she was hungry and her feet were sore, and she welcomed a stop for the night. She paid a few rupees to get bread from other refugees, and she and her aunt ate some of their dried fish with the bread. She wondered how long their money and gold would last. After she ate the last piece of bread, she crawled under a tree to sleep. She worried a little about all the men walking around, but there were other people nearby, and sleep soon overtook her. Sleep was not easy or particularly restful, however, on the hard uneven ground; she did not sleep well. Dawn came with a suddenness to which she was not accustomed. She was jarred awake by noise all around her, and she soon realized that the long line of refugees had in fact already formed and begun to move out. There was not much time for her morning grooming. She massaged her feet before she put on her sandals, took her aunt's hand, and they started walking again.

Around noon, the sound of planes could be heard in the distance. The refugees ran for the trees. CeCi sought out the largest tree and pulled her aunt to cover. In her haste she stumbled on a half buried body, falling forward and bruising her cheek. It would be the first but not the last time this would happen. Her aunt helped her up, and the two continued their run for cover. "No time to grieve for the dead," CeCi thought with horror. As soon as the planes were gone, the line formed again, and the refugees plodded along. It was hot, and sweat ran down her cleavage. Her tongue and the mucus membrane in her mouth were dry, almost cracking. She assessed the military-type can of water she was carrying. It was low, but she took a sip.

CeCi noticed that the refugees tended to cluster in groups. Chinese with Chinese; Indians with Indians; and Anglos with Anglos. She realized that a larger group would be safer, and began to cast around for others with whom she and her aunt could join. Behind her, she saw an Indian man smiling at her and shyly waving to her. It took her some time, but she finally recognized him as Lingham, Peter's manservant from Rangoon. Even in the best of times he had owned few physical possessions; now he had only a small parcel wrapped in a dhoti. She pulled her aunt toward him and greeted him kindly. In broken English and Urdu, he recited his journey.

As rumors of war had grown in Rangoon, he had sought out his friends at the toddy shop. "My friends say 'the mighty British will protect the country,' and I wanted to believe that," he explained. But in the end he had not been able to believe his fellow servants. When he learned that a group was leaving soon, he quickly finalized his plans. "I hoped that the Thomases would leave so that I could be with the family," he said wistfully. "But Mr. Thomas was essential." So Lingham had slipped out the back door and joined up with a group of laborers heading to Prome. In his halting English he continued "But they stop us. Government police and army send me back," he explained. "I walk back to Rangoon–Mandalay road. Go to Myitkyina." Lingham described how the road north had been crowded and how he had actually felt safe with all the people and military lorries. "When the group is small, the group is weak," he noted. Day after day, in the blistering heat and with little water, Lingham had walked north until he finally reached Mandalay. But the city had been attacked by the enemy air force and was burning; it was in chaos. It was burning. He and his fellow laborers had replenished their meager supplies, then set out again toward the great Sagaing Bridge. Normally at this time of the year, traffic would be light, but he found it packed with an assortment of cars, trucks, carts, and refugees on foot, who slowed down the transit. The cars were full of British and European women and children; the people on foot were mostly Indians with bundles on their heads or across their shoulders. "Then, just as I reach bridge," Lingham related with a wry smile, "the enemy come." Low-flying fighters had swooped over the refugees and fired indiscriminately. Pandemonium had ensued. Some people fell off the bridge. Lingham crawled into a gutter, and when the firing was over, the bridge was being closed. He could not go any further. Even if it opened again, he knew that it would be a target for Japanese airplanes. Knowing that he could not cross the wide river, he waited till he found some rafts going to the other side. Wet, frightened, and tired, he got to the other side and resumed his journey again, finally arriving in Myitkyina. Now he had joined the exodus from Myitkyina. He depended on his fellow Indians, labor like him.

CeCi had listened in fascination at the poor man's plight. "Walk with me and my friends," he urged CeCi and her aunt. "Do not stay in small group. Too dangerous." Gratefully the two women accepted his offer, knowing that they would be safer with the larger group. Lingham dreamed of going to the Ganges River to bathe in its holy water. "It will bring me luck," he said with his happy-go-lucky grin that CeCi remembered so clearly. She knew it was just a ritual, but hoped that he would fulfill his dream.

Day after day the refugees walked onward. Frequently, in the heat of the day, they rested at the side of the road. When they could, they would stop for the night at an ethnic Kachin village, where they would try to buy food supplies and replenish their water. CeCi was especially worried about water. Working in a hospital, she knew that to drink water from a stream was dangerous; the water here carried the Vibrio bacteria, which causes severe dysentery and cholera. As the days wore on, she noted that the group's composition changed. The groups grew ever smaller, shrunken by deaths from hunger and malaria.

When her feet hurt too badly, CeCi took off her shoes for a while and walked bare foot. Her aunt seemed to move more slowly each day, staying with the group only by starting early and getting a head start. Nonetheless, each evening CeCi and her aunt—attended closely by Lingham—were the last to reach camp. "How much longer must we walk like this, day after day!" moaned CeCi one night. The group had stopped at a small mixed Shan/Kachin village. As always, when approaching a Kachin village, the refugees were anxious. But the villagers appeared to be friendly and welcomed the refugees. They had cooked rice and had some dried fish, which they shared with the refugees. In the middle of the village was a small church, which made CeCi feel quite safe. Her aunt sank to the ground under a tree to rest her weary limbs. CeCi took a few rupees to buy a pair of Kachin loafers for her aching feet.

CeCi was desperate for knowledge of the area. She asked the village headman about the land around the village. "A short distance from here the jungle will close, and there is a range of mountains," he described. This, she surmised, would be the Kuoman range. "Beyond this range is a long valley with many small streams," the headman continued. He looked at the sky and told them, "When the rains come, the streams become impassable."

CeCi felt fairly safe in the village, and she and her aunt slept well in a safe place that the headman showed her. In the morning, the little group bought whatever supplies they could carry and whatever the remote village could supply, mostly a variety of wild animals, dried fish, and smoked meat. Then they resumed their long march. "The days of walking are monotonous," CeCi remarked to her aunt, "but there is no room for boring thoughts, as we run for our lives from the Japanese and their collaborators. What they might do to us is unimaginable." For CeCi and most of the others making this long trek, it was that hope of getting to safety, and fear of what lay behind, that motivated them to push beyond the limits of endurance.

As the days passed, the terrain changed. The hills looming ahead turned into mountains. It was difficult climbing to the top, and once there, CeCi was surprised at how narrow the ridge was. While two people could probably walk side by side, it was not safe to do so. Instead, they walked single file. Once she glanced down over the edge of the ridge, where the land fell off sharply. There, hanging on the branches of the densely packed trees, she could see bodies of dead animals lying grotesquely. "Don't look down," she instructed her aunt. CeCi diverted her gaze, keeping her eyes on the trail and trying not to imagine what it would be like to slip off the trail.

The group walked for hours and kept walking, and as usual welcomed the end of the day. The long rays of the sun brought relief from the searing heat, and CeCi knew that she would rest soon. She and her aunt found a place under a large fig tree and sat down. They engaged in their daily ritual of nibbling some food, massaging their feet, and then soon falling asleep. This night CeCi fell into the kind of sleep that produced dreams, and she was transported back to Rangoon. In her flashback she saw the American flyers and their antics, and she went with some girlfriends to the Silver Grille, which was crowded. In their Hawaiian shirts and casual slacks, half of the young men were already worse for the wear. Soon a handsome flier bought her a drink, and in the blink of an eye she was dancing cheek to cheek with him. He plied her with drinks, and she soon found herself in the back seat of a car and then in a beautiful house on the lake. In the morning she found herself almost naked and could not find her panties. Eventually she dressed hurriedly. The young flier was nowhere to be found. She knew that she did not belong in the English house, a large lakeside home with meticulously groomed lawn and gardens. When she went outside, a tall Indian servant—the senior cook—shook his head. In Hindi he told her that the owner would soon be back from breakfast and would be most upset to find her in his house. "You should leave right now. You have no right to be here," he said as he guided her to the road and hailed a tonga for her. She had a headache, probably from too much to drink, so went home and to bed. The next morning, she told her mother that she would have to go to work and would be home early, but instead of going to work, she walked down Montgomery Street and Sule Pagoda Road. On the patio of the cinema, she saw the young man from the previous evening in the company of other Americans. She tried to catch his eye, and even waved to him, but he completely ignored her. CeCi woke up with a start. As she pondered the dream she began to cry and could not get back to sleep. "That is probably how I'll be treated by the British in India," she thought bitterly.

In the cool of the morning, the group set out again, joining other small groups to form a long line of weary refugees that stretched forward and backward as far as the eye could see. They climbed ridge after ridge, on narrow and unforgiving trails. One misstep would mean the loss of footing and a tumble over the side of the ridge. CeCi shuddered and moved her weary legs slowly. In the distance she could see the tops of the mountains that were covered with thick mist. The cool morning temperatures gave way to burning heat. The plants on the ground seemed to give up their water, adding to the steaminess. Steam seem to drip from the leaves! On the open ridges the ground was still dry, but in the heart of the jungle and the valley, the air was humid and heavy, adding to the discomfort. Even in the day it was dark in the jungle, as the sun's rays could not penetrate the thick canopy. Only occasionally would the color of a flower or fruit break the monotony of the green jungle. Everywhere it was green, a green hell. Worse than monotony were the inhabitants of the jungle: flies, small and large, and, worse, a small flea that had a painful sting. It could penetrate through clothing and could bite where scratching was impossible. In the heat of the noonday sun, the group rested, and CeCi nursed her sore feet. She could not bear to look at her feet; they were red, raw, and blistered. Water was scarce.

A continual stream of refugees passed by, barely noticing them and rarely making eye contact. "We are becoming inhuman," she sighed to her aunt.

Soon after the group eased their way back into the refugee stream, the land rose again. The trail narrowed, and then another mountain range came into view. The walk became slow, and the higher they climbed the narrower the trail became. Once again, they were forced to walk single file. Late in the afternoon, CeCi heard a commotion behind her and craned her neck to see what was happening. The noise was from a man with a mule, which was being stubborn and would not move. CeCi took the opportunity to sit and rest her weary feet, watching the man and mule as though they were a cinema show. With the man pulling and others prodding, the stubborn animal finally started to move again, and soon the group resumed its march. CeCi heaved herself to her feet, helped her aunt up, and resumed the long climb up to the ridge. On the ridge the air was cool, but everybody was tired. They had two more hours of light, so kept walking until dusk. They selected a spot at a small clearing for their night's rest.

By now, the group to which CeCi and her aunt had attached themselves had set up a protocol, which determined who would cook and who would do other chores. CeCi's job was to attend to the medical care. She was not a nurse, but she knew some nursing principles, so she was glad that they trusted her. Unfortunately, her duties were becoming increasingly frequent, as the refugees suffered from the effects of lack of food and water, from insect bites and Naga sores, from exhaustion, and from sheer lack of hope. Many of the refugees seemed to have no other purpose in life than to put one foot in front of another, hour after hour, day after day.

That night, after a meager meal, CeCi fell into a light sleep. Around midnight she felt a man too near for comfort. She awakened with a start and screamed. She heard footsteps running away. After she was calmed by her aunt, the men in her group arranged themselves around the women as a perimeter, to protect the women. But CeCi still lay awake the rest of the night. She knew that at night deserters walked about looking for food and sex, and she had seen the way they had looked longingly at her over the past few weeks. She vowed that she would not be taken by surprise.

Morning could not have come soon enough for her, and CeCi actually was relieved to begin walking again. She counted the number of ridges she had climbed and tried to assess where they were. Soon the group came to the top of a serrated ridge. CeCi joined a small group of men who were discussing the road ahead. She surmised that the great obstacle was the mountain range that lay directly in front of them. She vaguely remembered reading about the Kumon range and the forbidding "Valley of Death," the Hukawng Valley. "This must be the Kumon range," she thought.

As usual, the trail at the top of the ridge was no more than a foot wide, and the sides fell sharply away. CeCi kept her eyes on the trail ahead, but it was not hard to see dead animals over the edge, pack mules that had been weighted down by the cargo they carried and that had lost their footing. The loss of cargo had sometimes been too much for the hungry and tattered refugees, and occasionally an unfortunate man had ventured down the slope to take what he could from the pack mule, only to die in the effort.

Late in the afternoon CeCi could see a small village ahead. Despite the pain in her feet and legs, she rushed with others in her group to village, not knowing if it was friendly but desperate for rest and possible supplies. Much to her relief it was a Kachin village, with friendly villagers. The group settled down under a tree, where they would spend the night. Suddenly an old man approached CeCi. In spite of his advanced years, he stood straight. He wore a wide-brimmed jungle hat that had a number of emblems and pins on it. The battalion emblem was faded but still discernable. He wore the hat folded up on one side like a Gurkha, and he wore it jauntily and with pride. He held a mug of hot tea in his hands and smiled at CeCi and spoke to her in halting English. His craggy face was kind, and CeCi noted that his eyes were soft; when he smiled they would twinkle. "Do you know where are you going?" he asked.

CeCi responded honestly. "I really don't know," she said. "All I know is that I am leaving the conflict in Burma for the safety of India."

The man lit a big Burmese cheroot. He seemed to take a fatherly interest in her. He saw the fear in her eyes and tried to put her mind at ease. He directed his young daughter to bring a cup of steaming tea for CeCi and another for her aunt. After they had gratefully taken a few sips of the hot brew, he told her, "I was one of the first Kachins to serve in King George's service. I was recruited to the newly created first Kachin battalion." He stopped. "I really do not like the label 'Kachin'; it is a pejorative term, the label that foreigners use to describe my people." He explained, "Here we are Jingpaw, our language is Jingpaw." He seemed to enjoy an audience of English-speaking women, so continued to tell his story.

He had been recruited as a levy at first, but soon advanced to the position of rifle man. He had volunteered to go to the Middle East in World War I. He had been an eager young man and had wanted to travel, and when he came back he was promoted to Naik, a corporal. He saw action against a large band of dacoits, and the company commander recommended that he be promoted again. After many long years of service, he rose to the rank of a subedar, the glass ceiling beyond which he could not hope to advance. It was in the military that he had learned his English, and when he returned to his village he became a *duwa*, a headman.

The headman looked carefully at CeCi and her aunt, then at the Indian laborers with whom they were traveling. "Can you depend on your traveling companions?" he asked.

"Yes," replied CeCi. "I knew one of them from Rangoon, and so far his companions have been very helpful. They have protected us." CeCi remembered the attack from last night with a shudder.

The headman looked kindly at her. "You are a pretty young woman. You face not only the perils of the jungle but also the perils of men, especially deserters." The man spat in the dust. "These men are not proper soldiers," he said. "They are retreating in disorder and do not hesitate to rob people . . . and do other terrible things." He puffed on his cheroot and proceeded to tell her of what lay ahead, especially the jungle. "The jungle is like a beautiful and seductive woman," he explained. He winked at her for using that analogy and then expounded. "But the green beauty of the jungle hides frightening things, both small and big. Every inch of land under your foot will teem with ants, fire ants, black ants, scorpions, fleas, and biting insects." CeCi shuddered. "Do you know mosquitoes?" he asked. CeCi nodded. "They bring malaria," he stated. "There are some types of malaria that makes the urine like wine. Few survive that condition." CeCi nodded again and the old man continued. "You should look at your body for ticks. The small tick carries the debilitating typhus." Then he went on to warn about the valley of many streams. "In the muddy waters lie unseen dangers. The worst of these are the big leeches." He held up his thumb.

"This big. The Bengal leech." He warned that she should not pull the leech off, as its teeth would remain buried in the skin. They would not fall off but would stay lodged in the skin, causing a infection. The infection would turn into a sore that does not heal. He turned his head in the direction of the hut and called out to his son in his Jingpaw language. The son brought a small bag filled with a white grainy powder. "In our mountains this is precious." He paused. "It is common salt," he said as he handed the bag to CeCi. "If you find a leech on your body, put some salt on it and wait a while. Be patient. In time the leech will fall off, taking its teeth with it. This is how my people avoid the Naga sores, for which there is no cure." CeCi had already seen some Naga sores. The sores ate the skin, muscle, and tendons down to the bone. There had been nothing she could do for those suffering the sores. The headman continued. "Then there are the Dim dim flies. They inflict a painful bite that too will fester into an ugly, dangerous sore." He warned, "Do not scratch too much." Then he stood up to take his leave.

CeCi thanked him profusely. "You have been so kind and generous. I will never forget you," she said. She stored his advice in her head and vowed to use it when the time came. He finished with a warning. "This is the last village in Burma. The next time you see a village, it will be in India. With luck, you will find some friendly tea farmers." Then the headman gave her one last warning. "Pray that it does not rain. If the rains come too soon, the result will be horrible. Even we who live here find it hard to navigate in the rains. The trails turn into rivers of mud, in some places up to the knee." He shook his head and continued. "Shoes are useless in mud like that."

CeCi clutched the bag of salt to her breast and thanked the old man again. For the first time since leaving Myitkyina, CeCi felt safe here. The young Kachin girl brought some rice and the traditional Burmese fish dish "nga hpi." CeCi had abhorred *nga hpi* all her life because of its foul smell, but she was so consumed by hunger that she ate with gusto this night. Much to her surprise, it tasted good. Then the young Kachin girl brought her hot tea again. CeCi touched the face of the girl, drew her close, and kissed her cheek. She was struck by the kindness of these strangers in this remote village, and remembered something that her Italian nun had taught her at the convent school. She could not remember the Latin version, but the message said, "I am a human: nothing human is alien to me, including kindness."

The next day the group of refugees set out again early in the morning. CeCi waved to the headman and his young daughter. For days the group trudged up and down on narrow dirt trails. It grew increasingly difficult as the mountains became higher and the refugees became weaker. Finally they descended into a broad valley. CeCi glanced at her aunt, who was finding it increasingly difficult to keep up with the group. "Thankfully our group will now rest before we set out on the next leg of our journey," she said. CeCi covered them from head to foot in the now-filthy blanket, drawing it tightly closed. Winged flies buzzed and whizzed all night, and when the buzzing stopped, CeCi knew the sun would soon rise.

The path they took in the morning led soon to a small stream. The women had to walk through the water balancing on small rocks. They almost lost their footing but managed to keep their balance. The trails led next into a thick jungle. "It is so dark in here," CeCi's aunt complained.

Ci Ci looked around her at the limitless number of large trees and other dense growth. Huge fig trees were enveloped with vines that slowly suffocated their host. Vines hung down to the valley floor and clung to the ground. They were everywhere! But where the sun came through, small plants grew profusely and twisted and turned to seek the life-giving sunlight. Even though they were terrified of the dense and dark jungle, the refugees welcomed the relief from the searing sun that the thick canopy provided. "It is also a protection from possible air raids," thought CeCi.

The trails through the jungle were covered with dead leaves, and the ground was criss-crossed with roots, small and large. CeCi held on to her aunt's arm tightly. Now and then a large log blocked the trail. This would slow the column of refugees, as women and children would have to be helped over the obstacle. Ants large and small marched across the trail; long columns of worker ants followed one another in long lines, carrying to their nests loads larger than their weight. CeCi warned her aunt, "Be careful; those ants will not hesitate to attack humans. We must be careful to avoid not only the roots but also the ants."

Sure enough the weather changed. Clouds began to gather, and the wind picked up. With startling swiftness, a full storm began, driving sheets of rain against the weakened bodies of the refugees, taking its toll. CeCi looked around for shelter. At some distance she spotted a Banyan fig tree.

The center was like a small room that provided some shelter. The middle of the large empty area was where the host tree had been smothered to death, leaving just a few roots that could provide shelter from the horizontal sheets of rain. Soon the rest of the group arrived, and CeCi felt a little safer in the group. She glanced through a opening and thought she saw a fuzzy animal briefly appear, but soon it disappeared. The rain did not let up, so the group remained in the semi-shelter. After the sun set, the group huddled around a small fire, which provided some warmth. Just after midnight, the group was awakened by a blood-curdling scream. CeCi heard something being dragged and heard soulful cries. The group huddled together in stark fear. They had to wait till morning to take a count, and soon she heard a shriek from the mother of a child. A tiger or leopard had carried away her child. The mother ran off, following the animal tracks, but the men soon grabbed her, despite her wails and kicking, They carried her back to the shelter. "It is no use," they said. "The devil carried your child away." CeCi was struck suddenly by the realization that to be a child on this dreadful journey meant that the odds of reaching adulthood were indeed small.

CeCi sought out her aunt and held her hand firmly. The group did not linger but set off in the early light. By midday they arrived at the river that the headman had told her about. The refugees stood on the river bank despondently. "How will we ever cross?" the women wailed. The answer soon became apparent. The Indian men had become saviors. They had harvested young bamboo, then split it and lashed it together to make crude rafts. In an organized fashion, the men would ferry a group of refugees across the river, then one would return to ferry the next load.

As she climbed onto the raft, CeCi fell into the water. She was quickly helped onto the raft by her fellow travelers and immediately, remembering the Kachin headman's warnings, looked at her legs. No leeches! She said a small prayer. As the raft approached the bank the raft began to tip and the passengers were thrown into the water. After she rested on the muddy bank, CeCi noticed a slimy black thing on her inner thigh. She let out a scream, then calmed down and took out the bag of salt which the headman had given her. With a shaking hand she put salt on the leech. She fought desperately the desire to pull the damn thing off but ultimately resisted. After what seemed to be an interminable time, the now-engorged, ugly, wiggly thing fell off. Quickly CeCi ran behind a tree to look up her crotch and was relieved to find that there were no ugly things clinging to her privates.

For endless days, it seemed, they walked. Each day CeCi cried, and each day she thought she could go no further. Her aunt had fallen almost silent, unable to do more than place one foot in front of the other. But CeCi knew that if she was going to survive and reach civilization again, she had to summon the last ounce of courage to carry on. So each day she found enough strength to go forth. Frail as she was, her will was indomitable. When she began each day, she wondered what the day would bring. She no longer thought of the next day; she just struggled to get through the present day.

As she glanced around at her fellow travelers, CeCi realized that the composition of her group had subtly changed. Many faces were missing. She knew that the ones she did not see were all dead or dying, victims of malaria, hunger, malnutrition, snake bites, and even some pitiful souls dragged away by tigers. She had been so busy keeping up her own strength that she had not really noticed the losses, nor did she note the ghost-like appearance of many of her fellow travelers, many deformed from loss of fingers, toes, and other ravages inflicted by the cruel jungle.

Ahead CeCi could see a very dense jungle. The trail led straight into it! As they entered the jungle, CeCi noticed that it was almost like dusk, even darker than the jungle through which they had passed previously. The canopy of the tall trees was so dense that very little light penetrated to the jungle floor. The ground was soggy thanks to incessant rains, and the trek became even more arduous. "No sunlight can penetrate the canopy," CeCi muttered, "but rain can. That doesn't seem fair." The mud was ankle deep. CeCi did not bother with her frayed shoes; like the rest of her group, she trekked barefoot across the rugged and soggy land. She had left her dignity behind, and each time she looked at herself in her tiny mirror, she was horrified. She hardly recognized herself. Her cheeks were hollow; her eyes had lost their sparkle, and they were sunken deep into her orbits, like some ghost. She wondered if she really had died and now walked these horrid mountains in purgatory, waiting for the angels to rescue her.

They finally left the broad plain and started to climb once again, up the ridge where there was no vegetation. The trail remained muddy, because of the many people who had used it. And there was trash littered along the trail.

Late one afternoon, she spied a group at the side of the trail, sitting around a dead camp fire. They were all huddling together. "Perhaps it is a family," she thought, "and they were so tired that they stopped early." As she approached the group, CeCi noticed no movement at all, and as she went to get a closer look, she found to her horror that they were all stiff, all dead. When she touched the littlest child, the body was cold. Maggots were already devouring the eyes. CeCi uttered a shriek and started to cry. Her group had passed the scene silently and was getting ahead of her, so she ran to catch up with them.

As the days progressed, this scenario became routine, and soon CeCi noted the smell, the smell of death. The bodies were now beginning to rot. CeCi could tell from the smell that there were corpses lying off the side of the trail. The worst thing was the maggots coming out of the body cavities, particularly from the eyes. If she looked at the bodies, she became nauseous and vomited, then had to stop for a while, then run to catch up with her group. She finally inured herself to the smell and the sight, walking past the dead bodies without looking. But at night, when the group stopped for sleep, the scene kept recurring endlessly. It would wake her, and only with difficulty could she doze again, but the same nightmare would recur again and wake her up again, until finally she would sit up and wait for the group to start their new day. She knew she was abusing her already frail body, but she had no control over her dreams.

Her aunt looked more frail each day. One evening she became truly ill. She developed a high fever and became lethargic and limp. Large blotches appeared on her legs, and she broke out in a rash that spread rapidly. Her eyes were bloodshot. CeCi tried to bathe the rash and put a cloth on her forehead, but there were no medications to be had. Nobody she knew to be a doctor was in her group, and even if there was a doctor, what could he do? CeCi cried. She dismissed the notion of looking for help, knowing that her aunt was past help. By midnight her aunt became delirious; her mumbling and moans kept CeCi awake. After some time, the mumbling diminished, and by morning she was dead of scrub typhus. CeCi placed her aunt's body under a tree tenderly. She had no strength to dig a grave. One of the Indian women in her group brought her a cup of strong tea. Then the group set out again. CeCi felt even more lonely than before, and worried that the worst was yet to come.

PART VI

To India

Chapter 26
"Head Northward to India"

Back at Waw, General Burnett had stoically watched the survivors of the battle for the Sittang straggle in, stunned by their experience. He had seen to it that they received what little food and water he could find, then he moved them out overland to Pegu. From there they would be directed southwest to Hlegu, thence west to Taukkyan, where they would finally pick up the Rangoon–Prome Road, the only motorable road leading northward that was not threatened by the Japanese.

Now all was quiet at headquarters; just his aides and he remained. In a brisk and decisive voice he ordered, "Now it is our turn. Destroy all equipment and papers, load the staff car, and abandon Waw. We will establish headquarters at Hlegu. From there, I can stay in touch with any straggler units coming from Moulmein, Sittang, and Pegu and can also stay in touch with General Taylor and his forces moving northward from Rangoon."

His chief of staff asked, "Where are the Japs, Sir?"

"That's a good question!" came the reply. "Word is that they are moving toward Pegu but are taking trails north of the Waw–Pegu Road. Probably heading to block the Rangoon–Mandalay Road. We must get to Hlegu before they do, or they will cut the Rangoon–Pegu Road. If they do that," he continued, "the British retreating from Rangoon will be trapped. We must hold Hlegu until the Rangoon garrison has completely withdrawn. From there, we will either fight the Japanese or retreat northward to a defensible position."

In Pegu, Jeremy and Peter joined up with remnants of their battalion. Although there was joy at seeing old comrades again, there was great sadness when the men recognized how many of their number were missing, presumed dead. After receiving reassignment to a hastily cobbled-together unit, the men were directed to Hlegu.

The situation in Hlegu was fluid. Rumors were rife that the Japanese had already been sighted west of the city. The cacophony of traffic alone was enough to give the men a headache. Tanks from Rangoon had arrived in town, and British civilian cars as well as slow-moving carts were choking the roads. Military police were trying desperately to keep traffic moving, ordering slow cars off the road to allow tanks, fully loaded lend-lease trucks, and two-ton lorries to move out of their exposed positions.

Jeremy looked at the sky. "An attack by the Japanese would create havoc," he remarked. Anxious to know of his family's whereabouts, he tried to see if he could make a quick trip to Rangoon. He managed to get a lift to Taukkyan, just southwest of Hlegu, on the Rangoon–Prome Road. But there a military policeman barred him from going any further south.

"If the enemy captures the city," the MP explained, "the exodus out of Rangoon will come to a screeching halt. We cannot impede traffic in any way." Despite Jeremy's pleadings, the MP remained obdurate, and Jeremy returned to Hlegu despondently.

"There is no chance of going south," he reported to Peter, "no chance to learn the fate of our families."

Peter consoled Jeremy and himself. "All we can do is hope that they have already left the city, that they will not be trapped there."

Both men were silent as they considered the situation. Rumors abounded that Rangoon was a desperate city, that it would be evacuated, or that it would be declared an open city to prevent its destruction. "I wonder how long the British can hold out," Jeremy worried.

Their battalion had been badly mauled by the White Tigers and had lost most of its officers and many of its men. The only senior British officer was the Battalion Major, who now gathered his despondent men and told them, "We cannot relax. There is trouble ahead. The Chinese divisions holding Toungoo are collapsing and retreating north. The Japanese have opened a new front and are advancing from the east, from Bowlake, on the Mawchi–Toungoo road. This is a good all-weather road, and the Japanese armor is advancing rapidly. They can arrive at any time now."

Peter paled, thinking of Amy working in the hospital at Bowlake. Her parents had insisted that she return home, and now the front was approaching that town of supposed safety. Although he was not a religious man, Peter found himself thinking, "Please let Amy be safe."

The Major continued his briefing. "Pegu is being threatened from the east and the north. The Japanese fleet in the Bay of Bengal threatens

Rangoon, and the Rangoon garrison is being evacuated. General Burnett will watch things from Hlegu. As soon as General Taylor and his men pass Taukkyan, General Burnett's forces will follow him, and all British units will move north on the Rangoon–Prome Road." The Major paused here, clearly uncomfortable with what he was going to say.

"India is our goal. We must get there before the rains." As he heard murmurings among the men, he explained. "From India, our army can regroup and launch a well-planned counter-offensive against the Japanese. Our retreat now preserves us to fight another day."

The men listening to the Major wondered what role they would play, and soon the Major clarified. "Our unit has been ordered to move northward in advance, to help defend the oil fields at Chauk. We are being charged with assuring that the oil fields stay in British hands. The Japs are too close to the fields; they are near Toungoo."

The men of the battalion looked at one another. They had endured horrific losses at Sukli Point, Moulmein, and the Sittang Bridge. Their battalion was battered. Their commanders had been killed, and many of them were worried about family in Rangoon and its outskirts. Yet when the Major ordered, "We will break up into small groups and retreat upriver through the oil fields," the men gathered their equipment and set out westward.

Peter and Jeremy managed to join the same patrol. The men set out single file, three feet apart from one another. They walked silently, one on each side of the road. They did not detect hostile fire until they reached a small village north of Wanetchaung. They slowed and were on high alert. In the darkness they could see dead bodies but could not identify them. The village was quiet and appeared to be deserted. Nonetheless, they waited until morning before entering the village.

Peter and Jeremy were sent ahead as scouts. As they crept into the village, they discovered that it had been a predominantly Indian village, with a brightly colored temple. Bodies were strewn about; the men had been murdered in cold blood. Some of them had tried to escape to the temple, it was clear from the cluster of bodies lying just outside it, but they too had been bayoneted or hacked to death. Here and there were clusters of frightened women, half naked, obviously raped. Even the children had been cruelly murdered. At the small courthouse, they discovered the bodies of an entire

British family that had been murdered in the Government bungalow. Other than the weeping women, not a soul was alive in the village. Peter and Jeremy were silent, with grief and horror. Then Peter gave a low whistle, indicating to the patrol that it was safe to enter the village.

Their subedar sent the patrol out to search the trails, but they found no enemy; just more bodies. He radioed the Major, who cleared it with headquarters in Hlegu, and by mid-morning other patrols in the area arrived at the village. When they arrived and saw the carnage, some of the men became crazed; they went looking for the enemy, intent on revenge. They found a small group of Burmans hiding in a small dry *chaung*, and surrounded them. In their rage, the men did not wait for orders; they fired into the group. Some of the surrounded men tried to surrender, but there was no stopping the battalion; they fixed bayonets and went on a rampage, bayoneting and beating every last Burman to death. Peter was aghast: the killing on both sides was gruesome. Finally the Major arrived and gained control of his men. He gathered them around him and gave them instructions.

"I have heard from headquarters at Hlegu. Frankly, I don't think either General knows where his advance troops really are. The Japanese are determined to encircle and annihilate the British army; our orders are clear. We are to secure the oil fields." Again the major paused. "We are a small battalion, tired and decimated. The Japanese are proving to be a resourceful enemy, and they are receiving assistance from some of the local population. Our best course of action is to break up into small groups so as to escape notice, then regroup at the oil fields." Again the major paused before giving his final orders and counsel. "In small groups, you will not have access to headquarters. You will have to use your wits and judgment. If for some reason the plan to secure the oil fields fails, remember that our final objective is India. Head there by whatever means you can."

Peter and Jeremy looked at one another, as did the other men who hailed from Burma. They knew that the dry season would soon end, and that the monsoon, with its great sheets of rain, wind, thunder, and lightning would turn the land into a sea of mud. Walking would be treacherous. They shrugged. What choice did they have? As ordered, they broke up into small groups again and headed west to Prome, where they would join up with the rest of the retreating Rangoon garrison.

Chapter 27
The Japanese Enter Rangoon

7 MARCH 1942

Tin Oo woke up to hear the radio. It had been weeks since the radio had last broadcast. Now it came alive again. He heard the Japanese command radio announce, "The glorious Imperial Army has conquered and liberated Rangoon from the hated British. They have destroyed the British Army. People of Rangoon: do not fear. Remain calm."

The city indeed was outwardly calm. The shops were all closed. Some had shutters like garage doors, others telescoping metal gates, but all were shut and padlocked. There was no water to be had, no power, and no fresh food. The mangy pariah dogs seemed to be the only life on the street; they had the run of the city. Rats scurried around in broad daylight, some as large as cats. These were what the locals called *bandicoots*—ugly and ferocious, fearful of neither man nor cat. People sheltered in their homes, fearful of dacoits, looters, and the future. The British had fled, and the Japanese would soon arrive.

Indeed, now, Sato's column entered Rangoon from the west. He was followed by his regiment carrying the regimental flag and a large Japanese flag bearing the rising sun. The city was deserted, but behind closed doors and through the narrow windows, eyes were watching. The odor of rotting garbage, the stench of decomposing dead bodies, and the smell of dead animals was overpowering. Sato held a white handkerchief to his nose.

Soon his party came upon a railroad bridge, where he found a group of people. From a distance, he assumed them to villagers hiding, but the nearer he got he knew that there was something horrible about these people. They raised their hands in surrender, and the first thing Sato noticed was that fingers were missing, noses had holes in them, and large welts were visible on the cheek bones. He realized the situation immediately. He whispered to his aide, "these are the dreaded lepers that I heard so much about in Japan." Sato waved his handkerchief ineffectually. "Draw up an execution detail," he ordered. "But tell the men to sheath their bayonets and not go near the people. Have them use guns." Sato then took his revolver, raised it, and shot the man closest to him who was waving his horribly disfigured hands in surrender. After the first shot rang out and the man fell, there was much crying and wailing, but it was cut short by a volley from the troops. After a brief pause, the troops let off another volley, and then it was all over.

Only after all the lepers were dead did the sergeant pass word for the troops to withdraw. "These were the lepers from the abandoned hospital," told them. "Do not to go near them." He turned to a small gathering of local people on the horizon. "You," he ordered a small squad as he pointed to the local people, "gather those people to burn these bodies."

The squad rounded up the local people who, despite their abhorrence of the act, duly burned the lepers' bodies, under the threat of the bayonets wielded by the Japanese squad.

Sato took a detour around the bridge then left the scene.

As they marched, the Japanese came upon a wounded British officer, hiding in a low bush. They pulled him out of the bushes and brought him in front of Sato. Sato looked at the unfortunate young lieutenant with contempt and called his sergeant again. No words were exchanged. The soldiers fixed their bayonets and lunged at the desperate man. Finally Sato took his pistol and emptied it into the dying body.

In fact, Sato was rather puzzled; he had expected the Burmese people to welcome him and his men as liberators. But the Burmese people were very cautious, and their welcome very tepid. Only after a few hours did some people dare to venture outdoors and watch the Japanese columns advance into the city. One or two waved to the victorious Japanese army, but the rest stood silent.

Sato had been assigned one of the many colonial buildings at the university. He took the University Building for his headquarters and quartered the troops in the men's dormitories. This would be the first time in weeks that the men would sleep in beds and would have real bathrooms.

As the men settled into their quarters, Sato turned his thoughts to provisioning. His men had fought valiantly and bravely, but they were tired and hungry. They needed to replenish their strength. Sato looked around him at the beautiful campus, only half destroyed. Suddenly he had an idea. He quickly assembled a small squad of men to search every building on campus for stores. It was not long before the squad returned with a respectable number of parcels and barrels. Just as Sato had suspected, in the dying hours of the British government in Rangoon, looters had managed to find stores and hoard them in the half-burnt university buildings. Sato curled his thin lips into a smile. Tomorrow he would mount a more serious campaign to gather food and supplies. But today at least, he and his men could eat well. The looters would never risk trying to recapture their ill-gotten gains.

General Maida had set up his headquarters in the old Governor's mansion and began to plan a victory parade in the city center. Colonel Sato wanted to situate the reviewing stand in front of the Governor's mansion to rub in the Japanese victory over the British, but the General overruled him. "We have to hold it where it will be seen by the majority of the people," he explained. He turned to his Adjutant and barked his orders. "The parade will be at the center of the city. It will start at Fitch Square in front of the Sule Pagoda." Troops immediately began work on a dais and dragooned local workers into the effort.

The next morning, Sule Pagoda Road was bedecked with flags emblazoned with the rising sun of Japan and the peacock of Burma. Battered uniforms were replaced with fresh clean uniforms or repaired. Guns were cleaned. A dais was erected in front of the city hall in the center of the square. Finally, carrying large Japanese and regimental flags and with the band playing martial music, the Japanese troops marched proudly, swaggering through the streets. They had cleaned up their long thin bayonets, and these glistened in the sun. They carried their rifles high on their shoulders, and on some of the shorter men, the rifles looked taller than the men themselves. The soldiers wore caps that were high in the front and low in the back, most with little extenders attached to keep the flies and heat from their necks. The officers wore tan jackets and brown jack boots finished to a brilliant shine. They marched in blocks, soldiers followed by 105 mm guns, lorries, 75 mm guns, drawn horses, and then the mountain guns. As they marched to the drums and music, they sang their martial songs. Following the army troops marched the Japanese air force, and bringing up the rear was the Burma Defense Force (BDF). General Maida stood on the dais to take the salute from the passing troops. He was dressed in tropical uniform. The parade lasted until noon. After the troops had passed, he made a speech which was translated into Burmese by a Japanese interpreter.

Again, Sato noted, the expected jubilation of the Burmese people was not forthcoming. Only a few stood along the streets to watch the parade, and they were distinctly sober. One young man caught his eye, however. Tin Oo stood in front of the church, clearly jubilant. He thrilled to see the Japanese soldiers who had chased the hated British from Rangoon. But he was most proud of the BDF, marching side by side with the victors. As the heat increased toward noon, the people slowly melted away.

The following day, Sato assembled his men to forage for food. His soldiers went knocking on doors of nearby buildings. If the building was empty, they broke down the doors and entered, taking whatever they wanted. Then they placed a notice on the exterior, next to the door, claiming the property for the Japanese Army. The notice was in the Japanese language, written in gold letters on a red background.

At some homes, the Burmese received the soldiers with food, but even so, the Japanese soldiers went about their work with their customary crudeness. They yelled "Kura!" and with fixed bayonets, while the people cowered, they pocketed everything in sight, especially food. The people who had believed that the Japanese would be liberators were surprised and dismayed at the crude mannerisms of the soldiers and the rough, unfriendly manner in which they were treated.

When the soldiers stumbled upon a houseful of British, Indian, Chinese, Anglo, or Burmese who seemed overtly sympathetic to the British, they nearly went berserk. Using their bayonets and shouting incessantly, the soldiers would prod the unfortunates out into the street, and then other soldiers would use bayonets to round them up into a small group. Then a horrible scene unfolded. The soldiers fell upon the suspects, bayoneting the men viciously. The victims and bystanders screamed, but the Japanese laughed. They acted as though they were practicing at a training course! After the first thrust, they would pull the bayonet out and repeat the ghastly procedure until the screams from the suspects died out, blood poured out of the victims' chests and the bellies, and bystanders fled. Blood pooled at the feet of the bent and broken bodies.

All day the soldiers rampaged through the city like this. Sato knew that the *kempeitai* would eventually sort out the friendly Burmese from others, but Sato wanted himself to punish British sympathizers, spies, and looters. His men were systematic, brutal, and ruthless. The population soon cowered in terror as the troops ran through the streets. Even the Burmese who had welcomed the ejection of the British by the Japanese were surprised by the brutishness of the soldiers.

That night, back at his headquarters, Sato smiled in satisfaction. His men were exhausted. But he had gathered all sorts of supplies. Not only did he now have plenty of food for his men; he had enough to sell for profit. He also had acquired jewelry, gold, and collectibles for himself. He was most delighted by the cache of Scotch whiskey that he had found. He knew that his men would have pocketed similar articles, but that did not bother him. "They deserve the spoils of war," Sato thought. "And those British sympathizers deserve what they received as well." He laughed and poured himself a large glass of single-malt whiskey.

A few days later, a group of Japanese led by a *kempeitai* sergeant arrived at Tin Oo's house. Tin Oo quickly took out a piece of paper to show the Japanese; it was a form from the BDF stating that he was a member. The *kempeitai* asked his interpreter what the piece of paper meant. The Burman looked at it, gestured his head toward Tin Oo, and whispered to the Japanese that he was a member of the BDF. The sergeant grunted and waved the paper back at Tin Oo. Then he brushed past him rudely and searched the house thoroughly. Finding nothing of great value, the soldiers took some food and left. This was the first time that Tin Oo had come face to face with a Japanese. He excused their rude behavior with the explanation that they were front-line troops. "When the garrison troops arrive, they will be more accommodating," he told himself. He was convinced that the army that drove the British and their lackeys out of the country would be good for Burma. "Yes," he reassured himself, "soon Burma will be free."

Chapter 28
The Sad Journey Home

The Thomases were frightened and tired after their long and dangerous journey, and beginning to wear on one another's nerves. It was wearying to stay confined on a boat for so long. Especially the women, who had been confined completely to the lower decks, were easily offended by trivial matters or perceived injustices. Benjamin was relieved when the boat arrived at the small jetty. "If I have to moderate one more fight between my sisters," he sighed to Reddy, "I don't know what I'll do!" Reddy laughed. But then both men thought of Mr. Thomas, who lay listlessly on his mat on the lower deck.

The family quickly disembarked and headed to home. The walk to the house was frightening. "The rice mill has been damaged," Benjamin noted to Reddy. "And so were many other houses," came Reddy's reply. Indeed, many houses were empty.

When the family arrived home, the first thing that they noticed that the doors stood open. Mother gasped. Next to the door there was posted a large sign in Japanese letters, written in gold on a red background. Reddy motioned the family to stay away while he and Benjamin cautiously entered the house. All the beds, tables, and fixtures were missing. "My mother will have a breakdown!" Benjamin moaned.

He and Reddy went outside and briefed the family. "You will be surprised and saddened," Benjamin said. He glanced at his father to see how he was taking the news. "In essence, we have a house, but nothing else. All its contents have been looted."

Mother began to sob and the girls began to cry. Grandmother pointed to the large sign next to the door. "What does that mean?" she asked.

Just then Reddy appeared with a neighbor. The neighbor, an elderly Burman whom the family had known for many years, was wringing his hands nervously. "It was terrible," he said as he described the situation after the British abandoned the city and the family had left. "There was no security. Dacoits roamed the streets with impunity. None of us were safe."

He hung his head. "We were afraid. We did not stop them from ransacking your house." He lifted his head and continued. "Then came the Japanese." He spat. "They came to take whatever the dacoits and looters had not found. They took all our food and ripped the jewelry off my wife's neck!"

Benjamin pointed to the sign. "What does this mean?" he asked the neighbor.

"That is a *kempeitai* notice. It notifies all that this house is Japanese government property. The Japanese claim it by virtue of the fact that the people who formerly owned this house worked for the enemy." The neighbor hung his head again. "I am sorry." He hastened away. But soon he returned with his sons and a few other friends who brought some rice and helped with the clean up.

The family walked slowly into the house, scanning the walls. They were intact, but without furniture the house seemed unwelcoming. Grandmother found a broom in the back and began sweeping. "Put your bundles in your rooms," she scolded the girls. "What are you waiting for? Do you think that if you look hard enough your beds will materialize again?" She swept more vigorously. "Go to the back yard and pick some mango fruits," she told her daughter. "You men," she glared at Mr. Thomas, Reddy, and Benjamin, "you decide how we can get rid of that horrible Japanese sign. Or I'll tear it down myself!" She bustled away into the back room, sweeping the corners of the room energetically, as though she could sweep the essence of Japanese out of the house entirely.

Benjamin knew that the first order of the day was to secure the doors. He and Reddy gathered lumber and bamboo and tools from the neighbors and from abandoned houses and reconstructed the door, making sure that it locked. Mr. Thomas helped half-heartedly, but took frequent breaks and was silent. After the doors were secure, the men sat down to contemplate their next move. "Really," Benjamin said apologetically, "I don't think we can think straight at this point. I think we should rise early tomorrow and discuss the future then, when we are rested."

Reddy agreed. "I'll be staying here now," he said simply. Benjamin nodded. Mr. Thomas was silent. He did not say what bothered him, but it was obvious to the whole family that he had fallen into a pit of despondency and despair. He went to his bedroom and there lay down on the mat next to his wife. He fell into a deep sleep. He did not wake up in the morning; his wife found him dead.

The family was gripped by grief. Despite the dire times, the Rangoon rumor mill worked overtime, and friends and family soon gathered for the funeral. They said prayers and sang the old hymns, "Rock of Ages" and others. To the strains of "Abide with Me" they buried Mr. Thomas at the Christian cemetery.

After a few days, most of the relatives left, afraid to leave their own homes unoccupied for more than a day or two. An eerie silence set in. Benjamin felt the weight of his new role as head of the family. He knew he could count on Reddy, his devoted uncle, but he also knew that as the eldest son it was his responsibility to provide for and protect his mother and sisters. If truth be told, he was terrified of the future. "How will the war turn out?" he wondered. "Will the British come back?" Most importantly, he worried, "How will we survive the grim days ahead? How will we raise money to feed the family?" That night there was another air raid. The family huddled in the dark house. After the all-clear sounded, the city was deathly quiet. The fires that had consumed the city had subsided, leaving a pall of smoke.

Benjamin and Reddy sat in the dark and laid plans. "First we need to take stock of what money and gold we have," Reddy advised. "Then we need to lay in supplies, if we can find them. Prices will only go up; we should buy now." That made sense to Benjamin.

"Will you do that, Reddy?" he asked. "I think my mother and grandmother might be more willing to talk with you about such things. Meanwhile, I need to attend to that blasted sign and its implications."

The next day Benjamin left the house early. Life was slowly returning to the city. There were more people on the streets, and some of the produce markets were open. Benjamin walked towards the big concrete building off of Insein Road, the civil occupation headquarters. The building sat at the end of a tree-lined, shady boulevard. Many of the trees had been uprooted. The closer he got to the building, the more Japanese soldiers he spotted. He also noticed sand-bagged defenses, and at one, a machine gun manned by a sullen Japanese soldier. As he approached the building he saw a long line of people waiting to enter the building. Many were people he knew, civilians. Most appeared distant; their eyes met, but there was little said. The sign outside the building said, in Burmese and Japanese, "Occupation Headquarters / Gunseikan-bu." Benjamin saw that the building had suffered some bomb damage but was being repaired. To his surprise, he saw that British soldiers were cleaning the rubble, guarded by Japanese soldiers. Every now and then the soldiers would prod the British with their bayonets and yell "Kura! Kura!" "I wonder what that means," he thought.

As Benjamin stood in the endless line, he cast around for someone who could help him. The building and its courtyard teemed with activity. Then he spotted a colonel in full uniform. To his shock, he recognized the colonel as the dentist, Suzuki, who had used to wait for him outside the Port Trust building and ask him questions. Benjamin raised his arm and waved. The colonel recognized him and summoned him to his side. They walked in silence, and Benjamin braved the stony stare of those who had been in line ahead of him. The colonel took Benjamin to a office, sat him down, and then asked, "What can I do for you?"

"My family was away in the country when the city changed hands," Benjamin explained obtusely, leaving out all mention of the actual reason for the family being away. "When we returned, there is this sign on the door. I think it means that the home my father built has been declared enemy property. I want to know how to get that proclamation reversed."

"Is that all?" asked the colonel. "You cannot imagine the intractable problems I face. I'll take care of it. No problem." He then waved Benjamin away.

As he walked home, Benjamin still worried. "Did I give up too easily?" he questioned himself. "Will the colonel really do something about the sign?" But a few days later, two Japanese appeared at the house and took away the red sign, much to the relief of the family. Grandmother took her broom to the wall, again sweeping away any vestige of the enemy.

General Maida was now the military administrator in Rangoon. He established the military administrator office, the "Gunseikan-bu." This was a propaganda program, a program designed to brainwash the people. The policy would force all people to learn the Japanese language and to do the bidding of the Japanese. After indoctrination, they would "accept the Japanese as the master race."

Each morning the radio blared the Japanese anthem, the Army anthem, and then homage to the Emperor. All the people outdoors were forced to bow to the east, in the direction of the Imperial palace, and join in the chorus. At the local schools, the day started with calisthenics. On a high branch of the mango tree outside the school, a loudspeaker blared the program for the day. Even those too old to go to school, like Benjamin, could be reached by the blaring lesson. Each day began with the Japanese national anthem:

> Miyo Tokai no sora akete
> Kyokujitsu takaku
> kagayakeba
> Tenchi no seiki hatsuratsu
> Kibo wa odoru oyashima
> O seiro no asakumo ni
> Sobiyuru Fuji no sugata koso
> kino muketsu yurugi naki
> Was Nippon mo hokori nare.

> [See the sky is opening over the eastern sea,
> When the rising sun lights up the heavens,
> Our hope dances on the Eight Great islands.
> Filled with the life and vigor of the world
> Oh, in the fine bright clouds of morning
> The shape of Fuji towers on high
> Firm as a rock, perfect like a vase of gold
> and to the great and glorious home land,
> and ended with the pride of our Japan.]

Next came the Burmese national anthem, and then came the numbers: Ichi, Ni, San, Si. The lessons went on and on. The students sat at crude shelters and followed the radio commands. During recesses, they broadcast propaganda programs about the latest battles and the "running dog British and their lackeys."

Each morning, Reddy stayed in the home to protect it and the family. Benjamin went out to look for food. There were only a few vendors of fresh vegetables; meats and other foodstuffs were not to be found anywhere. Benjamin traversed the city streets on foot, going from one shop to the next, bartering furiously so as to conserve the family's money. One day a strong memory struck him: he remembered the stall near the railway station, run by a lame man whose specialty had been lentil patties. Benjamin's stomach began to growl and he began to salivate. "Oh, for a lentil patty!" he thought. The stall had used to be open seven days a week, closing only during Ramadan. Now, like most of the other shops, it was closed. And now, most days, all Benjamin could bring home was a few wilted vegetables.

When he would arrive home, the young children, as he expected, could not be consoled. They cried as they spooned their soup with its sparse vegetables. But soon the darkness and fatigue forced everybody to sleep. There were no beds, so each one of them staked out a position in the big bedroom and went to sleep on a mat on the floor.

Benjamin knew that without meat, the children especially would become seriously malnourished. For days, all they had was boiled rice and a few wilted vegetables. If they were lucky, Benjamin could find a small piece of dried fish to add to the gruel. In desperation, he set out one day for the house of a trader whom he had known before the war to deal in black-market goods. He crept up to the front door and found that the metal gate was closed. But inside he saw the friendly face of the young woman he had known, the trader's daughter. She gestured him to the side door and quickly let him in. "There is not much fresh food," she said, "but I have some tinned Norwegian sardines and some biscuits."

Benjamin gave her some rupees and his best smile. He thanked her and put the food in his pockets. He then slipped out the side door, cautiously entering the street again. About a block away he spied some soldiers, but he could not identify which army they belonged to. To be safe, he ducked into a lane, hoping that the soldiers did not notice him. He waited until he saw their backside, then ducked out and hurried home. This time he was greeted as a hero by the children. They greedily ate the biscuits and sardines, cleaning out the tin with their fingers until it was perfectly clean. Benjamin looked at them as they squabbled over the oil remaining in the tins. Their abdomens were protruding, and their extremities were beginning to look like sticks. "Classic signs of malnutrition," he thought sadly. "Somehow, some way, we need to earn money to buy food regularly on the black market."

Benjamin faced a moral dilemma. He needed to work, in order to support the family. Without income, they would starve. And he knew that if he wanted to work, he needed to pretend to cooperate with the occupiers and have a working knowledge of the Japanese language. Moreover, without a job he might be at risk. Rumors flew down the streets and through the alleys of Rangoon that unemployed people disappeared. The *kempeitai* snatched them and took them to a camp. There the *kempeitai* promised them a good job and food if they would sign up to build a railroad. It was finally sinking in that any hope for an early return of the Allies was futile.

Chapter 29
The Retreat Continues

Peter and Jeremy set out from the small village north of Wanetchaung in a group of two. Jeremy made a entry in his small journal: the last week of March. Their progress was slow, because they were cautious. One evening Peter heard the sound of tanks. "But they could be enemy," he whispered. The two young men hid themselves by the side of the road and were comforted to find that the tanks were British. Identifying themselves, they talked to the men.

"There is a block ahead," they warned. "The Japs are good at racing past us through the jungle and then setting up a block." It was just before sunset, and Jeremy and Peter joined the tank column, bringing up the rear. As darkness closed in, the tanks halted for the night. The men slept fitfully, as the night always held terror. The Japanese were good at night attacks.

The days that followed had a sad repetitive rhythm to them. The men would get up before sunrise. After a meager breakfast the tank column would move slowly down the road. Jeremy and Peter brought up the rear, followed by an ever-growing column of refugees on foot. Most of the refugees were Indians, their retreat slowed by the fact that they were starving. Soon enemy planes would arrive overhead. The fighters were especially horrific: they terrorized and killed with their merciless guns, mowing down the hapless refugees. Each day there were more refugees, even though each day many would be killed by Japanese fighters.

Jeremy and Peter had mixed emotions. They were a part of the British Army, and the British Army was retreating. As it retreated, it was leaving Indians to their fate, which would not be pleasant. They felt a mixture of anger, guilt, and compassion about the scene in which they found themselves. Peter passed out biscuits when he could, but he and Jeremy had little access to food themselves and knew that they needed to keep up their own strength. The dusty dry season added to the misery. Drinking water was scarce, and the shortage of water caused panic among the troops and refugees alike. "Pani, pani!" the refugees wailed, begging water. But the military were themselves on strict ration and had none to share. Finally, one day, the tank commander told Peter to take to the jungle. "We will soon abandon the tanks. No petrol," he said simply.

Jeremy and Peter faded into the jungle the next day, following the small trails used by villagers. They approached villages cautiously, assessing their friendliness before approaching to ask for fresh water and food. Each evening when they bivouacked, Peter took off his shoes and saw that his feet were red and sore. No amount of massaging could comfort them. For three days they marched on the jungle trails, when suddenly they came upon a road. "A real road!" exclaimed Jeremy with excitement. They spotted some lorries headed west, and even though they were full of soldiers, Peter and Jeremy found a place to hang on. Jeremy was almost lighthearted as he swung from the bars. "What a relief to not have to march on the hot dusty trails!" he shouted rather gaily. Peter agreed readily, glad to spare his aching feet another day of marching.

For two days they traveled with the military convoy and had no contact with the enemy. "Maybe we've outrun them," Jeremy said hopefully. Finally they arrived just short of Prome, at a small river town of Shwegyin. It was late in the evening, and the men bivouacked. They set up a defense perimeter and soon fell asleep.

A few hours later they were awakened by gunfire coming from across the river. "It's a full-blown attack!" shouted the men. With no tanks, the men felt vulnerable. They fought from their fox holes, firing continually at the elusive enemy.

Just before dawn, Peter whispered to Jeremy, "This is another dead end. The Japanese will overrun our perimeter, and we will all rush into retreat, being picked off one by one. The men we are with have no tanks and no armored vehicles. They are no match for the Japanese. Let's get out of here while we can."

Jeremy, his experience at Sukli Point still clear in his mind, agreed.

Before the sun rose, Peter and Jeremy crawled out of their foxhole and ran into the jungle for cover. They stayed together and followed the narrow trails, hoping to circumvent the Japanese. The trails were soggy and muddy, slowing their progress. They could still hear gunfire, when suddenly, out of a bamboo grove, two soldiers in Japanese uniforms came at them. Soon they were in hand to hand combat. For the first time, Peter came face to face with a Burman in Japanese uniform. He was so surprised that he momentarily froze, and it was Jeremy who fired from behind him and killed the enemy. When it was all over, Peter said with awe, "It is now clear that we are fighting not only the Japanese but also their Burmese allies. We are really in trouble now!"

Jeremy was a little shaky himself. "I know we had to kill them, or they would have killed you. But these men are Burmese! What if some of them are our friends?" The two men were silent. Their thoughts turned to their friend Tin Oo. Was he now on the other side? Would there would be another encounter with Burmese collaborators? What would they do?

North of Prome the gunfire stopped. The allied defense had crumbled. Prome was now in enemy hands. "We've got to go directly north now," Jeremy said desperately. "We have to get to the oil fields quickly. So far we have beaten back all attacks. I just pray that our luck lasts."

Peter agreed and observed. "Then, once we get past the oil fields, we will have three enemies: the Japs, the Burmese collaborators, and the most fearsome enemy of all, the green hell of the Burma's jungle."

They checked their dwindling supplies of ammunition, groaned at the small amount of food and water they had, and set out northward, without guide posts. If they were lucky, they would join up with other retreating British soldiers. There was always safety in numbers. If they could make it to the oil fields, they comforted themselves, they would be able to join their fellow soldiers and fight off the Japanese. Or, they could make a run for the safety of India. "I'm not going to be captured by the Japs, that's for sure," vowed Jeremy. They set out cautiously, guns drawn.

They walked for days, lost in the wild country. Having shed most of their gear, they rested during daylight hours and set out each night as darkness fell. "Remember that boring course in astronomy?" Jeremy said wryly; "it may be what will save us." Peter chuckled, a rare moment of humor in their lives now so fraught with fear and danger.

In the inky blackness. Peter said, "Well, we have to find north. Let's put that boring course to work."

In the sky, the Orion constellation was rising. "Orion lies in the eastern sky," remembered Jeremy as he pointed out the constellation.

Peter shifted his scrutiny northward in the sky, identifying additional stars until he definitively pointed out the north star. "There!" he pointed excitedly. "We are headed north, so we follow the north star."

The men moved cautiously, ever on the alert for sounds of other men. They might be friendly troops, but they could also be Japanese or, as they had learned from their earlier experience, collaborators. For a long time they remained silent, until finally Jeremy whispered, "This is so different from Rangoon! The people are all farmers; there seem to be no foreigners or ethnic people. And it seems so isolated. They probably don't even know that there is a war going on." After a few moments he blurted out, "It is frightening, and it is at times like this that you draw on your god."

Peter remained silent, lost in his thoughts. Finally he said, "Unfortunately, I have my doubts; I no longer believe. I know I was brought up a Christian, but after college I began questioning, and after what I have seen in the past few weeks, my views have changed." He continued. "I often wondered about heaven and hell, and used to talk to Mother about it. She was very firm in her beliefs, but I never shared that certainty." Peter remained silent for while longer. "Then one experience pushed me into unbelief. Just before the war, my youngest sister was two years old. She was the prettiest little girl, with curly black hair and big limpid brown eyes. She was so playful; everybody loved her, and she was especially close to me. She woke up ill one morning, with a racing heart. The local physician listened to her lungs and diagnosed pneumonia. He gave her a small injection of camphor in oil and prescribed aspirin. That evening the family prayed almost continuously. I carried her close to my chest and prayed and prayed. By midnight she died. It took me a while to get over the fact that she was gone, in spite of all the prayers."

Jeremy interjected. "But not all prayers are answered, Peter. Sometimes we are tested."

Peter answered quickly. "That is so facile! Reddy, too, would always say that God works in mysterious ways, but I somehow cannot reconcile the two teachings. And after I began to start questioning, the questions never ceased. Writings of Spinoza and Russell and, of course, Darwin. Spinoza, the seventeenth-century Jewish writer, was particularly compelling. He believed that the universe is ruled only by the cause and effect of natural laws and believed that the god of this universe was a non-interventionist, whose essence is best described as Nature." Peter had warmed to his topic now and became expansive. "You know I was brought up in an American Southern Baptist household, sometimes a conservative and at times repressive one. My sister used to always say that Buddhists and Hindus cannot go to heaven, and she was adamant. But I cannot believe that a supposedly benevolent God would condemn Hindus and Buddhists unless they converted to Christianity and were baptized."

Again Jeremy tried to explain. "That is what the Bible teaches, though," he said.

Peter shook his head. "I cannot believe that." I used to see the high-caste women in the train who abhorred people unlike them. And my sister in turn despised such women, the type who treated the untouchables as unclean." He paused, then continued. "The Japanese were supposed to be Buddhist and have respect for life, all life, at least some. But they are cruel, bestial, and inhuman towards all people. They care little about people except their kind. The British, too, murder Burmese whom they suspect of being collaborators. And the Burmese in turn kill Karens and non-Burmese indiscriminately, especially the Indians. Frankly, I cannot believe that a merciful God would let these horrors occur."

"In my readings I came across this: 'there are no atheists in foxholes'," Jeremy said slowly. "Maybe that is why I find comfort in my God right now. But I must confess that I, too, have questions, although my roots in religion are strong. I always questioned the doctrine of Limbo, why all the people born before the advent of Christ could not be saved. And I cannot find any reason for the slaughter of the innocents in the air raids in Rangoon."

For a while both men remained silent, then Peter said, "You know, I thought war was glamorous, at least that is how the cinema portrays it. But in real life, it is unbelievably vile and horrifying." He motioned with his arms. "Look at us now. We are scared stiff, we don't know where we are, we do not know friend from foe. I guess it is at times like this that you draw courage from your beliefs."

Both men had been seared by the war, each with his own worries about the future. Jeremy confessed, "I try to have courage, but I do worry about the future. I wonder what we are defending. I had always thought that I belonged to this country and, in fact, was well placed, but now I keep remembering the words of Sir Walter Scot, "breathes there a man with a soul so dead that never to himself has said, this is my native land?" And I ask myself "what is your land, Jeremy?""

Peter tried to console his friend. "Jeremy, we will see our homes, family, and friends again."

Jeremy appeared to weep. "I worry about my family and, especially, CeCi. Did they leave Rangoon? What if they are out there walking through the jungle, the dreaded uncharted green hell. In spite of her appearance she is quite vulnerable emotionally, and being here, I cannot do anything to protect her."

"While we are in a reflective mood, and making confessions to one another," Peter said with a little self-conscious laugh, "let me tell you this. I have overcome my fears. I feel that I am a man now. Death has no terror for me." He continued. "What I do fear, however, is a lingering death, or the sight of the screaming enemy running me through with a bayonet. I want to go in a flash."

"I know what you mean," Jeremy shuddered. "The sight of all the suffering, wounded, and dying men haunts me every day." He remembered Carl Pinto, left behind by the retreating troops near Moulmein.

It was still early; the sun was just rising. They walked in silence for a while, then Peter changed the subject. "Let's talk about something else," he suggested. "Tell me about girls; it's easy for you," he prompted.

"You meet them mostly at dances," Jeremy explained. "You have to be a good dancer, know all the new steps. You need to spend a lot of time in practice at home and in the clubs. Then you see someone that you like, you ask her to dance, and after a few dances you hold her close and tell her how pretty she is and how light she is on her feet." He began to sound wistful now. "Then you sit down between dances and talk. You tell her what you like about her and so on; that you like her hair and what a good dancer she is."

"When do you get to the good part, like kissing?" Peter asked.

Jeremy laughed. "That, my dear fellow, takes time, and the setting has to be right. It is not easy in this crowded world to find the right spot; it takes time." He turned the tables. "What about you, Peter, did you ever . . . do it?"

Before Peter could answer, the tall grass east of them waved in the wind and they heard some rustling. They instantly froze and readied their guns, then dropped to the ground. They remained quiet. They thought they saw some shadows, but could not be sure, They thought they heard voices, but could not be sure. They found this territory so strange. Peter whispered, "I think I hear Japanese. Probably a patrol, or a predator stalking them, or an enemy with a *dah*." He put his index finger to his lips and gestured with his hand to stay low.

The two men remained hidden in the tall brown grass. Soon the sounds receded, but they decided to stay hidden. As night fell, Peter stayed awake while Jeremy tried to sleep, but sleep was always light. The slightest noise could arouse you to full alertness, and soon both men were alert to a new noise. It drew closer. Peter took out his binoculars. It was difficult to see anything in the dark, but he could see the shape of hats outlined against the moonlit sky. "It is a mixed patrol of Japs and Burmese," he whispered to Jeremy. He crossed his fingers while Jeremy prayed silently. They were afraid to move, hearing periodic movement throughout the night. Only in the early morning did the noise abate, assuring them that the enemy patrol had passed.

"I'm not sure it is any safer to move at night and rest during the day," Peter observed. "At night, the enemy is active, and we cannot identify them. Let's continue today in the daylight." Jeremy nodded assent, and the two men moved out.

They walked silently through the jungle. The heat was stifling, even early in the morning. In the dry belt of Burma, even the nights were oppressive, and in April, the dirt and rocks and everything around would heat up to the point that to put your hand on the ground would burn the skin. Clothes would be soaking with sweat in an hour. The shallow wells had all run dry. On the macadam roads, the tar would melt; and the rubber soles of shoes would soften and become mushy, transmitting the heat to the feet and making the wearing of boots unbearable.

At midday the they crawled under a tamarind tree, where they would rest till it cooled down. Jeremy mused, "I hope it rains; it would bring relief from this heat."

"But the pre-monsoon storms will bring their own horrors," Peter countered. "The humidity will rise, making the outdoors unbearable. And the worst of it will be that the mosquito larvae will mature in the heat and humidity. They will become ravenous and fearless. They'll buzz you until you turn mad and leave you full of red bites." Having given himself the jitters, Peter searched for repellent in his haversack. "Do you still have your mepacrine tablets?" he asked Jeremy. "We better start taking the medicine. I hope it lasts till we get to the forward bases." He shook his water bottle, then shook his head before taking a tiny sip. "We have to find potable water soon or we will die of thirst."

As the temperatures cooled in the late afternoon, the two men set out again, continuing their march northward. They knew that they were in a race against time and the monsoon. By evening they came upon the outskirts of a village. They stopped, not knowing whether it was friendly or hostile. Peter surmised that it was a ethnic village, because foot-high earthen mounds surrounded a central square, and in the center was a house on stilts. Chickens were running in the yard, and next to the house was a well with a draw bucket. "It should be safe," he said, "but I don't want to get too close." Under a banyan they found a pot of water. They filled their water bottles, but still avoided going through the village.

Soon, in the distance, the two men could see the top of oil derricks. "Look!" cried Jeremy excitedly. "The oil fields! We have finally arrived!"

But dense smoke emanated from the ground, enveloping some of the derricks. "It looks like we may be too late," Peter remarked. "Let's go closer, but carefully. If the Japanese control the oil fields, they will have outposts."

As the two men crept closer to Chauk, it became apparent that the British had decided that they could not protect the oil fields and had set them ablaze as they evacuated. They did not want to leave supplies behind that the enemy could use. Jeremy and Peter watched the black smoke billow skyward and knew that they now were on their own. They would have to find their way to

India without the support of a commanding officer or radio communications. Wordlessly they bypassed the oilfields and moved warily northward.

"We have to find the Myittha River," Jeremy said. Without motor transport, getting to the river would be difficult, and even then, finding a country boat would be even harder. Soon they heard the sounds of battle to the east. They crawled down a dry *chaung* and, once they got to the top on the other side, ran away from the firefight. They were safe for the moment, but now they were lost. They had totally lost their bearings, and the map was useless. For days they wandered aimlessly. Dehydration was a constant companion.

Peter complained, "I feel weak. My tongue is thick and dry as sandpaper."

"I feel the same," said Jeremy." But still they walked. At sunset they sat down to rest but decided to spend the night. They just did not have the strength to get up and walk any more.

The next morning they felt a bit better and continued their trek. Presently they came upon a large village with a cluster of huts around a central well. They could see young boys playing on the outskirts of the village. Jeremy was not only hungry but also thirsty. He started to walk quickly to the village, but Peter held him back. "This area is not known for its friendliness," he whispered.

The men stayed hidden, watching. Beyond the huts they could see the paddy fields, which were dry now. At the far edge of the paddy fields were tall trees, and almost hidden in the trees were two huts, some bullocks, and cows tethered to the trees. Just to the east of the huts, chickens ran around clucking, chased by a large male cock. The noise they were making indicated that they were oblivious to the presence of Peter and Jeremy. "A typical rice-growing village," noted Jeremy. "Maybe there is an earthen pot of water nearby, set aside for travelers."

"A great tradition. The Burmese are different," Peter thought to himself as he watched the village. "Unlike the Indians, whose mean-spirited caste system would not allow such an act." But neither man could spot a traveler's water station.

Peter said, "You stay here, Jeremy. I will approach the village to see if they are hostile. That way, at least one of us can get away." He took out his empty water bottle and walked slowly up to the boys, motioning one to come forward. "I am 'thaga gyin,' a friend," he explained. Then he asked, "Ye shee la?" [you have drinking water?].

The young boy hesitated a moment, but soon broke out in a smile. "Ye see-day," he replied.

Next Peter asked if there were any Japanese.

The young boy said, "Yes, there is cool water, but no Japs." He led Peter to the village. Peter was still nervous. He had heard about Burmese villages that lured soldiers in and then turned on them. He approached with trepidation and fear, calling "We are friends; we only want water" as he walked.

"Ye see la," the old man who seemed to be the head of the village replied. The man took him by the hand and gave him the ladle. Peter was scared but was so thirsty that he took the risk and drank out of the coconut cup. It was so satisfying! He said to the old man, "Let me call my friend. He, too, is thirsty."

The old man nodded. Peter gestured to Jeremy that it was safe, and Jeremy came quickly to the well. Both men drank deeply and filled their water bottles. They turned to the old man gratefully and said "Chesu" [thank you] before leaving.

Back in the safety of the tall grass, they rested. Jeremy prayed. They waited until dusk before setting out again. They started to climb uphill, and in the distance they could see blue-green hills. The vista looked peaceful, hauntingly beautiful, and serene. They walked late into the night before they sought cover again for a brief sleep.

The next morning they set out away from the sun, heading west, towards the hills. They found a trail they thought would lead to the Myittha River, where they hoped to meet up with the main body of retreating British army. They stayed off the trails, feeling safer hidden in the high grass that could protect them from being seen. By noon they had run out of food and water and sought a spot to rest. Continuing to walk in the midday heat would be suicidal. They crawled under a tree and fell asleep, awakening at three in the afternoon. The air was still dry, and it felt like air coming out of furnace. Peter asked for the map. Jeremy fretted, "I hope the river is not full of Japanese patrols."

Peter looked at the map and guessed, "The Japanese will be advancing to the big river towns. Even as we speak, they are probably racing to the town to cut off our retreating units."

Jeremy went silent for a while. Then he said with determination, "We must get to the town of Pauk soon. From there we can head northward to Gangaw, which is on the Myittha River, and once we are at the river, we can follow it northward to Kalemyo, where we should be able to cross over to the safety of India."

Peter said worriedly, "The trail to Pauk is through the dry zone. At this time of year, water is a precious commodity. We've just experienced what thirst can do to us."

By now Jeremy was so weary that he just nodded. They walked till noon. Peter tugged at Jeremy's sleeve. Ahead in the distance was a shimmering golden spire. Jeremy rubbed his eyes and turned to Peter. "You know that means there must be a village nearby." He quickly consulted his map. "I think we have reached Pauk!" But was the village friendly or not?

"Pagodas are always built on high ground," said Peter. "Let's observe the village for a while, to see if the Japs are already there." They hid and remained quiet. Jeremy took out his binoculars and watched the village. It was a small village, just a few huts surrounded by coconut trees. In the center, the largest hut was built on stilts, and in front of the house was an area that was cleared. "Is that a man with a spear?" Peter pointed.

"Maybe," Jeremy said. "Can't really tell. Let's wait until dusk. If we see a pot of water, we can fill our water bottles. But we may also find fruit, some guavas, or maybe some bananas."

When dusk fell, Peter crawled toward the village on all fours. Jeremy covered him. His progress was slow, and the dry grass was at times so sharp as to penetrate his uniform, but soon he came to the edge of the village. He saw a patch of green and, under a tree, a traveler's water pot. He crouched and looked intently to see if he was detected; then he stood up and advanced to the tree. Peering into the pot he was pleased to see that it was not empty.

He had managed to fill the two water bottles with the ladle made from half a coconut with a bamboo handle, when he heard a noise. He ducked and took cover behind the tree. He saw a man in uniform go up the path to the pagoda and disappear behind the building. Luckily, the man did not see Peter. As soon as the man disappeared, Peter grabbed some fruit from next to the water pot and then ran in a crouch to rejoin Jeremy.

They probably should have moved on, but their hunger drove them to take more risk. They waited to take another run to the house, looking for more food. But as they approached the house, they heard shouts, then gunfire. They did not return fire, as they were out numbered. Instead, they ran in a crouch. The firing continued but soon died out. "Thank God," Jeremy sighed. "We should not have been so greedy."

The two men walked briskly in the dark, anxious to get far away from the pagoda. Jeremy consulted the map quickly. "We should get as far as possible tonight. If we don't get to the river soon, the enemy will get there first and cut us off."

But between the men and the river were mountains—the Pegu Yomas. There were no roads through the mountains; the men would have to use the jungle trails—the very same trails that the enemy would use. Peter and Jeremy moved cautiously through the night, starting at every crackle and rustle in the jungle through which they passed and pushing their legs to the limit as they climbed the mountains.

As the sun began to rise behind them the next morning, they could see the river ahead, glistening in the sunshine. "Oh, how good it will feel to wade in the cool mountain waters!" said Peter.

"It looks close," warned Jeremy, "but it will be a full day more of trekking before we reach those cool waters."

The next day they reached Talin, a fishing village on the bank of the Myittha River. "I hope it is an ethnic village," Jeremy said. "If so, they will probably be friendly."

As they approached the village carefully, they encountered a villager. He turned out to be an ethnic Chin, and a friendly man. Peter addressed him in Burmese, begging him for drinking water and asking if he could sell him and Jeremy some food. The man was friendly and told them to follow him. Peter and Jeremy did so, but they kept careful watch all the time.

"Could we rent a sampan?" Peter asked the man.

"Yes, I have one," the man replied. "But it is dangerous. There are enemies all around. You will have to hide under the tarp." Peter and Jeremy followed the man to the river, boarded the sampan, and covered themselves as instructed. The man rowed upstream, then stopped at a distance from the village. "Stay hidden," he instructed. In just a few moments he returned with some dried fish and clean water.

As the sampan lay at rest in the river, they heard planes overhead. "Enemy planes," remarked Jeremy, the voice of experience. But they flew over without action.

The man said, "I will take you to the next village. That would be Gangaw. It is a Chin village. It will be friendly." When they arrived at Gangaw just after midday, they were relived to find the people friendly. A most inviting smell was coming from a kitchen nearby, the smell of *Kausywe*, fried Panthay noodles. Soon Peter and Jeremy joined other villagers nibbling the noodles topped off with fried chicken eggs. It was the first time in a long time that they ate a hot meal. Even so, they kept a careful eye out for the enemy. Peter cradled his gun between his legs even as he ate.

"Kalemyo thaw may" [we are going to Kalemyo], he said in Burmese to the noodle stall proprietor. The man replied in Burmese, "My son will take you near Kalemyo, leave you outside the town. You will have to find your own way up the river into town. I cannot tell you if the Japanese are there, and we don't want to find out." Peter nodded.

They got in the small boat and kept their heads low. The young man rowed upstream for hours. Then he stopped. "This is as far as I will go," he said. Peter paid the man and looked at the city in the distance. Jeremy and he climbed out of the sampan and waded in waist-deep, cold water to the muddy bank. They climbed up, cleaned their shoes and uniforms, and walked along the bank, hoping that they would not be detected. They were worried about being on the east bank; it could be in enemy hands.

Suddenly they heard voices and were beside themselves with joy, to hear what they thought friendly voices. Even so, they moved cautiously, and when they got closer to the voices, it sounded like Japanese was being spoken. The enemy was already there. Disappointed and still wary, they withdrew to rest for the night and decide on a course of action.

Peter argued, "We cannot cross here; we might be captured. We have already heard and seen the enemy. We need to get up to Kalemyo and find a crossing there."

Jeremy looked at the map again and said, "There must be a ferry in Kalemyo, although the jetty there is surrounded by a wide basin and mountains. If the Japanese are there, we could come under murderous fire."

"It will be dangerous no matter what we do" observed Peter. The two men were silent for a few moment. "But when we get across the river, we will have only a short distance to travel before we reach the safety of India. We need to take the risk."

Chapter 30
Pangsu Pass

Since her aunt's death, CeCi reflected on life. She could hardly believe the changes she had experienced since the Japanese had unexpectedly come up the Irrawaddy and advanced on Myitkyina. Although it seemed a lifetime, she had been walking for weeks. When she thought about her life in pre-war Rangoon, it seemed like a cinema, not reality. Reality was where she was at the moment: trudging, climbing, slogging, and nearly starving every day.

"Thank God for Lingham," she thought. "He helped us so much, and now that aunty has died, he is my only friend." Just as those thoughts crossed her mind, she realized that Lingham was not at her side; he must have fallen behind! CeCi retraced her steps, looking for him. She asked some of the other Indians in her party if they had seen him, and they just looked backward down the road. CeCi hurried back along the road, and soon found Lingham under a tree. He seemed to be sleeping. He been wracked with fever the last few days, had not eaten, and had drank little. He had complained of headaches and vomited. Now CeCi noticed how much weight he had lost weight and how dry his skin was. She held his hand to feel his pulse, and found it weak. She touched his skin and found it burning hot. He opened his eyes and began to mumble, then threw his head back. He shivered and shook, even though his skin was hot to the touch. His eyes, CeCi noted, were sunken and yellow and with hemorrhages. A man sitting next to Lingham, and who looked just as weak, told CeCi that Lingham's urine was like red wine. Suddenly CeCi recalled the dreaded "black water fever" for which there was no cure. "Lingham!" she wailed. But there was nothing more that she could do for him. Soon he was dead. He would never realize his dream to bathe in the Ganges River. Again there was no time for burial, no time for cremation. CeCi gently set his body under the tree and hoped that the carnivores would not find it. She left quietly and then hurried to rejoin her group. As she walked, her thoughts turned again to home, her brother, and her friends. "Now I am really alone," she realized, and a tear slipped down her cheek.

Each day, somebody in her group took ill and died. The stench was overpowering. Each day the refugees grew more desperate; some gave up all hope and surrendered to death. Water was getting scarce, and the refugees would drink from streams. Then they would become ill. It would start with frequent bowel movements, then the victim would fall behind the group, with painful watery diarrhea. The victim would appear ghoulish, with deeply sunken eyes, dry wrinkled skin, and a very dry tongue. Then one day the victim would simply lie down by the roadside and die. Counting the dead was useless; they were too numerous. The smell of death was always overpowering and toxic. "Strange," CeCi thought to herself, "all the bodies smell the same. The Chinese, British, and Indians all look the same in death, smell the same in death."

It had been six weeks since they had left Myitkyina. Frail, weak, and walking like zombies, the pitiful long column of refugees had doggedly continued their trek day after day. They dared not look back, lest they see the enemy. They had lost track of the days and weeks. "Since the monsoon has arrived," CeCi calculated, "it must be April or May. But beyond that, I have no idea of what day it is or, even where I am."

Then one evening she saw a range of mountains that looked different: in the midst of it was a pass, or a small break. She said a quiet prayer and crossed herself. If nothing else, it would be the end of the pestilential green hell. Then her heart leapt and her spirit soared. She remembered what the old Kachin headman had told her of the Pangsu pass. "This must be the pass!" she cried, and pointed to the break in the mountain. Others, those strong enough to care, looked up as well, and CeCi heard a few excited voices. Finally, they had reached the last ridge, and in it the infamous pass. Like the rest of the refugees, CeCi thought she was past fear, but it put in a fresh appearance now—a deep fear that at the very pinnacle of success, she would fall short of her goal. She shook her head as though the fear was a fly that could be shooed off. "A silly childhood fear," she told herself.

Ahead in the foothills she thought she saw some huts. "Stop dreaming!" she admonished herself. "It is only a mirage." But the closer she got to the mirage the more convinced she was that it was real. Finally, she knew there was no mistake. She could see a group of huts! She was so weary, and she knew it would be hours before she would reach the huts. But there was no denying her excitement, and she did manage to pick up her pace slightly. Even the infirm started to pick up their speed, dreaming of food and a bed.

Presently they came upon huts and some wooden sheds. CeCi took a deep breath and rubbed her eyes to make sure that it was not a mirage. If she remembered correctly from her Kachin friend, this would be the Tea Planters Association Center. As CeCi approached the site, she saw normal well-fed humans for the first time since leaving Myitkyina. Helpers bustled out of the huts to help the refugees. CeCi was carried to large well-kept compound. Outside the compound were some mules and elephants; inside were porters, either Nagas or Kukis, she didn't know or care which. To the right of the compound were two long huts: one for women and one for men. Even here, she noted, there was a house set aside for the British. She knew she would never see the inside of that building, but at this point she did not care. Like the rest of the refugees, all she could think about was taking a shower and maybe getting some clean clothes that were not torn. She walked to the hut where the kitchen was located. To one side was a space reserved for Europeans, and she saw that it was stocked with biscuits, soup, bully beef, and chocolate. Her mouth began to water; she had almost but not totally forgotten about how they tasted. But she knew that she could not pass for a European, especially in her current condition.

She sat down on a long bench at a table with other refugees, gazing at the heaps of rice and curry on the table. She looked around for a spoon, but there were none. Like the others, she put her hands into the hot rice and curry and ate with gusto. "Don't overeat," warned one of the attendants. "It is best to eat small amounts. You can always come back for more." The attendant smiled.

"Thank you," CeCi said politely, thinking about how long it had been since she had seen a smile. The curry might not have been the best she had ever eaten, and she had always abhorred the custom of eating with her hands. But she could hardly remember the last time she had eaten a hot meal. Listening to the attendant's advice, CeCi did not go for seconds, even though she was still hungry. Instead, she hastened to the communal shower, to wash off the accumulated sweat and grime. In the communal shower she could not strip down like she would do at home, but bathed Burmese style, wrapped in a *longyi*. The warm water caressed her body, and she sighed with pleasure. She washed the sores on her feet, then washed her clothes. She was given clean clothes and hung her own to dry. "Tomorrow," she vowed, "I will go to the clinic. But first, I want to sleep, in peace." She headed back to the women's hut eagerly, and within moment of lying down on the mat on the floor, fell into a deep sleep.

The next day at the clinic, she told the Indian doctor that she had acted as a "nurse" for many of the refugees. "There are many more refugees in dreadful condition," she said. "Some have the dreaded Naga sores. The worst cases have been left behind, because they cannot walk. But they may still be alive. Teams should be sent to fetch them."

The Indian doctor thanked her but said sadly, "We really do not have the means to go collect the sick. If they make it to us, we will treat them. But we have no transport ourselves, and as you know, the trails are narrow and clogged with refugees." When CeCi began to object, the doctor patted her shoulder. "Rest assured that we are doing our best and that we are treating everyone we can." CeCi nodded, knowing that the doctor spoke the truth. Still, it made her sad. So many people had been left behind!

CeCi knew that before she could set out again, she had heal herself, physically and emotionally. The camp that the tea planters had set up allowed her and her fellow refugees to do just that. Soon the thick exudate of the open sores around her ankle diminished. Each day they hurt less and looked less angry. The poultices seemed to help, and the skin around the sores started to grow in. The regular nourishment improved her strength. As she recuperated, she thought wistfully of her father and mother, and her brother, wondering what they were doing and where they were. After three days, she felt reborn. She had clean but spartan attire and had, with some effort, gotten some tinned food: tinned sardines, which were difficult to get.

Soon after the refugees arrived in the camp, they had been taken in groups to the big *basha* for instructions. The British camp administrator had addressed each ragged group. "All of you can stay here and have a medical checkup. Then, when it is safe, you will proceed to the railhead and head to Calcutta." All along, CeCi had noted that refugees straggled into the camp and others—stronger after their rest and medical treatment—left the camp. She knew that soon it would be time for her to leave.

As remote as this place was, it was strangely beautiful. One evening she walked over to the edge of the hill, sat down on a grassy spot, and looked back at the trail she left behind. She was overcome with unbelievable grief. And she realized how much she had changed from the carefree, even arrogant, young woman who had frequented the dance clubs in Rangoon. The British had all but abandoned her kind, but her fellow Asians had accepted her. She had come to terms with the situation and had adopted some of the customs that were common to ordinary Asians, like eating with her fingers. She had been forced to throw in her lot with the Asian people, and they had been good to her. She felt great compassion for all those who had suffered with her—her aunt, Lingham, other Indians in her group, Gurkhas, and the nameless Anglos and Burmese who had become displaced persons in their own country. On this trail of death and privation, of hunger and starvation, of disease and death without dignity, she had learned about the high-castes, the low-castes, and the untouchables; yet the ethnic hostility and hatred seemed to be held in abeyance while on the road of death. The refugees had set aside their differences, and their underlying humanness and humanity came to the surface. They had helped one another. She had seen great sacrifice and kindness. While most of the refugees became inured to the suffering of their fellow refugees, they were not callous. Many who themselves were hungry and in pain would stop and help those in greater pain.

"I wonder if it will make any difference, now and in the future," she mused. "Will our stories ever be known?" Her own family had been torn asunder, and she was just one of thousands who had endured the horror. She doubted that their suffering would be noted. It was not only her and her family whose lives had been ripped apart and destroyed; all the myriad people of the continent had suffered alike. She wondered about these people, "What are their names? What did they look like? Were they single? married? mothers? fathers? daughters? sons? Were they good people? Even if not, did they really deserve this? Did they have dreams?" And she concluded that no one would ever know how many hundreds of thousands had died. "The world will never know of their pain and desperation, and even if they know, they will probably not even care," she thought bitterly. The British and Japanese, she knew, would list all their dead at the end of the war, in well-kept, well-manicured war cemeteries. When peace treaties were signed, they would honor their dead; they would write eloquent epithets. "But what of the refugees," she thought, "who fled the terror of a war that they did not understand? What of the nameless, faceless common people who perished? There will be no lists, no burial sites, no well-maintained cemeteries, no places of remembrance. Their loved ones far away will not even know where, let alone how, they died. They will forever ask themselves, 'did they suffer? did death come quickly?' and they will never know." CeCi thought about the terrible tragedy and hopelessness of the war. She wondered whether she would ever see her mother, father, and brother again. She began to weep.

She was grateful for the help and kindness the tea planters had shown her and her fellow refugees, but her bitterness against the British rulers, the Japanese, and their collaborators was intense. Her tears soon turned into a steady flow, then she convulsed and heaved. She felt gentle hands on her shoulders; a woman sat next to her, staring out over the trail they had traversed. The two women sat in silence. There was no need for words; none were adequate to express their sadness and fear. They sat for awhile until darkness began to set in. Then the woman said, "It is not safe to stay out here in the dark, even so close to the camp. Camp policy requires us to go indoors after dark." Slowly the two women walked back to the hut, embraced silently, and settled in for the night.

The next morning, CeCi went again to the *basha*, this time to receive instructions from the camp guides. "Dangers still lurk," the guides warned. They gave directions and advice, then wished the departing refugees godspeed. The refugees gathered their meager belongings and walked out of the camp.

After they reached the western crest of the pass, CeCi saw a small sign. "Assam State, India," it read. She turned to look back. She felt great relief that she left Burma behind, but she felt sorry for all the people who could not leave, and those who had died in the attempt.

As they crossed the Pangsu pass, the land became flatter, and homes and terraced farms came into view. Then they came upon a motor pool.

With other refugees, CeCi boarded a relief vehicle, the ubiquitous 1500-weight lorry. The seats were wooden benches on the sides, and the refugees were crammed in cheek by jowl. Belongings were stuffed under the benches, and the few children who had survived the trek were seated on the floor, packed into the narrow space between the benches. After a bumpy ride and interminable waits for military conveys to pass, they arrived at the rail head. The narrow-gauge railroad station was crowded, but CeCi felt a comforting sense of familiarity. At one end of the station was the water tank, and beyond it was the coal and wood shed. She could almost envision her father talking to the railway men at the shed. There was a first-class waiting room and another for second class. A few shops were open for coffee and "sweets." The rail head was a virtual beehive of activity. British officials, Assamese, Bengalis, and Manipuris thronged the platform, along with the hordes of refugees. CeCi was comforted by the trappings of civilization, although when she went looking for a bathroom she found it a mess. There seemed to be troops everywhere, and in the siding there was all manner of military equipment—tanks, bulldozers, and earth-moving equipment.

Presently the government agent approached CeCi's group and said, "There will be no other train today." He guided them to the maidan in the center of town, where tents were erected for overnighting refugees. CeCi was surprised to see Americans. "Probably going to their American base at Ledo," she thought, trying to remember what she had heard about the Americans a lifetime ago in Rangoon. In spite of her tattered clothes, CeCi was still beautiful, and as she walked to the tents she heard cat calls. The troops winked at her, and soon it seemed as though they were closing in on her. She was not prepared for this and was wary of them. She knew that they would offer sex and would take her away from the ugliness of the war for a few hours, but that was not true escape. She turned her head and continued to walk away from their attention.

In her tent, which she shared with several other women, who were strangers to her, she wondered again about her future. She knew nobody in India. All she had was the names of some distant relatives. She wondered how they would receive her. "Will they be as welcoming as aunty was in Myitkyina?" she wondered. And the worries mounted. Where she would find work? Where would she live? "No use worrying now," she told herself firmly. "Time enough to worry about those matters later."

In the morning they boarded the train. It was a long goods train, with some passenger coaches attached. There were no amenities, just hard wooden seats. The small narrow-gauge engine sounded its whistle, bringing back memories of her father again. The small engine chugged and then got underway. The carriage swayed and rocked, but the clickety-clack of the swaying carriages soon lulled her sleep and into dreams of riding on her father's train when she was a little girl. She awakened when the train stopped, and was directed by agents at the stop to disembark. The refugees were led to a ferry, then they had another train ride on a broad-gauge rail. Finally they arrived at a huge busy rail station. Calcutta.

Calcutta itself was in the grip of food shortages. CeCi asked directions to the nearest convent, and as she walked the streets leading to the convent, she looked at the city's inhabitants. To her shock and distress, she saw that there were many starving people in the street. "Did I escape one hell only to arrive in another?" She asked herself.

Chapter 31
The Indo-Burma Border

Under cover of darkness, Peter and Jeremy crossed the Myittha River from east to west at Kalemyo. Their worst fears had not been realized; they had not come under fire from the enemy. They were now astride the mountain on the east side in the Kabaw Valley, although still in Burma's dense jungle. They still had to cross the ridge before they would be safe.

This was the wildest place on earth. Eons ago it had been an open sea, but tectonic collisions between the Indian and southeast Asian plates had created a long range of mountains and hills running from the north all the way to the ocean in the south: the Zibyu range; the Patkai, Naga, and Lushai ranges; and the Chin Hills. Dinosaurs had walked here; now their descendants were still here, other creatures, the deadliest creatures on the planet, snakes—the cobra, the viper, the spitting Russell viper, and the Burmese python. Predators large and small as well as elephants roamed the humid jungle. Even more deadly were the organisms that could not be seen by the naked eye: mosquitoes, ticks, and fleas. Here was prime breeding ground for malaria, typhus, and dengue fever. All of these kept man from pillaging this pristine land and allowed other creatures to live and thrive here: beautiful butterflies and beautifully plumed birds—especially the kingfisher bird, with its vivid blue plumage.

In the morning, Peter and Jeremy crested the mountain and descended into the broad valley. They immediately heard gunfire erupt from the high ground, and they hid, not knowing what was going on. Jeremy crawled through the jungle, then returned to report. "These are the mixed Burmese and Japanese forces, probably spies. . . ." Before he could continue, mortar bombs exploded near them, and then from a distance in the west, from India, allied artillery opened up. The Japanese guns were silenced.

The two men lay still, trying to protect themselves from the crossfire as best they could. "We must be near allied positions," Peter said. But as they listened, they could tell that the heavy guns were still some distance away.

When all fire ceased, they continued their descent into the west valley and soon approached the outpost of Fort White near dusk.

On the outskirts of Fort White, Peter and Jeremy sat under what seemed to be billions of stars. They found the place strangely peaceful, and could have stayed out all night. They were still in a daze after months of retreat and being on the run. But soon dark roiling clouds obscured the stars and hung low in the mountains. With a loud crack, they burst with thunder, and a bolt of lightening shot to the earth. Peter laughed. "My grandmother used to pray to the god Arjun, the fire god, that he would not shoot his thunder-bolts at her and would, instead, direct them toward the enemy. Maybe I should try it." No sooner had he finished speaking when the sky parted and the rain came down in endless torrents. No matter what they did, they could not find shelter from the rain. They climbed partway up the small ridge to the west and found a few sticks to build a temporary shelter. But the cold air added to their misery. For them it was something new; they had not experienced this degree of chill before. They pulled their blankets around them tighter, but the water seeped into the ground and made the ground soggy. And they had to continually stave off attack from insects, leeches, mosquitoes, and god knows what other sort of insects and creeping things that also sought shelter from the rain and cold. But eventually fatigue made them sleep. The next morning they were up early and set out again. They soon came upon the road and found it choked with cars, carts, and lorries, pony carts and even some bullock carts, all driven westward by refugees desperate to reach the safety of Imphal in India's Assam province. Peter and Jeremy joined the throng.

There were many sad sights. In a small frontier post they saw bodies in various postures: they lay where they had died; some skeletons seemed to be hugging together, families huddled together in a death embrace. Some of the bodies were still covered with strips of clothing, some showed signs of attack—deep gashes in the bones and missing limbs. Human waste and decomposing body parts were scattered on the roadside, as were dead mules and bullocks. Jeremy was overcome with nausea; he pulled over and vomited, then forced himself to keep his eyes on the road ahead. Occasionally they would find a live person sitting with a faraway gaze. Once or twice Peter went to look and talk but received no response. He was overcome with compassion and pity, trying to share with these pitiful souls a soggy biscuit or two. But most of these souls were beyond caring. Everywhere, the smell of death was overpowering. "It won't be long before we cross the border," Peter reassured Jeremy, in a voice tinged with desperation.

Finally, as they crested a ridge, they saw a large flat plain ahead. Jeremy consulted the map. "This should be the Imphal Plain," he cried excitedly. "Imphal cannot be far!" The men picked up their pace, as did many of the stronger refugees. Soon they came upon the border crossing, marked with a small sign reading "India." A tiny smile crossed their faces. "Finally!" Jeremy said with feeling. "We have arrived!"

At the border, the refugees by and large were allowed into the country and then directed to various camps. The two men, wearing their uniforms, were challenged by the Indian Battalion patrolling the sector. They were taken to the intelligence tent, where a British Captain interrogated them in great detail as to their unit, numbers, and where they had been. Peter was surprised at the suspicion shown by the Intelligence Captain and the length of the ordeal. But soon the Captain realized that they were not spies or collaborators. He debriefed and cleared them, explaining that there were many spies—Burmese and Indian—who had defected to the Japanese. "Moreover," he warned them, "the enemy is east of the river, and lead units of infiltration are just waiting to cross." The Captain pointed to a mess tent with tables set up in front. "Head over there. You can get a good meal and new uniforms. Talk to the aides at the tables to see if they can give you information about your unit."

Peter and Jeremy didn't need much urging. As they headed for the mess tent, Peter said to Jeremy, "I hope we find our unit. I don't even know if it is still viable or if it still exists, but we must try."

"I doubt it still exists," responded Jeremy, "but I may be more hopeful after I have a good meal." After filling their bellies, washing, and donning new uniforms, they talked to the aides at the information tables. "We are with the BurRifs," they said. "Have any others of us made it here?" To their chagrin, they were told that there were no other BurRifs in the area. There was, however, a battered but friendly remnant of the Burma Brigade. The presence of the Indian Black Cats unit was reassuring, and they were attached to that unit. Happy to rest, they made their way to the Black Cats headquarters. As they reported for duty, they discovered that the BurCorps had been disbanded. By now the two young men were so tired that they merely shrugged and looked for a place to sleep. This would be the first safe respite they would experience since they had left Pegu, and nothing was going to deter them!

The next day, after a breakfast that seemed delicious, Jeremy sat down to write a letter to his family. He had not received any letter from his family for a long time, nor had he been able to write himself. He had been deterred from sneaking into Rangoon to learn their fate, but had given it much thought over the past several weeks. "They would not have stayed in Rangoon. I know my father wanted to get CeCi out, by rail to Myitkyina and then by plane to Calcutta, where he has some distant relatives. If they made it there," he explained to Peter, "the Indian Red Cross will be able to forward this letter to them." After chewing on his pencil for awhile, Jeremy wrote:

My Dear CeCi,

I am at the Burma-India border, near the town of Tamu. I cannot say where, for security reasons. I will not bore you with my travails; suffice it to say that Peter and I barely escaped capture by the enemy and are now together. You know, Peter is a fine fellow. We could not have survived if we did not fight and run together. It was touch and go all the way. While in Burma, I was never certain what each day would bring. For the first time in what seems like the longest months of my life, I have a sense that I am in a friendly place.

For many days I have been thinking about you, Mother, and Father. Father told me before I left that he could not flee Rangoon but that he would see to it that you got out of Burma. He would not leave Mother alone in Rangoon. I attempted to see them while I was in Hlegu, but the roads were blocked. I worried about them, don't know where they are.

The worst thing is, I don't know where you are, and how you are. I can only pray that you got out to India and Calcutta. I hope that you got out of Myitkyina by plane, as Father planned. I cannot imagine that you could have walked out through the jungles of Burma. Having walked out myself, I saw how difficult it was for civilians. As we retreated, we saw thousands of refugees. It was pathetic: men, women, and children covered with tattered and dirty clothes, sick and hungry, with eyes so sunken that they looked like ghosts. The stench of death was everywhere. Maggots crawled out their eyes. I could not look; I covered my nose and looked straight ahead. I considered myself lucky that I carried a gun. Peter and I had some money and gold to buy food, but those poor beggars had nothing.

There is nothing but bad news coming out of Burma, especially about how the Burmese collaborators and Japanese are treating people like us, and the ordinary Burmans, the Karens, the Kachins, and the Shans. They suspect us. I worry especially about all the pretty women. The war is far from over, even in India. I cannot tell you more.

I hope I can get away to see you in Calcutta. Write to me, care of BurCorp, Tamu, Assam. I need to know where you are and if you are safe.

Your loving brother,

Jeremy

He re-read the letter to be sure that it contained nothing that would rouse the ire of the censor, then went looking for the Red Cross hut to hand over the letter for mailing. The censor read it dispassionately, then told Jeremy he could seal it. Jeremy did so, then kissed the letter before handing it back. He turned to leave the hut before the censor could see the tears in his eyes.

Chapter 32
A Troubled Occupation

For General Maida, the Japanese military victory was easy, but occupation was less so. To the extreme north, in the Kachin state and northeast India, the Americans had established an air base to supply China. The Japanese plans to subdue and defeat the Chinese did not achieve success; the nationalist government did not crumble as expected. At the same time, the British were furiously expanding and building the British-Indian Army in Assam and Manipur.

Most annoying, the age-old Burmese chauvinism, which the British had suppressed, was now resurfacing, with the number of Burman attacks against the Karens and Kachins increasing by the day. The Japanese hoped to contain this internecine fighting, lest it tie down Japanese forces controlling the country and impair their offensive capability. Nonetheless, in spite of valiant efforts by the Japanese Imperial Army, the long-simmering conflict between the Burmans and the Karens evolved into a full-blown Karen resistance movement. These armed and determined Karens posed the biggest problem for the Japanese. Yet the Japanese clandestine organization encouraged this ethnic conflict, because they saw all Karens as British spies or enemies.

Burma's Karens, who like the Gurkhas had fought fiercely on behalf of the British, now faced dark days. They feared the Japanese but were even more fearful of the Burmese collaborators. Many high-ranking Karen had taken refuge in the delta town of Maungmya, the home town of Saw Lu, Benjamin's friend from Rangoon. General Maida was acutely aware that harsh measures against the pro-British supporters would create problems. But before he could bring order to Burma, Burmese collaborators gathered in Maungmya to settle old scores. On the pretext that some Karens were working for the British K-Force, the collaborators surrounded the village and closed the two roads that led in and out of the town. They ordered British sympathizers to leave the town and surrender, but, not surprisingly, no townspeople emerged. In the late afternoon, the collaborators attacked the town, firing trench mortars randomly into the town. Few homes in Maungmya were of solid construction; most were made of timber and bamboo. The flimsy homes soon caught fire, sending the terrified villagers to the roads to escape. But the collaborators had set up a light machine gun on the road leading into the town, and they fired the gun at the desperate people who were fleeing their burning town. The collaborators shot anything that moved. The people then turned to the jungles, in hopes of fleeing down the jungle trails, but the trails, too, were covered by the collaborators, who mercilessly shot them down. Next the collaborators moved into the village and massacred any men and women who had hidden in underground shelters. They killed the prominent Karen leader and his British wife, with no thought of the repercussions.

General Maida had feared such a massacre, and ordered Sato's regiment to the delta. Because there was no direct road, Sato and his men had to travel part of the way by river and part way by land. He arrived too late. Even Sato was shocked by what he found. In the finest house in town, he discovered that an elderly man of importance and his British wife had been hacked to death. They had numerous deep gashes all over their bodies and had their heads severed. The woman's body was naked and abused in the most grotesque fashion. Sato had the bodies cremated and sent a radio message to General Maida, reporting the carnage.

General Maida was furious. He summoned the commander of the BDF to his headquarters. He demanded that Colonel Koga of the Minami Kikan, the Japanese liaison with the BDF, be present at the meeting. When they were all assembled at headquarters, tension was high. General Maida was visibly upset. His chief of staff stood rigidly behind him, and the two men who had been summoned stood at attention before him. "What explanation do you have for this massacre?" Maida demanded.

Colonel Koga bowed his head and tried to explain. "A mis-communication," he mumbled.

Maida dismissed this explanation by a wave of his hand. He then turned to the Burman. "All activities of your units will cease immediately." He then ordered Colonel Koga to disarm the BDF. "I order you to remove all machine guns and other guns from these units. All Burmese units will be assigned a senior Japanese officer. Disobeying these orders and any other such massacre will be dealt with most severely."

General Maida's anger was not necessarily over the loss of life. He had a larger concern on his mind as he prepared to meet with his superior in Singapore. The Japanese had just experienced their first reversal in the war: the American navy had defeated the Japanese navy at Midway, the radio reported, and had sunk many Japanese ships, especially the big aircraft carriers. American submarines now active in the southern seas were sinking Japanese supply ships. He wanted to show his superior that in Burma, at least, the Japanese were still in control.

Maida was awed that he would personally meet with the commander-in-chief and was nervous as he flew to Singapore. The morning conference opened with little ceremony. The chief of staff of the Southern Army said in somber tones, "There must be no mass killings in Burma. Such events would upset the timetable for future operations. We have promised the Burmese their independence, and to get the cooperation of the Burmese, as well as the Indians, is important to the progress of the Greater East Asia Co-Prosperity Sphere."

Maida blanched. Had the Supreme Commander heard of the massacre at Maungmya? The chief of staff had looked directly at General Maida as he said this, and despite his best efforts, Maida shook his leg nervously.

Sitting quietly next to the chief of staff was a slender man, a highly decorated senior general. Maida turned his attention to this man. What he found remarkable about the General was his moustache, something quite unusual for a Japanese. This was General Tanaka, from the general staff in Tokyo, and now it was his turn to speak. "I just returned from Tokyo," he said softly. "Headquarters is looking for new victories. As you well know, our navy experienced defeats in Tugali and Bougainvillaea, and the program is not going well in New Guinea. I propose that we revive plans to invade India." He paused and looked around the room at the astonished faces. "I have been promised help from certain leaders of the Indian independence movement. Soon, the Indian leader from Germany will arrive in Singapore. He promises us two Indian national divisions."

The men in the room listened in silence, then turned to General Maida. Maida cleared his throat. "Going past the Chindwin River would be dangerous, General," he said tentatively. "Supply lines would be exposed, and we do not have air support." He hesitated, then decided to brave it. "And we have internal problems in Burma. The ethnic groups all hate one another and are bent on exacting revenge for perceived past injustices. With respect, sir, I think that we should consider postponing the plans."

Tanaka continued his briefing as though Maida had never spoken. "A unit of the Indian soldiers of the former British Indian Army is being readied in Singapore now. When it is ready, it will be the nucleus of an Indian National Army, the INA." He paused, then went on. "The Indian National Army will fight alongside the Japanese in the forthcoming invasion of India."

As the meeting ended, Maida took aside the chief of staff. "There are many pro-British elements amongst the Burmese, Karens, and other ethnic groups. Do you have suggestions as to how my units should control these elements and eliminate spies and supporters of the British?"

The chief of staff replied, "Send a request for help from North China. Request help from the biological warfare group known as Unit 731. They know how to kill undesirable people and enemies of Japan, without resort to gunfire or violence." He clapped Maida on the back. "Come. Now let us join the victory party." Sake flowed and geishas entertained the men till late in the night. With a splitting headache and an omen of impending difficulties, Maida returned to Rangoon the next morning.

Just one week after Maida returned to Rangoon, a bomber arrived in great secrecy from Manchuria. Sergeant Takahasi descended the stairs from the plane, carefully carrying a brown box under his arm. As he walked toward the small bungalow, two sentries ran forward to help him with the box. Two *kempeitai* approached Sergeant Takahasi and ushered him to the front seat of a waiting car, loading the box into the back seat, between them. The car took the only road from the aerodrome. The car bounced around as it rushed down the winding road in the dark Burmese night. Soon it arrived at its destination: the compound of the Harcourt Butler Institute.

Inside the Institute, the men carefully opened the box, wearing long protective gloves. They removed a bottle almost reverently and poured its contents into several slim tubes, then lowered the open tubes into a pen that contained big black rats. The technique was painstaking. Fleas from the rats investigated and ingested the contents of the tubes, then returned to the warmth of the rats. The rats began to die. New rats were introduced into the pen to provide new hosts for the fleas. The dead rats were removed and sectioned, and slides were made of the glands to confirm the presence of the plague. The plan was now ready. The head of the unit was Major Hata. His biggest challenge now would be how to keep the infection from going out of control and spreading to the Japanese Army.

Every chair around the table was taken. Major Hata stood stiffly at the head of the table. When General Maida nodded towards him, he opened his portfolio and presented the report. "The experiments are now complete. As soon as we identify the enemy, the infected rats will be introduced and will quickly infect the inhabitants. Once that happens, we surround the home with steel sheets, thus isolating the home. We will remove the inhabitants, who will never be seen again." In a matter-of-fact voice, he continued, "The neighbors will be told that the family died of plague."

When the men in the room all nodded agreement, Major Hata continued to lay out his plans. "We need to find local doctors and workers to carry out the plan. I recommend recruitment of unemployed local doctors."

All heads turned to General Maida. "That will be easy. There is ongoing recruitment for the railway in Siam over the River Kwai. Many who come forward are unemployed local doctors."

The men discussed the details of the people to kill. "There is a big fifth column," General Maida explained. "This includes people left over by the British. Some are Indian, others include the Karen and the Kachin, who remained loyal to the British." He warned, "the Burmese and the Indians will be difficult. It is not easy to identify those loyal to the Japanese empire."

Major Hata interjected. "Even if we kill some innocents with this method, it is better than the alternative. Crude methods such as surrounding and massacring hostile villages will harm the Imperial cause." He looked hard at General Maida and smiled. "This is a very subtle method of destroying British collaborators and spies. Nobody will ever suspect."

As he left the meeting, General Maida remained worried. He knew that the Japanese occupation was not winning the hearts and minds of the local population. Too many of them were too hungry. And too many Japanese troops were themselves too hungry for food and women. "This better work," he mused.

Indeed, months after the Japanese entered Rangoon, their promises for a better life had not borne fruit for the local population. Farmers could not find seed to plant. The Japanese Army had first call on food supplies, and prices for remaining stocks were sky high. News from overseas was adding to General Maida's fears, and try as he might, he could not seem to stamp out all radios among the population.

Benjamin hid his short wave radio under the roof of the back-yard shed. He knew the consequences of discovery: instant execution. But the pervasive presence of the *kempeitai* did not deter him. In darkness he would go to the shed, making sure that everybody was sleep. He would listen to the radio, keeping the volume low. On good days he picked up Radio Australia. He knew that the invincible Japanese war machine was running into difficulties in the South Pacific.

One morning Benjamin was summoned to the house of a neighbor. The neighbor's young son was complaining of severe abdominal cramps. It had at first been just an upset stomach, but then he became quite nauseous; an hour later he started having frequent bowel movements, which would not abate. Within hours he became bedridden. His eyes became sunken, receding deep into their sockets, and soon he became comatose. Benjamin knew that the boy had to get to the hospital, because the only thing that would help him would be to restore the fluids that he had lost. The father hired a rickshaw, and Benjamin took the young boy to the General Hospital while the father stayed home with his wife and young daughters. Benjamin was horrified when the Japanese guard pointed his rifle at him and his charge, forbidding them to enter the hospital. The Japanese had reserved all hospitals and doctors for the Japanese Army. Benjamin had no choice but to take the boy home, where he died a few hours later.

That evening before supper, Benjamin told Reddy what had happened. With a long face, Reddy admitted, "My early enthusiasm for the Japanese is now in tatters. The Japanese are animals! But I still hold out hope that things will change. I still believe in independence."

When the family had gathered for their meager supper, Benjamin agonized whether he should bring up the subject. Finally he decided that it was imperative for him to do so. He cleared his throat. "I have seen terrible things today, and it is not the first day. We must be prepared for a very long and difficult conflict. There will be shortages, hunger, and disease, and the Japanese will treat us brutally. They slap people at random, for the slightest perceived disrespect. I have seen even the lowest soldiers slap men till they to drew blood." The family was silent and Benjamin shuddered. "I have seen worse, also. I have seen men tied to a tree, forced to stand all day in the sun. Any movement brings them a beating."

Reddy supported Benjamin's tale. "The Japanese have issued an order that any person caught with old British gold or sovereign coins will be considered a spy and could be executed summarily." Reddy did not voice his own memory, of having once seen a *kempeitai* cut a man's throat circumferentially, then stick his finger under the skin to try to lift the skin off the man's face. Reddy shuddered involuntarily as he remembered the terrifying screams the victim emitted as the *kempeitai* got the skin halfway up the neck and jaw, then tugged again and again without success. This caused horrible bleeding from the rich blood vessels of the victim's face, and he was to die in a horrible, painful, lingering death.

Benjamin then announced, "Nobody must leave the house. We must keep the windows covered. Girls," he turned to his sisters, "you must not, under any circumstance, open the door. Either Reddy or I will be here at all times, and only we will go to the door."

Mute, Benjamin's grandmother, mother, and sisters nodded their agreement.

Just the next day, while walking down the main road in the center of the city on his quest for food, Benjamin became aware of a noisy crowd ahead.

He heard the familiar Japanese shouts, and saw Japanese soldiers in full combat gear herding a long line of Burmese and Indian coolies. "Some kind of recruiting," he thought. He hesitated just a moment and then turned around to get out of sight. He heard footsteps behind him and a solider grabbed him by the arm and pushed him towards the line. Benjamin had heard the Indians talk about work being offered at a railroad in the jungle. Now the Tamil interpreter was telling the crowd of men that if they signed up for work, they would be fed and paid well by the Japanese Service Corps. Benjamin desperately glanced around for some means of escape. "I am not going to work like a coolie on a railroad for the Japanese!" he vowed.

He quickly realized that the Japanese soldiers were separating laborers from educated men. Benjamin moved toward the group of educated men. The Burmese interpreter asked his status, and Benjamin replied quickly. "I am a physician." The soldiers quickly took him to an office, where he met a Japanese officer. The officer spoke English quite well and asked Benjamin several questions, probing his knowledge. The officer then suggested, "You could work for me. You would not be conscripted. You would be paid. And, you would get a pass that will keep you from ever being sent off to the "jungle railway construction."

Benjamin was stunned and mumbled his gratitude. The officer continued. "I will give you a pass, inscribed in Japanese, which will prevent harassment by the army. We will extend this protection to all of your family."

With no work and little choice, and remembering the thin limbs of his sisters, Benjamin accepted. He was told to report the following day to a unit headquartered about two miles from home.

Many Karen soldiers who had not retreated with their British regiments had stayed behind in their villages on the outskirts of Rangoon. Maungmya, which had been so ruthlessly attacked by the BDF, was just one of several such villages. In their villages, the Karen soldiers found comfort and security with their families. Some, however, continued their efforts on behalf of the British, by joining the clandestine K-Force, an intelligence unit of the Special Operations (SOE) exchange.

The Japanese knew about the K-Force and thus viewed all Karen men as potential enemies and collaborators. They wanted to eliminate the

Karens, and Major Hata had arrived in Rangoon to oversee the extermination of spies by plague. It was really an experiment, to introduce infected rats so as to start an infestation of plague. Their first attempt was to bury sheets of steel in the ground to keep the infected rats in. Then teams spread rats in the village. A few days later, the villagers caught fever and died horrible deaths. But the experiment was actually a failure, as the infected rats burrowed under the steel sheets and spread the infection to other villages. "Nonetheless," Major Hata insisted, "the concept is sound."

Benjamin was only told that there had been an epidemic of plague in a nearby village. "People there have contracted sores, have high fevers, and have died. We need you to determine what the cause of this illness and death is," he was told. The Japanese supervisor of Benjamin's unit drove him to a nearby Karen village. When they arrived in the village, Benjamin found a Karen man who had complained that morning of a chill. By mid-morning he was feeling hot and began to cough. He had dismissed this as a simple cold, but by late afternoon his coughing worsened. He had laid down to rest, and his mother had offered him some soup. He had not been able to eat, and looked hot and flushed. Now he lay on his mat and was muttering incoherently. The Japanese supervisor stood back as Benjamin examined the young man. Soon the mumbling stopped, and Benjamin touched the man's forehead. It was damp, but cold. Benjamin knew that the young man had died.

When Benjamin and his supervisor returned to the unit headquarters, Benjamin saw Japanese soldiers in special quarantine suits carrying cages of rats into the headquarters. The soldiers were being hosed off in the back courtyard of the headquarters. Suddenly Benjamin understood. He realized that he was a tool of the infamous 731 unit, which used disease as a instrument of war. He was overcome with grief at the indiscriminate killing of innocents. Benjamin made his way home. He was overcome with disgust, and to assuage his guilt he stopped at a roadside restaurant. He didn't want to eat, only forget. He motioned to the young waiter dressed in a shirt and *longyi*, "Bring me a bottle of XXX rum." As Benjamin drank, he was overcome with helplessness and anger. The enemy was going to use biological warfare against the Burmese people. They were going to exterminate any people of whom they were suspicious. "If only I had not agreed to work for that officer!" he thought to himself, forgetting that if he had not agreed, he would be working on the jungle railway at this very moment. "I wouldn't know about this and could continue to live in ignorance." Benjamin knew that biological warfare went against all his medical training and the Hippocratic oath. "'The moral depravity of the Japanese knows no bounds!" he thought to himself. "Worse, have I put my family and myself at risk?" He poured himself another drink, and continued to drink until closing time. Benjamin paid the waiter and staggered out, to stumble home in the dark.

Sickness and hunger spread to Benjamin's family. Marge, Benjamin's older sister and the family cook, fell ill. The next day she noticed a redness on the outside of her foot, and the sore gradually increased in size and started to drain. Benjamin cleaned the eschar. While doing so he heard airplanes come over the city in waves, but Marge could not go down to the shelter. When Benjamin came up from the shelter after the raid, Marge started to feel soreness in her groin and by nightfall began to notice lumps. The pain became intense, and by morning the lumps were the size of hen's eggs. Every move was excruciatingly painful, and she remained still. Her chills and fever worsened, and she became moribund and delirious. Benjamin noticed red patches on her abdomen that turned dark and slimy. Her delirium worsened, and she would cry with pain when she moved. Then as night fell, the boils burst, exuding a foul dark pus. Marge's last moments were torturous. Her light brown skin turned black and she became smelly.

Benjamin knew that medically, Marge may have had a fighting chance. But it was hope less, because there were no hospitals for the local people, and medicines were scarce. Most of the chemist's shops, such as that of E. M. De Souza, had been looted. So Benjamin watched Marge fade away. Her abdomen began to distend, and she fell into a coma. Tears formed in Benjamin's eyes as he realized that the typhoid had eaten through the intestinal wall, leading to peritonitis, from which there was no recovery unless emergency surgery could be done. Marge never gained consciousness. The family saw her take her last breath, and they immediately planned the simple burial. As they lowered her into the grave, Benjamin mourned, "These burials are now an everyday occurrence."

Burma's "Independence"

To entice Burmese co-operation, Japanese Radio announced the granting of Independence to Burma. A Prime Minister was appointed, with much fanfare. He came from the gem city of Mogok and had served a short stint the previous colonial government. He was a vainglorious, pompous, and morally corrupt politician. He took great pride in his physique. He was of some sort of mixed ancestry; rumors were that he had a little Anglo blood, and he said that his grandfather had been Portugese. Indeed, he had sharp features and white skin, especially after he had painted himself with make-up. He was fond of saying that his skin was whiter even than that of most Japanese, which ired the Japanese. But the Japanese governor needed him, so overlooked his many peccadillos.

The new puppet Prime Minister set out to build a government, largely through radio propaganda. Each day's broadcast began with a blaring wake-up call in Japanese, urging the youth to join the country's new army, which would fight side by side with the Japanese. After the martial music, the puppet Prime Minister spoke with a high squeaky voice, "Burma owes a debt to the Mighty Imperial government. We thank the great Japanese General and the great Japanese Emperor, who with great benevolence have agreed to grant Independence to Burma." He droned on. "The time has been set by astrologers, and the most auspicious moment for our nation's independence will be 4 A.M."

Duly at 4 A.M. on the appointed day, Burma was declared independent. The Prime Minister intoned, "Burma is now in a state of war against the government of the United Kingdom, its empire, and the government of the United States of America." His voice became even more high-pitched, and he almost shouted, "The Japanese will rearm the Burma Defense Force so it can join the great army of Imperial Japan to prevent forever the return of the British."

Tin Oo listened to the radio breathlessly. He had proudly joined the BDF. Each morning he arose to the call of the Greater East Asia Co-Prosperity Sphere. He learned Japanese at the only schools that were open. He spent more and more time away from home, training for future warfare. Rumors were rampant that the Japanese were suffering defeats in the South Pacific. Tin Oo was determined to protect his country from re-entry of the British colonial armies. He ignored and excused all ill behavior of the Japanese. "They are fighting to make us free," he told himself.

But the Japanese were not winning the hearts of other civilians. In desperation, off-duty enemy soldiers would often prowl the neighborhoods looking for food and women. They swept through towns and villages and took what they could, adding to the woes of the local population. Marauding Japanese soldiers periodically came around looking for livestock as well. Benjamin's grandmother, a feisty diminutive woman, raised chickens and ducks for eggs and kept a cow for milk. She would exchange the eggs and chickens for rice and other staples, keeping starvation at bay. One day a group of soldiers was attracted by Grandmother's chickens in the back yard, and they plunged in, trying to catch the birds. The chickens scattered in all directions, and Grandmother rushed out of the house, brandishing her broom. "The matriarch of the family fearlessly stood up to the Japanese," Reddy related with pride, as he told Benjamin of the day's happenings.

The high-level Japanese officers went to geisha houses in Rangoon to ease their sexual frustrations. The foot soldiers frequented the "comfort stations" on Barr Street, where young women who had been seized and forced into prostitution were kept as sexual slaves. Some desperate soldiers turned to young boys, bribing them and asking them for "ziggy ziggy Askane." The young boys at first were mystified as to what the Japanese were looking for, then the older boys figured out what they wanted: girls for sex. The Japanese were trying to turn the young boys into pimps.

The only women on the streets were the very old or children; all the young women hid in their homes. From to time the Japanese soldiers would turn desperate and become violent. One day they suspected a young girl was hiding in a house and they broke down the flimsy door, pulling the young girl out and gang raping her. That evening, the poor wretch, pretending to fetch water, in desperation jumped into a well and committed suicide.

Only poor quality broken rice was available for the civil population. The Japanese Army commandeered the best crops. The children suffered from multiple vitamin deficiencies and beri-beri. The lack of fresh food caused bloated stomachs, swollen legs, and ugly sores. Skin turned leathery, then ulcers developed in the mouth and on the tongue.

By early 1944, war came closer to Rangoon. New long-range bombers were pressed into service, the most fearsome being the American-built B-29 super-fortress. They carried a large number of huge bombs. They came in waves from the southwest, striking terror into the hearts of Rangoon's residents and sending civilians for cover during the daylight hours. Sometimes it would be near sunset before it was safe to leave the shelters. A wave of these giants approaching and flying overhead and dropping their heavy bombs was most frightening. Their heavy drone could be heard for fifteen minutes before they appeared overhead, unlike the high-pitched noise of the light fighters. The houses would empty and the children would all be bundled into the shallow air raid shelters. The big bombs whistled before they hit their target, shaking the ground all around for as much as a mile away. If they missed, they would kill civilians. The Japanese barracks at the university were a favorite target, and great plumes of fire followed by smoke often would arise from that area. Dust would shoot skyward, in another terrifying plume.

Benjamin walked the two miles to his work at the health unit. He still had to work there to prevent the Japanese from sending him to the front. Benjamin had set off to work one unusually cool morning when he heard the familiar drone of heavy bombers. There were no air-raid sirens, no warning. What was different was that the wave of planes was coming from the east and north. "That is an unusual flight pattern," Benjamin observed. He counted eleven big American super-fortresses, metallic, shining silvery in the bright sunshine. There were no Japanese fighters in the air, only a few puffs from the anti-aircraft guns. Benjamin almost laughed. The puffs always fell short of the high-flying planes. But today, he noted smoke emanating from the left wing and engine of one plane, and it quickly exploded and broke up. Then another plane started to trail smoke, and then another! The planes kept flying but soon lost altitude and started going down. Then another plane burst into flames, and then another! Benjamin had never seen anything like this, and he watched, mouth agape. Soon tiny parachutes started to pop out of the plane. They grew larger and larger, until he could see the shape of humans. While his focus was on the parachutes, on the ground there was frenetic activity by the Japanese. In open lorries, with bayonets fixed, the soldiers rushed to the site where one of the parachutes was coming down. Benjamin joined the rush of people to the site. The local people approached warily, not wanting to provoke the Japanese soldiers. The man was young and injured, an American. He was quickly captured by the Japanese, who began to scream and shoot in the air to disperse the crowd of locals. The man was wounded, but the angry Japanese soldiers handled him roughly, loading him into the lorry and taking him away.

Benjamin returned to work but was curious as to what happened. That night he went to the secret hiding place of his radio and listened to the SEAC radio. The announcer mentioned the raid on Rangoon, but the familiar phrase "all aircraft returned to their bases" was missing. Then he heard on the Japanese radio of the "marvelous achievement of our crack ground battery; they intercepted the enemy raiders. Giving full play to their skillful and effective firing tactics, they instantaneously hit and shot down six enemy planes in rapid succession," screamed the Japanese announcer. This was a game the two sides played: the Japanese overstated the number of allied planes that they shot down, and the allies claimed that they hit only military targets. Benjamin soon developed the uncanny ability to discern the truth from these bombastic statements from both sides.

Chapter 33
The British Regroup

For the Japanese, it had been a spectacular victory and a triumph. With the exception of a few border areas, General Maida had conquered Burma. His victory would have been complete had he been able to trap and destroy the 17th Indian division and the BurCorps. His troops had nearly wiped out the BurCorps and had battered the 17th, but they had failed to annihilate either.

The British retreat from Burma began at Victoria Point in southern Burma, and ended on Burma's northwest border with India. It covered 700 miles and was six months long, the longest retreat for the British Army. The Indian states of Assam and Manipur, and Manipur's capital city Imphal, would be the bases from where the British would not only defend her colony but also launch any effort to re-capture Burma. Here the stragglers from Burma were absorbed into new units and underwent training for new battles to come. Rajputs, Punjabis, Jats, Baluchis, Gurkhas—all the ethnic peoples of India and Burma trained together.

Like so many other men, Jeremy had been sorely shaken and demoralized by his defeat and retreat. Peter tried to reassure him by saying, "We will go back eventually." He had read a report about a new division that was being formed, mostly from remnants of local units. The British had few troops to spare, and there were not many Aussies available. "The British, I think, are already planing to recapture Burma," he consoled Jeremy. "And we will be a part of that effort."

Both men awaited reassignment and were ordered north to Imphal to receive orders and training. As they marched northward with the Black Cats, an Indian battalion, Peter observed, "Northeast India is so different from the steamy plains of Burma. It seems like the most remote place on earth!"

Jeremy nodded agreement. "The monsoon here is close to being over, thank God. Look at the clouds, though, still hanging low over the mountains."

Indeed, thin wispy clouds draped the high peaks on the cool mornings, sneaking down into the valleys like fingers of fog. Still, on some days, the sky opened up and the rain came in sheets. Those days also brought cold, damp, and gloomy weather, which chilled to the bone. "I may be Indian," Peter said, "but I don't think this Indian weather is in my genes! I find it depressing."

The men remained jittery and jumpy, and arguments were not uncommon. Although they ate regular meals, they still had not eaten enough to put meat back on their bones. Jeremy and Peter were worried about being accepted by the other troops, especially the Black Cats.

"I always think that, behind our backs, they are talking about how unreliable BurCorps is," Jeremy complained.

They finally arrived at Imphal. It stood at the top of the broad Imphal plain. To the west was a large lake, Logtak lake, and to the east were hills up to the border of Burma. A narrow, winding road headed north to Kohima and thence to Dimapur. Astonishingly, the men learned that in order to get to Calcutta from Imphal, one would have to traverse this road northward to Dimapur. At Dimapur a narrow-gauge rail line headed south to a river ferry, and only on the other side of the river did a broad-gauge rail line run down to Calcutta.

"What a quiet place!" Jeremy commented. Used to the large city of Rangoon, he and Peter found Imphal a very small town.

"But for now," Peter responded, "I am thankful for the quiet here. The war seems to be suspended, and I feel as though I can concentrate on restoring my health."

Both men were anxious for news from Burma. Every chance they had, they would listen to the enemy radio, which announced, "Plans for the formation of the Indian National Army are going well. Many Indians, former soldiers of the British, are joining. The core will be formed with remnants of Indian divisions form Malaya, to be led by Subas Chandra Bose." Each broadcast would end with martial music and the usual victory shouts of "banzai!" In the mess, among the Indian troops, broadcasts such as this created a great deal of curiosity and heated discussion.

The months spent in Imphal gave Peter and Jeremy ample time to recover from their arduous retreat through the length of Burma. Uncertainty was very unsettling. Their greatest disappointment was to learn that their new orders would require them to leave the Black Cats battalion that they had been training with. They were told to take transport north to their new assignment.

They rode northward in a new American-built lorry, bigger, stronger, and more comfortable than the British-made vehicles they were used to. The narrow road zig-zagged and hugged the side of the mountain. Steep gullies and ravines fell off the side of the road, and every now and again the road would enter a narrow tunnel. The sides of the mountains and hills were covered with trees not seen in the dry plains of Burma: thick clumps of pine, eucalyptus trees with their distinctive smell, cedar, and oak. For miles there would be no houses. It was eerily quiet; the only noise was the wind rushing through the valleys and the rustle of the leaves. Jeremy and Peter were impressed.

"This land never ceases to amaze me," Peter remarked. "Here it is hauntingly beautiful, but remote and inhospitable."

Just as he spoke, a large lake came into view, and in the bottom of the valleys rivers could be seen. The sun reflecting off the water added to the beauty.

"It may be beautiful," Jeremy said through clenched teeth, "but it is also terrifying!"

He held so tightly to the railing of the lorry that the blood drained from his fingers. Their lorry had just approached one of the road's many hairpin turns and confronted another lorry coming down the ridge in the opposite direction. The road allowed for only one vehicle at a time, and both lorries stopped. Then began a dangerous vehicular dance, in which each lorry would inch forward, then backward, like shunting engines, until one could edge past the other and continue its climb. Jeremy sighed with relief.

"It is a miracle that the lorries do not run into each other!" he exclaimed.

But the drivers seemed oblivious to any danger, careening downhill so fast that before long, both Jeremy and Peter were holding their breath in fear. The sun was behind the tall mountain to the west when they finally arrived at their destination: Kohima, the capital of India's Nagaland. The men alighted, sore and unsteady.

The next morning, the Intelligence officer, an Englishman, told them at their briefing. "Few companies of your BurRifs survived the retreat. Right now, various remnants are northeast of here, at a place called Phek. You will stay here to train for a short while, to acclimatize yourselves before being reassigned."

The two men quickly settled into their new surroundings. The setting was beautiful, but remote. Although just a few miles separated the place from the fury of the bloody and brutal war to the east, it seemed far away. Their days were filled with drills and weapons training. They dug foxholes and bunkers, and felled trees to roof over the bunkers. The nights were chilly and sometimes windy and cold. There was nothing much to do, so the men explored their new environment with interest. They found some of the Naga tribal people friendly, but found others, such as the Kuki, indifferent. The Nagas had a fearful reputation, but seemed in reality to be quite peaceful. They lived separately in their villages, in an uneasy peace with the Kuki.

When they had free daytime hours, Peter and Jeremy took long walks through the tea country just north of the town. The green hills and shallow valleys were covered with tea plants. The mild climate and plentiful rain had brought British tea planters to this remote land many years ago. The tea plants had originally come from China and had taken to the hills with a vengeance. Obstreperous British planters had set up little villages, with bungalows in Tudor style, teak houses, plentiful servants, including *mali*s [gardeners], gardens, well-manicured lawns, and tennis courts.

On one of their walks, Jeremy confided to Peter, "I have always dreamed of building a house on stilts like these, with a wide veranda and servant quarters in the rear, all enclosed in a secure compound. I would enjoy breakfast on the veranda and savor the sunset in the evening."

Peter agreed. "I've had similar dreams. Especially now, after everything we've been through, this tranquility is very attractive."

Peter gestured to the east. "It is hard to believe that the horror of the war over there will soon replace this tranquility."

"Yes," said Jeremy sadly as he looked around at the idyllic setting. "Maybe it is just a pipe dream. Maybe there will be nothing left after the war." Rumors among the Indian officers were that times were changing fast and that the British club in town, too, welcomed others, not just the white tea planters.

"Let's see if those rumors are true," Jeremy cajoled Peter. "Before the war, mess halls were separate for 'native' officers and for the white officers, and that tradition is now being shattered by the war."

Peter was hesitant. "Do you really think the planters will have changed their attitudes?" he asked. "They have not fought with us; they probably still cling to their traditions."

But Peter was thirsty, so acquiesced, and the two men went to the club. The club was built on a high terrace, just below the main garrison. From the outside, it looked like all the other buildings—long and low—but inside it looked like a true British pub, complete with draught beer taps, dart board, and pool table. The bar and tables were toward the far end. Compared to the temperature outside, the club seemed warm and inviting. Peter and Jeremy entered nervously and sat together, not quite sure how they would be received. They didn't see any men from their company in the club. After a wait, the Assamese bearer, himself an Indian, looked at them with resentment, then asked them "What do you want?"

"Do you have Empire beer?" asked Peter.

"Yes," the bearer replied.

"Then bring us two," Peter requested.

The bearer strode off without another word. The two men looked around and took stock of their surroundings. The club was getting crowded, and most of the seats were taken. There was just one free stool, at their table. Presently a young English lieutenant of the Assam regiment entered the club. Looking around for a seat, he spotted the free stool at Jeremy and Peter's table. He hesitated a moment, then made his way to the table, avoiding eye contact with Peter and Jeremy. He didn't say a word; just drank his beer down as quickly as possible and left.

"He probably doesn't want his fellow officers to tease him about having shared a table with WOGs," Peter observed wryly. "We may march together and even fight together, but socialization is still impossible and probably will never change."

The two men took their beers outside, where the air was cold but fresh. "Fresher than in that stifling club," Jeremy agreed.

The very next morning, Jeremy was summoned to the command tent of the newly formed battalion. He saluted the major and accepted his invitation to sit, wondering why he had been summoned. Their ensuing conversation astonished him.

"How much Burmese can you speak?" asked the Major.

"I can speak but cannot read, Sir," Jeremy replied.

"Do you have any radio background?"

"I have some familiarity with Morse code, Sir."

"Good. You will be re-assigned. You will receive some communications training, including more morse code, radio operations, and encryption. Upon completion of your training, you be assigned to Force K, the spy agency. You will be sent back into Burma, sometimes behind enemy lines. Your task will be to ascertain Japan's intentions. Needless to say, this assignment will mean the utmost secrecy. You cannot reveal it to anyone, even your closest friends. Do you understand?"

"Yes, Sir," Jeremy saluted. "It will be an honor, and I will do my best."

"I'm sure you will, son; I'm sure you will," smiled the Major. "Dismissed."

Stunned and honored at the same time, Jeremy returned to his tent and sought out Peter, feeling guilty that he could not share his news with his long-time friend.

"I have been reassigned," he said, "but I cannot say where."

He embraced Peter, gathered his few belongings, and left for the new training camp. Peter was envious of Jeremy, but also happy that he seemed energized by his new assignment, whatever it was.

Chapter 34
Kohima Ridge

The reformed battalion was full of new faces. Now it had more Indians, Assamese, Karens, and other remnants of the Burma Rifles than it used to have. The troops trained vigorously and incessantly in anticipation of a Japanese attack. Although Peter got on well with the other men in his unit, he missed Jeremy. They had been friends from childhood and had endured difficult times during war. Peter managed to get hold of some books and spent hours in the mess catching up with reading. But he also was interested to learn more about the environment in which he found himself living and training. He knew that a major battle was looming, as the Japanese were intent on capturing the British bases in India as well as driving them out of Burma.

Now alone, Peter decided to take a walk by himself, to get a sense of the geography of the place. Kohima was actually a series of outposts atop seven hills, spread for about one mile along a sharp and narrow ridge. The main road from Imphal reached Kohima from the south and wound around the eastern side of the ridge, taking a sharp bend before heading west to Dimapur. The northernmost point of the Kohima ridge was a Naga village, located on a flattened area above the seven hills. The village was now deserted, its inhabitants having fled into the forest. They would provide invaluable service later.

Peter climbed to the Naga village and observed that its largest structure was a long, low *basha*, a communal warehouse with open sides and a thatched roof. In the middle of what had once been the village, Peter spotted a small church and assumed it was a Baptist church. "Once they hunted human heads," he mused; "now they have been converted by the American Baptist Mission." He wondered how the American Baptist Mission had arrived in this remote place of Britain's empire, and why they had come such a distance; clearly they had succeeded in converting the people and building churches.

From the abandoned Naga village, Peter got a panoramic view of the entire Kohima area. To the east lay the dense jungle-covered Somra Hills, with a few trails leading into the hills from the Naga village. Further east, he knew, lay Phek and the Chindwin River, but they were too far distant to see. Any Japanese attack would come from the east, he was sure, but through the Somra Hills? Or from further south?

To the west were dense wooded hills as far as he could see. Dimapur lay to the west, but there were many miles of jungle and woodlands between Kohima and Dimapur. Peter shivered. He had read that the Bengal tiger and the Indian leopard, both cunning and dangerous, lived in this area. He looked around him at the evergreens, pines, alders, and tall cedars interspersed with giant teak, padauk, and tamarind trees and wondered what was lurking within them. He felt small and vulnerable.

He looked to the south and could see the hills of Kohima clearly. Closest to him was Treasury Hill. Treasury Hill was actually a low hill. From the buildings on Treasury Hill, the colonial bureaucracy and the deputy commissioner had administered the semi-autonomous state.

Just to the southwest of Treasury Hill were a number of terraces, with the road hugging the edge of the lowest terrace, actually a mound, closest to Treasury Hill. The main road cut into the hillside here, then bent to the west toward Dimapur. Beyond the mound was a series of terraces cut into the mountainside. On the first terrace stood the District Commissioner's bungalow. Peter had explored it previously and knew that its architecture was typical for the country. A wide veranda spanned the entire front of the bungalow, and smaller verandas wrapped around both sides. It was surrounded by well-manicured lawn, with beds of multi-hued flowers. The kitchen lay beyond the bungalow, separated from the bungalow in typical colonial style. East of the bungalow and kitchen was a low building, narrow and long, which was the garage, where vehicles were stored and maintained. On the next terrace, just above the bungalow, were the servants' quarters. Above this narrow terrace the land rose steeply to a large, flat area. Here a tennis court had been built, running north to south along the breadth of the flat area. The tennis court had somehow seemed out of place in the remote jungle, but Peter supposed that it had allowed the tea planters, in better times, to enjoy a little taste of home. Now, he remembered from one of his previous exploratory walks, it looked forlorn: the net was sagging, and the white lines were barely visible; grass grew in the many cracks that ran across the surface. Above the tennis court was yet another steep rise, upon which stood the British club. To the south of this entire terraced sector, the land rose gradually then, dipped into a gully, and then continued upward to form the base of Garrison Hill.

Further to the west of the bungalow sector lay Hospital Ridge, which consisted of a ridge and, beyond it, a spur, where two Indian General hospitals were located. Beyond that ridge the land dropped off sharply into a heavily wooded ravine. Peter frowned. The ridge looked utterly indefensible to him, and he wondered if medical services would remain centralized in this location much longer.

Beyond the bungalow sector and Hospital Ridge were, in order, north to south: Garrison Hill, Kuki Hill, Supply Hill, Detail Hill, and Jail Hill. Barely visible in the distance was a low ridge called Transport Ridge by the men.

On the summit of Garrison Hill stood a large house, part school and part meeting place. "In peaceful times, the tea planters and their families must have admired the magnificent scenery from that position," Peter thought. He spotted a trail behind the house. "I can just see the ladies taking long walks along that trail," he speculated. Then his thoughts turned to the reason he was here at all. "It is probably the best defensive position, as it is situated right in the middle of the all the hills."

Peter hiked down from the Naga village, revisited the DC bungalow sector, and climbed Garrison Hill. Between the tennis court and the summit of Garrison Hill, but high on the slope of Garrison Hill, he passed the battle command post that had recently been established. It was located in a large trench covered with a corrugated iron roof and allowed a clear view of both the DC bungalow and the Naga village. From this point, Peter could also see the hospital and began to see why the garrison commander had located his battalion command post here. Located below the ridge, it provided safety for the command post but could also provide access to and communication with all the hills along the Kohima Ridge.

Compared to its neighbor Garrison Hill, Kuki Hill seemed small. It was so called, Peter recalled, because a unit composed of Kuki tribesmen had been stationed there in the Naga War of 1879. Now it was just a landmark, defended by a small contingent of troops cobbled together from various regiments.

But further south at Supply Hill, there was quite a bit of activity. The men had cleared the land and for months had been storing ordnance there for the forthcoming battle. Lately, lorries had been busy all day, dispersing supplies to each unit along the ridge. The commander was keen to protect the supplies and wanted to decentralize their location. Peter remembered also that medical teams had arrived at each unit, and he suspected that he was not the only one who feared that Hospital Ridge might be indefensible.

Detail Hill, still further to the south, was where the mess was located and where the garrison's food was prepared. Peter, still remembering his days of hunger, thought very fondly of Detail Hill. Like Kuki Hill, it seemed low in comparison to its neighbors.

Very close by, just across the road, lay Jail Hill. It was higher than Detail Hill and sharply peaked. It took its name from the fact that it had once housed the local jail. Now it housed another ammunition depot and a petrol depot.

Further south of Jail Hill and somewhat to the west was Transport Ridge. There seemed to be a variety of cookhouses and *bashas* there, but Peter was not sure what really went on there.

Peter walked the length of the mile-long Kohima Ridge, all the way to Transport Ridge. From there he turned to the southwest and came face to face with the formidable Aradura Spur. He paused briefly and looked heavenward, where the peak pierced the sky. As his eyes traveled back downward, he identified both deciduous and evergreen trees. Slowly he climbed the trail that he found, passing many spirit houses and places of offering along the way. As he approached the top of the spur, he became short of breath and found himself huffing and puffing, unaccustomed to the altitude. His breath formed little clouds in front of his face in the cold air. He finally reached the top of the spur and gazed around him. "This must be the abode of the Naga spirits and gods," he mused. His thoughts ran freely. "That makes sense. Like the Greek gods on Mount Olympus, the Naga spirits and gods can observe the comings and goings, the failures and triumphs of mortals from this vantage point." Then he thought pensively, "they will not be pleased with what will soon transpire here; they will witness the ultimate folly of man, as the Japanese and British armies collide."

As he returned to his tent that evening, Peter pondered all that he had seen. To him, Kohima seemed defensible, even though it stretched a full mile. There were few trails coming from the east, which would undoubtedly be where the Japanese would come from. He was heartened by the preparations that seemed to be going on, decentralizing ammunition, food, and medical services. He knew a battle was coming, and he knew it would be difficult. "But at least this time we are making a stand and have a chance to plan," he thought. "Not like at Moulmein." As he stood there he was startled by a strange noise. Instinctively he took cover and looked up to see an enormous bird with a huge yellow crown and a beak: a great Indian Hornbill. In the days that followed he would note a great number of beautiful birds; in this remote place there was great beauty of nature.

Chapter 35
Life in Occupied Rangoon

More than two years after the start of the war, at the headquarters of Japan's Burma Area Army, some of the assuredness and arrogance was drained from General Maida. Tokyo sent an emissary to Rangoon to gain a military appreciation of the situation. Nervously pacing in the Lion Throne room of the former Governor's mansion, Japan's leading generals of the 15th Army awaited the arrival of the veteran general, Isomura. Finally he strode into the room, and the generals took their seats. The meeting convened.

Isomura opened the meeting with Tokyo's assessment of the Imperial Army goals. The men listened in disbelief. It took some time to sink in. General Maida took the opportunity to question the army's goals. "We cannot maintain normal operations without more supplies," he objected. "Even Japanese staples like rice are in short supply, and the morale of my troops is diminishing in direct proportion to the amount of food and weapons they receive."

Isomura listened patiently and then responded, "Shipping is difficult. Allied submarines are sinking unescorted transports."

Maida was quick to interject, "Where is the Navy? Why is it not defending the transports?"

Isomura was surprised at Maida's tone. He avoided answering the question and instead said, "Soon the Burma–Siam Railroad will be completed. I will make sure that you get more supplies then," he promised. "In the meantime," he continued, "you will proceed with the plans I have laid out." He handed the details of the orders from the Imperial Army high command, and the meeting ended. General Ugaki, from Maymyo, engaged the veteran general in a quiet conversation, its topic kept secret from the other generals in the room.

After the meeting, General Maida expressed his frustration to his chief of staff. "Supplies from Japan and Singapore are dwindling, and allied submarines are sinking almost all the surface ships plying the South China Sea. I see the morale of my troops sinking ever lower. I cannot snap my fingers and get those supplies from Japan and Singapore to this theater." He drummed his fingers on the tabletop, then directed his chief of staff, "Call the Prime Minister of Burma here."

Dressed in his long silk *passo*, tied in a large knot, Burma's Prime Minister sat uneasily next to his Japanese advisor. After a period of silence, General Maida began to lecture the Prime Minister. "The war is now almost three years old. We have liberated all of Burma from the yoke of colonialism and given you independence. But you and the Burmese seem not to appreciate what the Emperor and the Japanese empire has done for Burma." He continued, "You must energize the flagging support for war in Burma among your people." He paused for the fact to sink in. "The civil population must share the burden of the war, and any opposition to doing so must be dealt with most harshly."

The Prime Minister shifted uncomfortably in his chair while he listened to General Maida lay out his plan.

"Exhort your people to support Japan's Burma Area Army and the Burma Defense Force. Their rice and staples must be given first to the glorious Japanese Army." He went on, "Exhort your people to fully co-operate with their great Japanese friends. Admonish your youths to join the Independence army. We must fight shoulder to shoulder to protect Burma's newly won independence, and to prevent the return of the British and their lackeys."

The Prime Minister managed to gasp out a tentative objection in his high-pitched voice. "The Burmese people already are starving. Resentment is growing." He then went into a tirade against the British, but the Japanese general cut him short with the comment, "Recruitment for the army has in fact gone quite well. You need to speed it up and increase the numbers."

The Prime Minister was taken aback by the tone of the Japanese General. He suppressed his resentment at the plight of his own people, but knew he was complicit in it. Hunger and malnutrition were stalking his people; there were no hospitals for the Burmese and no medicines for them. The lack of supplies, arms, and motor transport was affecting the fighting capacity of the fledgling army. He knew he should complain about the harsh treatment of civilians by Japanese soldiers. His people suffered continual physical abuse, and endured slapping even for minor offenses such as not bowing to the Japanese. But the Prime Minister, being a coward, could not bring himself to complain. Instead he meekly offered, "air raids have totally disrupted our planting. Besides, there are no goods trains, and there is no petrol available for lorries, so transport of food to urban areas is difficult."

General Maida waved away such explanations. All the Prime Minister could do was bow and promise to make the farmers grow more crops, fully knowing that it was not possible. "We will redouble our efforts," he murmured. Secretly, he worried about the loyalty of the civilians who remained in Rangoon. Their lives were becoming difficult, if not desperate, with each passing day, as food and medicines were siphoned off to the Japanese troops.

At the Thomas's home, the cupboards were bare. Even though Benjamin was being paid for his work, food was scarce. What was available had to be purchased by gunnysacks of worthless Japanese notes. The children were continually hungry; the rice and dried fish Benjamin brought home barely nourished their growing bodies. One evening he asked Reddy what he thought. Reddy looked sad and was silent for a long time. Then he spoke.

"I must confess that I took satisfaction in seeing the British soldiers humiliated. But how wrong I was about the Japanese! Their behavior is sordid and inexcusable. I think, however, that the tide is turning against them and their collaborators." Reddy looked at Benjamin sadly. "You can see yourself that the city is becoming shabby. Garbage is piling up in the streets, causing an abominable stench that is pervasive. The stores are empty; even rice, which was always plentiful before, is scarce."

"Not only that," interjected Benjamin, "medicines, even aspirin and bandages, are costly, if they can be had at all. But," he continued, "my gravest worry right now is food. How to feed the family."

Reddy advised, "you have to get to the market early, before anybody else gets there, even before the market opens. Then you have to use your contacts. I am not as well connected as you."

"Thank you, Uncle," Benjamin said. "You have done much for our family, and we are grateful. Every day when I am at work, I am thankful that you are at home, protecting the womenfolk. These are awful times!"

The next morning Benjamin rose early and walked to the east end of town. He wore sandals whose soles were made from old tires, because traditional Burmese slippers were no longer available in the marketplace. Walking in these crude sandals was difficult. The heat penetrated the rubber soles and burned his feet. He noted that many people he passed wore only rags and crude clothing made of gunnysacks. Yet he continued on. He was headed for a small fishing villages on the bank of Pazundaung Creek where, in spite of the war, small fishing boats went out to the sea each day. They were harassed by Japanese patrol boats and allied aircrafts, but each day they brought their catch back to the little port. Here the villagers made *nga pyi*, the pungent fish paste that the Burmans so loved. But they also salted fish and then left it out in the open to dry in the intense sun. Benjamin walked to the fish market. Flies covered the fish, and the women waved the flies away so he could pick well-cured fish. He pointed to the fish he wanted and the seller cut it into inch-thick cubes. Benjamin paid her with a stack of Japanese 100-rupee notes and hurried home, pleased with himself. At home he washed the fish and instructed his mother. "Add just one cube to each meal. It will provide protein and other nutrients for the family and will last. I don't know when I'll be able to get more. It takes an entire gunnysack of Japanese money to buy just one meal!" His mother nodded wearily. So much had changed in her life! She took the wilted vegetables that Benjamin had found in the market the day before, added water and one cube of dried fish, and cooked them over the charcoal fire. Her spices were dwindling also and were irreplaceable. Their meals were becoming increasingly bland.

Indeed, with each passing day inflation rose, making the Japanese currency less and less valuable. The blue-green notes were imprinted with "The Japanese Government promises to pay 100 rupees" and so on, but 1000 rupees could not buy a cup of rice and a sprig of greens. As soon as he received his salary, Benjamin spent the money on food, knowing it would buy less the next day. On the streets, he noted that the young children looked increasing ill, with bloated bellies. Reddy had told him of rumors that the allies were adding to the woes of the civilian populace by torpedoing most supply ships, and Benjamin's information from the radio reports seemed to confirm this. "Odd," he thought, "how in war our allies make our lives more difficult and dangerous as well as the enemy."

Tin Oo too was also feeling the despair. He worked for the Minami Organ, a small group of Burmans who had trained in Japan and had now returned to Burma to liberate the country. He had followed the exploits of the Oki detachment and had been thrilled to learn how it had liberated the coastal city of Tavoy in 1942. He had been inspired by speeches delivered by the Japanese colonel Koga, who had exhorted the army, "We must now land a final blow to the colonialists and their lackeys, the British-Indian Army!"

Tin Oo had joined the Burma Defense Force (BDF), had competed his officer training, and had advanced quickly through the ranks. Now he was a lieutenant. His unit had been attached to the northern expedition force of the BDF and had received orders to move north. The unit would attack and clear the area across the Chindwin River, to the Burma border. Tin Oo was eager for action and excited about his orders. Nonetheless, he wondered about supplies, as in Rangoon food was becoming scarce and rumors were rife that ammunition was limited.

Before he left for the front, Tin Oo went to see his mother in her home village. She had lost weight and now looked aged. "The Japanese soldiers are getting brutal in their theft of food and livestock," she complained. "I have not had any chicken or oil for cooking in weeks. The vegetable market is rarely open, and when it is, the prices are always higher than they were the previous day." She spat out the words. "Life under the British was better, my son." She admonished Tin Oo, "don't you believe all the propaganda that the Japanese tell the public; instead, look at what they do."

Tin Oo listened in silence, not wanting to admit that he had already come to the same belief. He knew that things were not going well and that the high command of the BDF was beginning to doubt the Imperial Army goals. But he put on a brave face. "Don't worry, mother," he said. "I will be all right, and the house will be all right, too. Tin Hla and her husband will keep an eye on the house; in fact their son and his wife will live there, so that it is not vacant and does not present a temptation for looters. Soon the war will be over, and we will return home and live in a free Burma."

His mother spat again. "Where exactly will you be going?" she asked.

Tin Oo dodged the question, telling her that he would not receive his orders until the next day. He patted her hand. "Don't worry, mother. I will write and will keep in touch with you."

With a heavy heart and a degree of angst, Tin Oo left his mother and returned to his unit. The next day the unit reported to the train station for transport north. In front of the engine were two open carriages filled with firewood instead of the typical coal. The coaches showed their wear; without parts from the Scottish company, they were held together with a variety of ropes and wires. Jury-rigged to keep it running, the train looked like it might not go the distance. The troops boarded the coaches in silence, and the train pulled out of the station after dark. The coaches were dirty, and many of the seats were broken or missing. The coaches needed paint, inside and out. The men received their orders to go north to Mandalay, then disembark and proceed by foot to Shwebo and, thence, to their assembly point. Tin Oo settled in for a long ride and tried to get some sleep.

At Mandalay, the weary troops climbed down from the coaches. A Japanese commander greeted them and sent his RMS to examine the ragged-looking troops. Then he addressed the troops, repeating all the usual Japanese propaganda. He closed his address with the admonition, "Be brave! Great victories lie ahead!" he said, and then turned on his heel and entered the waiting staff car.

The troops set out on foot. They had two days of slogging through the jungle ahead. Some of the trails were marked, but more were unmarked. Finally they arrived at Tamanthi, across the Chindwin River, where they bivouacked and began to prepare for the offensive. Within days, many of the force were felled by malaria, typhus, and various other fevers. Nonetheless, they were ordered to continue their preparations. The drills and training seemed endless, and the marches left them worse for the wear. The young men were made to shout "banzai!" three times as they started and again when they returned to the barracks. Finally they were deemed ready for action and were ordered to march northward again.

As they moved north, they encountered enemy troops, who seemed to be well equipped, well supplied, and well fed. The enemy troops did not flee this time but held their ground and fought the Japanese. In contrast, the Japanese were showing fatigue, and their equipment was inferior to that of the British. Still, they persevered and hoped to conquer the rest of Burma that remained in British hands. Fighting off enemy attack, the troops continued their northward march. They were attacked by enemy aircraft almost every day, and there was no mistaking the origin of the aircraft; the RAF markings were clearly visible. The men took cover as best they could, then set out again. Without air cover from their own side, the road to the border was difficult, and the men began to grumble to themselves.

After one long day's march, the men rested on the outskirts of a village. They hastily dug shallow trenches and foxholes for cover. Suddenly the darkness was shattered by lighting and thunder, then the sky opened up and the rains came. The deluge poured rain into the hastily prepared trenches, and the weary men clambered out to seek better shelter. They wrapped themselves in their rain ponchos and clustered together in small groups to wait out the night. Even the fierce Japanese were no match for the Burmese monsoon. Mud, mud, thick grey mud, seas of mud would not allow anything to move, and the troop movements were delayed.

The Japanese commander was anxious to break through to Imphal, where the Allied headquarters were located. He sent a Burmese officer on a scouting mission ahead, to assess enemy strength. Tin Oo went along on patrol, along with several of his comrades. As dusk began to fall, they approached an area of dense clumps of bamboo. Over on the ridge they could see some huts. Tin Oo and his patrol were not familiar with the north country but nevertheless went on gamely, braving the elements. Suddenly a shot rang out ahead, and the Japanese point man fell on the spot, shot through the head. Tin Oo immediately jumped into a shallow ditch, just as a machine gun came alive and sprayed fire. The patrol backtracked and approached the machine-gun nest from the side. Advancing through the high grass, they spotted heavily armed Naga tribesmen. Tin Oo put his finger to his lips, crawled through the grass, threw his stick grenade, then buried his head. The explosions took his breath away, but the firing stopped. This was the first time that he had killed a man, and he was strangely shaken and exhilarated at the same time. He quickly made his way back to the patrol through the grass, and the patrol moved forward to assess the enemy dead. When they approached the machine-gun nest, triumphal shouts of "banzai! banzai!" erupted. The Japanese examined the bodies, discerning that they were Nagas. The Japanese winced: Tin Oo had heard reports of captured Japanese who had endured terrible torture before they were killed by the Naga. It was said that they put sharp sticks up the prisoner's penis. Tin Oo shivered. He took some maps and papers and left the bodies as they lay.

As the patrol returned to camp, Tin Oo observed something that shocked and deeply troubled him: one of the soldiers failed to salute the Japanese major and in consequence was slapped, then beaten. Before he could process what he had seen, however, artillery shells exploded all around. Tin Oo had not heard or experienced such heavy gunfire. The guns seemed to be heavier than those the Japanese had. The fire was so accurate and intense that the men could not move from their cover. Finally, during a lull, the patrol beat a speedy retreat back to camp. Tin Oo accompanied the patrol leader as he informed the battalion commander of the strength of the enemy. "Sir," he stammered, "I don't think we can stand that kind of fire power." The commander agreed. "Our first encounter with the new British enemy did not go well. We will not retreat, but we will take a different route to our destination." He ordered Tin Oo and his comrades back across the Chindwin River, to Pakoku.

While awaiting further orders, Tin Oo heard rumors from Rangoon. Increasingly, the Burmese people felt that the independence they had been given was false, that they were worse off than before the war. The puppet Prime Minister continued to support the Japanese, but the Burmese people were becoming restive. Even the new soldiers were grumbling about inadequate weapons and training. The BDF battalions were under-strength; they had no other offensive weapons. The Burmese officers commanding the small army were dissatisfied, and there was talk of revolt.

One night, one of Tin Oo's fellow Burmese officers whispered, "Japan cannot win the war against the allies. In the high circles of the BDF there is a secret plan to revolt, especially if the allies take central Burma."

Tin Oo was shocked. But his mother's words rang in his head, and he recalled vividly the soldier who had been slapped and beaten for such a minor infraction as not saluting a Japanese officer. He continued to move with the Japanese until they arrived at Pakoku.

At Pakoku, the same Burmese captain surreptitiously called a conference of a handful of his fellow Burmese officers. "A very important man from the BDF headquarters is here with an important message," he whispered. Tin Oo recognized the man immediately. After swearing the officers to secrecy, the visitor informed the officers that there would be a secret meeting at the Pongyi *chaung* that night. "Come. You will hear an important message from the BDF. You will need to use this password." In a low voice he imparted the password, and the men returned to their tents.

Tin Oo took a catnap, and at midnight he walked to the nearby monastery. When challenged, he used his password to enter. Inside he met his fellow officers, all looking a little worried and nervous. Very quickly, and much to the men's surprise, a high-ranking officer from the BDF came in through the back door, accompanied by a major. Tin Oo immediately recognized Major Maung Maung from Rangoon. The Major made the assembled men take a vow to secrecy, then introduced the high-ranking officer: Colonel Kyaw Khin, from headquarters in Rangoon.

"My fellow Burmans," the colonel said slowly and softly, yet with great import. "A great change has taken place. Major Maung Maung here and I have left Rangoon. Our whereabouts are secret. We have endured much at the hands of the Japanese. They have betrayed us. The independence they promised us was a sham. Our country has been ravaged, our women have been insulted, and now they have turned against the *sanga* [brotherhood of monks] itself."

He paused. Tin Oo was shocked, but a thrill ran down his spine. Here were Burmese officers expressing exactly what his mother had expressed and what Tin Oo himself had been considering.

Colonel Kyaw Khin continued. "You will receive a coded message. After you read it, follow the instructions. At a pre-arranged moment, you will sever all communications with the Japanese army. You will break with the Minami Kikan and only respond to our Burmese commanders. Do not engage the Japanese. Instead, disperse. Attack the Imperial Japanese army only as a last resort. Hide your weapons. Wear civilian clothes. Root out any spies for the Japanese and exterminate them."

After Colonel Kyaw Khin spoke, there were murmurs of assent among the men. They then sang the national anthem and dispersed. In his tent, Tin Oo listened to the heavy rain beat down on the roof and found it soothing.

Chapter 36
Japan Prepares to Invade India

The garden city of Maymyo, located northeast of Mandalay, was the hill station where the British took refuge from the heat and humidity of Rangoon in colonial times. Even before the British arrived, it had been a bucolic setting. The hills surrounding it were full of wild flowers, jacarandas, and rhododendrons. British botanists set up a botanical garden, where they studied the flora. The gardens were quite cool and peaceful then. It was different in 1944. On the north end of the green quadrangle stood a Tudor style mansion: the former British governor's mansion. The British had used this hill station as a refuge from the "unhealthy climate, the heat and humidity of the plains of Burma." Here, *memsahibs* had retired to escape from Rangoon's oppressive climate. From here, the British governor had ruled Burma in the summer.

General Ugaki of the 15th Imperial Japanese Army now sat in the same chair as the British colonial governor had in past years. This was the headquarters of Northern Army Command. From here, Ugaki prepared for the invasion of India. In fact, his grasp was greater than his reach; his enthusiasm for the invasion of India was greater than that of his boss in Rangoon. Ugaki had a history of recklessness and a propensity for dangerous adventures. The new commander of the Burma Area Army in Rangoon, General Kobiyashi, was preoccupied with the precarious supply line necessary to feed and supply his army. General Ugaki, in the comfortable setting of the hill station of Maymyo, bypassed the cautious Rangoon command and, using his connections in Tokyo, engineered approval of a plan by the High Command to launch an attack against India. He busied himself with retraining newly arrived divisions, and his staff had worked on war plans until, finally, they were ready.

After their time in Rangoon, Sato's regiment had fought two campaigns in the Arakan against the British. The first had been successful, but the last battle did not go well. Sato found himself languishing in the Arakan, nursing his wounded pride after having been pushed eastward by the British in the second Arakan campaign. Now, Sato received a summons to go north to Maymyo; his regiment would follow. "Maybe," he thought, I will be able to conduct another campaign that will be as successful as my march up the Tenasserim to Rangoon itself."

Sato had not been to the hill country before. He boarded the train with anticipation. As the train chugged northward, he noted how much the terrain differed from that of lower Burma, around Rangoon and throughout the Tenassarim. From the last switchback, he looked down at the valley below, which spread for miles to the east. In the distance, barely visible, was the city of Mandalay. In the late afternoon, the train stopped just east of Maymyo. The mood at the station was decidedly festive: he noted the profusion of flowers, plants, and greenery, which reminded him of his home. Tropical trees were intermingled with deciduous trees. A large tan Humber staff car was waiting to take him into the city. The corporal standing next to the car approached Sato, saluted, and took his bags. He then opened the back door, secured it after Sato had seated himself, and chauffeured Sato in style to the city, depositing him at the Tudor-style mansion where General Ugaki was waiting for him.

Sato surveyed the mansion with interest. Although many of the buildings in Rangoon had a British colonial flair, this mansion looked to be British through and through. Inside, Sato noted, the walls were of the rare beautiful red padauk wood, whose reddish color added warmth to the rooms. He knew that the hill station enjoyed cool evenings and nights, and knew that the rosy glow of the rooms would take the tinge of cold off of the nights. The rooms had fireplaces, the first he had seen since he had left Japan. From the window of the meeting room he could see residences of lesser officials below the government hill. Even the natives here lived in solid cottages arranged on well-ordered streets. His troops, he was told, would be quartered at the former British Jungle Warfare school, which consisted of a row of red colonial-style buildings. Sato felt altogether comfortable in Maymyo. He would like living here, even if it was temporary.

From here, plans would be hatched for the Japanese invasion of India. While the high command in Rangoon doubted the wisdom of pushing into India, General Ugaki had bypassed the Rangoon command to contact high-placed officers in Japan. Now he had received orders from Japan to proceed with an attack on India. At breakfast the morning after he arrived, much to his surprise, Sato encountered officers from other regiments. They told him, "Something big is going to happen. We don't know what, but there are rumors about action. And about intense debate over that action."

At 9:00 A.M., the officers were ushered into the large room that had once been used as a theater by the British governor. The room soon filled with more officers, some of whom Sato recognized from the 15th and the 18th Divisions but others who were new to him. "It must be something big," he thought to himself. Then it struck him: an invasion of India and a win there would give a tremendous boost to the morale of the Imperial Army and Navy. He had heard about General Ugaki's legendary toughness and his reputation as a maverick. Some of his friends compared Ugaki to the Tiger of Malay, the conqueror of Malay and Singapore. Sato was eager for the meeting to start.

General Ugaki soon strode into the room. He was a imposing man, big and burly. His broad face was pockmarked and rough, his hair was cropped short. His olive-green uniform was well pressed and bore white stars on its collar, indicating his rank of Lieutenant General. On his chest were many medals, including the Mukden star, in acknowledgment of his instigation of the Mukden Incident, which began the Japan-Sino War. His wide belt was gleaming, and attached to it was a gold-gilt samuri sword. His brown jack boots were polished to a shine. As he entered the room, the officers leapt to their feet. They raised their fists and shouted "banzai! banzai! banzai!"

Following the General was his chief of staff, a short and slender man. General Ugaki sat on the elevated dais in the front of the theater room. After Ugaki was seated, the chief of staff invited the officers to sit down. In the very first row sat the staff officers; structure was all-important in the Japanese army, and hierarchy was the norm. Behind the staff officers were rows of other officers. Sato sat in the middle of the room and concentrated on the imposing General. He looked stern and unforgiving.

General Ugaki began to speak. His voice was low and menacing. Sato shuddered. "I would not want to anger him," Sato thought. "But I could follow him anywhere! He represents all the fierceness that a military leader should convey." From time to time, Ugaki's measured tones rose to a shout. "You are privileged to be here," he admonished the men. "You will be part of a great enterprise of the Greater East Asia Co-Prosperity Sphere. Your work will bring greater glory to the Emperor and the Empire of Japan."

Ugaki smiled, took a sip of water, and continued. "The Japanese Army is invincible! When we strike our objective, it will be with the speed and velocity of wildfire. Despite obstacles of river, mountain, and weather, we will sweep aside the paltry opposition from the weak British forces that we will encounter. We will defeat and annihilate them, and add luster to army tradition by achieving a victory. When we reach our destination we will unfurl our flag, proclaiming to one and all our victory in . . . India."

A whisper of anticipatory excitement swept through the room. "The time is not far off," Ugaki continued. "When we reach India, I promise to share the Churchill supplies with you, especially the whiskey."

Whispers among the officers grew louder . . . and happier. Ugaki concluded, "We will throw the white colonial rulers out and establish a Greater East Asia Co-Prosperity Sphere from the Pacific Ocean to the Indian Ocean!"

Thunderous applause broke out, and shouts of "banzai!" filled the room. General Ugaki stood to accept the men's salutes, then left the room.

The officers milled about, discussing the news. Sato overheard one officer comment to another, "the General is probably on the way to his favorite geisha, at the former Maymyo Club. It has been fitted out with tatami and paper and wood screens, and the General will be served warm sake while his favorite geisha entertains him, massaging away his cares."

His companion laughed and added. "Yes, and that entertainment and massage will be followed by a sumptuous dinner of fine Sehikan, rice with red beans. Then he will retire with his favorite geisha, for the pleasures of life, sake, and more sake. The two men giggled. Then the first turned serious and remarked with a bitter undertone, "However, while the General will enjoy sex with his favorite geisha, and fine food, we, the troops, will survive on half rations."

The chief of staff now called the men to attention and took over the meeting. His aides brought forward the maps and posted them on the wall, then handed him a pointer. Even from his vantage point, Sato could see the maps clearly enough. The chief of staff discussed unit formations and explained which various units would be attached to the division. Then he went into the details of the operation:

This will be a large offensive against Assam, Manipur, and Naga states. The main focus will be Imphal and Kohima. We can then cut off the road to Dimapur and prevent supplies and reinforcements from reaching the British garrisons now at Imphal and Kohima. From Dimapur, we will be just a stone's throw from Bengal. Ours will be a three-pronged attack: Tiddim in the south, Imphal in the center, and Kohima to the north. Each of our formations will be at divisional strength, with additional units. Our preparations are almost complete.

The staff officer passed plans and order of battle. Sato's heart raced with excitement and his breast swelled with pride when he heard the chief of staff explain that his own regiment, the 212th, would be the lead unit to attack the main British base at Kohima. He could hardly wait to look more closely at the order of battle.

The chief of staff continued, "Our first objective is to destroy the 15th and four other Indian divisions at Imphal. Once we capture Imphal, we move north to Kohima. Our plan is to be a hook and a block, between Kohima and Dimapur. This will trap the British and Indian troops and destroy the enemy army once and for all."

The officers in the room could hardly contain their excitement. A low buzz spread through the room. Sato overheard one of his neighbors murmur, "The Indians did not fight well in Moulmein, but they might put up a better defense when they are defending their own country."

Just then the chief of staff addressed that very concern. "Fighting alongside our sons of Japan will be troops of the Indian National Army.

Their presence will inspire a revolution in Delhi," he stated with conviction. The room was full of nodding heads.

He went on to detail points of the future fighting, but Sato could not concentrate. He barely heard the chief of staff's acknowledgment that there were enemy strong points at Jessami and further north at Sangshak and Urkhul, as well as at Kharasom in the south. Sato was already dreaming of victory and glory and the spoils of war. Licking his lips with anticipation, he envisioned his return to Rangoon as a hero. He was wrenched back to the present by the chief of staff's next words, however.

"The date of the invasions depends on the end of the northwest monsoon, which is typically in January. Here in Maymyo the temperature is cool, but in northern Burma it will be humid and hot from the monsoon rains. The mountains will be cool, but wet, moist, and foggy; the valleys will be hot and full of irritating insects. Northwest Burma can be a dangerous place, as the hills and streams are breeding grounds for malaria. The pools of standing water left behind by the monsoons will be filled with larvae, which will begin to hatch as soon as the temperatures begin to rise. The danger of typhus, dengue, and hemorrhagic fever are also low in January but will rise with the temperature. The streams and rivers will teem with the ugly blood-sucking leaches no matter what the month."

The attendees turned somber, but the chief of staff concluded with an allusion to Ugaki's speech. "In the end we will overcome all these obstacles and will achieve success," he declared. The officers rose to their feet yet again, shouted "banzai!" and the chief of staff left the room with his aide. The meeting ended, the officers excitedly made plans for an evening of carousing.

Now, the officers agreed, it was time to forget the coming horrors of the jungle and the unknown perils that lay ahead. It was time to get drunk! The mid-level officers did not have access to a geisha house, but they could go to Maymyo's comfort houses. There they could pay a pittance for sex with the Anglo-Indian and Burmese women who had been forced into prostitution. After sex they would drink till the wee hours of the morning.

Fortified with sake, Sato boasted to his fellow officers of his experience in the Arakan. "The ridges will be treacherous and the valleys steep. But my soldiers are veterans; they are used to this. They drove the British and their lackeys from Moulmein to Rangoon and then northward into India. They could not stand up to us."

None of his colleagues questioned him. None of them considered failure. In their minds, the Japanese Imperial Army was invincible, and their mission of establishing a Greater East Asia Co-Prosperity Sphere was noble. They looked forward eagerly to their campaign as they stumbled back to their beds.

HIKARI KIKAN

At the headquarters of the Indian National Army (INA) in Rangoon, the anticipation was palpable. The men had spent months marching, drilling, and training, and anticipating the arrival of their new commander. Finally the much-heralded day arrived. Colonel Patel arrived from Singapore, and the troops welcomed him exuberantly. He had trained in Japan and received rave reviews for his leadership.

The next day, Colonel Patel, with his Japanese liaison officer from the Hikari Kikan, led the INA troops north toward India. As the men marched out from the Moghul palace in Rangoon, they sang,

You drink too much whiskey
And swirl gin.
You cannot shoot straight.
When we meet in battle
We will set you straight.
We will defeat and kill you.
And retake our sacred land.

As the parade passed in front of the Thomas's house, the girls peeked out from behind the curtains in awe. Leading the INA was a unit of women soldiers! The girls were shocked to see women in uniforms and jack boots marching alongside men. These were the Rani-Ki-Jhansi, who would fight along side their male counterparts in the INA.

Reddy listened with interest to the songs and slogans chanted by the marching troops. The INA had only a few weapons but seemed to be in high spirits. For months they had trained here, and now they were prepared to answer the call by the Japanese to liberate their own country. They handed out pamphlets as they marched down the street. Reddy snatched one and read out loud, "Sepoys of India, do you always want to live like second-class citizens and be treated like dogs? Wake up my friends! Support us! Be prepared to shoulder the burdens with us! We will liberate India and defeat the British. Change your colors and come over to us to kill and destroy the English and the Americans."

Reddy shook his head as he showed the pamphlet to Benjamin. "I want to believe," he said, "but I fear for these brave young men and women. I fear that they have been deluded."

Benjamin crumpled the pamphlet and threw it away. "You know as well as I do, Uncle, that the Japanese will simply use them, as they used the Burmese. Don't believe a word they say." He turned his back and walked back into the house, admonishing his sisters to keep the curtains drawn.

Weeks later, this unit would reach the front in northwest Burma. From there, the Japanese liaison officer, Colonel Fukuhara, the head of the Hikari Kikan in Burma, sent his most trusted Indian intelligence captain, Captain Dutt, to India. His task was to assess the mood of the Indian political establishment and ask the Quit India movement for support. The support was not forthcoming, and the denial of support came with a warning about the Japanese. Captain Dutt, while a Kings's soldier, was a Indian patriot who had been a prisoner of war in Malaya and had joined the INA there. Now he was conflicted, worried whether he was doing the right thing, given his oath to the King and Emperor. But the cry for independence had become like the waves of the sea, gaining momentum all the time, and now Indians had started to take very forceful action. Captain Dutt assured himself that the only solution was to join the INA and work to defeat and then chase the allies from India. He rejoined his unit somewhat worried about the lack of support from the Congress party and the Quit India movement, but nonetheless committed to his course of action. He reluctantly joined with the Japanese to invade India.

Chapter 37
The Road to Imphal

Sato said goodbye to the cool comfort of Maymyo. But before he left, he took time from his frantic schedule to send a letter to his wife. He had not had contact with home in the two and a half years since he had left Japan. He had left a wife and young son there. He knew that his father was getting older, and he worried about his mother. By candlelight, he penned his letter.

... I cannot tell you where I am or what I am doing, but I can tell you that I am embarking on my greatest adventure. In a few weeks, you will hear of my great success and achievement. My regiment's efforts will bring great glory to the Emperor and to Nippon. ...

Tell my son of the way of the samuri and of the great Emperor. Make him stand tall and teach him to be courageous. When his time comes, he will be a soldier like me and will fight for the empire of Japan and our Emperor. ...

Please care for my father and mother.

Your loving husband

Sato and his troops set out in a long caravan. He had limited provisions and depended on capturing supplies to feed his troops. In the meantime, he would make do with commandeered materials. From Maymyo, the army traveled past dusty Mandalay and then westward. The caravans pouring out of their bases looked more like those of the Roman army than a modern one: thousands of horses, mules, the muleteers, goats, cattle, and even elephants. The goats and cattle were "food on the hoof" for the Japanese. Unlike the British and Americans, who had canned food and a good supply chain, the Japanese were stretched too thin from their source of supply and resupply in Rangoon.

Before long, the dry zone gave way to low hills, beyond which was the high jungle. East of the Chindwin River, Sato established a camp at which he would further prepare his troops for the coming offensive. He drove his troops mercilessly in their training and exhorted them to find additional mules and other pack animals to carry their supplies and ammunition.

Sato went over the plans yet again. His troops would cross the Chindwin by ferry, raft, and small boat, and he also had to get the "food on the hoof" across the river. Once across the river, the supplies of rice and oil would be packed onto the mules for transport, enough for the three weeks that the battle was calculated to take. Sato gave one last briefing to his officers. Then he advised them, "At 06 hours we move out."

As the officers dispersed to ready the troops, Sato was exited. He was satisfied with the great endeavor. At the head of his troops, he looked back at the long line of the convoy as they approached the Chindwin River. The mules were heavily laden, and Sato worried about the mule teams making the sharp, steep, and dangerous ridges on the other side of the river. Mules were sure-footed and could climb sharp mountain ridges, he knew, but they also could be stubborn. Once they crossed to the west side of the Chindwin, Sato planned to direct his men to gather more elephants and their *ozzies* [elephant handlers] from the Kuki villagers; these would also carry large quantities of supplies.

One thing nagged at him, however: up here in northern Burma, the Burmese, Shan, and Naga peoples were unwilling to part with their livestock and were hostile; only the Kukis could be trusted, as they disliked the British, who had at one time sided with the Nagas against the Kukis. If this situation held, the troops would be faced with supply problems, but Sato was confident his troops could move in and out of northeast India before any such problem arose. A greater concern was discovery by the British Royal Air Force (RAF), or the Lysanders of the Royal Indian Air Force, which flew over the area from their bases in India. Secrecy was important to the success of the mission.

It took two days for all the pack animals to assemble for the river crossing. Sato anticipated difficulty once the troops crossed the river and reached the jungle, but much to his chagrin, the troubles began even as they prepared to cross the river. The rafts broke down, and many animals drowned. The weary troops assembled on the west side of the river, but Sato could not let them rest if he was to adhere to his schedule. He pushed them forward into the wild green jungle of north Burma.

For days they climbed the sharp ridges and followed the jungle trails into the rain forests. Finally they arrived at the assembly point in India, without being detected from the air. Now came the really difficult part: climbing the tall mountain ranges. The mountain tops turned to narrow ridges. These were so narrow that the men could only walk single file, and the sides of the trails fell off into deep jungle-covered ravines. Even the sure-footed mules lost their footing, and some tumbled down the ravines only to become impaled on the sharp branches and roots and die a horrible death.

After scaling the mountains and traversing the ridge trails, the troops then descended into the valley, where the creeks were swollen with monsoon waters. After wading through the water, the soldiers would notice blood on their shoes, above the leggings, and when they looked under the leggings they could see huge black leeches clinging to their skin. Over and over the sequence repeated: mountains, ridges, valleys, water, and leeches. Sato's medical officer and staff had warned Sato about potential health risks, and now they were very busy.

Sato worried as he consulted his map. He had maintained radio silence so did not quite know what the other units were doing. "I hope they are overcoming their challenges as I am," he thought to himself. "We all need to assemble at the same time." He glanced at his horse: even his horse showed signs of strain from the jungle. For the umpteenth time, Sato opened his secret plans and re-read his directions. The 33rd division would cross the Chindwin near Kalewa and would assault Imphal from the south. The 15th would cross the Chindwin near Thaungdut and would surround Imphal, cutting the Kohima–Imphal Road. And his regiment, part of the 31st, would attack the northern sector, the Kohima ridge, and cut the Kohima–Dimapur Road. The 31st had actually split into three columns: one crossed the Chindwin near Homalin and was moving westward to Urkhul; from thence it would move northward to Kohima. Sato's own column had itself split into two columns, crossing the Chindwin both north and south of Tamanthi and then moving, pincer-like, toward Jessami, the last village before Kohima. The southern column would take Kharasom before turning westward toward

Phek and Kohima; the column he led would take Phek to the north and head directly to Kohima.

At his morning meeting, Sato held a meeting with his senior staff. His chief of staff read the orders aloud. "The 31st will attack the Kohima ridge. We have been charged with taking ridge and the hilltop position of Jessami, east of Kohima, as well as the small, isolated post of Phek. Then we move on to attack the Kohima ridge."

Sato's intelligence officer advised him that Jessami was a tiny garrison. With the exception of a British lieutenant who commanded the troops, all the men were Assamese or Gurkhas. "They are second-tier units, Sir, not the best. The second in command is an experienced man, Subedar Singh."

Sato grunted his acknowledgment. "They will be no match for us," he boasted. The troops set out that night. Sato was keen to annihilate the garrison of Jessami. But just east of Jessami, Sato would be surprised.

HILL 42

The British commander in Kohima, Colonel James, had sent out a strong patrol to monitor Japanese movements. The patrol established their observation point on Hill 42, east of the hilltop town of Jessami. Major Murphy was in command of this small unit comprised of Assam Rifles, Naga tribesmen, and Burma Frontier Forces, including Jeremy Rawson, who was to act as interpreter and oversee communications. Naga guides and levies who had been waiting for them guided them to their positions on Hill 42. Major Murphy directed the men to dig defensive bunkers as they awaited reinforcements. Jeremy and the other communications specialists set up a wireless, using a tall tree for the aerial. The generator would be run by hand. The men tested the setup and found it successful. Major Murphy quietly informed all the men, "No fires. The entire operation has to be conducted in secrecy."

The Naga tribesmen were essential to the success of the patrol's mission. They would operate the generator and go on patrols. They knew the land intimately and would guide and advise the allied troops. The troops them-selves were mostly Assamese, Burmese, and Anglo-Indians who were un-familiar with the rugged terrain. The next morning, even before the mists lifted, a small patrol set out. The men climbed up a treacherous ridge from which they could watch the Chindwin River and the track that led from the west bank of the river to Hill 42. They settled in. Now it was a waiting game.

Jeremy scanned the area and noted its features. The morning's mist still hung heavy in the area, and the land was still. Then he reached into his pocket and brought out a small packet of mail that had been given to him just before he had left Kohima. It was the first mail he had received since he had left Rangoon, and he was savoring it. He had recognized one letter addressed in his sister's writing. Now, finally, he opened it with excitement and trepidation. "She must have received my letter," he thought. "And since I am receiving a letter from her, she must be safe."

My dear Jeremy

The Red Cross brought me your letter. When I recognized your handwriting, I fainted. I cannot tell you how happy I was to get a letter from you. I had been so worried! Now I am so relieved that you are safe and in India. Even though I cannot see you, I am filled with joy that I cannot describe. I feel close to you now.

I am in Calcutta, staying at the convent. I work for St. Johns Ambulance and live in a hostel for girls. Calcutta is in the midst of famine. There are food shortages here, and people are really dying of starvation. Sometimes there are dead bodies on the street, but we cope. I have some medical problems, but I do not want to burden you with my problems; I will tell you all about them when I see you again. The city crawls with troops—British, and some Americans. The dance halls are full every night, but I avoid them.

I last saw father in Myitkyina. I was to be evacuated by air, but as you well know, the last planes carried only the last of the British; they had no room for us. I had begged father to go with me, but he was adamant. "I have a responsibility to drive this engine," he insisted. You know how much he loved his engine and mother. I think after his family, he loved that engine most, and took very seriously his responsibility to the government, even though the British looked upon him as a half-breed. I worry about what happened to him. As for mother, she has many Anglo friends at our old home, and if anything ever happens to Father, she will probably seek their help.

I cannot ask you where you are and what you are doing as that may be a breach of security. I only pray that you will be safe wherever you are. This has been a nightmarish year and a half. I pray every day that this horrible war will end soon so that we can be a family again.

I will close for now; my address is listed below.

I love and miss you,

Love, CeCi

Tears welled up in Jeremy's eyes. He was happy that CeCi was safe, but his anxiety only increased for his father. He wished he had time to write, but there was work ahead. Not to mention the difficulty of posting a letter from where he was!

The mists still blanketed row upon row of hills, ridges, and valleys. But soon the sun burned the mists away, and he could feel the warmth of the sun on his back. He took out his binoculars again and looked intensely at the footpath. He moved the binoculars from his eyes and then replaced them. From the edge of the silvery river, he could see movement! He could make out the shape of humans and animals, large and small—mules and elephants, heavily laden elephants slowly lumbering through the forest. As he concentrated, he saw that the column stretched to the horizon. It seemed endless! As the column got closer, Jeremy could make out their shape. They were Japanese! He whispered to Subedar Singh, "this is not a patrol; it is big—a full regiment and more! Maybe a division, with animal transport!"

The subedar and he crouched low and ran to the Major, directing his attention to the concentration of men approaching their position. As the men watched, they discerned that there were in fact two columns, one coming directly toward them from the south and the other seeming to circle northward, possibly bypassing them. "Get ready to send the signal to Corps headquarters," the Major directed Jeremy.

The Naga radio man started to pump the radio. It crackled and gave a long whistle. The Major turned to his code book and wrote out his message, then warmed his fingers and began to transmit.

From K-Force Hill 42. Enemy forces in strength crossed the
Chindwin and are advancing to our forward position. Soldiers,
elephant, mules, and hoofed animals, in two long columns, all
heading west. They will reach us in approximately half a day. Have
Urkhul and Karasom fallen?

Just as he finished his transmission, a first shot was heard from an advance
Japanese patrol. "Take defensive position," ordered the Major. With the sun
behind them, the allied troops saw the Japanese charge up the ridge,
accompanied by screams, trumpets, and cries of "banzai!" From the high
ground, the defenders withstood the attack and inflicted heavy casualties.
The Major went from bunker to bunker to assess the damage and the loss
of life. He called up stretcher bearers to gather all the badly wounded.
"Evacuate them at night," he ordered.

The Major returned to his command post. Although his men had fought
off the enemy, he knew that other attacks would soon follow, and he knew
that his men would be grossly outnumbered by the enemy as the Japanese
troops made their way westward.

When the second charge came, it too was repelled, but again with heavy
losses. With each attack, the enemy gained ground, and finally they gained
the higher ground. They erected a machine gun there and opened fire on the
beleaguered defenders of Hill 42. The perimeter was fast closing. The
Major called his trusted subedar, Singh. "Destroy all codes books and maps.
Leave the post, and take the jungle trails back to Kohima. You and your
men have done a splendid job."

The subedar demurred. "Sahib, I will not go. I will stay."

Major Murphy looked into the eyes of his trusted subedar. "This is a
direct order. You will leave the post with the men. Report to Jessami. Be
careful and good luck." With that, Major Murphy turned his face away from
his subedar.

Subedar Singh could do no more. He knew he would never see his
commander again. For a brief moment he hesitated, then he turned on his
heel and slowly walked out to the edge of the ridge where his men were
waiting. He did not look into their eyes, just said "chalo" [go].

The Major would stay true to his orders from Brigade headquarters.
They had been very clear, "last man, last bullet." Major Murphy would stay.

He knew that he would die on this hill. He looked around at its features frequently, as though memorizing them. He kept his pistol next to him and prayed softly that his end would be swift and not be too painful. He did not want to be captured by the soldiers of the Empire.

The men waited with Subedar Singh for the right moment, then in inky darkness slipped over the ridge and descended the mountain. The Nagas led them to the trails that only they knew, and the men made for Jessami. Just as they reached the valley, they heard gunfire, intense gunfire, and grenades from the position they had just evacuated. The subedar knew that his commander was dying. In silence, the men walked in single file. The trail wound around great trees and clumps of bamboo, making progress slow. Some of the men fell behind, but there was no time to go looking for them. If they did not get to Jessami to alert the garrison there, it too would be overrun. Jeremy froze every time he heard a noise. By morning they arrived at Jessami's perimeter. "Johnny don't shoot, Johnny don't shoot!" the men shouted. The defenders asked for the password, which the men from Hill 42 did not know. They pleaded, and after an agonizing moment, with guns pointed at them, they were allowed to enter.

JESSAMI

Sato was chagrined. He had done all that he could, but now he was behind schedule, due to the delay at Hill 42. That fact tempered his pride in how swiftly his men had routed the defenders of the hill. That, and the information he had received from headquarters. He had sent a signal to his division at Indaw. Division headquarters had responded with disappointment at the delay and new orders. "You have one day to take Jessami," came the order. "Then proceed directly to Kohima."

Sato exploded in anger. "That schedule is far too ambitious," he shouted to his chief of staff. Nonetheless, he ordered his chief of staff to get the battalion ready to proceed forthwith.

The next night, Sato put in an attack on Jessami. The defenders on the top ridge waited in their foxholes while intense artillery fire wracked the mountain for an hour. Then came silence, and the defenders readied themselves. They knew what was to come. In his foxhole, Jeremy trembled.

Without wire and strong bunkers, the defenders were weak. He heard some rustling of leaves and narrowed his eyes to better concentrate. He saw something move, then stiffened and pulled the trigger. He felt the recoil of his gun, then shouts of "Tusokome! Tusokome!" Swords flashed, then came the clanging of cymbals and the shrieks of the Japanese soldiers. Jeremy jumped out of his foxhole and retreated to the second line of defense. Mortar shells and trench mortars were exploding all around, and the shrieks of pain were heart-rending. Silently the enemy crawled into the positions just vacated by the defenders.

Sato's troops were seasoned and experienced, but Sato was surprised by the fierce resistance shown by the British and the lead Indian troops. They had fallen back but had held their position, and the Japanese had sustained high casualties. The first Japanese attack had been only partially successful. Now his men would need to mount another attack on the hilltop.

From the defensive box, a rifleman opened fire, and then came the Bren guns. The Japanese again suffered many dead. The defenders in their bunkers continued to fire into the night. They waited patiently until they saw the flash from the Japanese weapons before they fired, thereby making their defensive fire deadly. The crossfire was intense. Finally the Japanese broke off their attack, but Jessami's defenders fired into the night whenever they saw movement. This was only the beginning. The defenders knew that the enemy would be back soon.

Indeed, soon their scouts reported another column approaching from the south, bigger and with elephants, bullocks, and mountain guns. The defenders were somber. There would be no reinforcements coming from Kohima. There was no way out for them. Nonetheless, the men were united and determined in their efforts to defend their position. Every day, every hour that they staved off the Japanese was another day or hour that the defenders of Kohima could use to strengthen their position so as to repel the Japanese and keep them from invading India.

Water was in short supply in Jessami. The men collected water on tarpaulins and carefully doled it out. The Japanese attacks continued, and as the defenders suffered losses, they retreated to fallback bunkers. The perimeter shrunk. The defenders were exhausted but still fought on. But then a mortar bomb tore a hole in the barbed wire, opening a gap in their defenses. The commander knew it was just a matter of time before the Japanese discovered the gap and poured in like rushing water. He gathered his officers and advised them. "Hold out till the next attack stops. As the Japanese regroup, we will break up into small groups and head for Kohima. Run for Phek first. There is a small BurRif company stationed there. Warn them, and all fall back to Kohima."

The officers nodded, saluted and returned to brief the weary men in the bunkers. As the next Japanese attack waned, the defenders slid down the ridge in silence and descended to the valley. In the darkness and silence, some of the defenders got turned around and took the trail southward to Kharasom instead of the trail northwest to Phek. There they met up with the retreating defenders of Kharasom, which had fallen to Japanese attack earlier. Eventually they found their bearings and headed northward to Kohima. The small unit at Phek, warned by the retreating men from Jessami, also headed westward to Kohima.

In small groups the retreating soldiers took to the jungle trails, guided by trusted Naga tribesmen. They walked throughout the night, under most difficult conditions and always wondering if there would be an ambush at the next bend. Late in the morning they approached Kohima, terrified, dispirited, hungry, and some wounded. The defenders of Kohima thankfully recognized them as comrades and allowed them through the perimeter. They stood in silence as the stragglers stumbled past them. Aides rushed from the commander's headquarters to separate the healthy from the wounded and usher survivors to the commander for debriefing. Jeremy was anxious to meet up again with Peter, but knew debriefing was top priority.

The intelligence officer questioned them intensely about units, strength, maps, etc. He and the commander thanked the men for their stout defense. "By delaying the Japanese attack, you gave us valuable time to prepare. You were on a lonely little outpost on a high ridge deep in the jungle, and you conducted yourselves with honor. These words will never make up for the loss of life, but this is war. You take whatever Fate hands you."

The commander instructed that all the men be fed at the mess hall and examined at the hospital before being attached to units. He knew that he would need to rely on these men to supplement his own troops, and wanted them to be strong and ready.

Chapter 38
Battle of Kohima

ON THE KOHIMA RIDGE

Kohima's garrison commander, Colonel James, reviewed all the information that he had gathered from his patrol and the Naga scouts, and sent his appreciation to the Corps commander.

> I have seven hills to defend, two under-strength British battalions, and other under-strength units. The latter include men from Assam State Battalion, Assam Regiment, and Assam Rifles; companies of Gurkhas, two platoons of Maratha Light Infantry, and a company of Royal Kent Battalion. I have some composite Indian non-combat administrative personnel and remnants of two Burmese companies, mostly domiciled Indians, Eurasians, and ethnic Burmese. Experienced British infantry commanders are short. I must consider good Indian officers. Forces arrayed against us are far superior in number and include the fearsome White Tigers of 31st Division. Request reinforcements.
>
> Colonel James, Kohima

The reply from Headquarters came rapidly.

> Signal understood. All indications are that enemy in division strength are headed to your position. Intentions uncertain. May bypass your position, cut road to the west, head to Dimapur; may head south to Imphal; may attack you directly. No reinforcements possible.

When roads are cut, you will be isolated.
Prepare for a long siege. Good luck.

                              Headquarters, Comilla

Colonel James was worried but resolute. He called his commanders together to share this latest appreciation. "We must plan to patrol aggressively. We will use information gathered by our Karen spies, also known as K-Force, and our own units to learn about the movements of enemy."

The colonel then detailed his plans for the defense of Kohima's seven hills. "The Royal Battalion will defend the vital northern sector on which the tennis court, the DC bungalow, and the club stand. This sector will likely be the first to be attacked, as the enemy strives to take Garrison Hill from the east, from the Somra Hills along the trails from Jessami and Phek. Garrison Hill will be defended by a company of the Assam State Battalion, commanded by my own second in command. The nearby Hospital Ridge will be defended by a division of Assam Rifles and the Assam Regiment, also under his command."

The officers shifted in their seats uncomfortably, thinking about the attack that was sure to come. Colonel James continued, "I have assigned British infantry commanders to the following positions. Kuki Point will be defended by a composite mix of British and Assamese troops. Two platoons of the Maratha Light Infantry along with K-Force will defend Detail Hill. The jailhouse will be defended by a platoon from the Assam Regiment and two companies of Burmese troops. A composite company of Gurkhas and another of Indian infantry will defend Transport Hill. Treasury Hill will be defended by a small mixed unit."

Colonel James paused and looked around the room. "That leaves no British infantry commander for Supply Hill, which is a vital position to our overall defense. Supply Hill will be defended by the Royal Indian Service Corps," he said, "comprised of Indian troops, a unit of Indian Pioneers, and other small units, including men from Phek and Jessami, mostly Assamese and some Gurkhas. Major Rajendra will command the sector."

There was some murmuring and grumbling among the other officers, who questioned the wisdom of appointing an Indian to such a command position. But Colonel James had searched for an officer to command this unit and had found in Major Rajendra a very capable man with battlefield experience. Colonel James stared his men in the eye and stated firmly. "All our positions are in good hands." He continued, "This will be a long siege. I cannot tell you how long it will last. There are no fresh troops available, as they are all busy in the Arakan. When the attack comes, we must make do with the troops available."

Again the officers murmured, this time with some anxiety. Colonel James concluded, "I have one piece of good news: to the west of us, at Jotsoma, there is a highly respected Indian artillery, part of the 24th Mountain Field Artillery. They are battle-tested and one of the best in the Indian Army. They will provide cover for our garrison." There was a collective sigh of relief as the officers were dismissed and filed from the room.

SUPPLY HILL

Peter was assigned to Major Rajendra's unit and soon learned that he was a highly respected officer. He had an imposing stature and military bearing. He was a tall man, not unusual for his ethnic group, and he stood ramrod stiff. His father had served in one of the storied British Indian calvary units, which had allowed Major Rajendra to go to a good school. Then, by sheer dint of smarts, he had been to staff college at Quetta and now was one of the few officers who had commanded an infantry unit. Peter was satisfied that he could serve this man without question.

Major Rajendra briefed his officers, and Peter's admiration grew as he heard the Major speak. "Defense of Supply Hill is our responsibility. We must prepare for a long siege." Major Rajendra carefully outlined where the defenders should dig foxholes, bunkers, weapons pits, and tunnels. He explained where they should lay telephone lines so that they would be best protected. As soon as they were dismissed, the officers set their men to work on these tasks.

Evenings came early in this mountainous land, and the jungle came alive with calls from its inhabitants. For Peter, the crickets were the worst; it was hard to hear anything above their infernal and incessant noise.

Parakeets kept up a cacophony of song, flitting in and out of bushes and trees, quite oblivious to all the human activity around them. In fact, the trees and bushes literally teemed with exotically and vividly plumed birds of every hue. Below the crest of the hill, in the wetlands, teal, snipe, pigeon, and crane all went about their lives, eating and buzzing about, cooing and doing their mating dances.

As Peter rested after his day's work, he thought, "This is really a peaceful and placid setting. The only animal out of place in this setting is man, who brings his differences and disputes." He thought about the days to come and continued his musings. "We will shatter the trees, burn the fields, bloody and pollute the waters, and settle our thirst for booty, resources, and conquests. All of us young men—yellow, brown, white, and even the black men from far off Africa—will shed their blood in these hills. They will not have time to savor this wonderful setting. Instead, their lives will be shattered, their limbs will be severed, and countless numbers of them will die."

Peter returned to his tent for a restless night. Nothing happened that first night, but in the morning another signal came through from headquarters that set the men at Kohima on high alert. "The road to Dimapur has been cut," the signal informed them, "and there is some uncertainty about the Imphal–Kohima Road. If that road is cut, your situation will be grave."

Colonel James had also received a report from the spies of K-Force and shared it with his officers. "There is enemy movement in the Somra Hills. We don't know where the first attack will fall, whether from the north, the south, or whether it will be a general attack on a broad front."

His officers looked grim as the colonel continued. "Air supply is not forthcoming. The USAAF at Ledo is busy supplying China, so that they can continue to tie up Japanese divisions. The few RAF Hurricanes in our area will not be able to provide us with support either, although a few planes may be used supply Kohima." The officers returned to their units to rally their men's morale for the attack that was sure to come.

In his bunker on Supply Hill, Peter wondered about his family. Were they safe? Was Reddy still with them? Surely his father and Benjamin were no longer working, now that the Japanese had taken Rangoon. Was his family even in Rangoon, or had they fled along with countless other

Indians, trying to trek to India? Were they even alive? How long would his family's savings last? What if the gold and jewelry had been stolen or discovered by the Japanese? He wondered when he would see his family again. His thoughts turned to his youth, when he was just a young boy. The onset of the monsoon was crystal-clear in his mind. The dust, dirt, and grime would be cleansed from the road, and the lakes and gutters would fill with small fish that had washed there when the swollen river had flooded the street. Peter remembered trying to catch the fish with his bare hands, with very little success. He had been more successful getting mangos from the trees in the large compound of the Moghul Palace across the street from his home. Peter and his friends would sneak into the Moghul Palace compound, trying not to make noise to awaken the gardeners. One day while there he had heard a hiss; glancing toward the noise he had seen a large snake coming towards him, hissing and spitting venom. He had been unable to move fast enough, and the viper had bitten him. Before running home, he had grabbed a large stick and had struck the snake in the middle of its body; half-paralyzed by the blow to its spinal cord, the snake had stopped, unable to move but still able to hiss at him. Remembering his Uncle Reddy's admonitions, Peter systematically hit the snake until he smashed the head. Only then did he run home to tell his grandmother of the bite. In fact, his life had hung in the balance, and without his grandmother's ministrations, he would not have lived. He could not remember all the things she had done, but his sister still told the story of the Hindu medicine man who had treated the wound. "Did I live because of those ministrations?" he now wondered. "Or was I just lucky enough that the snake's poison sack contained only a little venom?" He knew that the same type of snakes slithered around here, and hoped that if he encountered one of them he would be that lucky again.

He also wondered about Jeremy. He had not heard from him since he had been transferred. Where had he been assigned? What had he done? Is he still safe? Tormented by worries such as this, Peter had difficulty sleeping in his bunker.

After he had been released from the hospital in Kohima, Jeremy again had wanted to look up Peter. But instead he was immediately transferred to the northern sector, with the units who were to defend this vital position. In his bunker there, Jeremy cleaned his gun and looked at the dark sky full of stars. He wondered if Peter was still in Kohima. As he sat in the cold damp shelter, his thoughts turned to home. After reading CeCi's letter, he now wondered if his father was still alive; his fears were that his father had been captured or dead. If so, how did his mother manage? CeCi's assurances that neighbors would help their mother notwithstanding, Jeremy worried. His mother was a small woman, and if his father was not with her, she would now be thrust into a position of responsibility with no means of income except for the gold and jewelry she possessed.

EAST OF KOHIMA

The victorious Japanese troops set out for Kohima. Like their enemy, their challenge was to not get lost in the dense jungle, but they were at a disadvantage. They had no Naga guides. Sato had now captured Hill 42 and the hilltop position at Jessami, but he had paid a big price for a small gain and had fallen further behind schedule. As they walked through the jungle, some of the troops got lost, thereby delaying the amassing of all the troops. Also, Sato had been surprised by the fierce resistance he had met. He was appalled by the unanticipated high casualties his men had suffered, so his joy was tempered by those losses. He was worried about being behind schedule for the main attack on the primary target, Kohima. But he consoled himself that he now possessed Hill 42 and Jessami, and he had learned that his southern column had captured Kharasom. He was relieved that he did not have to take Phek before moving onward to Kohima; his scouts had informed him that the small British unit there had already fallen back to Kohima. Japanese troops should also have cut the Imphal–Kohima Road by now.

Sato, now on his horse, rode through the jungle. Although his prize was within sight, he was becoming worried. He had received orders from Headquarters: "Capture Kohima quickly." However, his ammunition and supplemental food supplies were delayed, forcing him to delay the offensive.

Furious, he summoned his Captain in charge. "Your failure to move the supplies to our forward position has resulted in our delay. If we fail to take the main target by our deadline, the fault will be yours. You will be responsible for our failure to inflict punishment on the British and Indian units, like I was able to do in Moulmein."

The Captain trembled. "I promise to do my best," he murmured humbly. He went on to explain, "It takes four mules to carry one gun: one for the barrel, one for the base, and then two for the ammunition. We have lost many mules, making this a great challenge."

"I don't care what challenges you face!" screamed Sato. "I want the supplies here. By tomorrow morning!" With that he waved away his Captain curtly and summoned his other officers.

"We are faced with the challenge to take Kohima soon," he explained, "but our supplies have not all arrived. I have given orders for the supplies and ammunition to be here by tomorrow. But if they do not arrive, we will attack anyway. We are Japanese! We will be like Genghis Khan; we will sacrifice some pack animals for food. We will attack with the guns and ammunition that we have."

His men cheered him, moved by his words. Sato continued his exhortation. "We will annihilate the defenders of Kohima. That outpost is now cut off from Imphal. We will rout them!"

Again, cheers erupted among the officers, and they hastened back to their troops to give them their orders. Sato sat alone in his tent, fuming. He was angry with the short timetable he had been given and angry at the fact that his supplies had not arrived. For the first time, he worried about the outcome of his venture. The defenders of Hill 42 and Jessami had shown a valor that he had not expected. Would they meet similar determination at Kohima? If the defenders of Kohima put up as much resistance as those of Hill 42 and Jessami had put up, would he have enough food and ammunition to wage a long siege?

THE SIEGE AT KOHIMA

Assamese patrols detected a heavy concentration of Japanese forces south of Transport Hill. The Japanese were on the Imphal–Kohima Road. After an exchange of gunfire with the enemy, the patrol returned to base and reported the enemy coordinates. All the troops then knew that the battle was imminent.

The morning mists still hung over the ridge, as the warming rays of the sun filtered between the trees. Sato had positioned his men for attack during the night and now shattered the peace. Mortar bombs exploded on Transport and Jail hills, then came a shower of grenades. Accompanied by screams and the clash of cymbals, the Japanese attacked these two lightly held positions and by mid-day had overrun them both. The British tried a counter-attack but failed to dislodge the attackers. Nonetheless, the Japanese suffered losses as the defenders put up stiff resistance. The fall of Transport and Jail hills exposed the road and the approach to Supply Hill. As night fell, Sato kept up some sniping and positioned his men for a new attack in the northern sector of Kohima Ridge. His plan was to methodically engage and wear down the lightly held positions before launching the main attack on the more heavily defended northern sector.

Sato moved his headquarters to the Naga village, on the high plateau from which he could survey the entire ridge. He was pleased that some supplies and new troops had arrived, allowing him to mount simultaneous attacks on several of the northern allied positions.

The next day, Sato ordered his men to begin shelling the DC bungalow sector. The defenders sustained heavy casualties. Then Sato turned his guns to the Indian gunners at Jotsoma, where he wanted to take out the Indian Mountain Artillery regiment. He also kept up an attack on the Hospital Ridge and spur, tying down the British defenders in these areas. And he sent a patrol to the northwest to Kuki Point, where they severed the only pipe that supplied water to the entire garrison. Sato smiled as he envisioned the plight of the men in the garrison, who would have no water for showering or other personal hygiene. The garrison was cheered by one small piece of news: a company of Rajputs had broken through the ring of enemy and had arrived from the west to reinforce the garrison.

Sato bombarded the DC bungalow sector again, including the tennis court area, then marched up the road that abutted the steep cutting there. The men climbed up onto the flat land on which the DC bungalow stood, dragged up the light machine gun, set it up, and opened fire on the bungalow. The firefight went on all night, and although the Japanese held their position on the terrace, they failed to capture the bungalow itself or the tennis court.

As the sun rose the next morning, the Japanese attacked again and advanced to the "ad" court of the tennis court but then ceased their attack. The high table remained in British hands. The British had lost one third of their number. Sato observed the stretcher bearers removing the wounded defenders and taking the dead to be buried or cremated.

The bearded and smelly defenders climbed out of their bunkers to clean themselves, all the while ducking sniper fire. Colonel James came down from his bunker atop Garrison Hill and congratulated the defenders of the DC bungalow sector. "I'll be getting additional supplies and ammunition to you in the next few hours," he promised. The men were weary and exhausted, and Colonel James also ordered some of the battered but valiant British regiments to withdraw, to be replaced by the Assamese regiment. Then he descended to Detail Hill to assess its security. By late afternoon, the changeover was complete, and the British were once again ready to defend the tennis court and bungalow.

Detail Hill was a long narrow hill, crowded with old huts and *basha*s. To the north and west end of the hill was an ammunition depot. Colonel James was worried that if it took a direct hit, his ammunition stores would go up in smoke. He ordered ammunition to be dispersed to the various units defending the seven hills of the Kohima Ridge.

That night, from his vantage point on Supply Hill, Peter noted flashes of gunfire emanating from Jail Hill and piercing the darkness. Shells fell on Detail Hill and on the approach to Supply Hill. The huts on Detail Hill soon went up in smoke. A moment later, he heard a faint noise and went on high alert. The sentry also heard the same noise and was similarly on alert. Peter's eyes narrowed, and he kept his gaze on the place where the noise had come from. Yes! He saw something move! He called out and pulled the trigger, feeling the recoil of his gun. "Tusokome! Tusokome!" came the cry from the advancing Japanese. A sword flashed, then cymbals clanged as Japanese mortar shells exploded behind the bunker. Peter heard shrieks of pain from wounded men as the enemy attack focused on the thinly defended line to the south. He picked up a few hits himself. When the gunfire finally abated,

Major Rajendra ordered stretcher bearers to take the wounded away while the survivors waited for another attack that they were sure would come.

After two hours, the enemy put in another attack on both Detail Hill and the south face of Supply Hill. The defenders returned fire, in a cacophony of noise. For several hours, machine guns and Bren guns, shrieks and cymbals rent the air. The defenders were forced to give ground and retreat to the second line. The enemy had advanced north of Detail Hill and now were in the gully separating that hill from Supply Hill. Major Rajendra worried that the Japanese would be able to come up from the gully to Supply Hill and overrun it.

Just as he thought, the Japanese mounted another advance, from the gully. Ducking sniper fire, he led his men in a counter charge. With *kukris* flashing, the Gurkhas and Assamese vanquished the forward Japanese soldiers and pushed them back. They advanced all the way to Detail Hill and re-took that position. But their elation was short-lived. From one of the big *basha*s used as a cook house, Japanese hidden between the huge ovens opened fire on the allies. Soon a shower of grenades drove the Japanese out of the *basha*, and the British killed them to a man. The battle became very confused, and smoke hung heavy on the air. It was difficult to discern who was in which *basha*. The fighting went on all day, back and forth. Peter was confused by the incessant gunfire; he kept shooting at the smoke, not knowing if he hit anything, and he took cover from incoming fire. The situation was very fluid: the Japanese flowed northward, the allied troops flowed southward in a continual see-saw battle. In the end, the Japanese retook Detail Hill, and the allied troops withdrew to Supply Hill. At this point, Supply Hill was in a precarious position, exposed to Japanese attack.

Japanese gunners on Detail and Jail Hills bombarded Hospital Ridge and spur, causing heavy casualties among the wounded men there. The exploding shells re-wounded many men and killed many others. The operating theater was directly hit, killing two of the doctors. The hospital was swiftly evacuated, with the men and equipment being transferred to new bunkers.

Peter crouched in terror as shells exploded all around him. They hit targets on the entire ridge, including Supply Hill. As they exploded close to the bunkers, the ground shook. The logs on top of the bunker came loose, and mud and dirt fell onto the men in the bunker. The defenders along the ridge had only 25-pounder guns to respond to the heavy Japanese shelling. For a moment, the shelling of Supply Hill ceased, but increased commensurately on the northern sector with its tennis court. Shells rained down on Supply Hill again in a few moments, and as the enemy advanced on the hill, Major Rajendra called for artillery fire. A fire pattern was laid out so close that some of the allied shells fell on friendly foxholes and bunkers. The enemy then, with fixed bayonets, charged Supply Hill. Major Rajendra ordered a platoon of Burmese to counter-attack and sent reinforcements of Assamese and Gurkhas to their assistance. Finally, at the end of the day, the Japanese were stopped, just short of the bunkers.

In the night, in the northern sector, the Japanese mounted another fierce attack on the tennis court. The intensity of the fire made the allied soldiers give ground and abandon some of their buildings to the enemy. The next morning, the Assamese jemedar climbed out of his bunker to assess the damage. "Fifty enemy dead," he reported. No count of dead allies was given to the men; they could see for themselves who was missing.

The garrison commander called a meeting of his officers, to assess the losses and review strategy. In a different situation, he could expect that the lost men could be replaced, but this was not possible. He and his men were cut off from any possibility of reinforcement. They could only re-group with the surviving men. "If the northern sector should fall," he warned his second-in-command who was in charge of the entire northern sector, "the command post and the entire garrison will be vulnerable to attack and probably lost."

Sato reorganized his troops. Having failed to take the DC bungalow sector, he turned his attention once again to Supply Hill. He waited until nightfall to make his attack, although he kept pressure on the northern sector throughout the day. He wanted to confuse the defenders and keep their main strength in the northern sector. Sato's plan was to rotate the attacks from one position to another, to gain ground with each attack, and thereby demoralize the defenders. He hoped that this would rout the defenders or force them to surrender.

As darkness set in, fear and anxiety gripped the men in their bunkers on Supply Hill. They cleaned their weapons obsessively, re-stocked ammunition, and awaited the next inevitable attack.

The anticipated attack came with a fierce bombardment, followed by screaming Japanese soldiers streaming up the hill with fixed bayonets. Some of the green troops, especially the Burmese, fled in terror. Soon their positions were overrun. The defensive perimeter around Supply Hill had now shrunk considerably. By morning, half of the hills on Kohima Ridge were in Japanese hands.

At the garrison command post during the morning conference, the commander expressed concern about troop strength in the south. He wanted to know if a new Japanese regiment had come up from Urkhal in the south, which the Japanese had captured recently. He addressed Major Rajendra. "We need to send a patrol to gather intelligence on this matter urgently."

"Yes, Sir," came the major's reply. "I will organize a patrol." When he returned to his men, he called Peter to his bunker, along with Naik Pun, a courageous Gurkha, and three Assamese riflemen. "You will go southward stealthily, to gather information, maybe take a prisoner. Even a dead enemy would be good, if you can get his insignia, papers, and/or maps." The Major turned to Peter. "Will you lead the patrol?"

Peter was more than eager. "Yes, Sir," he said. He then went over the details with the commander, who gave him a detailed map.

"I expect you to set out at dusk and be back before the night attacks," the commander said. "Good luck." Then he added, as if Peter needed a reminder, "Be sure to identify yourselves when you come back, or the men will shoot at you." With that he dismissed the control.

It was four P.M. Peter had two hours to prepare. He went over his gear, took his pistol and Tommy gun, stripped them, and cleaned and oiled them. A wide grin broke out on the broad face of Naik Pun, who took the smaller of two *kukri*s out of its sheath. As he sharpened it, it shone in the dull light. When he was satisfied with the edge, he gave it to Peter. "Sahib," he urged, "you will need this more than the Tommy gun." Then he went on to show Peter how to use it. "The knife must cut the neck in a single swipe, from left to right." He laughed. Peter took the *kukri* and practiced. He shuddered at the thought of cutting somebody's neck, but this was war. Kill or be killed.

Peter consulted his map and memorized the main features of the land they would traverse. One wrong move on his part and the patrol would walk into a hornet's nest. He picked out a trail that he knew to be thick with bamboo, which would give the patrol cover. He briefed his men on the trail and other details, as well as the password.

At twilight, as the sun disappeared and darkness set in, the men climbed out of the bunker. Silently they assembled below the ridge, remaining undetected. Men in other bunkers had Bren guns at the ready, fingers crooked on the triggers. The patrol disappeared into the darkness.

Naik Pun was in the lead, with Peter and the three Assamese behind. The crickets chirped here and there, then the chorus was joined by the high-pitched noise of an animal in distress. "The noise will be a advantage," Peter knew. The night was cold and damp. It was quiet for a while, then the bamboo rustled. A mist that had gathered on the leaves dripped on the men as they moved through the dense thicket, wetting their clothes so that they clung to their bodies and made them even colder. Gusts of wind penetrated their skin and made them shiver. The descent was steep. They had to step very carefully in the dark, lest they slip or make a noise that could give them away. Peter hoped that there were no deadly snakes, as a poisonous snake bite would end life quickly.

Just beyond a clump of giant bamboo, they came upon a clearing, beyond which they could see movement. They also heard voices, indicating the presence of the enemy. The men went into a crouch and waited to adjust their eyes to the new surroundings. Peter turned to Pun and nodded. Pun took his curved *kukri* and put the blunt end in his mouth. Peter did the same, and on their hands and knees they crawled about fifteen yards in silence. Suddenly Pun's hand hit a pocket of ooze, a small mountain stream not on the map. He slipped on a moss-covered stone, and his body hit the stream with a light splash. He and Peter froze in their tracks as a shout of "Kura! Kura!" arose from the far side of the clearing. The men stood frozen, hardly daring to breathe. Peter could feel something wiggle up his leg, and although he knew it was a hungry leech, he made no attempt to deal with it.

Finally the shouts from the Japanese ceased, and Peter and Pun began to slowly crawl forward again. A sentry came into view. Peter's palms became sweaty. The sentry now had his back to them. The Assamese behind Peter and Pun tensed as they covered the men ahead of them. Fast as lightning, Pun grabbed the sentry's helmet and, before he could even cry out, sliced the sentry's neck in two. In a single bound, Peter jumped on the second man, an officer, keeping in mind all the things that Pun had taught him. He knew that he had only once chance; if he blew it, all would be over for him and his men. The *kukri* slashed the man's skin and cut the fat and muscle. The cold knife was thrust deeply, and Peter felt the first gush of warm blood from the carotid artery. Blood covered his hands and his shirt, the man stopped struggling and became limp, soon the flow from the blood vessel stopped, and Peter pushed the man down. Both Japanese now were dead.

Pun wiped his *kukri* and systematically went through the pockets of the officer, collecting papers and maps. The three Assamese men joined him and went through the sentry's pockets, taking his insignia. Pun then sliced off both men's ears to give to his commander. Peter went through the officer's satchel and took it with him.

There was a shout, then a challenge in Japanese. The men did nothing and said nothing; instead they waited till the shouting receded. Then they crawled backwards, hoping to escape undetected. But more shouting ensued, then a Very flare pierced the darkness. The men broke into a run as flashes of orange flame and bursts of automatic fire pursued them. Thankfully, from the bunkers on Supply Hill came return fire and mortar bombs. Peter realized that Pun was not with him, and when the firing ceased, he crawled back to where Pun lay. He was not moving. Bullets had gone through his neck and abdomen, killing him instantly. Peter gathered the papers and the ears from Pun and headed back. More gunfire broke out, and bullets whizzed over his head, but he and the three Assamese made it back into their position.

The Intelligence captain was waiting anxiously, along with the Gurkha commander and Colonel James himself. Peter gave the ears to give to the Gurkha commander and reported Pun's death with great sadness. "He was responsible for the success of our endeavor," Peter said. Then he handed over the satchel and papers to the Intelligence captain, who promised to review it and report to Colonel James the next morning. Colonel James congratulated Peter and his men, sending them to their bunkers for a well-earned rest.

That night, the Japanese continued their attack on Supply Hill and the CD bungalow sector. The next morning the Intelligence captain reported to the Colonel's tent, where the officers were awaiting his report. He brought alarming news. "Apparently there is a new division operating in the south," he reported. "The 15th Division. We had thought that this unit was in Myitkyina, but now they are here."

Colonel James mused. "So. Two full divisions surround us." He turned grave. "We are in for a bloody fight, in for a long and bloody siege." He turned to his commanders and announced, "I expect every unit to perform to their limit. Go and prepare." The officers returned to their bunkers, made sure that they were re-supplied, and prepared for another night of terror.

That night the enemy gunners resumed their shelling of the hospital. Once again the medical orderlies and doctors were under great strain, and once again many of the wounded men died in the bombardment. Yet each morning, stretcher bearers carried the night's wounded to the hospital. Water was becoming scarce.

Sato also launched another attack on Supply Hill. Major Rajendra called on the Mountain gunners and gave them the coordinates. Soon the boom of the guns could be heard, then the whistle, and boom! boom! they put a precise pattern against the enemy advance. The guns took a terrible toll on the enemy, but the Japanese kept coming. They managed to capture more of Supply Hill, forcing the defenders to fall back and draw in their perimeter yet further. The defenders were so nervous that even wind whistling through the dense brush set off another round of defensive gunfire. Peter fired his Bren at noise and shadows, as well as at attacking Japanese, and finally the engagement was broken.

The next morning, fresh reserve troops appeared on Supply Hill, to replace the men who had lost their lives in the previous days' fighting. One such was a tall Rajput havildar, and he was assigned to Peter's bunker. The havildar had straight black hair, which he combed back, smooth brown skin, and he carried himself with traditional military bearing. In short order, Peter got to know his new bunker mate. "I am twenty-four," he told Peter. "I am married and have two young children at home. I have been in the service for almost six years." He smiled. "My specialty is the Bren gun."

Sato had been able to refit his battalions and once again turned his attention to the northern sector. He knew that if he could continue to chip away at the southern defenses while attacking in force in the northern sector, he had a chance of taking the Kohima Ridge in its entirety. He had his own worries, though. His supplies were running low again, and he needed to restock and resupply. He had gained a few yards of barren land on the tennis court but had not managed to move further.

"We will mount a full-scale attack on the remainder of the tennis court," he announced to his officers. "This will be psychological warfare; we will cause fear and panic with night attacks," Sato explained. "This technique was very effective in the battle for the Sittang Bridge. We were able to sow fear, confusion, and terror."

As his officers left him to rally the troops, Sato turned to his chief of staff and whispered, "But it was different then; now it is not easy to rattle the enemy." As night fell, a cold drizzle began to fall, adding to the misery of the men on the ridge. In the rain, Sato began the attack.

Peter and the havildar had cleaned up the bunker and re-stocked the weapons pit. Then they hunkered down for the night. As expected, the Japanese gunners opened fire again. From the high ground, Peter and the young havildar fired the guns until their guns glowed red from the heat. Peter saw a Japanese soldier approach the bunker and point his gun at the havildar. Just as he was about to pull the trigger, Peter shot the man at close range. The Japanese soldier fell into the bunker, but once they assured themselves that he was dead, the two men continued to fire ceaselessly. Suddenly a shell burst right at the edge of the bunker, its shrapnel shattering the young havildar's skull. The skull exploded, scattering its contents in every direction. Peter was horrified, but through his tears he kept firing.

The shelling and gunfire continued as the enemy advanced, then came an order from Major Rajendra: "Fall Back! Regroup at the command tent!" With the remaining men, Peter dashed out of the bunker to regroup, yielding their position to the Japanese. At his command tent, Major Rajendra ordered his men, "Retreat to Kuki Point. We will join the troops defending that position." The men wearily but hastily beat a retreat northward to Kuki Point.

The British unit defending the tennis courts was just as cold and miserable as the Japanese soldiers and came under the same sort of fierce attack as the men at Supply Hill. Worse, they were short of water. The siege had taken its toll on their health, but their morale was still high. They were able to fend off the Japanese attacks for awhile, but then Sato used elephants to bring a mountain gun to the "ad" side of the tennis court and began shelling their defensive positions. The defenders put up a noble and monumental defense, then launched their own attack against the enemy. Disregarding personal safety, some of the men charged into the Japanese gun position, lobbed grenades into the gun pit, and rendered the mountain gun ineffective. All of the Japanese in the gun position were annihilated. By morning, after a bloody, all-night fight, Sato admitted that things were at a stalemate and withdrew his forces yet again.

As morning broke, the scene surrounding the tennis court showed most of the buildings gutted. Shellfire had destroyed virtually all of the tall pine trees that had surrounded the court. Broken branches hung grotesquely from the tall alder trees. Many trees smoldered from the battle, sending puffs of smoke skyward and burning the men's eyes. The shifting wind blew the smoke in various directions, sometimes obscuring the Japanese lines and sometimes hiding the British lines.

From Kuki Point, Major Rajendra ordered a last-gasp attack on Supply Hill. The men managed to re-take the position, but Major Rajendra knew that they could not hold it for long. He managed to track down Colonel James by phone, and the two men had a conversation.

Colonel James: "How are you holding up?"

Major Rajendra: "They keep coming up the hill, we keep killing them, yet they keep coming. Last night we had to withdraw, but we managed to retake Supply Hill today. We can hold it if we have more men. Request reinforcements."

Colonel James: "Unfortunately, the northern sector was battered severely last night, and I have had to send reinforcements there. All I can spare is a Rajput platoon, under a very able subedar, Singh. They should arrive before sunset."

Major Rajendra: "Thank you, Sir. We have enough ammunition. Our morale is high. We will hold on as long as we can."

As he hung up the phone, Major Rajendra had mixed emotions. He hoped that he and his men could hold the hill, and now that reinforcements were on their way, that hope was possible. But he also realized that it was quite possible that Supply Hill would fall to the Japanese for good.

That night, the Japanese attacked all along the ridge, from south to north. They hit every position. They re-took most of Supply Hill, reducing the defensive perimeter to Garrison Hill, the northern sector, and part of Kuki Point.

Sniping continued throughout the day, but the Japanese did not mount a daylight attack in force. The defenders of the shrunken garrison were able to clean wounds, assemble ammunition, and regroup in new positions and new formations. At night, though, the Japanese attacked and took Kuki Point. In the northern sector, they managed to occupy the DC bungalow itself. Part of the land on which the club sat also fell to the Japanese.

As morning broke, only a small portion of Supply Hill, Garrison Hill, and the Hospital ridge remained in British hands. Miraculously, the Japanese had abandoned Kuki Point, ceding it back to the British.

Sato had thrown his troops in ceaseless attacks, sometimes recklessly, not minding the losses of men and ordnance. He still clung to his plan to continue the simultaneous assaults. He kept counting on victory, but with each passing day he began to have doubts about the sacrifice of men and ammunition. Each morning he counted his losses, which mounted with each attack. The dead lay where they fell, bloated bodies smelling of death and decay. Ammunition was beginning to run low, as was food, and replacements of men, ammunition, and food were not forthcoming. "All this for a few feet of gritty, pock-marked land," he thought. He became increasingly irritable and short and was not pleased to receive a call from his division commander.

The division commander was angry and frustrated. He himself was under pressure from General Ugaki in Maymyo. The division commander expressed anger at the lack progress. "You should have taken Garrison Hill by now," he railed. Sato made no reply, and the division commander continued to rant. "You have failed to keep to the schedule and achieve your goal. If you do not plant the Rising Sun on Garrison Hill, you will be removed. I may be removed as well. Attack and take the tennis court, and enter the base of Garrison Hill." He continued, "By tomorrow morning, if this task is not accomplished, you will be court-martialed and dismissed." The phone went dead as the division commander hung up.

Sato was livid. Headquarters assumed no blame for the failure! Then his anger was supplemented by fright. He sent an immediate reply by signal. "The enemy we face here is not the enemy we faced in the paddy fields of the south. Here they are more resolute, better supplied, and stronger. A few months ago, the British and Indians would have run away, but now they stand and fight. In contrast, my men are nearly starving. We need supplies. We have not received rice or salt in over a week. We need ammunition. We need mortar bombs. We have lost many soldiers; we need more men. We cannot fight for much longer."

Sato did not even wait for a reply. He signed off the wireless and returned to his tent, shaking with anger. "I must devise a successful plan," he insisted to himself. "I cannot count on Headquarters; I have to do it myself." Sato had not slept for days, and had not eaten any hot food for weeks. He walked out of his tent to have a smoke and to think. He knew that his weakened men were not going to overcome the determined defenders of Garrison Hill. He had to try another tactic. After a long period of pacing, smoking, and thinking, he called his chief of staff and gave him instructions. "Take the remnants of our strongest units to attack the tennis court, and the table of land it stands on. This will expose the base of Garrison Hill to attack and will isolate the hill and the command post." He now reorganized again.

It took all day to transfer his strongest units to the north. Sato drove his men relentlessly to get in position for the attack on this difficult position. By early evening, his men had climbed the steep bank from the Dimapur road, a stupendous feat. A few hours later, as darkness set in, they positioned themselves on the open land of the ground surrounding the tennis court. The darkness deepened, the crickets ceased chirping, and a deathly silence prevailed. Soldiers on both sides were tense. Then the silence was shattered by the sound of mortar bombs exploding in the scarred hills. Blood-curdling yells heralded a new and deadly attack by the Japanese, focused most intensely on the narrow piece of land on which the tennis court stood. The fighting went on all night. Darkness did not deter the defenders from charging at the enemy positions, even if sometimes they were only shadows. The Japanese too charged recklessly, but the defenders held their positions tenaciously. They fought all night courageously. The incessant shelling and banzai charges took their toll on the defenders, but the Japanese only gained a few feet on the "ad" side of the tennis court; they could not even reach the court's midpoint. They did occupy one of the out-buildings, pitilessly bayoneting all the defenders.

General West, with his new British division and an Indian brigade, had been preparing to break through the roadblocks that Sato had set up. From his base in Dimapur, he planned to relieve the defenders of Kohima Ridge. After a back-and-forth battle that raged all day, he was finally able to break the last Japanese roadblock. Now he could resume signal traffic, and he informed Colonel James jubilantly, "The last roadblock has been demolished. You will be relieved soon."

At his morning conference, Colonel James, his spirits somewhat buoyed by the news he had received from Dimapur the night before, knew that the British attack against the Japanese encirclement had started. He called all his officers and congratulated them. Peter listened eagerly as Colonel James told his officers and men, "Relief is imminent. Forces were being held up at milestone 12 from Kohima, but that last barrier has been crushed." The men cheered, looking forward to their relief. Then Colonel James con-tinued. "Unfortunately, the same cannot be said for Imphal. The Battle of Imphal and the Imphal plain continues, although reinforcements are being flown in from the interior in order to relieve the 17th Division there and prevent its annihilation for the third time."

The undernourished, tired, and hungry men returned to the bunkers with some hope. Soon, the distant sound of aircraft coming from the west commanded their attention. Gazing warily at the sky, although no Japanese aircraft had put in an appearance for two weeks, the men saw that the planes bore the unmistakable RAF roundels. A collective cheer went up. By the time the planes were directly overhead, every head was turned skyward to look at the planes, and all arms were waving in delight. As the planes made a circle and came in low to drop supplies, cries of joy erupted from the men on the ground. As the hungry and battered men watched in agony, half of the supplies plummeted over the edge of the ridge into the hands of the enemy. Thankfully, enough were rescued to raise the morale of the troops.

Jeremy heard a low rumble. "Could this be another attack?" he wondered. But no, the noise was coming from the west. It grew louder, and when the defenders looked west, they could see in the distance the outline of British tanks. Another cheer arose from the dirty and hungry men. "The siege is over!" they cried. "British tanks have broken through!" From the tennis courts in the norther sector they could see a convoy of British and American lorries; the 2nd Division, attacking from Dimapur, had broken through. The first troops to arrive in the northern sector were the men of the Punjabi brigade; then came the all-British Division, tanks first and then the armored cars. The long sixteen-day siege had finally ended.

The garrison was relieved, but still the enemy mounted attacks. Much fighting lay ahead, but with fresh troops, the position could be held. At last the men could move more freely around the garrison, and all did not have to be on alert at all times. Jeremy wasted no time in seeking out Peter. Was he still here? Was he still alive? Word came that Peter Thomas had been attached to Major Rajendra's unit on Supply Hill, had withdrawn to Kuki Point, and then had fallen back to the foot of Garrison Hill. Jeremy slipped away and made inquiries. He was pointed to a small bunker near the foot of the hill and spotted the back of Peter's head. "Peter!" he shouted, running toward the bunker. Peter spun around and, when he saw Jeremy, climbed out of the bunker and ran himself toward his friend. They embraced, to much laughter and tears. Their delight in finding one another safe and alive was contagious, and soon all the men nearby were sharing in the joy.

Chapter 39
The Tide Turns

As the British troops celebrated their deliverance, a stunned and fearful Sato was called to Headquarters in Indaw. Incensed by the lack of support—food and ammunition—that he had received from Headquarters, he knew that he would be blamed for the failure to take the British positions at Kohima.

At Indaw, Sato's division commander had already received an angry phone call from General Ugaki in Maymyo. "The plan is behind schedule and the attacks have not brought the anticipated success!" Ugaki had raged. "Why is this?"

General Watanabe, the Division commander, had tried to explain. "Resistance was unexpectedly strong and determined."

Ugaki had interrupted, "Excuses; that is all excuses. You are all cowards!"

Watanabe had pleaded. "The enemy is being supplied by their air force, while our supplies are being interrupted by the local people, especially the Kachins." A short silence had ensured. Then Ugaki had broken into a rant.

"The struggle is between our spiritual strength and the enemy with their material strength. You will continue the task till all your ammunition is expended. If your arms are broken, fight with your feet. If your hands and feet are broken, use your body. If there is no breath left in your body, fight with your spirit. If you run out of ammunition, use your bayonet, if you do not have your bayonet, use your teeth; bite your enemy to death. Lack of weapons is no excuse for defeat."

The line had gone dead, and Watanabe had hung up his phone with a trembling hand. "Now I must face my field commanders," he had sighed. He signaled his chief of staff to usher in the field commanders, Colonel Sato from Kohima and his counterpart from Imphal. He faced his two field commanders from the Kohima and Imphal fronts and asked curtly, already knowing the answer, "Why did your attacks fail?"

Sato angrily complained about the lack of supplies. Then he continued, "This is a new and determined enemy. The theory that the British are weak and will quit fighting to either retreat or surrender as they did in lower Burma is no longer valid." Watanabe looked askance. Sato added, "They also receive supplies by air."

The field commander from Imphal added, "British agents steal our food and ammunition. Plus, the British air-drop supplies to the resistance as well as the troops."

General Watanabe looked at his two field commanders. They were unshaven, with long hair; they were lean and hungry. He knew that his field commanders had fought with bravery. He knew they had not received supplies. He suspected that the new American-built planes were better than the fearsome Zero. But he needed to boost morale. He promised more supplies, especially rice. Sato asked if there would be air supply, as the British were doing. The division commander knew that the Japanese air force was depleted, that many planes from the motherland were being lost in the South Pacific. Nonetheless he lied. "Yes, air supply will come." The meeting ended with tepid shouts of "banzai!" There was not much sake at hand, so there was not much celebration. The meeting ended before dusk. Sato went to his quarters wearily, bewildered at the events of the past two weeks.

KOHIMA RIDGE, BRITISH SECTOR

The British troops on Kohima Ridge were ebullient. In the best British tradition, the commander had been directed to take a well-earned rest before reassignment. The men bid him good-bye with heartfelt respect. They congratulated him mightily on a magnificent job. Then the recently beleaguered defenders enjoyed a warm breakfast—the first eggs and hot coffee they had had for weeks—before moving to the rear.

The fighting was hardly over, but the British were already making plans for the next phase. The new garrison commander would make plans for re-entry into Burma, in order to chase and annihilate the retreating Japanese. "It is like killing a cobra," Peter thought. "You have to crush and bury the head, lest it revive and come after you." But now the British had faith that the "invincible" Imperial Japanese Army could be beaten.

There was still some fighting at Imphal, but the tide of the war was clearly turning in favor of the Allies. The men on Kohima Ridge tried to enjoy the lull in activity and build their strength. It was inevitable that they would see action again soon, and they needed to build their strength again if they were gong to succeed and survive that action.

Peter used the time to reflect on the events of the last few weeks. His favorite spot was overlooking the DC bungalow and its tennis court. At college he had played some tennis but had lost more games than he had won. As soon as the game would start, his opponent would pump balls to Peter's backhand, which was weak, and Peter invariably lost. Somehow those memories helped him to realize that if he was to win in life itself, he had to overcome adversity. He promised himself that, should he ever return to normal civilian life, he would work to overcome all his weaknesses. But normal civilian life seemed far away right now.

Some nights, he and Jeremy would sit on the ridge. Often they sat in silence; other times they vented their feelings.

"It is shocking that this formerly pristine land has been so devastated: trees broken and uprooted, some still standing but split in half," Jeremy lamented.

Peter's eyes turned to the flowers that had been trampled by the hundreds of soldiers and crushed by wheels. Jeremy read his thoughts. "You are worried that they will never grow again. Peter, if we leave them un-disturbed they will revive; nature has a way to recover."

The men fell silent. In the distance, the plaintive call of the peacock and parrot could be heard. Peter now changed the subject.

"Jeremy, let's talk about us. Can you believe that it is three years since we left the comfort of our homes? We were young then, full of hopes, dreams, and the bright future we faced. We are older now. We have lost our innocence and youth. We have given some of our best years to a war, whose outcome is still not certain."

"Yes, we are battle-tested," Jeremy said sadly. "I guess we will leave soon, but I will never forget this place. That said, I am anxious to move on and go home. More than anything, I want to be home with my family."

"I have been haunted lately by what might have happened to my family," Peter admitted. "Who lived and who died? Where are our neighbors, our friends? Life will never be the same again, even if we return home safely."

"The war is hardly over," said Jeremy sadly. "We have a long slog and a long way to go yet."

The evening was closing. "Let's go listen to the radio news,' Jeremy suggested.

They retired to the mess and tuned to Radio Kandy from Ceylon. The familiar voice announced, "Tanks and personnel carriers, supported by RAF bombers and Mosquitoes, finally dislodged the enemy. The Battle of Imphal is over. The Japanese are in full retreat. British and Indian troops are now in pursuit of the enemy across the border." The mess erupted in cheers as the announcer continued, "The RAF has raided Rangoon again. All planes returned safely to their bases." More whoops of joy rose from the tired men. With that, the broadcast ended, and the men, energized, poured out of the mess to share the news.

In a short time, Jeremy and Peter had both recovered their strength. Peter's eyes were still yellow from all the Mepacrine he was taking to fight off his bout of malaria, but excitement overcame his lassitude. The battle at Imphal had ended, and two columns of the famed 17th Division, one from the south and another from the north, had joined up. Now that division was entering Kohima. Its General would be the new commander of all the troops.

Peter joined the troops gathered to get a glimpse of the General of the 17th. He had to crane his head but was tall enough to see over the heads of the mob that surrounded the tall General, congratulating him on the turn-around. The General took time to meet his men, walking slowly through the crowd and shaking hands. He announced that he would be giving medals and citations, and both Jeremy and Peter hoped that they would be included. They also knew that they would soon move out from Kohima in pursuit of the Japanese.

After several days of re-shuffling and reorganization, all units were at full strength again, reinforced with new arms and equipment. The road to the heart of Burma lay open, broad, and straight. The army was ready for the cross-border offensive. Jeremy was full of anticipation. "The rumor is that we will cross the Irrawaddy River at a still-secret place. Then we will race to central Burma," he reported to Peter.

Peter observed thoughtfully, "What a great irony, that this war has come full circle. The hunter has now become the hunted. Now the Japanese will be the hungry and beleaguered soldiers that we have been since Moulmein."

THE JAPANESE RETREAT

Sato was inordinately frustrated. He had been unable to take Kohima and unable to get support from Army headquarters. He had promised his battered troops supplies. "Army Command will send food and ammunition within days,' he had announced. "Then we will drive the British off the ridge." Yet days had passed, and no supplies had arrived. The troops now were not only hungry and haggard; they were also beginning to grumble. Sato was stymied as to what to do. He had received no orders to retreat. His troops were in no condition to march southward to help in the taking of Imphal. He was unsure of what to do next. He called Division Headquarters again, explaining the plight of his men and reluctantly requesting approval of his decision to temporarily break off his engagement with the enemy. "Food is in short supply," he explained. "Half the oxen are dead, and the rice is wet. Please favor us with more food. We also need ammunition. All ammunition for our field guns and mortars is exhausted. Without food and ammunition, we will be unable to achieve victory."

Watanabe remained silent, so Sato continued. "We have been bombed by the RAF, who use their bases in India. The Kachins raid us and take our supplies; they seize the mule trains that are supposed to bring us our supplies." With a note of desperation in his voice, Sato said, "I must break contact with the enemy until I receive supplies."

Watanabe again made no response. He knew that the promises he had made to his field commanders at Indaw had been hollow. After they had left his headquarters, he had called General Ugaki in Maymyo again, pleading for resupply. The General had been livid, telling the division commander that if the troops had taken Imphal, as they had been directed, they would have plenty of "Churchill supplies." "They failed because of poor leadership!" General Ugaki had railed. The division commander had tried to explain.

Division: Without resupply it is impossible to take part in any further operations.

Maymyo: For the great Imperial Army, "impossible" is not an option.

Division: We need rice, meat, and protein.

Maymyo: Send your quartermaster to Sangsak; there are supplies stored there.

Division: Sir, sending a contingent to Sangsak will expose our front to enemy attack.

Maymyo: You are aware that you are disobeying a direct order?

The division commander had taken matters into his own hands and had broken communications with Maymyo. Now he told Sato bluntly, "Maymyo will not send supplies. You must retreat to east of the Chindwin River."

Sato hung up the phone shakily, and his stomach was churning. Retreat?! This tasted too much of defeat! But what other choice did he have? His men were slowly perishing before his eyes. Quickly he gave orders to his officers for a "redeployment" east of the Chindwin. No shouts of "banzai!" greeted this announcement. Instead the officers silently took their leave to ready their units.

The dispirited men crept down the ridge under cover of darkness. Sato left two companies to act as rear guard and detached one as an advance guard. The sick were carried on bamboo stretchers, and sick animals were abandoned. The unit's meager supplies were loaded onto the surviving but now-starving mules. Sato feared not only the British but also their allies, the dreaded Kachins and the Nagas, who were such good jungle fighters and enjoyed tormenting stray soldiers. "Keep a tight formation," he admonished.

As they slowly retreated down the ridge from Kohima, the soldiers were given three rounds of ammunition and were instructed, "use your bayonet first." Their clothes were muddy and torn, and there were no replacements. The troops had been on half-rations for so long that some of them stumbled and fainted, causing delay and risking detection. Within days, the desperate soldiers who protected the mule trains slaughtered the mules. But even cooking under cover of darkness was dangerous, as spotters would get coordinates. Any attempt to get food to bolster the strength of the troops was fraught with hazard.

Sato had lost weight along with his men. His clothes no longer fit him. He had chronic diarrhea, which had weakened him. His men had endured hard times before, but this was different. His officers told him of wild rumors of rebellion; that the General had quit; that the new army commander was ill; that the old army commander would return soon. Sato did not know what to believe.

The next day, Sato heard the high-pitched whine of fighter planes. The whine sounded different. "Take cover!" he screamed. Indeed, these were twin-engine fighters coming in from the south. They screamed over the ridge, and the next thing Sato knew was that he and his men were taking cover wherever they could, dodging machine-gun fire from the fast new RAF Mosquitoes. The fighters came in waves, screaming and dropping their bombs. The whistling bombs dropped among the Japanese columns and exacted a severe toll. Sato was angry. He had been told by his division commander that the RAF had no bombers, and now he knew that he had been lied to. He was surprised at how fast and deadly the allied planes were. After the last wave finally departed, Sato came out to assess the damage. Many of his men lay dead, and Sato moaned in anger and disbelief. Darkness would soon descend, and there was no time to remove the dead. "Keep moving," he barked at his stunned men. He did allow the men to remove small items from the dead to send home to Japan, however.

The troops stumbled down the narrow and treacherous trails on their way to the river. Once they reached the river, Sato would have to figure out a way of getting all the troops across it. He had not heard from the two advance units he had sent ahead as they departed Kohima, so he sent scouts forward to assess the best crossing point and report on how best to cross the river.

The scouts arrived at a large village, now empty. But smoke indicated that people had been in the village recently. As the scouts crept warily toward the center of the village, they came upon fellow soldiers from the advance unit who seemed to be sitting in a stupor. As the scouts crept closer, they saw that the soldiers were naked from the waist down. To their horror, they saw that the men were impaled on sharpened bamboo, a technique that the Nagas had refined. Some had sharp bamboo slivers driven into their penis, and their testicles smashed. The scouts were horrified, knowing that the men had probably been fully conscious when they endured such torture.

The scouts sent a runner back to Sato. When he came upon the scene he saw that his men were weeping openly. He issued orders swiftly. "Remove the men from the bamboo. Cut their fingers to send to their families in Japan. But leave the bodies lying on the ground; we do not have the time or the means to give them a proper burial."

Knowing it was not wise to stay at the village, Sato hastened back to the main body of troops and pressed them to move onward. He was sick at heart, worrying about what had happened to the rest of his advance units. Unfortunately, as the troops moved onward toward the river, they discovered the fate of many of the men in the advance units.

From time to time the main body would come upon the bodies of their fallen comrades. Often the bodies had been mutilated by the unseen enemy spies and tribesmen who had surprised them. Typically, the soldiers' clothes were removed, and always all the insignia were missing. Those who miraculously were alive and had strength called to their brethren, "give us grenades; let us die in dignity." The retreating soldiers, under orders from Sato, ignored them, not because they did not empathize but because they could do nothing. They could not spare any ammunition; they needed all of it for the fight ahead.

Sato was relieved to be out of hostile India and into Burma proper. "Surely," he thought, "we can get help from the Imperial Army now."

He set a course for Homalin, on the east side of the Chindwin River. If he did not find the Imperial Army there, he hoped to find friendly Burmese. He remembered that villagers from Homalin had provided cows, rice, and salt to the Japanese as they had marched from Burma into India. Sato did not want to think about any alternative; he needed desperately to feed his starving troops. But he would be surprised.

The forward-most Japanese units arrived at the west bank of the Chindwin and gazed at the swollen river with its strong current. Advance scouts had learned how to build a raft from tender bamboo and tree bark. Sato set work parties to cut down 8-foot lengths of bamboo with their bayonets and lash them together with thin strips of bark from young trees. The rafts assembled, the men awaited the arrival of the rest of the straggling troops and orders to cross the rain-swollen and tempestuous river.

When all the Japanese arrived at the river bank, Sato ordered the sick and the wounded on stretchers onto the flimsy rafts and pushed them off. Then the rest of the troops crowded onto the quickly built rafts. Sato himself boarded the last raft and set out. Some rafts got across the river, but others, including Sato's, got caught in the strong current and were swiftly carried away down the river. The rafts twisted and spun helplessly and started to break. Men fell off of the rafts, and some of the poor swimmers bobbed their heads in the water a few times and then disappeared forever. Sato knew that a falls and whirlpool lay ahead, where the river fell off precipitously. "Hang on!" he ordered his men. As the remaining rafts entered the falls, they were lashed back and forth. Sato's raft fell into the whirlpool, and he heard a tremendous roar. Miraculously, the whirlpool spit the raft out again, and as the raft moved rapidly downstream Sato heard the pitiful cries for help from the men on rafts that were not so lucky. The cries tore at Sato's heart, but he could not do anything to help his men. It was all he could do to gain control of his own raft and finally maneuver it to the river's east bank.

As the wet and exhausted men lay panting on the east bank, Sato walked up the muddy bank to regain his bearings. He knew that many of his men had drowned, others had bashed their heads against the rocks and died from the blow. He and his comrades had been among the lucky few to survive the cauldron. How different was this crossing from the time he had crossed the same river in the opposite direction! Then he had been so optimistic; he had not considered the possibility of failure. Now he was tired, beaten, and worried.

Sato returned to the survivors, still lying immobile on the river bank. "Do your best to get to our old base at Indaw. We will meet up with the rest of the regiment there. Move in small groups to avoid detection from the British or their allies."

The men shuddered as they remembered the scene in the Naga village. Slowly they pulled themselves to their feet and moved toward Indaw. Sato was the last to leave. If they could reach Indaw, he could feed his men, replenish his supplies, reorganize his regiment.

Most of the men reached Indaw and met up with the rest of the regiment, those who had not been swept southward by the river's current. But the men discovered only an abandoned town. Not a Japanese in sight. Not a Burmese to be found. No evidence of Nagas. On the precipice of panic, Sato dispatched a small unit to gather food, but they came back empty-handed. "There is no rice at all," the unit reported wearily. The lack of friendly Burmese in and around Indaw puzzled Sato. "They have been our allies for so long; they should be fighting alongside us. But now, when they are most needed, they seem to have melted away." It was beginning to get dark, and there was no time to move on to another village. Against his better judgment, Sato advised his men to forage for whatever food they could find and spend the night; they would move out at first light.

As the hungry Japanese soldiers filed out of Indaw the next morning, they came under small arms fire. "Take cover!" Sato directed. "Take defensive position!"

The assault sopped in a few minutes, as the enemy faded into the tall grass. Sato was sure that it had been Nagas who had fired upon them. They were a stealthy people, able to sneak up on soldiers and pick them off one by one. They would not mount a full-scale attack on his men, but they could pick them off slowly. Then the survivors would be terrorized. Sato realized that the men faced yet another threat: malnutrition, cholera, and malaria. These diseases were beginning to take a severe toll on his men.

As the men followed the river as it turned eastward, they heard gunfire ahead. Sato motioned them down and waited. He surmised that the fire came from K-Force shooting at his advance units. Soon the firing ceased, and he sent out a reconnaissance patrol. The information they brought back sent a chill down his spine. They brought papers and maps in Burmese! Now he was fighting the Burma Defense Force as well as the British and Indians!

Sato thought quickly. "The Burmese were our allies," he mused. "Something must have gone terribly wrong in Rangoon. The Japanese high command there must have somehow bungled the independence, turning the small BDF against the Japanese." Sato fretted about this but did not share his fears with his officers. "My troops are not prepared for this. The BDF is not large enough to face us in static warfare, but they can play havoc with our food supplies and communications. Like the Nagas, they can harass us, especially small isolated units like this." He hurriedly called his senior officers together to draft a plan and route. After consulting the maps, the men agreed to head to Monhyin, from where a road would take them to Mandalay. They immediately mustered their men and began the march.

After two months, Sato and his men were still struggling to move eastward. Disease and hunger, as well as guerilla attacks by Nagas and Kachins, had demoralized and reduced their number. Now they faced the Irrawaddy River, which they needed to cross before they could cross the Shwebo plain. Sato despaired, and with each failure his despair grew. His increasing anger and frustration were made worse by the loss of most of his radios. So he was uncertain as to what was happening to the other regiments since they had left Kohima. Were they moving in the same direction as he? Why had he not met up with them? Was the enemy ahead of him or behind him? Would they stop his progress? He still could not bring himself to call his progress "retreat," although it was taking on all the characteristics of a retreat. Wearily, Sato had called his RSM and directed him to send a small patrol ahead of the main unit, to gather intelligence. And now it had been two weeks, and he had not heard from the patrol. Sato's position was becoming increasingly tenuous.

THE BRITISH OFFENSIVE

The enemy was in fact behind Sato, hard on his heels. The re-formed BurRif battalion had been attached to the 17th Indian Division, the old battle-tested unit. They had left Kohima, crossed into Burma, and were now chasing the desperate Japanese, first toward the Chindwin, now toward the Irrawaddy. The 17th had been ordered to make all deliberate speed to cross the dry zone and then cross the big river, the Irrawaddy. The men knew that they were heading to the Irrawaddy but did not know the precise crossing point. Only the Corps Commander and his closest advisors knew the precise location.

Like others in the BurRif battalion, Jeremy and Peter were eager to return to the country of their birth and to see home and family again. They were now in new Bren carriers. Jeremy was in high spirits. "Look at all the transport and armor!" he enthused. At one stop they ran into the West African division, and Jeremy extended his hand in friendship to an Askari soldier, whose uniform and emblems signified that he was part of the 81st West African division. "So many men from so many backgrounds, all pursing the same goal: to drive the Japanese out of Burma," Jeremy exclaimed.

The advance continued. The main column turned southward. The land looked familiar to Peter; it was *deja veu*. He pulled out a map and turned to Jeremy. "Look," he said, pointing his index finger at the map. "We are heading to the Irrawaddy River, and I think we are close to Gangaw, from where we retreated three years ago."

Just then, RAF planes flew overhead in large numbers, heading eastward. Soon the men heard thunder. Obviously bombardment had started to soften up the targets. Finally, after much secrecy as to their destination, the division now received their orders head to Pakokku. When they arrived at the riverbank, the sappers were ready with rubber boats. They were already laying down a pontoon bridge. The troops waited until dark, then climbed aboard the rafts and headed to the opposite bank. They fully expected fire from the opposite bank, but no response was forthcoming. It was a complete but pleasant surprise to reach the opposite bank without encountering resistance.

The beachhead was quickly established. Water-craft transported the heavy weapons, and the division reassembled on the east bank of the Irrawaddy. Again Peter thought of the retreat three years ago. This time was so different: the American-built jeeps and the shiny new olive-green lorries impressed him. There was food—C-rations and chocolates!—and ammunition enough to make the men feel strong and confident. For a few days, the division waited for the deep thrust into Burma. The junior ranks were kept in the dark as to where they were headed, but they knew the upcoming action would be big. Soon the orders came: move to Kyaukpadaung.

Peter again opened the map and pointed as he remarked to Jeremy "Look at the map. The big prize must be the rail and road junction of Meiktila. If we capture that junction, we bisect the Japanese at the waist."

By late morning, the race towards Meiktila gained momentum. The column split in two: the northen pincer would trap the enemy divisions from the north; and the southern pincer would prevent reinforcements from the south. It would be a classic military maneuver to trap and annihilate the enemy, their old enemy the White Tigers.

As they moved, Peter saw that some of the oldest calvary units of the Indian Army would lead the attack. They had such romantic names— Deccan Probyn's Horse, for example—and the men wore exuberantly colorful turbans. Now the calvary used motor transport and tanks instead of horses, but the old romance still prevailed.

MEIKTILA

Meiktila was a once sleepy village, where Burmese kings had dammed a small river, creating a lake. The British colonial rulers had improved the dam and divided the lake in two, with a bridge bisecting the lake into a southern and northern lake. They made it a rail and road junction. They had created a beautiful city in the center of the dry belt, dominated by two lakes. The lakes were situated at the north and south of the city and were joined by a narrow creek. The city was like an oasis. Tall trees, shrubs, prickly pear cactus, flowers, and brightly plumed Burmese birds as well as cranes and herons added to the beauty. It was a prosperous city, with red brick colonial buildings for the British and with solid teak wood houses for the middle-class and wealthy Burmese. Of great military importance were the four airstrips that were in the four corners of the city.

The commander waited until all his units were in place. He positioned field guns just outside the city. When they were all in place, the order to fire came down. They thundered in unison for hours, shells falling into the Japanese lines. Small 25-pounders and tank guns joined in. Great plumes of fire shot skyward, and spouts of water jutted upward like spectacular fountains when the shells fell into the lakes. There was no way to avoid hitting non-military targets. Suddenly the big guns ceased, and the men and armor rolled toward the center of the city. At the outskirts, the dug-in enemy opened fire and fought with great tenacity and ferocity. They suffered tremendous casualties, but few, if any, surrendered. Instead, they fought till they ran out of ammunition and, when they faced capture, committed suicide by the dozen. Some would wait in their foxholes with explosives strapped to their bodies, then detonate the explosives as the allied tanks rumbled over them.

Other Japanese troops had already been sent eastward, past Mandalay, and into the safety of the Shan hills. But nothing could slow the allied advance. Escape became harder as armored cars and lorries raced south, to take the southern airfields and cut the roads that allowed retreat. In the north, a tank brigade column of the 17th raced past the city and blocked any Japanese retreat to the north. Too late, the Japanese commander realized that the attack was not a feint but a major attack. Too late, he recognized the full power of the allied tanks and armor trained upon his position. He called Rangoon General Headquarters, "Large enemy forces crossed the Irrawaddy, led by tanks and armor. They have now reached Meiktila. This is not a feint; it is the main attack. Some units have moved eastward to the Shan Hills, but the enemy has cut off all escape. Situation desperate."

The 17th Division was slowed by the suicidal actions of the Japanese soldiers, but they soon sent out squads tasked with shooting and killing the suicidal Japanese first, thereby allowing the tanks to advance with no threat. By morning, the tank advance, supplemented by the Hurricane fighters and ground support, broke through the enemy resistance and took the city. Peter's company reached the center of the city to join the old brigade of Gurkhas.

Despite the allied success, a bloody battle for control of the city went on for days, as desperate Japanese made a last-ditch effort and fought to the end. One group even captured a British tank and turned it on the British. The Gurkhas took casualties but held their ground. The momentum was with the British and their allies.

Meanwhile, Sato and his men were creeping eastward into this very maelstrom. Sato was unkempt, half starved, and ghost-like. He had not paid attention to himself; his hair was long and oily, and he looked sick, but his determination was still steely. He was adamant that he would lead his men back to their parent army. His scouts had returned and had reported no enemy ahead, but Sato was still worried. He had few radios left and was wary of making contact with headquarters, for fear of alerting the enemy to his position. Nonetheless, he needed to know where the enemy was and where his unit should head to join up with other units of the Japanese Army. After much effort, his signal made radio contact with headquarters. "Moving eastward to Monhyin," Sato reported. "Situation bleak. No food or supplies. Advise of enemy in area."

When the reply came, it was bad news. "Mandalay is under attack. Avoid Mandalay. The enemy has cut the Rangoon–Mandalay Road. One enemy pincer north of Mandalay is coming down from Thabeikkyin. Move south soon to avoid being trapped. Head to Mount Popa and join the Arakan Army there, the 28th Japanese Army. You will be under their command."

Sato and his chief of staff were stunned. "How could this be happening?" Sato wondered aloud. He swore the radio man to secrecy, and then he and his chief of staff talked late into the night and pored over maps, trying to grasp the difficult situation in which they now found themselves. In the middle of the night, Sato called his officers together and advised them of the plan. He had no illusions about how difficult the coming days would be but presented as confident a demeanor as he could.

"British tanks and planes are in the area, attacking Mandalay." His officers looked stricken as he continued. "We cannot outrun them. We will head south to Mount Popa and join the 54th Division of the 28th Army under General Sugiyama. We leave at first dawn."

The officers seemed calmed by the idea that they would join the 54th, and after Sato dismissed them they hastened to inform their men. Sato sat alone, pondering his situation. Half of his men had been lost; the remaining half suffered from malaria, cholera, and beri-beri. All were stunned, weakened, and dispirited. The march to Mount Popa would be difficult, but Sato knew he had no choice. Like his officers, he looked forward to serving under such an illustrious commander as General Sugiyama. He admired the General, remembering him as a slender man with deep-set eyes and a shaven head. If anyone could find a way out of the trap in which the Japanese found themselves, it would be General Sugiyama. Sato's thoughts returned to the victory celebration in Rangoon fewer than three years ago, when he had first met General Sugiyama. He found it hard to believe that the fortunes of war could have turned so abruptly.

The next day, he led his sorry men southward, toward the big lake. At the south of the lake was a road and railroad. If he was lucky, he might find transportation there. But first they had a three-day walk ahead of them. In good times, it would be much quicker, but his men had been so weakened by the lack of food, the heat, and the terrible tropical diseases that they could hardly walk.

As the Japanese marched onward, they came upon Burmese villages that were totally deserted. There was absolutely no food to be found; no pigs, chickens, or even rice. Sato suspected that the villagers were somehow being tipped off. His men had not had food for days, and many of them had no hope left. They would drop behind the main column, gather in a circle and pick straws; the man who drew the short straw would pull the pin on his grenade, and the metal casing of the grenade would tear into the men's weakened flesh. Shards of muscle, pieces of liver, and intestines were spread afar. Men who did survive for a few moments would moan, then take their bayonet and commit Hari Kari. Villagers who watched this desperate act from the jungle slowly returned and ghoulishly took valuables, even the gold from their teeth by smashing the heads and jaws and picking out the gold.

THE BURMA DEFENSE FORCE JOINS THE ALLIES

The 17th Division had received much intelligence from the Special Operations Exchange (SOE) and their Karen spies (K-Force). The latest news was that the Burma Defense Force (BDF) had surreptitiously left their Japanese allies and now sought to join the winning side. This was the first time that the Japanese-trained army had turned against the Japanese. The BDF had contacted SOE and K-Force, who had forwarded the information on to Army headquarters in Comilla, India. Commanders in the field were suspicious about the intentions and commitment of the BDF; they wanted advice from headquarters as to how to proceed. Comilla in turn sent the information up the chain of command to Southeast Asia Command (SEAC) in Kandy.

The SEAC commander was delighted with the progress of the military operation so far, but he, too, was suspicious about the intentions and commitment of the BDF. He asked his chief of intelligence, "What do you know about these men?"

The intelligence chief replied readily, "Frankly, I am unimpressed with their principles. The Prime Minister in Rangoon is nothing but a puppet. These young men received some training from the Japanese military, especially the Minami Kikan, but they are still inexperienced, ill-equipped, poorly led, and undisciplined. None of them went to staff college. The Japanese do not seem to have used them in important operations. I think they will have limited ability to help us." He paused. "We cannot have them fight in our cohesive units."

The chief of staff interjected. "I advise keeping tight control of them and using them only as part of the underground forces. We must keep them away from the Karen of K-Force, or they will be at one another's throat."

The Corps commander nodded his head. "It is agreed that they entirely serve under our command. I understand that a delegation from the BDF has requested a meeting with the command of the 17th. I will have my staff draw up a written memo and get it to the 17th via the 4th Corps."

17TH DIVISION HEADQUARTERS, MEIKTILA

By the time the BDF delegation met with the commander of the 17th Division, the latter had received the memo from his Corps headquarters:

```
April 1945
Burma Defense Force wants to switch sides.
Allow them to present themselves, and if they
defect from the Imperial 15th Army, accept
their cooperation. Direct them that while the
country is under military administration, all
elements of said army shall place themselves
```

```
unreservedly under the direct command of the
local British commander. They shall not
interfere with your operations in any way.
They shall not engage in offensive operations
independently. They will be totally subject
to our command in the destruction of Japanese
elements in Burma. The only legal government
in Burma is the military administration set
up by the Supreme Commander under the
authority of the King and Emperor. No written
recognition, no payments, no monetary rewards
will be made. All units must make regular and
full reports on activities and progress.
```

In the commander's tent, the taciturn General read the text of the memo from SEAC to the BDF delegation and asked if they agreed to the terms. The delegation agreed, and the commander of the BDF summarized: "The BDF and its allied Patriotic Burmese Forces (PBF) are now at war against the brutal Japanese Imperial Army. The BDF will do its best to avoid conflict with K-Force and the British-Indian Army. Our role in the fight against the Japanese units will be to stage ambushes and harass the enemy; also to provide intelligence. We will obtain permission from the local British commander before we attack the enemy."

The commander thanked the delegation for their understanding and their efforts. He then explained, "You will receive weapons and supplies from the British and Indians. But this will happen only if you coordinate with and take your orders from the British Army."

The agreement was duly signed and witnessed. Arrangements were made to dispense weapons and ammunition to the BDF, through the delegation. Then the BDF delegation faded into the jungle to inform their foot-soldiers. At their base, the delegation's leader was asked questions about giving in so easily to the British. The leader maintained, "This is the beginning of our drive for Independence. Regardless of the agreement, our troops will defend towns, villages, and the Burmese people from Japanese soldiers and any other enemy."

When the information that the BDF had joined the allied effort reached the British troops, the reaction was mixed. They were not happy with their new erstwhile allies. They viewed the BDF with deep suspicion, as turncoats. "Embrace of this force is ridiculous!" many charged. "Any contribution from the BDF will be worthless," they added scathingly. Nonetheless, they grudgingly accepted the value of more on-the-ground intelligence. Thus the British command cautiously welcomed the BDF into the alliance against the Japanese, only to end this dreadful war.

The corp commander from Meiktila signaled to GOC Comilla, "Will continue operations and will continue to support K-Force. We parachuted SOE operatives a week ago to contact the Karen levies. Karens who stayed behind have joined those in the Karen hills near Toungoo and have become a strong resistance unit, with new rugged transmitters. One of our English operatives is with them." It was easy to recruit Karens. For three years they had lived in fear of the Japanese, and many had been captured and tortured in a most hideous manner; many had been killed on mere suspicion. Now it was their turn to take revenge against their tormenters.

Chapter 40
Desperate Japanese Breakout from the Pegu Yomas

Peter and Jeremy's BurRif battalion was dispatched from Meiktila to the battalion headquarters near the important town of Pabwaye, on the Rangoon–Mandalay Road. It was imperative to do so, as there was evidence that an important, high-ranking Japanese General was in the city. The British wanted to surround the city and prevent the Japanese from escaping into the surrounding jungle.

Peter was summoned to the battalion headquarters. After he entered the command tent, the colonel motioned for him to sit down. Peter was taken aback; such an invitation was unusual. The colonel spoke. "I want to compliment you on your perseverance. You have been with the army from the very start of the war, and you are among just a handful of men who stayed. As you know, many of your comrades deserted or disappeared. You stayed with the battalion all the way, and now I am promoting you. You will receive your paperwork later."

Peter was speechless, and honored. The colonel drew on his pipe and then continued.

"As you know, we have reached a critical point in the re-conquest of Burma. I have a new and dangerous assignment for you, behind enemy lines." He waited for the message to sink in, then asked, "Are you ready?" He waited for Peter's nod and then continued. His intelligence officer brought forward a map and showed it to Peter. The officer pointed to a place to the south of Pabwaye. The major then explained. "We have a number of operatives in and around the town and in the hills: the Jedburg unit (SOE) and K-Force." Peter looked puzzled, and the Major explained.

"Special Operations Exchange, SOE, is a highly secretive unit. Their Jedburg unit and K-Force are working together. They have been operating in Pabwaye for six months, but we recently lost contact with one cell. We do not know whether they have been captured or are laying low to avoid detection. Given your background and your language skills, we think that you could find this unit and rescue it, if it is still extant."

Peter was surprised to be offered such an assignment, but also a little frightened. As if he could read Peter's mind, the major said, "of course, you will be at considerable risk." Then he dangled an inviting prospect. "By the way, we think that General Kobiyashi, Sato's commanding officer, may be in the vicinity. Information about him or his capture would be most helpful."

Peter's heart was racing with excitement. To think that he might help capture Sato, the man who since Moulmein had been a thorn in the side of the British Army and Peter himself. "I will accept this task, Sir," he said resolutely, "and will do the best I can."

The Major shook his hand with warmth and led Peter to the intelligence tent, where he went over the details of the operation. "There were at least three men in this cell," he explained, "one British, one Karen, and one Kachin. All were highly trained to operate radios, and their job was to find General Kobiyashi, who, we believe, is in the area." The Major said rather obliquely, "we believe that his capture would be of value to the SEAC. Our cell had obtained evidence that Kobiyashi was in a monastery. Just as the SOE was about to capture him, we lost contact with the cell. Your job is to find out what happened to our operatives." The Major paused, and then added, "We also want to know what is happening in general in Pabwaye."

The intelligence man gave Peter detailed maps and explained more signals and details of the operation. He was to leave after dark, with six other men. When the Major was satisfied that Peter understood everything perfectly, he clapped Peter's shoulder and wished him well. Peter saluted the Major and left for his tent, to prepare himself for the operation.

Like Jeremy had done to him back at Kohima, Peter now explained to Jeremy that he had been given a special assignment, the details of which he could not share. Jeremy chuckled, then turned serious. "I know, Peter, that we will always find one another again. It is our destiny. Go and do well." The two men embraced and Peter left on his mission.

The seven men left as dusk set in. They ran down into the *chaung*, which had only a small amount of water. They kept their heads down and reached the outskirts of the enemy positions. Ahead they could see a monastic school. Peter paused and brought his men together to give whispered orders. "If the SOE unit has been captured, they will likely be held in the residence of the headmaster. We will break up into three groups, two men staying behind to cover the others." Peter signaled his men to stay quiet and headed for the headmaster's residence. They broke open the door, Peter leading the charge. Shooting their way out the back door, the enemy fled. Among them was a young man and a middle-aged man of high rank. Peter knew that this was Kobiyashi, but he and his men were distracted by the scene inside. Blood and bodies lay grotesquely about. A white man with his neck slashed and some of the others were still, clearly dead, but one man was still breathing. The small party immediately went to his assistance. Peter bandaged the man's wounds, then dispatched two men to support him as they headed for the *chaung*. Peter stayed back to go through the papers, maps, and other records. He put them in his satchel and left the residence. As he and his men approached the *chaung*, the two men who had remained there called out. All hell broke loose. From behind the men, gunfire erupted, and under cover from fire from the two rear guards, the men ran to the *chaung* and hid. They returned fire until the enemy fire ceased. Quietly, Peter calmed his men and re-assembled his party, which now included the wounded man. He knew that it was important to get the paper and maps they had found back to headquarters, and knew that there was little risk that the Japanese would follow him. At the same time, he wanted to take a look at the city's defenses. "Return to Meiktila with the material and the operative," he instructed his second in command, handing over his satchel. "I will follow you after I look about the city." His men reluctantly returned to Meiktila, and Peter lay quietly for awhile before emerging from the *chaung*. He was able to observe the defenses at Pabwaye and noted that they were good defenses. He also saw many units heading south. He returned to his base exhausted, but knew that he needed to report to Intelligence immediately.

At the Intelligence tent, men were already busy analyzing the data that Peter's squad had brought. The Major looked up. "Good work, young man," he said.

Peter reported further to the Major, "I was able to take a closer look at the town. I think it is being rapidly evacuated, but that they were retreating southward rather than eastward. I guess that is because our forces have blocked any escape to the east."

The Major nodded his head. "The information we have gleaned supports that. The entire avenue of retreat to the east was cut off by the SOE and K-Force. Word is that the enemy has promised to hold Pegu, but only till the Rangoon garrison can retreat to Moulmein. The general in command there has already fled Rangoon, and the garrison will retreat as best they can." He then told Peter what the army expected to happen in the near term. "We believe that various units of Japanese who are retreating from the Arakan and the Irrawaddy delta will assemble in the hills overlooking the Rangoon–Mandalay Road somewhere around Toungoo. These combined forces will stage a breakout."

The Major asked Peter if he had heard or seen anything that might confirm this expectation or shed light on where the Japanese would stage the breakout. "Regrettably, Sir," replied Peter, "I do not know. I heard nothing about such an assembly or movement."

The Major thanked Peter for a good job and sent him to rejoin his unit. "Your first order is to get some sleep, young man," the Major said dryly.

IN THE PEGU YOMAS

Rangoon was captured by the allies. A detachment of the 70th Gurkhas had parachuted to the south of Rangoon, and the 26th Indian division was now on the outskirts of Rangoon. The vise was now closing. Japanese troops from Meiktila could not retreat to Rangoon. While the Burma area commander had fled Rangoon, heading for Moulmein, Sato and his troops were marooned in the Pegu Yomas, a range of low hills that formed a barrier across the southern spine of Burma. The Pegu Yomas were not very high, but they were covered with dense forests of bamboo and teak jungles, making travel from west to east difficult. The area was remote, and tropical diseases were rife. For Sato there was no air cover, and retreating through the Pegu Yomas would be hellish. The Karen lived here, and they would take sweet revenge on the Japanese. They knew all the hill trails and hiding places, and they harbored a hatred for the Japanese. Where, exactly, were he and his men heading, and what would await them when they arrived? Events were overtaking him.

Sato was correct to fret about the Karens wanting to take revenge on the Japanese for their treatment of the Karen people. After surviving the disaster at the Sittang Bridge, Saw Travis had joined his fellow Karens in the hills. They hid from the Japanese in limestone caves and now had emerged, happy to fight the enemy. They knew the hills better than the Japanese, and jungle warfare came naturally to them. They were being reinforced by air drops of weapons and radios from the allies.

It had been more than three years since Saw Travis had contact with the British. On a clear night, he directed his men to place crude kerosene lamps along a clear patch of earth. An RAF Dakota flew into the valley and descended. The men watched in great anticipation as the planes seemed to slow, almost stall. Then the cargo doors opened, and objects seemed to be flung out. Parachutes opened above the objects: heavy cans, rice bags, ammunition boxes. As the first supply plane left, another came and dropped more goods, including radio transmitters and receivers. The last plane dropped an Englishmen and some animals. Captain Eastman, with Britain's SOE, gathered the Karens and filled them in on the plans. As they hastened to a well-prepared bunker on the mountainside, Saw Travis told the Englishman how pleased he was to see him.

The Karens were ecstatic when they opened the bags and boxes and saw the new shiny guns, radios, Johnny Walker scotch whiskey, and Player cigarettes. Captain Eastman, who spoke both Burmese and Karen, opened a bottle of Johnny Walker, took a deep swig, and then handed the bottle to Saw Travis. It was the first time Saw Travis had tasted Scotch, and he found it scorched his throat. He had posted sentries, and the men rested for the night, knowing that they were safe.

In the morning, the radio was set up, the antenna being mounted on a tall tree. Captain Eastman established radio contact with the corps headquarters, reported his safe arrival, and received orders. He directed the Karens to break up into small groups and to spy on the Japanese positions. They were counseled to avoid Burmese units as best they could, although the position of the BDF was still uncertain.

For their part, the Burmese from their villages assembled on and beside the dense hills north of Toungoo. Their bunkers were well sited above the road, at each hairpin turn. From these well-hidden bunkers they waited for the enemy, armed now with Bren guns and sten guns from the British. They too would take their toll on the pitiful Japanese.

Sato's new commander, the wily and resourceful General Sugiyama, advised him, "The Rangoon–Mandalay Road is in British hands. There is no escape across the road to the safety of the Sittang Valley. All units will assemble in the Pegu Yomas, opposite the Rangoon–Mandalay Road. We will break out together."

Sato realized that troops from the Arakan and the Irrawaddy Delta would be the last to arrive, but that he and his men needed to make haste to the assembly point as well. He sent his RMS out on patrol, to make contact with other units. At dusk, soaking wet, the patrol set out. As the sergeant led his squad through the hills, the eyes of the Karens followed their every move, but the Karens did not fire, for fear of giving away their position. When the patrol was far enough away from Sato's headquarters, though, Very flares lit up the night sky, and a cacophony of gunfire erupted. Within minutes, half of the patrol lay dead, and the rest retreated in haste. Just before dawn, the sergeant returned with the unsettling news: "The Karens have infiltrated the hills around us. The hills teem with them, and they took revenge on us."

Sato asked, "What of our other units?"

"We learned that the 53rd division has already passed by, as has the Hikari Kikan, the Indian unit." The sergeant cleared his throat before he continued. "It is my estimation that the Black Cats division, as well as another Indian division, is astride the Rangoon–Mandalay Road."

Sato managed to thank the sergeant and dismiss him before venting his feelings to his chief of staff, "It is an irony that we, the White Tigers, have to fight the Black Cats all over again. But this time they are the hunter and we are the hunted. The White Tigers are weak, hungry, and sick. Can a sick tiger maul a well-fed cat. . . ?" His words drifted off and he fell silent. He still believed in the Greater East Asia Co-Prosperity Sphere, the Emperor, and, ultimately, victory. But he blamed incompetent army commanders for the situation he found himself in. He would fight to the end. He would not commit *seppuku* [suicide].

Sato looked down at his feet. His feet and ankles were swollen, and a ring of swollen skin bulged above his shoes. His feet were constantly wet. The skin between his toes was broken and infected. Foot rot had set in. His skin looked like that of an old woman. Nonetheless he ordered his troops, "Move out!"

He was surprised at how cold it was. A constant drizzle fell, adding to the misery. He pulled the burlap bag over his head, but the drizzle turned into rain, and the bag was soon rendered ineffectual. Walking was painful, yet they had to get to the assembly point as soon as possible. They were still a few days away. Rations were in short supply. His orders were clear: get to the assembly point. And Sato was anxious to arrive there. "Even though we will have to wait till all the disparate units arrived before we break out," he told himself, "at least the army will be assembling and readying itself."

Each day new stragglers arrived at the assembly point. In the hills south of Pabwaye, the rag-tag Japanese units prepared the best they could for the breakout. They did not know the precise time and place, so while they waited they practiced building rafts, oiled their guns, and simply waited. Half the men were sick with malaria, scrub typhus, or dysentery. Of the myriad of illness that plagued all the soldiers, dysentery was the most debilitating. One sip of the water from the streams was enough to cause dreadful bacillary dysentery. At first there were only loose stools; then the stools become watery; then, when all the food has been evacuated, the intestines themselves seem to fall out, increasing the dreadful cramping. It would not take much for a man to dehydrate and then lose all interest in living. Naga sores and starvation killed off half the men. Sato's men waited impatiently for the arrival of the "Kanjo force," the new designation for all the disparate units of the lost army, and the order to move out. Rains came in great torrents, hitherto dry *chaung*s were rapidly filling up, and in the distance past the road, the Japanese soldiers could see the water accumulate till the place looked like a endless lake. The ground was soaked till it could not hold any water. Sleeping was impossible, nor was there any time to attend to personal hygiene. The men sullenly waited in their wretchedness.

With the capture of Pabwaye and with the Japanese all but defeated, British armored units found the road open and were racing to Pegu. Jeremy received his orders to rejoin the Burma regiment, now reassigned to the 5th Indian division that was heading for Rangoon. Peter was ordered to stay with C Company of the BurRifs. He was proud to remain with the Black Cats, but he desperately wanted to be with the troops that would liberate Rangoon, his home town. Instead, he bade yet another farewell to Jeremy and headed to Toungoo in a new jeep.

Colonel Kyaw Khin and remnants of the BDF also began to head to Rangoon. Tin Oo's BDF unit east of the Chindwin had one by one melted away into the jungle as the Japanese retreated toward the Rangoon–Mandalay Road. Stealthily, they met up again in small bands and headed southward to Rangoon, avoiding the Japanese and, for the most part, the British. Tin Oo led one of these bands. He did not know the country well, but knew that he could find help from villagers south of Penwegon. There he came upon some hutments. He summoned the headman, who was a relatively a young man, and told him, "I am with the Resistance against the Japanese. Please do not cooperative with them. The BDF has ceased joint operations with and support for the Japanese." Then he asked for directions. He warned the young headman, "Do not reveal our presence, or else we will be hunted by the Japanese. Even though they are on the run from the British and the Indians, they are still dangerous."

The headman agreed. "I will post guards and warn others of the BDF," he promised. Then the man offered his best estimate of the Japanese position. "I think they are gathering in the hills west of the Rangoon–Mandalay Road."

Tin Oo was pleased and expressed his appreciation. The villagers cooked rice and fish for him and his men, the first hot food they had enjoyed in weeks. Tin Oo thanked the villagers again, then slept peacefully until he led his men out of the village at dawn. All night, he had tossed and turned, tormented by doubts and worry. Even though the Burmese had an army of their own, they were small and worn down. The euphoria of the war's early years had given way to uncertainty about the future.

Sato realized that he now had more enemies than the British had four years ago. It was July, and the monsoon was a month old. The men in the Pegu Yomas were wet and water-logged, sick, and tired, and hungry. Their only food was rice and bamboo shoots, an occasional lizard or fish paste. Each day one or two men would walk away into the woods, never to return. The sound of a pistol shot or the boom of a grenade meant a quick and merciful end. They awaited their orders to attempt break out, but they knew that the precise day and time and the actual place where they would run the gauntlet of British and Indian troops on the Rangoon–Mandalay Road would come at the last moment. The waiting was agonizing.

Finally General Sugiyama arrived and addressed the assembled troops. Sato was thrilled to finally meet the man he so much admired, the man who, in spite of his desperate plight, still had a commanding presence. "At midnight on July 18," the General announced, "the breakout will begin. Each unit will be given a time and place." He provided general details to the men, having already provided precise details to his commanding officers. "We will cross the Rangoon–Mandalay Road and head across the Sittang Valley. We will stay well north of Pegu. We will cross the Sittang River and head toward Moulmein, taking back roads in order to avoid the enemy."

General Sugiyama then retired to his tent. He sipped the last of his sake and remembered February 1942, when he had so brilliantly defeated the Indian Army's 17th Division. Sadly, he contemplated how different the situation was now. He and his men faced a rejuvenated British-Indian 17th, well armed and anxious to redress the drubbing they had received three years ago at the hands of the Japanese. The breakout was not going to be easy.

Sato's unit was merged into the Kanjo force. On the appointed day, after midnight, Sato gathered his men and gave them last-minute instructions and reminders. Then they began to move. The ghostly emaciated figures descended the hillside and entered a deep gully. Waist deep in water, they waded toward the railway embankment ahead. Those who could still fight led the column; the sick were carried on stretchers; and those who could walk but were too weakened to fight would help the sick. Some of the latter had weapons, but others had only knives or sticks. The smell of men sick with dysentery, malaria, and assorted tropical sores was overpowering, clinging to the column like a nasty cloud.

Sato was the first to reach the embankment, and when he had climbed it, he stepped aside to let his men pass. He flourished a little bamboo rod that he used to get the slower men moving more rapidly. Unlike in the past, the men walked quietly, without cries of "banzai!" or the clash of cymbals. In small groups they climbed the embankment and headed toward the only dry spot, the Rangoon–Mandalay Road. They would have to walk in the open to get to the road, and it was not long before the British fired Very light flares into the night. Sato halted his men until the flares stopped. Then, he ran up and down the column, urging the men to hurry and hitting the recalcitrant men with his bamboo rod. The men ran like scared rabbits across the road to the supposed safety of the other side, a distance of about one hundred yards. They crouched as low as they could. They were surprised at the rain hitting their back so hard it stung, pelting their backs relentlessly.

The darkness was pierced by the flash of gunfire like lightning, as the British, Indians, and Karens collectively opened fire at the ghostly figures on the open road. The enfilading gunfire was deadly. Any man who paused in his race across the road was mowed down. The gunfire was so deadly that bodies littered the road, making it an obstacle course for those who came after them. Many men lost their footing as they stumbled across the bodies, and they rolled down the slippery slope on the far side of the road. In the process, many lost their weapons and spent precious time re-collecting them. There were enough dead and wounded Japanese from whom they could snatch a weapon, if they could not locate their own. Then they continued running in terror through the inky blackness into the Sittang valley. Finally the firing ceased. In the mist and darkness, the survivors eventually found one another and congratulated themselves on their escape. Little did they know that their journey of horror was just beginning.

East of the rail embankment the valley was low and stretched to the horizon. The flat land was a vast lake fed by the overflowing banks of the *chaung*s. As dawn approached, the men spotted floating islands covered with high grasses and shrubs, and Sato directed the men to crawl to the islands and stay down. From the tenuous safety of their grass islands, the Japanese saw enemy planes fly low over their positions, but they held their fire, to keep their position secret. The enemy planes fired at anything that moved.

Sato's men slept by day and marched at night. Walking in the inky blackness had its own horror. Sato had no need to counsel against cooking fires, as there was no food to cook, not even rice. Water was everywhere, and the men found walking on the slippery mud agonizingly difficult. Brisk marching was impossible. The hills were full of enemies, human and non-human alike, and the enemy aircraft made their presence known all too frequently. The men were hard pressed to find hiding places, and their number decreased steadily. While the men lamented their fate in the present, Sato worried about their future; he knew what was ahead.

SITTANG CROSSING

Sato knew the peril of crossing the Sittang River. If not impossible, it would be extremely difficult and dangerous. Yet he had no choice. He and his men were on their own, facing an angry and determined enemy. No army in the history of warfare ever faced more dreadful conditions, and any other army under similar conditions would have surrendered. But in the Imperial Japanese Army, especially Sato's proud regiment, surrender was not a option. The Japanese soldier's field manual had no mention of it.

In the dry season, the Sittang valley was a lowland, a rich agricultural land. Eons ago, the Sittang River had been a tributary of the great Irrawaddy River, but in the great tectonic crushing of the land, the Sittang had been cut off, and its catchment basin had "shrunk." Now the river formed in the Karenni hills, from where, in the fierce monsoon, the waters ran rapidly down hills, in rivulets, into *chaung*s. From the mountains to the sea was about a hundred miles, which made the rise and fall of the river rapid, its current formidable. During the monsoon season, the river overflowed its banks and turned the land into a vast lake. The edge of the river was never easily identifiable even in the best of times, as its tidal bore could change by the hour. Swollen by the monsoon, the river/lake seemed to grow and shrink willy-nilly. The Japanese walked, ran, and swam whenever they could, dreaming of the sanctuary of Moulmein.

The men were careful to not draw attention to themselves. They ate only what they could find or catch, mostly fish or lizards, and ate them raw. There was no firewood to be had. Day after day they slogged through the water, which sometimes was waist deep and sometimes up to their neck. They had abandoned shoes long ago, and uniforms were now disappearing, simply rotting and falling way. Some of the men wore only white loincloths, soiled with feces. The diarrhea had weakened some so much that they just surrendered to the water and died. Sato heard cries for help and urged the good swimmers to help the less fortunate, but even the good swimmers could not help. The pitiful cries soon faded as they were pulled into the depths of the swirling water. The survivors passed the lifeless along with dead animals and debris. It was an awful sight and stench, but when the monsoon ended, the sea would recede and the land would cleanse itself. Sato had no intention of being in the valley when the monsoon ended. He had counted the number of survivors in his proud regiment and was depressed by the number. Still he drove his men toward the Sittang River. He knew all about its terrible current, having seen it sweep away his enemy three years ago. But if he and his men were to have any hope of survival, they would have to cross the river.

In early August, Sato's unit was just one day away from the river, heading for Pa-An, north of Moulmein. He was proud to have kept the unit intact, if diminished in number. The lake through which they slogged had seemed to swell by the hour, growing ever larger and deeper. But now the waters seemed to be steadily receding. The monsoon temporarily eased, but also, as the men approached the river, the land rose. The invaluable islands of reeds grew more plentiful, allowing the men to cut reeds and bamboo to make rafts. The men could rest on the rafts, giving respite to their sore and water-logged feet. The men also came upon country boats, which they pulled along with them with great effort. They could hear in the distance, and growing louder with every meter they traversed, the rush of water down the hillside into the Sittang River. The men were slogging through a wetlands formed by the overflowing river, but the river itself was ahead, still a discrete channel of water with swift current and swirling eddies.

It was daylight when they approached the west bank of the river, but Sato wanted to cross it immediately. He risked attack from the air during daylight, but risked ambush from the rear or the hills if he waited. The men assembled themselves, the rafts, and boats and pushed off into the raging river. The water swirled around and drew the rafts into the middle of the channel. Sato knew the crossing would be difficult, but even he was not prepared for the deadly force of the water. It tore apart the bamboo poles held together by flimsy rope and flung the men into the swirling water. The men cried for help, waving their hands and shouting "long live the Emperor" before disappearing under the water and being dragged past the broken bridge to the Andaman Sea.

Sato was lucky. His boat arrived at the high east bank, just below the Shwegin *chaung*. He was able to scramble up the slope, collect survivors, and for the first time in weeks enjoy the feeling of solid land under his feet. Ahead was Pa-An. It had been three years and three months ago that he passed through here after his success at Moulmein. He grimaced. He had received a friendlier reception then than he expected now. He heard the drone of planes and instinctively hid under a tree. He glanced upward at the planes and frowned. Peculiarly, they were not dropping bombs or strafing the land. Instead, the sky was full of paper floating down! After the planes left, Sato crept out from under the tree and picked up the pamphlet. It was in Japanese, and he read the imperial rescript in disbelief. It read, "The war is over. All units of the Imperial Japanese Army should lay down their arms, cease fire, and surrender."

Sato was incredulous. He could not believe his eyes, and suddenly they were welling up with tears. Three years ago he had been a young, determined, proud colonel of the Imperial Army. He had waged successful campaigns and had entered Rangoon in glory. Now he had aged. His hair was unkempt, long, and matted. He knew he smelled. The beard on his chin was longer than ever before. His eyes were sunken deep into their sockets, and his skin was much darkened. "I look like a Burmese," he admitted sourly, "and a pitiful one, at that." He sobbed. The last count he had taken of the men whom he had brought out of the Pegu Yomas was no more than fifty human wrecks. "What was the meaning of all this?" he wondered through his sobs.

Chapter 41
Tying Up Loose Ends

The road to Rangoon was now open. Together with his driver, Jeremy raced in his Jeep towards Rangoon. They passed the wrecked hulks of Japanese cars, lorries, and tanks. Dead and bloated bodies lay on the roadside, and the stench was overpowering, reminding Jeremy of the bleak days of his retreat. Past Pegu finally he arrived at Taukkyan. The village was nearly empty; only a few scrawny and emaciated civilians stood at the side of the road and stared at first vacantly at the allied troops as they entered the village. Then the civilians broke down. Their eyes filled with tears, and some down knelt on the rough ground and wailed, "thank God you are back!" Again and again Jeremy heard villagers repeat this refrain.

Jeremy was filled with pride to be a part of the liberating force, but he also was overcome with pity. He gave his own day's rations to the civilians as the jeep moved through the village on its way to Rangoon. "Rangoon!" he thought. "How many years has it been since I was home?"

When he arrived, the city was in allied hands, the Gurkhas had parachuted south of the city, and a brigade of the Indian National Army (INA) stayed behind as the Japanese fled, trying to prevent a massacre. At Sule Pagoda Road, he found the Gurkhas, with their jungle hats, and the British light calvary and assorted troops firmly in control. The skeletal civilians were in rags, but their fear was now replaced with joy; they even smiled at the soldiers. They filled the streets and welcomed the allied troops with great enthusiasm. "After the Japanese fled in panic," one man related, "the city was once again a haven for criminals." He continued sadly, "The police had disappeared, and we feared total chaos." Another man spoke up. "The INA protected us. That is why we stayed." Indeed, these men, who had fought first for the British and then the Japanese, who had remained in Rangoon after the British and then the Japanese had fled, now showed their mettle by staying behind to face the consequences. They hoped that the

British would show them mercy. Now they turned in their weapons to the British. One INA captain volunteered information about the Japanese and the fifth column: "The main command of the Japanese Army flew out of Rangoon ten days ago. The Burmese Prime Minister fled ignominiously along with Japanese. The head of the INA left by lorry along with the Rani-Ki-Jhansi regiment."

Scotch that had been hoarded for years mysteriously appeared, and toasts were drunk to the King and Emperor. The bottle passed from man to man. Slowly the people of Rangoon gathered around the victorious allied soldiers to thank them and tell their tales.

Meanwhile, Peter was ordered to follow the force to Toungoo-Bowlake, in pursuit of the 28th Army. Already his thoughts had turned more frequently to home and family. And Amy. Now thoughts of Amy took hold, and Peter could not rest until he found out what had happened to her. He requested and was granted personal leave to travel to Bowlake swiftly, in advance of his unit. The only means of transport available was by boat and DUWK, a long, slim boat-like vehicle with wheels and, at the rear, a rudder with a screw. This amphibian vehicle could be driven on rough terrain or on water. The heavy monsoon rains had turned the roads to rivers, so Peter was happy to be assigned a DUWK. He was determined to keep his promise to Amy that he would come looking for her, and that where he was headed. When he met up with some Karens of the K-Force, he enquired after Saw Travis. "He is in the Karenni Hills," came the news. "We can take you to him."

When Saw Travis saw Peter, he ran to embrace him. Peter was surprised by how much the war had aged the man. Then he remembered, "It must have been difficult hiding from the Japanese. And I suspect that I have aged, as well." Aloud, he asked Saw Travis, "It has been three long years. How did you survive?"

"We stayed close to the villages, prayed a lot, and played the guitar. Each evening we gathered around the fire and sang hymns and old American songs and ballads and kept to ourselves," Saw Travis explained with a grin. Peter remembered visiting Amy's village, where she had joined in the singing. She had been a good songstress. "I wonder if that is how she made it through," he thought. To Saw Travis, he said, "It is so good to see you. I am so happy that you are alive!"

Saw Travis took a look at Peter's three pips and congratulated him. "You look good in them," he teased. "I always knew you would make Captain."

Peter told him of his mission. "I will need your help in finding Amy." Saw Travis nodded his ahead in agreement and stroked his American carbine with pride.

It rained all night. The next morning they set out on the road to Mawchi, which was still open. In dry weather the trip would take three hours, but with roads under water, it would take longer. The driver deftly maneuvered the DUWK over the washed-out portions of the road and through the valley, toward the mining center. Soon they started a slow climb, into the cool mountain air. The road had been cut through the mountain, leaving steep walls. When the road had been built, the dynamite had dislodged large boulders that lay near the sinuously twisted road. It was prime ambush terrain. Saw Travis confirmed this when he said, "These boulders were great for hiding when attacking the Japanese." He pointed ahead to two large boulders, one on each side of the road. The jungle crept close behind the boulders, and right there the road took a sharp turn to the left. "We would wait here for the Japanese. We killed many of them."

Peter peered closely at the boulders and could see Karen soldiers poised there. Saw Travis continued. "From the top of the boulder and from the side of the road we shot them. It was usually a massacre. Eventually the Japs began to travel in convoy, and point men got out to clear the road before they could pass." Saw Travis smiled. "But there are many points of ambush! And the British supplied us with radios and weapons." The smile disappeared from his face. "The Japanese paid a high price. They deserved to, after what they did to us back at the Sittang. But they sought revenge by surrounding our villages and burning them. They would shoot the old men and children, and carry away our young women. They would carry them off and commit unspeakable acts of sex and depravity before they destroyed them." Tears streamed down Saw Travis's cheeks. "We, too, paid a terrible price."

The men journeyed onward in silence for a few miles, then Saw Travis spoke again. "I do not know what happened to Amy. Once we arrive at the base camp, I will take you to her village. But there are still collaborators, so I will send my men first. Then we will go in the evening." He chuckled grimly. "I don't want anything to happen to my Captain friend." They set out single file that evening along a narrow trail, climbing to about 4000 feet. After two hours it was dusk, and they arrived at the ridge. Saw Travis signaled to Peter. "There. It will take about ten minutes to go down to the village. I will send some scouts. If it is clear, we will go down. I know the trail, so it will be safe to arrive at night."

Amy's family came from a small village near the tungsten mines at Mawchi. The village nestled in a valley. In the center was a small Baptist church with a tall spire, and around it were built small houses and huts. It was picturesque, like a postcard. Peter heard a series of three short whistles, and Saw Travis took his arm. "It is safe," he said. "Follow me."

The two men walked quickly to the village and entered the church. The minister was reading the Bible by candlelight. He recognized Saw Travis and put a finger to his lips. There were no chairs, but the minister pointed his finger to several boxes. Peter and Saw Travis sat down, and the minister said quietly, "Even though the Japanese have been defeated, they are still in the mountains, trying to retreat to the Sittang. We are ever fearful."

Saw Travis whispered to the minister of their quest. "You know I arrived here recently," the minister said. "I do not know this Amy. I will ask tomorrow." He gestured to the corner. "Sleep here; it will save time tomorrow."

It was uncomfortable in the small cramped rectory, and Peter's sleep was tortured with fears about Amy. The tales he had heard about Japanese atrocities horrified him but did not surprise him. He had seen for himself how cruel the Japanese soldiers could be.

Peter got up early and looked around him. The sun's rays were just beginning to peek over the top of the mountain, and some of the tallest peaks were still shrouded in mist. In the distance he could see the silvery Salween River, glistening in the morning light. The minister approached Peter and said, "Let me find out. I will report to you." Then he slipped away. Peter waited impatiently, checking and rechecking the packs of cigarettes and chocolate he had brought. Finally the minister returned with an old man. They retired to the small office in the rear of the church and the minister told the old man to tell his story.

"The Japanese were eager to avenge the loss of their soldiers," the old man began. "They surrounded the village and the church and then went on a rampage," he continued. "They shot Amy's father, and she had tried to run and hide, but it was no use. A Japanese colonel grabbed her and accused her of being a spy. He grabbed her by the arm and forced her to the ground. Holding the bayonet to her neck, he pulled her *longyi* up."

Peter's eyes were wide and steely, knowing what was to come but still needing to hear it. The old man continued. "Then he raped her," he said simply. But he was not done. "When the colonel was done with her, he turned her over to his men, and they performed unspeakable sexual acts. When they left, she was so brutalized that she did not gain consciousness. By morning she was dead."

The men wept silently, mourning not only Amy but also other daughters, sisters, and mothers. The Peter pulled himself together and asked, "do you remember the emblem on the colonel's shoulder?" he asked.

"I will never forget it," the old man said. "It was a white tiger."

That was enough for Peter. It had been Sato's regiment that had gone through in March of 1942. He would pursue Sato. He would avenge Amy. Peter thanked the old man, who then left the church with the minister. Saw Travis rummaged through his rucksack and brought out a bottle of Scotch. He poured four fingers. "Drink it down," he commanded Peter.

Peter obeyed his friend and let the scotch sear his throat. In agony, he remembered his last day with Amy and admitted that, deep down, even then he had known that he would never see her again. But he had not envisioned anything as horrific as the death that had been described to him. "Pour me another four fingers," he told Saw Travis. "I'm going to get stinking drunk tonight. Tomorrow we will return to the base camp, and then I will take my leave and follow the White Tigers. They will pay for this!"

When Peter took leave of Saw Travis and headed for the river, he had grappled with his grief and had turned it to a burning white rage directed at Sato. "Go to the river," he ordered his driver. As they entered the Sittang valley, the mountains gave way to flat land and swampland. Weeds and grass grew almost shoulder high, and the men were on full alert. The river was half a mile wide and getting wider by the day. Peter in his amphibious vehicle progressed onward. He passed people on rafts and in the river. Many of them were in a pitiable state. Worse were the dead bodies floating in the reeds, their mouths distorted. The driver explained, "When the Burmese find dead bodies, they strip them bare of all valuables, even the insignia. Their mouths are gaping because the Burmese smash the teeth for the gold fillings." He was philosophical. "It is grotesque, yes. It is pitiful. But only a few months ago, the ones who are dead were committing some of the most heinous crimes themselves."

They picked up speed as they headed toward the town of Pa-An. There, Peter climbed out of the DUWK and began to interview people. "I am looking for the White Tigers," he explained to everyone he met. He knew that just three days earlier, the commander of the Japanese Burma Area Army had surrendered. Peter knew that Sato might have escaped already to Siam, but a sixth sense told him that Sato was here. The road was clogged with retreating troops, and Peter surmised that Sato would be weakened by his defeat and retreat. "His regiment was here," Peter thought. "And Sato himself is probably still here. If so, I will find him and bring him to justice."

Indeed, Sato was too sick to continue his retreat. He suffered from diarrhea and foot rot. He was exceedingly gaunt from lack of food, and his hair and beard were long and matted. He had stripped off his insignia and hoped that he could pass for an ordinary soldier. Throughout his long retreat, the thought of defeat and surrender had not occurred to him. But now, after reading the Imperial rescript and realizing that the Japanese Army had been defeated, Sato had no more fight in him. "I will rest here and hope for the best," he thought. "If I can rest for just one day, and can escape the wrath of the British, I can either be repatriated with the rest of the ordinary soldiers or can slip into Siam." His thin lips pulled into what passed for a smile these days. "They will not capture me," he promised to himself.

Peter doggedly walked through the town, looking carefully at clusters of dejected Japanese soldiers and asking questions. Late in the afternoon, as the sun was setting in the west, he spotted a group of such men sitting in the shade of a large peepul tree. His eyes narrowed as he surveyed the small group, and then his heart lurched. It was Sato! He strode purposefully toward the tree and took a closer look to be sure. The man he thought was Sato was no longer the dapper, swaggering figure he had been. He was suffering from the terrible ravages of the retreat, of the jungle, of disease, and of starvation. But Peter had formed an image of Sato and had burned it into his memory. He approached the group of men and said softly, "Colonel Sato."

But Sato sat stoically, looking Peter in the eye with a tinge of defiance. Peter returned the stare, as though he could bore into Sato's warped soul. Then the beaten colonel nodded wearily. It took Peter a great deal of restraint not to grab Sato by the scruff of his tunic and shoot him right then and there, but he controlled his rage. He shouted to the nearby MPs, "Hurry. Colonel Sato is here. He must be arrested." The MPs hastened over and took Sato into custody. Peter watched him shuffle away between the two MPs, then left himself.

By now, darkness was setting in. Peter returned to the DUWK but found it empty. His driver was nowhere in sight. Peter opened his rucksack and found the half-full bottle of scotch from which he and Saw Travis had drank the night before. He put the bottle to his lips and drank deep, without the niceties of water or ice. It seared his throat, but he drank again, as though he could burn the images of Amy's last hours from his mind. Then for a long time he just sat there, meditating on what the full force of the Burmese jungle, mountains, valleys, fevers, and the ferocious monsoon could do to even strong men.

The Sato who had so decimated the allied troops in Burma three years ago and who had, literally, chased the British from Burma to India must have been a strong man full of *bushido* [the way of the warrior] and swagger. The Sato Peter had seen this day had been hollow-cheeked; his eyes had been sunk into their sockets, and he was thin to the point of gauntness. But Peter had also seen the curl of Sato's mouth, his cruel streak. Even as he hated Sato, Peter felt sorry for the man. More, though, he was filled with nostalgia for Amy and saddened at how she had died. "Her last days must have been terrible," he mused. "Yet she was marked for death by her ethnicity, her religion, and her allegiance." Tears rolled down his cheeks. He had already had too much to drink and knew that he would be sick the next day, but he nonetheless finished the bottle and lay down in the back seat of the DUWK to sleep a troubled sleep.

The next morning, Peter groggily sought out the command tent and inquired about Sato. The commander told him, "You have rendered invaluable service to us. Now his fate will be decided by the authorities." Sato was ordered to a special camp for possible war criminals. He was then transferred to a Liberty ship bound for Japan. Guards kept the prisoners away from the railing, fearing that the prisoners would leap overboard to escape their trial and punishment. Sato stood at a distance from the railing and looked at the South China Sea. Memories of his glorious victories seemed pale and long ago. Now he worried about his future and considered suicide, even going through the motions. As a young officer he had been instructed to place the knife midway between the ziphiod bone and the umbilicus, then thrust the knife past the skin; as the knife pierced the peritoneum and caused a sharp pain, the knife should be advanced upward to pierce the main artery and the maze of arterial branches; death would be instantaneous. In a way, death would be merciful.

But suicide was not a viable option for Sato now. He felt that he had fought nobly for the Emperor and had now been betrayed, by the Emperor's surrender. The Emperor did not deserve Sato's respect, and Sato was not going to surrender his life for a man and ideals whose time was past. He would submit to the new authorities, accept his punishment, and hope to live another day in the new world that seemed to be emerging. He had a sudden hunger to see his wife and son, and vowed to survive by any means so that he could join them again. He would never breathe a word of his disappointment to his wife or son.

Peter wanted to take one last look at the Sittang Bridge site before he headed to Pegu and thence onward to Rangoon. The driver stopped on the east bank and Peter surveyed the scene. Memories of the terror he and his fellow soldiers had endured three years ago flooded his mind. "So many died," he mused. "And so much death and destruction followed." Then he pushed thoughts of the past from his mind and asked his driver to head to Pegu.

The next morning Peter rose eagerly and turned his thoughts to Rangoon. He thanked his DUWK driver and exchanged the DUWK for a military jeep, which would make better time and take less room on the roads to Rangoon. Home after three and a half years! He drove as fast as he could, hopes and fears crowing his head. Was his family alive? Were they healthy? Was the house intact? He knew he would soon find out.

PART VII

Post-War Rangoon

Chapter 42
Return to Rangoon

Peter reported to his new barracks and immediately requested a day of leave. "I need to see if my family survived," he explained. "I have been away for three long years, and came here even before I looked in on them."

Receiving leave, Peter headed down Prome Road and drove past the Moghul palace. He was pleased to see it intact, although a little worse for the wear. Then the family house came into view. He was dismayed at the state of disrepair. He stopped the jeep in front of the house and climbed out. His sister Kamala rushed out of the house to greet him, followed by the rest of the family like ducks following their mother. "Peter!" Kamala cried with joy, through her tears. "I always knew you were alive!" The rest of the family joined in the rejoicing, crying and laughing and talking all at once. Peter looked around for his father, and instantly knew something bad had happened. "Where is Father?" he demanded in his most military voice. "And Benjamin, Reddy, Grandmother, Marge?" The family fell silent, and his mother began to weep. Kamala ushered him inside the house and sat him down on a rickety chair. Then she began to tell him of the past several years.

"Let me begin with father," she said sadly but with a little smile. "For his entire life, he worked to feed and care for us. In February 1942, when the British left, he was without work. He worried about how long the savings would last. The Japanese were thirty miles from the city and rapidly approaching; criminals and collaborators were growing bolder by the day. Father was desperate to evacuate the family from Rangoon. Benjamin and his Karen friend got to the American lend-lease storage facility just in time to get two Dodge lorries, and we set out in them as the demolition teams were blowing things up throughout the city. Fire and smoke was everywhere. We thought we could drive to Prome, but just past the airport, there was heavy fighting ahead. At the Burmese village, we rented two bullock carts, left the lorries and the road, and headed for a nearby rubber plantation. But we were unlucky there also, as the Japanese had preceded us by just a few hours. So, we left the plantation and went to the Rangoon River, hoping to escape by boat. We were on the boat for four days, and father believed that we would be successful. But Japanese gunboats approached and forced us to take refuge in a friendly village; then the Japanese came to the village and beat father and other men cruelly. His spirits sank, and he never recovered. The brutal treatment at the hands of the Japanese was the end of him. Even though he was not shot or bayoneted, like they did to many, he was traumatized by the pain they inflicted on him. When we finally returned to Rangoon and found our home robbed so completely, that was the last straw. That, together with the loss of work, led him to lose his will to live. His death was the most terrifying thing for us."

Kamala's eyes filled with tears as she remembered those dark days. "But we gave him a fine funeral. He was buried decently, with most of the family in attendance. We sang all the old hymns, 'Abide With Me' and 'Rock of Ages," and all the others." Then she picked up the story.

"In summer, the air raids would grow in intensity. Rumors of invasion and fighting were constantly in the air. We would retreat to the country, to live in huts. Then, when the rains came and the bombers stayed away, we would return home. The gold and money started to get low, and the worthless Japanese money would only buy a little food. Benjamin and Reddy kept us together. And Grandmother," she said with another little smile. "Grandmother's cow, chickens, ducks, and eggs kept us going for a while. But in the later years, the Japanese too faced shortages. They would come in gangs and forage for food. Grandmother's livestock were prime targets." Here Kamala managed a little giggle. "With her bamboo stick, she would chase the soldiers, and they would scurry away like mangy dogs." Then she grew serious again. "But they always returned, and the livestock began to diminish. The slow ducks were the first to go. Grandmother then locked up the chickens, but soon even those were gone. Then, like Father, her spirit was broken. She slipped away one night, and we buried her next to Father. In the last year we survived on rice and a little dry fish. Sometimes Benjamin could get wilted vegetables at the market. But we womenfolk never left the house, for fear of the Japanese."

Peter opened his knapsack and handed over the cans of meat, chocolate, even sugar and salt that he had obtained from the quartermaster. Then he looked around at his sisters. "Where is Marge?" he asked.

Kamala sighed and continued her tale. "Marge was next, after Father and Grandmother. She took sick in the fall of 1944, and at first Benjamin thought that it was pneumonia. But her fever was unrelenting, and she became ever more listless. Benjamin visited with his friends and the pharmacies, but other than local medicines, there were no medicines. Eventually Benjamin realized that she had typhoid. There was nothing he could do for her. There were no hospitals for civilians. She lapsed into a coma; soon her abdomen started to enlarge and distend, which Benjamin said meant that the typhoid had eaten through the intestinal wall. There was no recovery. She, too, is buried near Father."

"Thank goodness Benjamin and Reddy have been able to help you," Peter said. "I was so worried while I was away, but I was either fighting or fleeing the Japanese myself. Jeremy and I tried to come here as we retreated from Moulmein, but the soldiers stopped us. I guess that was when you were trying to flee and ended up in the rubber plantation and on the river."

"Probably," Kamala agreed. "But now let me tell you about Uncle Reddy. This tale gets sadder and sadder."

Peter blanched. How much more news about disease, suffering, and death in his family could he bear? But he sat quietly, listening to Kamala.

"Uncle was a big help to us. Benjamin was working, trying to earn enough money to feed the family. I'll tell you about his travails next. And Uncle stayed here in the house with the womenfolk. Whenever anyone came to the door, he would shush us into the inner room and answer the door himself. Unless Grandmother materialized around the side of the house with her broom! One day fairly recently, Uncle went out. It was rare for him to leave the house, but Benjamin was home. Uncle was near the university when there was an air raid. He took a shrapnel to his foot, but it didn't seem serious. He walked home. But it became infected—the bone was infected. Green pus came pouring out of his foot, and he developed a high fever. He never recovered, but before he died he said, 'I am happy to die knowing that the Japanese never occupied India. India will find independence in a peaceful way, in her own time.' So, you see, he never changed. Always the great champion of India."

In spite of the sorrow, Peter laughed out loud as he remembered his uncle's fervent love of India. "He had so much passion! He and I had many spirited discussions; he was a good man." Peter worried about his mother "She has lost her husband, her mother, and Reddy," he thought. "She looks lost herself." When he turned back to Kamala, the look in her eye confirmed Peter's suspicions. Mother was like a shadow haunting the house, not fully partaking in or contributing to the family life. He felt a pang of sorrow on her behalf. "Now tell me about Benjamin. Where is he working? When will he get home?"

Kamala began to talk about what life was like in Rangoon, sliding away from the topic of Benjamin. Peter let her tell the story in her own way, at her own pace. He was anxious to hear all the details but also filled with trepidation.

"The last days of the occupation were filled with terror. There were not only air raids but also rumors of a naval bombardment and then a combined sea and land invasion. Then one day the enemy sentries suddenly disappeared. The Japanese soldiers no longer patrolled the streets. At the Japanese headquarters, the buildings were empty except for the Indian National Army. Ironically, we prepared for the second invasion in three and one-half years. That evening, many Japanese bombers and cargo planes flew out of Rangoon, and soon word spread that the Japanese high command had fled, leaving the city without protection from criminals."

During Kamala's tale their mother had slipped out of the room. Now she returned with a plate of rice and dried fish. She stroked Peter's face and handed him the food. "Let me feed my son," she said simply. Peter accepted the plate although he knew that what he ate meant less for his family. He didn't have the heart to hurt his mother. As he ate, he listened to Kamala return to her tale.

"As the Japanese retreated, they left many stores. Benjamin was desperate to find medicines, as well as food for the family. Rumor had it that there was a medical store near the chancellery of the University. In spite of his many fears, he went to the storage site late in the afternoon. He told me that he would be safe, that the British never bombed in the afternoon because they had to fly back to their bases in India. What he did not know, and what we learned later, was that the British had recently captured the Kyedaw air base at Toungoo and had stationed planes there. So on that day, almost at dusk, two British Mosquitoes from Toungoo flew over the tree-tops and strafed the storage sheds. The pilots probably thought that the people there were Japanese. The machine-gun fire was deadly. All the people looting were killed. We buried Benjamin also in the family plot."

Peter was appalled. "What about neighbors and friends?" he asked, almost fearful to hear the answer.

Kamala shook her head. "We don't know what happened to the neighbors next door. They left in March 1942 and never came back. Many others left also, and some returned, but many never came back. Many of your friends and their families are missing," she added sadly. "But you will be happy to know that Jeremy is in Rangoon. He came here after he went to his family home. His tale is sad, too."

That was the only glimmer of happiness in Kamala's long, sad tale. Peter was saddened beyond words and frightened about the future. "Can we put our lives back together?" he wondered aloud.

Kamala shook her head and frowned. "Our lives will never be the same, Peter," she said. "The best we can hope for is to begin new lives. There is no going back." With that she embraced him and walked slowly from the room. Peter left the house and drove thoughtfully back to the barracks.

Jeremy's homecoming had been just as difficult. He had arrived in Rangoon one week ahead of Peter and, as soon as he could get leave, drove a jeep up U Cho Street to his home. He turned left past a large estate now stripped of everything that was removable. Then he turned left once more and could see the house that he remembered so well. He stopped the jeep and walked to the house. He paused on the steps. The doors were open! There was no sign of his mother or his father! The house had been completely looted!

Jeremy stumbled outside and sat down on the steps, overcome by grief and worry. Were his parents alive? If so, where were they? How would he find them? He looked around. Squatters had built huts on every bit of empty land. Other than his own home, the area was nearly unrecognizable. Then inspiration struck. He leaped up and climbed back into the jeep. Carefully and slowly plying the streets, he found the small church. He knew that his father's old friend Mr. Minor lived next door to the church. "Mr. Minor?" Jeremy queried, as the door cracked open in response to his knock and a wary eye peeked around the door. Mr. Minor recognized Jeremy instantly and threw open the door. But Jeremy hardly recognized Mr. Minor; he had lost much weight and all of his hair, and he had aged dramatically. His eyes teary, they embraced for a long time. Then Mr. Minor invited him inside.

Jeremy was shocked to see that the house was almost bare. The once-fine furniture was all gone. Mr. Minor noticed Jeremy's surprise. "They stole everything," he whispered. His wife soon entered the room, also overjoyed to see Jeremy. She hugged him and asked, "Can I bring you some tea? I have only jaggery, though; no white sugar. We have not seen white sugar in a year." Jeremy nodded, and Mrs. Minor disappeared into the kitchen, emerging soon with three cups of tea. The three looked at one another, Jeremy afraid to pose the question he had come to have answered.

Mr. Minor broke the silence. "You no doubt want to know about your family." Jeremy nodded mutely. Mr. Minor looked downcast, then looked Jeremy in the eyes. "Your father drove the last train to Myitkyina and emptied its cargo, the fleeing British. He took CeCi with him."

Jeremy nodded. "I know. CeCi is safe in Calcutta now. I have a letter from her."

"Praise the Lord!," cried Mrs. Minor. Mr. Minor was just as happy. He continued his tale.

"After he returned from Myitkyina, your father was ordered to go to back south to Ye, to pick up wounded British soldiers and evacuate them to Myitkyina. On his return from Myitkyina, the train was attacked by enemy fighters. Word has it that your father left the burning train and took shelter in a village. But soon the Japanese captured the crew. I heard that your father was sent to Siam to build a railroad for the Japanese." Mr. Minor paused. "But I think he died before he got there."

Jeremy bit his lip and tried to contain his emotions. "I don't think many survived. I have heard that even those that survived the journey to Siam died of overwork, malnutrition, disease, and downright cruelty."

Mrs. Minor then picked up the story. "We advised your mother to go live with the nuns in the Catholic convent. For her safety. Without a man in the house, she would have been too vulnerable. She is still living there and will want to see you." She wrung her hands. "I have not told her about the true condition of the house. I only told her that some of the furniture had been taken. I didn't want her to take a risk and come back."

Jeremy thanked the Minors and excused himself. He went back to the jeep and brought back some tins of bully beef and chocolates. The Minors were delighted. "We haven't had foodstuffs like this in three years!" they thanked Jeremy gratefully.

On his way back to barracks, Jeremy had stopped by Peter's home. When he had knocked on the door, the curtains twitched but the door did not open for a long time. Finally Peter's sister Kamala opened the door and greeted him. "I only opened the door because I recognized you, Jeremy," she said. "We have no menfolk anymore. We do not open the door to strangers." Although the Thomas women were delighted to see Jeremy, the house was permeated by sadness and worry. Jeremy returned to his barracks relieved but also depressed and worried about the future.

Chapter 43
Rangoon Rebuilds

Within a few days of Rangoon's recapture, shops reopened and began a brisk trade in K-rations, C-rations, cigarettes, and tinned meat. The victorious British now prepared for their own celebrations. Big bulldozers cleared the main streets. Preparations were made for a grand parade. The excitement was palpable; the joy of victory could not be suppressed. Finally the General commanding the victorious 12th Army arrived in the city. It was time for the celebrations to begin.

It started early in the morning. The General dressed in his unassuming uniform. He forewent the traditional cap with the red band but instead donned his Gurkha bush hat of his old Gurkha regiment. The men shed their sweaty uniforms and donned clean dress uniforms. The parade began. Even the overcast skies could not diminish the pageantry. It started with the Scottish Pipes playing "Scotland the Brave," followed by divisions from West Kent, Yorkshire, and Gloucestershire; also sturdy, sunburned troops from Australia and New Zealand. All the storied commonwealth regiments were there: Indians, Nepalis, and West Africans. Tall Rajputs, Sikhs, and Pathans from India's northern provinces with their colorful turbans; small Bengalis and dark-skinned sappers and miners from the south of India; compact and powerful Gurkhas from Nepal with their bush hats and flashing *kukris*; the West African Askaris with leopard skins hung over their shoulders; Anglo-Indians and Anglo-Burmese of the BurRif units; and the Karens, Chins, Kachins, and Burmese units from Burma's ethnic states—every division that had fought so valiantly was there. The Black Cats of the 17th Division evoked wild cheers, and when they had passed, the cheers rose for the 5th Division, with their ball of fire emblem. The men in the regimental bands, dressed in clean khaki uniforms, marched smartly down the streets, playing their pipes and drums. They carried big drums strapped closely to their chests, and as the tassels on their flourishes flew through the air, their drums reverberated in unison. The sounds of the great military marches filled Sule Pagoda Avenue and reverberated through the narrow streets leading from the main road. Tanks and Bren gun carriers brought up the rear. It was a magnificent parade, like no other. It went on for hours, full of colorful flags of every regiment and the full pomp and grandeur of a victorious army, all manner of men marching as one. But it was also a sad moment, for it would be the last time that this army would march as one. Soon, this army would break up and pass into history forever.

Peter and Jeremy had marched with pride among the BurRifs and had been gratified by the cheers they had received from the crowds. They had also enjoyed the flower garlands placed around their necks by beautiful young Burmese women.

The next day they drove through the city to get a better look at their home town. They were awed by the destruction that the war had wrought. Away from the city center, row after row of buildings had been destroyed. The port was devastated, as was the railway station. In amazement, they tried to remember the times when they had accompanied their fathers to work, Jeremy to the railway station and Peter to the port, where his father had overseen the coal supplies for the railways. It was hard to remember the city when it had been intact and beautiful.

Peter said, "while we roamed the jungles of Burma, what I missed about Rangoon was the smells of food—the fragrant biriyani, that long-grained rice just dripping with ghee."

"Yes!" cried Jeremy, "with chunks of lamb, almonds, and even strands of silver! What I also missed," he added, "was the mohinga on every street corner and all the street food—the open grills and the smell of kabobs—and the ubiquitous *pan* [beetle-nut] shops."

With youthful grins on their faces, the two young men exclaimed at the same time, "Let's head to Frasier Street!" Laughing for the first time in a long time, they headed toward the street where the food shops had been concentrated in open-air stalls. But where so many food shops had once been located there now were just a few bleak stalls with battered stools on the sidewalk. Sobered, the two young men sat down, remembering the once-exciting city they had left behind.

The owner, a Muslim, welcomed them and, noticing their uniforms, thanked them for liberating the city, then complained of shortages of sugar and cooking oil. "All I can offer is tea," he said sadly, spreading his hands. Soon a young man brought two cups of steaming hot white tea. For a while the two young men said nothing, just tried to remember the scene, the crowds, the noise, and the smells of exotic food that had been such a part of their city before the war. Then they began to reflect on events of the past three years.

Jeremy remarked, "Things have changed so much! We have changed as well. Of course, we are older, but also we have been through the green hell. As I look around, though, I wonder. All the sacrifice, all the death—what was the meaning of it all?"

"I worry about the future," Peter responded. "How long will reconstruction take? Will the British stay to finish the job? Or leave in haste?"

"I think the British are exhausted, and probably broke," observed Jeremy. "And if the British leave, we—you and I and others like us—will be left to the mercy of whoever takes over. I shudder to think of the future."

Peter turned philosophic. "Japan's quest for hegemony in Asia ended on the plains of Imphal and Kohima. Yes, it was once again the white man winning, but it was not for any lack of ability on the part of the Japanese. Instead, it had much to do with Japan's motives. She was not truly interested in "freeing Asia"; she just coveted Asia's resources and markets and desired to be the master race to rule over the yellow and brown men. Japan wanted to replace the British. In part, her defeat was due to the refusal of the Asian people to submit to the overbearing Japanese and their brutality. I am proud that most of the allied soldiers who fought against the Japanese were Asian."

"You know," Jeremy said thoughtfully, "Britain may glory in the 'retaking' of Burma, but I don't think it will last. What we saw at the Sittang River and how the British were so thoroughly routed by the Japanese proves that the myth of the white man's invincibility is just that—a myth." He continued. "The British held the view that colonial people could not rule themselves, that it took the British to make things work. Well, this war proved how illusory that view was! In fact," he continued, "I think Britain's hold on the Indian empire will end soon, as will their hold on Burma."

"My Uncle Reddy would agree with you there," Peter laughed, with a tinge of sadness. "But I agree as well. There will be some hiccups, but colonialism—white men's control of Asia, as Reddy would say—has ended; their quest for riches and the stealing of our patrimony will end." He continued to muse, "Even though we worry about our place here and about our future, we should be proud to have participated in a mighty adventure and great victory. Collectively, we destroyed a sinister, brutal, and cruel enemy. We may not have fought for our country, and instead fought for our 'colonial overlords,' but the notion of 'country' cannot be defined in a narrow patriotic sense." He took a deep breath before continuing. "It may sound pompous, but I think of it in a broader sense—that we made a small contribution to free humanity from fear and depravity, to let people live in freedom."

Jeremy laughed. "You'll never change, Peter. You should be a professor, not a doctor. But I do agree with you. This war will change Asia forever. The Kuomintang Army in China is losing to the Communists, and in all likelihood the tottering Chinese regime will fail; America will be pushed out of China."

"Right now we need to get our lives back on track," Peter advised and rose from his stool. The two men paid for their tea and went back to their barracks. There was not much to do there. The men had plenty of time to recuperate and recover their bearings in the city. Mostly, they attended to family matters, trying to make up for the losses their families had endured and trying to assure that their future would be better.

Jeremy especially was absorbed with family matters. He spent much time trying to find out what really had happened to his father. He had moved his mother back home from the convent. He had been able to buy some furnishings in the markets—no doubt looted from the homes of others—but the house was still a bleak place, and food in Rangoon was scarce and costly. He received news that CeCi would soon return from India, and he felt the responsibility of caring for both his mother and sister.

On the appointed day, he went to the battered and pockmarked airport. The Dakota came in from the west. As it landed and taxied, the crowds had to be held back. He craned his neck trying to spot CeCi. She finally alighted and approached him. He held her for a long time, tears rolling down her cheeks. "Welcome home," he said gently, kissing her on the cheek. She looked older and thinner, but still beautiful. He gathered her meager belongings and took her home to their mother. CeCi hugged her mother for the longest time, and they did not speak for a while. Jeremy felt awkward, as though they shared an unspoken secret that he did not know. Finally they sat down, wiping their tears, and the three of them talked at length about their lives during the past several years.

Many of their friends had died or, if they had reached India, had decided to stay there. There was much discussion about Mr. Rawson, whether he was alive and where he might be. Jeremy assured his mother that as soon he was demobilized, he would start the quest for information. But demobilization was somewhat delayed because of unrest in the countryside. Jeremy was anxious to leave the barracks, so that he could be close to his mother and sister, but he—as well as many others—had to wait for official release from the civil government and the governor.

That night Jeremy, CeCi, and their mother gathered around the family dinner table for the first time in years. "What will you do after you are demobilized, Jeremy, and after you discover what happened to your father?" his mother asked. "Will you use the knowledge you gained in the military to ask for a higher paying job?"

Jeremy looked worried. "I'm not really sure what the future holds, Mother," he replied.

"Now that the British are in control again," his mother offered confidently, "they will rebuild the country."

"I'm not so sure of that," Jeremy interjected. "I really don't know about the politics of Great Britain. They are debating the future of their empire." Some of Jeremy's most cherished myths had been destroyed by the war. He wondered how long the British would stay in Burma and India. The recent elections in England had surprised him. "I had thought that the grateful British people would re-elect their great wartime leader, Churchill, who inspired the British to fight to the end," he explained. "But the British people are tired of the war. Churchill's party was defeated. The Labor government is more amenable to the notion of independence for India and Burma."

CeCi nodded. "My experiences in India point to that end as well."

"Surely the British would not abandon all the people who fought to save the British Empire!" Mrs. Rawson gasped.

Jeremy and CeCi looked at one another. It was clear that their experiences had changed their outlook on the world, and that Mrs. Rawson had not traveled that same path. She had been cloistered in a convent as the war raged around her. And CeCi had shielded her from the truth too. She had not told her mother all about her odyssey, wanting to spare her. She had only told Jeremy about her ordeal, slowly, in dribs and drabs. She had to deal with catharsis herself, and could only acknowledge her sufferings in small pieces. CeCi chose her words carefully as she explained. "While I was in India, the movement for Independence was strong and growing. It will happen. I don't know if Burma is ready for immediate independence, though. Perhaps it should wait until after the reconstruction."

"Why don't you think Burma is ready for independence?" Jeremy asked, interested.

Again CeCi chose her words carefully. "I learned on my trek that the Kachins do not want independence until considerable progress has been made to assure more autonomy for the ethnic people. Also, there are no Burmese technicians; Indians and Anglos ran the country. How can the Burmese run things?" She paused. During the last four years, she had grown up a lot. She was more aware of the world's problems, more knowledgeable about the world's economic woes. Building and maintaining empires cost money, and the war had drained the British. CeCi knew that the British did not have the money to rebuild, or the military strength to put down any Burmese rebellion. "If Burma's ethnic people rebel against an independent Burmese government, I think the government of India will withdraw its army. India has lost so many of her sons in the fight on behalf of the British; I don't think an independent India will be willing to make any more sacrifices for Burma, a county in which Indians are considered an inferior ethnic group."

Jeremy was startled by CeCi's words. She obviously had endured great hardships, and her new attitude was formed by her bitter experiences during her trek from Burma. Yet he knew that she spoke the truth. He and Peter had recently come to the same conclusions. He was overcome with nostalgia. He loved this city—its smells, its building, its pagodas, churches, and temples. He was saddened to think that he now faced the possibility of not being able to live in it, even though he had fought and suffered and had endured great hardship to free the country from the tyranny of the Japanese. He looked at his mother. Her face showed her confusion. He realized, as had CeCi, that his mother's view of the world had hardly changed over the past four years. She was not prepared for the change that would be inevitable.

"But we non-Burmans—like your father," she said as her voice broke, "have been instrumental in this country's growth. We fought to free it from the Japanese. We have a right to live here! And if by chance," she added, "the Burmans do not want us, then the British will take us in."

CeCi's spoke sharply, with sarcasm. "Like they took us with them when they evacuated Rangoon, Mother?" She snorted and continued angrily. "Mark my words. The British will go, and the Burmans will turn on us, as allies of the hated British. In Calcutta, I heard Anglos talk ad nauseam about 'going home.' That's a laugh. They don't want us. They consider us as a 'bit of the tar brush,' easy, and oversexed. Their attitude is 'sleep with them and then forget them.' Besides," she added, as she saw her mother's astonished look, "we would get too cold in England. And their food is strange."

The tension at the table was palpable. Mrs. Rawson urged Jeremy and CeCi to finish dinner, but they ate in silence. CeCi cleared the table and retired for the night. Jeremy reached over the table for his mother's hands. "Mother, I put my life on the line in the most important battle on mainland Asia. I saw things I still cannot speak of. You cannot bury your head in the sand and think that the future will be like the past. The fact is that this and other colonial possessions were seized by a few British soldiers. Now things have changed. The people here and in other colonies are fully armed. I think CeCi is right. The colonies want independence; the British do not have the stomach to fight any more; and besides, if they grant India independence they no longer have the Indian Army to police their far-flung empire. They will negotiate and grant Burma independence. Burma will be for Burmans."

His mother began to cry. "We have lived here all our lives! You were born here! Your father—whether living or dead—is still in this country! I refuse to believe that we cannot live here any more! Where will we go?"

Jeremy said firmly, "I'll figure it out, Mother." He held her hands until her crying ceased. He had sounded confident, but inside was not really sure about what the future held for any of them. He thought about his meeting with a colored American. He had asked what it was like to live in America, whether that country would welcome people such as himself after the war. The colored man had thought for a while before replying, "I'm not sure. Whites do not generally treat colored people—or Native Indians—very well." That reply haunted Jeremy and led him to believe that neither Britain nor America would welcome his family. "Maybe Australia," he thought.

The next day he broached the subject. "I am thinking about the possibility of going to Australia if we need to leave Burma," he suggested. "The climate is better than that in Britain and America, and the Australians are sympathetic to our plight. That does not mean that there would be no problems," he warned quickly," but it is a good possibility. What do you think?"

His mother began to cry again, but CeCi looked back at him firmly. "I think you should explore it," she said quickly.

As life slowly returned to some semblance of normalcy, other events were proceeding as well. An undercurrent of tension ran through the streets, as political events also were causing wariness. In the *Rangoon Gazette*, the news was bad. The Governor was negotiating with the Burmese political parties (AFPFL) and the leaders of the Burma Defense Force (BDF) about independence. The Burmese vernacular press exhorted the Burmese to strike for full independence, with no delay, and no commonwealth status. The rhetoric was, "We were independent once; we can rule ourselves again.

We are a rich country, rich in minerals, wood, and oil." The older and more moderate segment of elder statesmen, the old-line Burmese civil servants, cautioned against reckless adventurism. They wanted a gradual process that would lead to Dominion status. They pleaded that Burma did not yet have strong institutions that would sustain democracy, but their pleas were drowned out by the politicians and the colonels, who dismissed such arguments as old collaborationist views and accused the civil servants of being lackeys of imperialism. "Once we get rid of the foreigners and their nefarious influence," the hotheads argued, "We will prosper. We want the British to leave now."

Tin Oo was one of the young Turks. "Nothing should slow the quest for Independence for Burma," he thought. Although he was still making his way back to Rangoon, he, like Jeremy, Peter, and CeCi, had been changed by his experiences. Not all his dreams had been realized. He too had aged and learned more about the ways of the world. He worried that there were so many weapons that any future war of independence against the British would be bloody. Better to do it now, while the British were still weak. Nonetheless, his confidence wavered. He wondered whether his aspirations would end as ignominiously as those of the Japanese had ended.

At the Rangoon tea shop the radio announcer spoke in somber tones. "The entire cabinet was attacked earlier today. All were assassinated." A deathly silence fell over the tea shop. All were in shock. Then a babble of cries and wails broke out. Peter whispered to Jeremy, "This will be the end of gradualism and cooperation with the ethnic peoples. I do not think it is a good portent."

The teashop emptied in a hurry. Jeremy and Peter headed home to ponder the events of the day. "I fear for the future here. It is a mess."

Chapter 44
Independence

It was very early in the morning. The astrologers had consulted the stars and charts and had found this hour to be the most auspicious time for assuring a long-lived country. So, at this odd hour, four o'clock in the morning, to the sound of cymbals, the ringing of the gongs, and other assorted sounds, the Independence of Burma was proclaimed. Nearly 100 years ago, the English had come here to trade and subsequently conquer. It had been more than two years since the British had driven the Japanese out of Rangoon. Now an epoch was coming to an end. Crowds assembled at the old Fitch Square, now renamed Bandoola Square. Not all the people were enthused about the changes, though. The Karens gathered in a group in front of the American Baptist church, and soon they were joined by others.

To the north and east of Sule Pagoda and the traffic circle, stretching northward to the Municipal building, jubilant Burmese gathered. They were in a celebratory mood. They had brought with them noise makers, cymbals, and whistles, and they blew them with gusto. The Karens, Anglos, and Indians in front of the church were in a more somber mood. In the past, the British could be depended upon to maintain order among the various ethnic groups; with the British gone, the ethnic minorities feared for the future. Peter and Jeremy had joined the throngs, standing midway between the church and the Burmese crowds. They had resumed contact with their long-time friend Tin Oo, who soon joined them. He was ecstatic with the outcome of the war and jubilant about the granting of independence.

The sound of bagpipes was heard, coming from two directions, east and west. As the troops assembled before the Municipal building, the British band played "God Save the King" and prepared to lower the Union Jack. There was a moment of silence, then four soldiers bearing the regimental colors stood at attention. The soldiers moved to the pole and ever so slowly lowered the Union Jack for the last time on Burma's soil. The bagpipes struck up again and sounded like a wail, signaling the end of one era and the beginning of a new, uncertain future. The colors were presented, and the regiment started the march down the road to the riverside.

As the flags were changed, the Karen and Kachin women wept silently, not so much because their protectors were leaving or because of any romance that they could have had in their dreams, but for their way of life. They feared Burman domination and feared for the future. The Anglos likewise worried. Would they be able to continue to wear western clothes, listen to American music, go to Saturday night dances, go to their clubs, get British and American magazines, and buy nylons at the only shop just north of here? The Indians worried about their ability to practice their religion freely. Would they be free to move around the country and able to obtain jobs?

These minority groups had tried to tell the British to wait until their people could be protected. They felt that independence was being rushed, without regard for the safety of all Burma's peoples. There were no strong institutions, and the wrong people were in power. There were no promises for minorities, their safety and equality, and no guarantees of autonomy.

Tin Oo turned to Peter and Jeremy. "We have finally won," he said, then turned somber. "Burma is for Burmans. It would behoove you to think about your future." Peter and Jeremy were stunned by his forthrightness. Tin Oo continued."I don't know where you should go, but in this country there will be no jobs for you. All the jobs will be given to the long-suffering Burmese." He continued. "I say this as your friend, based on what I hear and know."

In the days and weeks that followed, Peter and Jeremy continued to rebuild their lives and prepare for the future. With help from family and friends, they had resumed their studies and picked up odd jobs for support. But underlying everything was the worry that Tin Oo's warning would indeed materialize. They saw the signs and talked about action. They made the rounds of the embassies of England, Australia, and America and gathered information about their chances to leave before they were forced to leave. But neither man could bear to leave the country of their birth, their homes, and their friends. They could not imagine taking their families with them, and they could not imagine leaving their families behind. So they stayed on.

Tin Oo likewise planned for his future, but he did so by consulting his astrologer. "What should I do," he asked the man. "Should I leave the army and resume my civilian life?"

The astrologer took out his many celestial charts, and read Tin Oo's palms. He asked him the exact time of his birth, the day and the year in the Burmese calendar. He mumbled as he pored over the charts and looked at Tin Oo's palms once again. Then he looked gravely at Tin Oo and said, "Your future is entwined with that of your country, There will be an assassination of a very important person, and then the country will be plunged into war again. This time the war will rage between the people of Burma itself: Burman against Karen, Shan and Kachin."

Tin Oo was astonished by the perspicacity of the astrologer, who continued. "The country will go through a period of economic hardship and turmoil. You should seek a peaceful occupation," he whispered, "like medicine. Else you will be caught up in the maelstrom." Tin Oo paid the man and walked home in a daze. Would this really happen?

Even though at Independence the astrologers had predicted a golden era that would surpass the era of the most powerful kings of Burma, that golden era remained elusive. The transition from war to peace was not going well. Hostility to investors led them to take their capital and leave the country. Corruption and mismanagement had brought the economy to a slow descent and then into chaos. There was a segment of the population, particularly among the ethnic peoples, that longed for the old days and silently hoped for the return of colonial rule. The Burmese promises of equality were gradually eroding, proving illusory. As the years passed, the infrastructure decayed. No new rolling stock was added to the railways. Travel by train became stressful.

In his small room, Peter was deep in study when he heard a pistol shot. At first he thought it was random firing by bandits, unfortunately a frequent occurrence during these times. But the shot was quickly followed by Bren gun and machine-gun fire. It was continuous. As Peter rushed to the front door, he looked northward and saw red and orange tracers in the night sky. People rushed from their homes. As firing intensified, they began to shout in panic and flee toward the safety of Rangoon. Peter ducked back into the house and shouted to his family, "Run to the police station and take shelter there." But he stayed in the house to protect it. Fighting continued for days. It was the beginning of the ethnic warfare waged by the government of Burma in Rangoon against the Karens and other ethnic groups—warfare that would rage for decades.

At first only a trickle of people left. But after the ethnic wars broke out and as conditions and future prospects worsened, the trickle grew into a strong flow. First to leave were the professional and affluent people. Then came the middle class, including the Indians who owned so much real estate. They sold their property and left the country. The diaspora from the country spread to the far corners of the world.

Peter and Jeremy saw each other infrequently. When the radio announced "Burma for Burmans," though, Peter knew the time had come to look seriously at his options. He and Jeremy arranged to meet at the bar in the Orient café. Peter ordered a beer, Jeremy arrived shortly; and before long they were on their second beer. Peter steered the conversation to future plans. To his surprise, Jeremy announced, "I plan to emigrate. I will miss this country. It may not be friendly to us now, but it was once very good to us. We lived our childhood and youth here, and we fought for its freedom in a horrific war. It will be hard to leave and go to an uncertain world, not knowing what future awaits us. But I see no option."

"Will CeCi go with you?" Peter asked.

"Yes." Jeremy said. "She insists she will not go to England; her experiences during the war made her distrust the British. But she says she would go to Australia." He put down his beer and confided, "CeCi has so much to heal! She still has so much anger and angst. We don't know how we will be received in Australia, but we hope for the best. Mother is not sure she wants to go, but CeCi and I are not giving her any choice." Then Jeremy asked Peter, "What of you?"

"I too will leave, to pursue studies in the U.S or England or somewhere else. Many details have to be worked out, but I know that I must leave."

Jeremy nodded his head. "And soon," he added. "Do you remember Tin Oo's words at the Independence Day celebration? We didn't fully believe him then, but he was right."

The two men finished their beers and left the bar. They walked into the darkness of the night. Before they went their separate ways, they embraced. "Good luck to you, Jeremy," said Peter. "We have traveled a rocky road together and came through it in the end. We will endure this upheaval too."

Jeremy, who had always been so optimistic and had kept Peter's spirits up during their long retreat during the war, looked worried. "I am not sure how much more I can endure," he confessed. "I am getting worn down by all the worry. I guess that means that it is time to leave. I will miss you, my friend."

The two men embraced again, and as they went their separate ways, tears rolled down their cheeks. Memories of times past—joyful and fearsome—filled their minds as they prepared themselves for the next chapter in their lives.

PART VIII

The Legacy of War

Chapter 45
Post-War Return to Rangoon

He had been anxious about emigrating, knowing that it would not be easy. He knew that the Aussies called the city "Black Perth" because so many Asians had emigrated there. But Jeremy was dogged. He went to school there, worked hard, got married, and raised a family. All in all, he had done well. Now his thoughts turned to his childhood and the country of his childhood.

Peter, too, had left Burma with much sadness, particularly because his family was also leaving, but not with him. They scattered to different continents. He had always planned to return to Burma after his studies. But when he finished his studies, the door to his return was closed. He realized that there would be no opportunity for him in Burma. He could make a better life for himself in America. His life was busy with career and family, and he, like Jeremy, did well.

But memories came calling The war had haunted him these many years, and he had lain awake nights trying to make sense of what he had lived through and what his family was still living through. On a visit to London's Imperial War Museum, he had walked into the bookstore and, much to his surprise, found row upon row of books on the war. There was even a special Burma section, and he bought as many as he could carry in his suitcase. Reading the books, he was filled with nostalgia about his childhood and the searing experience of the war. He had kept in touch with events in southeast Asia and Burma; now he felt the need to go back, to visit all the places that were beginning to fade from his mind. He felt the need to relive his youth and revisit the places that the war had taken him. He wanted to renew old friendships, especially with Tin Oo and Jeremy.

But the news from Burma was not good. Peter wanted some on-the-ground intelligence about the wisdom of visiting and whether he would be welcome in the country. On a whim, he placed an advertisement in the *Perth Spectator* seeking the whereabouts of Jeremy Rawson and asking him to write to the specified address. Many months later, much to his surprise and delight, he received a letter from Jeremy, and the two men resumed their friendship through correspondence and then a phone call.

"What do you know about Burma these days, Jeremy?"

"Not much. I have no family there anymore."

"Do you ever hear from Tin Oo? Do you know where he is?

"No, Peter. I lost touch with him. He is probably a bigwig in the army by now; you know how passionate he was about Burma's independence!"

Finally, Peter got to the point. "Do you want to go back with me for a visit? I want to go, to see the city of our youth again. But I would feel better if you came with me. We share a lot of memories."

Jeremy agreed, and the two men set up a plan, agreeing to meet in Singapore. Peter checked into the new Shangri-La hotel. His suite was large and luxurious, about half the price he would pay in America. He had a full day in the city before Jeremy's evening arrival, so he toured the city. Almost all evidence of the war was obliterated. The city was undergoing a boom, with construction cranes dotting the skyline. The new buildings were very modern, concrete and glass skyscrapers nicely landscaped. The streets were clean, traffic was orderly, and public transportation was excellent. Shops were brimming with goods. At the same time, the city had preserved its heritage and its unique southeast Asian flavor. Roti stalls were open into the wee hours of the morning, families strolled along the waterfront until late at night, and the historic Raffles Hotel, built by the Sarkie brothers who had also built Rangoon's Strand Hotel, was glorious and thriving.

They had agreed to meet in the hotel bar, and Peter gave himself time to bathe in his luxurious bathroom before the meeting. He wondered how the years had treated Jeremy. When he spied Jeremy across the room, he smiled, then jumped up and waved. Jeremy looked the same, perhaps just a little heavier. The two men embraced and laughed, teasing one another at how they each had "filled out" and looked like prosperous men. Over many Tiger beers they spent the evening catching up with each other's lives. Then they turned to the present. The news from Rangoon was not good. There were reports of revolution and a bloody coup d'etat.

"Are you still game?" Peter asked.

"I didn't come all this way for nothing!" Jeremy exclaimed. "I'm ready. We've endured plenty of hardships; this will be nothing. It will be fun!"

The next morning they brought tickets to Bangkok and then booked onward on the weekly flight to Rangoon. This was the only way to get to Rangoon. As they landed in Bangkok, they were startled by the modernity of the place. The old dirt strip they had flown out of so many years ago had been replaced by new runways and a new terminal. The airport was crammed with people, the bays and runways full of airliners. Bangkok was bustling, from what they could see, although they only passed down the busy streets in a taxi from the airport to their hotel and then back again the next morning.

For their flight to Rangoon, they boarded an old propeller-driven plane that was clearly showing its age. Peter heard Burmese being spoken. He found it difficult to understand. He asked Jeremy, "what did they say? There are so few Burmese people in America that I've forgotten the language!"

Jeremy frowned. "I speak it occasionally, but not often. But they are just giving us the usual instructions about seat belts and lavatories." The two men settled in for the hour and a half flight to Rangoon. From his window seat, as the aircraft descended, Peter could see the lush greenery of Burma. He and Jeremy both craned their necks to see if they could identify any landmarks, excitedly pointing out to one another the Irrawaddy River and the spire of the Shwe Dagon Pagoda far in the distance.

The landing at Mingaladon Airport was bumpy. The runway still bore the scars of the war and was still just one runway. "It is so different from Singapore!" Jeremy observed. The plane stopped some distance from the terminal building, and the passengers deplaned, walking single file to the terminal, watched by armed guards.

The small old terminal looked drab, in need of a coat of paint. And it was chaotic. It took the baggage an hour to arrive. Then it took another hour while the hostile customs and security opened their suitcases and examined every article. Jeremy and Peter were subjected to extra questioning when the officials noted from their passports that they had been born in Burma. In addition, there was the laborious process of filling out forms, listing every item, including currency, they were bringing into the country and promising to present all items upon departure. The smell of staleness and decay was everywhere, and to top it all off, the toilets did not flush! By the time they emerged from the terminal, they were exhausted. "I'm glad we are staying at the Strand Hotel," Peter said wearily. "We need a little ambiance!"

But when their wheezing taxi dropped them off at the Strand, the two men were shocked. The once-storied hotel, which had rivaled the Raffles and Penang's E&O Hotel, was now shabby. The paint was peeling, the teak flooring had many pieces missing, and there were precious few furnishings in the lobby. The few wicker pieces that remained were broken down. The hotel staff was now all Burmese. Slowly they approached the reception desk and endured the laborious process of submitting their passports and all the papers they had filled out at the airport. The desk clerk kept peeking at them as thought they were a new species. "Bumanus returnus," whispered Peter to Jeremy. Finally the process was complete, and they went to their respective rooms. They agreed to meet at the lounge in the afternoon, after a nap.

The lounge was dark when Peter arrived, although the long teak bar with its brass footrail still glowed. "I'll have a whiskey and soda," he said to the bartender, who was dressed in an open Burmese shirt and paso.

"No whiskey or foreign drinks," the man said sadly. "Only warm Mandalay beer." He raised two fingers. "Two left."

"I'll take both," Peter said, "one for me and one for my friend who will join me." As the man placed the large warm brown bottles on the bar, Peter asked, "Do you have peanuts or chips?" The man disappeared and after ten minutes returned with some stale peanuts. "Chesu," said Peter, remembering the Burmese word for thanks. The man's eyes widened but he said nothing, nor did he move from his position behind the bar, directly in front of Peter. Despondently, Peter munched on the peanuts as he nursed his sour beer.

There were few people in the lounge, mostly men in leather jackets with their hands in the bulging pockets. They seemed to have nothing to do; they didn't even talk to one another. The bartender leaned forward, looked furtively at the leather-clad men, and then whispered, "MIS."

Peter peeked at the man closest to him. He did not pay any attention to Peter, other than to watch him out of the corner of his eye. When Jeremy joined Peter at the bar, the man glanced up and then struck his nonchalant pose once again. When Jeremy tasted the beer, he exploded. "Blimey! This is the sourest beer I've ever tasted!" Peter just laughed and suggested that they take a walk, then head onward to Tin Oo's house.

They left the bar and went out the side door, where they were accosted by half a dozen touts and taxi drivers. The young men said, "We will trade cigarettes and whiskey for kyats." Peter hastened away, but one of the young men followed. "I will give you kyats thirty for a dollar," he pleaded. The official exchange was six kyats to the dollar, and Peter was tempted, but with the memory of the MIS man back in the bar, he decided it was too risky. One persistent young man ran up to them and offered to buy Peter's watch. Finally the two returnees escaped the touts and began to walk away from the river, toward the city center.

They walked up to the old Fitch Square. "The Baptist church is still here!" Peter cried with happy memories. "But it sure could use a coat of paint." Then he noted that all the streets had been renamed.

On Barr Street there were outsized red signs hanging from buildings and scaffolds. Jeremy walked over to take a good look at one of them. He read aloud, "Thwart the conspiracy of the treasonous minions within the Myanmar Naing-Ngan and the traitorous cohorts abroad! Be vigilant against colonists trying to re-colonize the country and enslave the Burmese people again!"

Peter and Jeremy didn't know whether to laugh or cry. Jeremy turned to read another billboard. "Guard against the colonial designs, and support the Tatmadaw [army], guardian of the Burmese people," he read.

"Stop!" said Peter. "You'll make me laugh, and we'll get into trouble."

An old Indian man dressed in a singlet and *longyi* approached them. "Be wary of talking to anybody," he said to Peter in Hindi; "there are intelligence men and spies everywhere. The army is everywhere. Don't trust anybody."

Quickly sobered by the words, Peter pressed a kyat into the man's outstretched hand. Indeed, the further they walked, the more the men noticed how oppressive the city was. Nobody smiled. Everyone seemed preoccupied and tense. With the exception of the old Indian man, nobody approached them. In fact, passers-by seemed to go out of their way to avoid them.

"I don't know about you," Peter said, "but I cannot walk very far in this climate. How did we do it when we lived here?"

"You've gone soft," Jeremy teased. "You ought to come to Perth some day." Then he added, "But I guess I've gone soft myself. I'm ready to go back to the hotel for a good night's sleep."

"No objections," Peter responded. "But tomorrow, let's take a taxi! we can swing by my old house, then go visit Tin Oo."

"I hope he still lives in the same house," Jeremy worried.

The next morning they hailed a "taxi": a tiny, battered, blue pick-up truck. Two people could just squeeze into the tiny rear cab. It smelled of burning oil and belched thick acrid black smoke out of its broken tail pipe. Peter gave directions to the driver and agreed on a price.

"From what I can see," Jeremy observed, "this country has been left frozen in time. I suspect everyone lives exactly where they used to, and that their homes have not changed one whit."

Peter was lost in his own memories. He remembered playing with his red fire engine in front of the house; he remembered the pre-monsoon season when the mangoes were ripening and he and Jeremy would foray into the large Mogul compound to steal the juicy fruits; he smiled as he remembered playing hide-and-seek with the gardener and trying to catch fish from the monsoon streams without a net. But what he remembered most was the meadow behind the house. Some squatters had moved in before he had left the country, but the meadow had still been pristine.

When the taxi arrived at Peter's old house, however, he was shocked and repelled by the destruction of the meadow. There were many people milling about, most of them strangers who had come after the war, found open space, and filled it with huts. The house was still standing but was not well maintained and was showing its age. The Mogul Palace was in even worse shape. The well-kept gardens were now overgrown with weeds, and mold and mildew covered the walls.

"Do you want to stop?" asked Jeremy.

Peter shook his head numbly. "I wouldn't recognize anyone; they've all grown up or left. They would be strangers." He tapped the driver on the shoulder and gave him Tin Oo's address.

When they arrived at the address, they found Tin Oo sitting on the veranda, wearing a singlet and smoking a cheroot. As Peter and Jeremy climbed out of the taxi and walked to the veranda, only Tin Oo's eyes moved. He had aged beyond his years; he was thin, even underweight, and undernourished. His eyes were nervous and seemed glazed, his pupils dilated. Not until Peter and Jeremy got to the stairs did Tin Oo seem to recognize them. A pale smile flitted over his face, and he slowly rose to his feet.

Peter felt reserved in light of Tin Oo's demeanor, but Jeremy, with his inimitable exuberance, ran up the stairs to grasp Tin Oo's hand. "We finally came home," he said. "And you are the first person we wanted to see. You can't imagine how often I thought of you over these past years."

Tin Oo's eyes narrowed, then that pale smile appeared again. To Peter, it almost seemed wistful. Or was it envy?

"Here," Peter told him as he stretched out his hand. "I brought you some cigarettes. I remember how you always loved to smoke."

Tin Oo looked at the pack for several moments before he took it in his own hand. He took time to smell the tobacco, then thanked Peter profusely. He seemed preoccupied, constantly looking behind him and from side to side as though he was in a prison. His handshake had been tentative, and as he held the cigarettes, his hand trembled.

"Tine" [Sit down], he said, gesturing to nearby chairs. "Do you still remember Burmese?" They nodded in unison. Tin Oo called his daughter to bring some tea and then lit a cigarette, carefully putting his cheroot out and saving it for a later smoke. After a short silence, Tin Oo's pretty young daughter brought hot piping tea, which the men sipped slowly, Peter and Jeremy murmuring about how good the tea was, how they could not find such delicious tea where they now lived.

Finally Peter asked, "How are you? What did you do after Jeremy and I left the country?"

With some pride, Tin Oo explained, "I reached the rank of Colonel in the army. Now I am retired—well, made to retire. I still had a few years left, but I had to leave. I now live on a small pension." He was hesitant to continue. "I am sorry that I cannot offer you any food or drink. You can see for yourself that things are not what they used to be." He snorted. "I can be frank! Nobody cares about an old colonel. Besides, we are old friends." The warmth seemed to be returning, and Tin Oo seemed to be coming alive.

"Why did you retire?" asked Peter, "if you did not reach retirement age."

Tin Oo puffed on the cigarette a while, then turned his head and blew the smoke away from his visitors. He began. "I was so hopeful after the war. I thought that independence would bring back the glory that was once Burma, the old kingdom that my mother constantly told me about. I believed that my children's future would be better than my own life. But," he continued sadly, "you can see for yourself that things have not worked out that way."

Tin Oo sat silent for a moment and then continued. "Before the British left, they made sure that the armed forces would be well balanced, not dominated by Burmese. To that end, they promoted a Karen colonel to the rank of general and then appointed him to be chief of general staff for the army. The air force was commanded by an Anglo-Burmese squadron leader, and the navy also had minorities in the higher ranks. General Kyaw Khin, my old commander and the post-war commanding general of the army, seethed at this perceived slight to him. And while the politicians were busy fighting among themselves, he plotted to consolidate his power. About this time, 1949, the Karens rebelled, agitating for their autonomy. This was the excuse that Kyaw Khin had been waiting for. He purged all minorities from the senior ranks of the armed forces and consolidated his power by appointing his own cronies to vital positions in the military. Then he bided his time, waiting for the politicians to stumble, so that he could seize full power."

Once started, Tin Oo seemed unable to stem the words. "Soon the civil government did stumble; it was riven with dissent, and nobody knew where the power really lay. There were ethnic tensions. The Shans were threatening to secede, and soon the tensions and dislocations had an adverse effect on the economy. The price of rice dropped. More rice was being produced in Thailand and other countries than here; can you imagine that? General Kyaw Khin seized the opportunity. He claimed that only he could prevent the country from breaking up."

Tin Oo sat quietly as he remembered. "Kyaw Khin overthrew the elected government by a brutal coup. He deposed the elderly and re-spectable Shan president, killed his son, voided the constitution, and abrogated full powers to himself. When there were riots in the streets, I was commanded to shoot at the protesting civilians. When I came home that night, I could still see the blood and could hear the cries of pain. The people could not believe that their beloved soldiers would shoot at them."

He shook his head ruefully. "I knew about the upcoming 'coup,' and, like many officers, opposed it. I believed that we were going back on our promises to our ethnic peoples. I expressed my deep concern and skepticism of the plan to overthrow an elected government."

Peter and Jeremy sat quietly, letting Tin Oo finish his sad story. "I was sent away to the country on a spurious mission," he said simply. "Then I was retired." After a pause, Tin Oo backed up and told Jeremy and Peter all about the years since the coup.

"General Kyaw Khin promised to restore the country to its old glory. This, he promised, would be accomplished by throwing out the 'blood sucking foreigners' who had 'bled the country dry.' He blamed all the country's ills on its past colonial masters and moved to eradicate all vestiges of colonial rule. He seized all the assets of non-Burmese—and many Bur-mese as well. He nationalized the entire economy, appropriated all foreign capital, and banned all capitalist enterprises. Only by doing so and em-bracing socialism, he promised, would the Burmese people be able to restore the glory of Burma. But these actions sent foreign capital fleeing the country."

Trying to understand how it all went so horribly wrong, and how Kyaw Khin could act so brutally against his own people, Tin Oo returned to the war years. "Unfortunately, the Japanese took advantage of our inexperienced, very young, very angry, and very ambitious men; and used them for their ends. History has shown that legions and regiments are built on long traditions and on professionalism, and that troops actually fight more for the regiment than for the country or, surely, any politician. In their training, though, the Japanese ignored that lesson; they preyed on young Burmese men's passions. Interested in creating a puppet army to do their bidding, they taught us to be like them—cruel, fanatical, and willing to kill without thinking."

"So," Tin Oo continued, lighting yet another cigarette, "when the ambitious army leaders mounted their coup and took over the country, they were totally unfamiliar with administration. They were inept." Tin Oo went on. "The people believed Kyaw Khin's promises, though, made in frequent speeches." He gave a wry smile. "Like so many others, I believed him. I *wanted* to believe him. I wanted our country to be strong, to assert itself. But General Kyaw Khin did not revive the golden age of Burma; instead, he ended freedom for the country's people and sent the economy into a desperate decline." Tin Oo waved his arm in a vague arc. "Today I hear about the armies of Singapore, Malaya, and India; they are all in the barracks, and those countries are growing economically. But here, we have rice and nothing else."

Unlike in his youth, when he had been a taciturn young man, now the words poured from Tin Oo's lips in an unstoppable flow. "They were not really socialists; none of them actually studied Marx. No, they were arrogant, paranoid, and naive men who had an inflated opinion of their ability."

Tin Oo paused and looked around to make sure no one was listening. "We called the General 'No. 1'," he said. "He was mercurial, ill-tempered, and sometimes behaved like a mad man. We were afraid to say his name, as though by doing so we would conjure up his evil presence. He believed more in mysticism, numerology, and astrology than in idealism, common sense, or socialism. He would establish a new road, he said, 'to socialism, the movement that is sweeping Asia and the world.' And when his promised riches did not materialize and the people began to grumble, he said that more socialism was the answer: the 'Burmese Way to Socialism.' 'We will seize every business from the leeches who sucked our blood!' he would rant, 'and we will send them packing!' He claimed that the state would own everything and run things for the people's benefit, thereby removing the evil profit motive."

"Hah!" Tin Oo snorted, "And although he preached a puritan and spartan life for the people, he lived a far different life. His appetite for women was legendary. He escaped this drab country for Europe from time to time, allegedly to consult medical specialists in Austria, but everyone knew he would spend weeks in the many flesh pots of Europe. He would take with him fists full of rubies from the famed Mogok mines, to pay for favors."

Tin Oo fell silent, and neither Peter nor Jeremy knew what to say. They knew Tin Oo was not yet done with his story and did not want to make him clam up in any way. With a sigh, Tin Oo turned to Peter and asked, "Do you remember U Nyunt, on 8th Street? He had several daughters. The oldest was a beautiful and voluptuous young woman. The General saw her at the university pagoda and became instantly enamored of her. One night he took a company of his personal guards to surround the house on 8th Street. It went on all night: finally the father was forced to arrange a marriage, much against his best judgment. She became his fourth wife."

Tin Oo lowered his voice and again looked around to see if anyone might overhear him. "People who did not agree with him or opposed him were accused of being sub-human and were destroyed." Then his voice dropped to a whisper. "The country is in worse shape now than it was under the British."

Peter was shocked to hear such words coming from Tin Oo, who had been so sure that Burma's difficulties were due to the presence of the British and who had been such a supporter of Burma's independence from Britain.

"Now," Tin Oo observed bitterly, "The country is a mess. There are no medicines in the country, no cooking oil or kerosene; and prices rise astronomically each year. Yet they hold parades and give speeches. The rest of the world has moved on, and we still have not overcome the ravages of the war. The General used the occupation and British colonialism to justify his ruinous policy. It is clear that other colonial countries, like Singapore and Malaya, have overcome their colonial past and have built their economies; their people have a much better life than us. British colonialism may have been wrong, but it was not responsible for creating the bleak conditions we now live under. Remember when we had the best university in southeast Asia? University of Rangoon was one of the best schools in Southeast Asia, but now it is not considered much of a learning center. Britain does not even recognize its diploma any more."

Tin Oo was breathing heavily. Peter knew part of it was the cheroots and cigarettes that Tin Oo smoked incessantly. But he also suspected Tin Oo was getting himself worked up into a frenzy of anger, like he used to when he was young.

Now Tin Oo fairly spat his words into the air, heedless of who might be listening. "No. 1 proudly proclaimed that the victory over the British was his alone. But his rule was strewn with victims, especially the old upper- and middle-class. He pushed them out of the country or eliminated them. He did this in a cold, calculated, destructive manner. He continued his philandering ways, his many wives and mistresses, and his heedless pursuit of hedonism, even as the country sank into an economic morass. He enforced his despotic rule ruthlessly through spy agencies. Children were encouraged to spy on their parents. Those who showed even the slightest dissent were thrown into jail for long periods and tortured at the infamous Insein Jail. Now, his personality disorder emerged clearly: paranoia, super-stitious belief in black magic, numerology, and an increasing seclusion."

With that, Tin Oo was spent. He lit another cigarette and slumped in his chair. "So, now this once-vibrant and cosmopolitan city is a drab and dismal place. Men like me, who once believed in change for the better, have been sidelined or, worse, killed. People walk about the city as though in a fog, afraid of authority, afraid of one another. Probably afraid of the two of you, too," he concluded.

It was getting late. Peter and Jeremy hardly knew what to say. "Tin Oo," Peter tried, "Jeremy and I saw some of this coming years ago. We felt the pressure and chose to leave. So I think we understand somewhat what you have experienced. I'm only sorry that you were not able to make a change yourself, to build a better life elsewhere. You were always so energetic and hopeful. . . ."

"You always were the lucky ones," Tin Oo said sadly. "When I first began to see what was happening, I also thought about leaving, but was too afraid to leave, afraid that I would not be accepted elsewhere. Then, when things got worse, I was too afraid to leave because I feared my family would be punished. So I hung on, trying to be unobtrusive and get through the days. But it finally caught up with me. I guess it is my own fault." He looked forlornly into the distance and said no more. Jeremy and Peter each patted his shoulder and took their leave, knowing there was nothing that they could say or do to change the situation or Tin Oo's thoughts.

On the way back to the hotel, Peter turned to Jeremy. "There is something about his eyes. He looks wild at times. I wonder if he takes drugs, which are so easily available here."

Jeremy at first joked, "You mean wilder than usual?" Then he turned serious. "Yes, his eyes looked dilated, and once he started, it was as though he could not stop; as though he were possessed. And then, I was shocked to hear him admit that he had been wrong. He is now sad and bitter. I suppose our visit wasn't heartening for him, just a reminder of how bad things are."

"Join the army in crushing the enemies of the state!" proclaimed another billboard along the roadside. Peter could barely suppress his mirth and he nudged Jeremy.

"Who believes those slogans!?" Jeremy asked incredulously.

Back at the Strand, Peter suggested that they stop in at the bar for a drink. "Maybe they've gotten two new bottles of sour beer," he said hopefully. Indeed, they were lucky: cold Mandalay Beer! As they settled at a table, Peter shook his head. "It is a fantasy that the army have foisted on the people, that the Tatmadaw defeated not only the Japanese but the British also."

Jeremy agreed. "The BDF turned against the Japanese in March of 1945, after all the major battles had been won by the British-Indian Army. They never fought a single major battle." He warmed to the topic. "You remember the bloody battles! We were almost destroyed! And then it was at the all-important battle of Meiktila, with the old 17th Division in the lead, that the Japanese were driven from the town and scattered into a retreat."

"Now that the visit with Tin Oo is out of the way," he said more calmly, "let's return to being tourists. There is a tour desk next door, and we can take the obligatory tour—Pagan, Mandalay, Taungyi—in a week. Or, we can choose just one place and do it in two days."

"I'm not sure we have time for a week tour on top of the time we've spent here. Besides, I'm not sure I'm ready to revisit Mandalay or Maymyo," said Peter. "Why not go to Pagan and then come back to Rangoon?"

Jeremy agreed. "First thing tomorrow, let's book."

They started their trip with a visit to the great ruins at Pagan, the old Burmese kingdom. After a grueling tour of climbing hundred of steps up countless ancient pagodas, they headed up the last and biggest pagoda. From its summit, with their legs dangling from the parapet and the sun setting in the west, they surveyed in silence the blue hills of the Tangyi range and the glistening water of the Irrawaddy River. Peter was lost in memories of long ago. "I remember crossing that river at night," he reminisced. "Time seems to have not changed much here." No comment from Jeremy was required, and before it got too dark they climbed back down the steep steps to the horse-drawn tonga that would take them back to their bungalow.

First stop was at the bar for a warm Chinese beer. Then they walked along the dimly lit path to the bend of the river. There they saw a large number of now-stooped and greying Japanese men; they looked like they were searching for something. Peter and Jeremy were wary; years of fighting the Japanese cannot easily be erased. They glanced at one another and silently agreed to return to the bungalow.

That night, when they sat down to dinner in the communal dining room, they saw several large groups of Japanese at tables. Peter asked the waiter, "Who are those people?"

The waiter responded, "They are the friends and relatives of the Japanese soldiers who fought here and died, many, many years ago. They have come to pay respects and to collect any objects remaining, so that they can be buried at the Yakusuni shrine."

Jeremy turned to Peter. "Do you remember that balmy February night in 1945, when the Punjabis and Gurkhas crossed the Irrawaddy and caught the Japanese by surprise? It was a short but brutal battle. The Japanese died by the hundreds. . . ."

The two men finished their meal in silence and then sat outside on the small veranda, each lost in their thoughts and memories of the war. Jeremy broke the silence. "It was a historic time, a time of fear but also of adventure. We survived, although I still have nightmares about the retreat and the battles in Kohima."

"I have nightmares, too," Peter confessed, "about many things. And I agree that those experiences will live with us forever."

The next morning they were taken to the airport for the trip back to Rangoon. The propeller-driven plane droned on and on, and a few clouds could be seen in the distance. As Peter looked out his window, he noted that the starboard engine was sputtering. Immediately, the pilot's voice offered some comfort. "I shut down the engine, but there is no fear," he announced. "We can land on the one engine we have left." First there was a frenzied buzz of questions among the passengers, then silence. The ride was bumpy, but they managed to land safely.

Peter observed, "I feel as though I have been in a fight, not on a flight. Travel here is so very debilitating!"

"Soon we'll be back at the luxurious hotel," Jeremy teased him. "And you can have a cold shower of rust-colored water."

Peter laughed, and the two men rode companionably back to the hotel. As they entered, the doorman pulled Peter aside. "I have a message for you," he said quietly.

Peter looked at the message. "This is written in Burmese!" he said to the doorman. "And I cannot read Burmese anymore. Will you translate?"

The doorman looked around, read the note, and then gestured Peter into the shadows. "Your friend requests your presence," he read. "He is not well."

The next morning, Peter and Jeremy took a taxi to Tin Oo's house. As he had at their first visit, he sat alone in the veranda. He did not look good. He had a tremor, and his hands shook. His eyes were glazed and his pupils were wildly dilated. With difficulty, he said, "We were young once. We had our dreams and our hopes." He paused for breath. "I was impetuous once.

I believed, like so many, that Burma's problems were all due to foreigners. I believed that if they were all gone, we Burmese would be well off again, but I was wrong." Tin Oo swallowed with some difficulty. "I want you to know that I am happy for both of you. You look good. My karma was not good. Things did not turn out as well as I had anticipated." He stopped speaking, and his breathing became more labored. Peter again looked at Tin Oo's eyes, whose pupils were even more dilated than before. The twitch on the right side of his face worsened. Just as Peter arose to suggest that they take Tin Oo to a doctor, Tin Oo stopped breathing and keeled over and died. Whether it was a drug overdose or a massive coronary, they would never know. Whichever, it was a release from the fetters of his dismal life.

Shocked, Peter and Jeremy offered condolences to the family. They knew that they were perceived as outsiders, despite their friendship with Tin Oo years ago. Quietly they took their leave and, saddened, returned to the hotel.

The next day at the Scott (Bogyoke) Market, they brought trinkets for their families and remarked at the goods they had forgotten about: carved teak animals; packets of sesame seeds, peanuts, and fermented tea leaves for *lapet*; lacquer bowls and bangles. Peter was intrigued by the store that sold currency, coins, and stamps from the time of the Japanese occupation, buying some as mementos. "Amazing that I am paying money for money that was worthless then," he laughed. "And my children will probably never understand what it means to me. But it is like a door to another time."

That night would be their last night in Rangoon. Jeremy said, "Let's celebrate our being here and our leaving. Where can we go?"

"I remember a stall along the waterfront that served delicious giant river prawns," Peter offered. So the two men walked to the water. The long orange rays of the late afternoon sun added to the gravity of the day's events.

"At least we saw him again," Jeremy said suddenly. Peter knew of what Jeremy was speaking. "And I think he had made peace with us, with his life. It must have been a sad one, these past few years. We were just lucky to get out when we did."

"Yes," Peter agreed. "But we were too young then to know how important it is to keep in touch with old friends. Besides, I was never sure that Tin Oo wanted to stay in touch with us. I know he liked us, but I also thought he resented us, as 'lackeys of the British,' or whatever." He walked in silence for a few steps, then summed up, "It was good for us to come back here, good for us to see him again, good to re-live the past. Let's celebrate those facts."

The food stall was just ahead. It was busy, run by a Burmese mother and her pretty young daughter with *thanaka* [sandlewood paste] smeared on her cheeks as a sunscreen. The mother procured two stools, cleaned them, and motioned them to sit down. Peter turned to the young woman and said in Burmese, "Ba zoon hin she la" [will you bring prawn curry]? She nodded her head and scurried shyly away to the kitchen. "Some of the best river shrimp ever are here," Peter said. "As big as a dinner platter!" He pulled out small half-pint bottle of Scotch. "I got it at the diplomatic store the other day," he said in response to Jeremy's questioning look. The young girl brought two glasses, and Peter poured the scotch. "We have to drink without water or ice," he said. "But this will nonetheless be a celebration."

The sun was rapidly slipping under the horizon. "What is it like in the U.S.," Jeremy asked. "Do you have sunsets like this?" Not waiting for an answer, he continued. "We don't have cold weather in Perth like you describe," Jeremy said, "but still I have often been stricken with a nostalgia for our youth. Everything in Perth seems new and functional; the buildings do not have the grace and history of old Rangoon." He leaned forward and confided. "And not only that. Everywhere I go, I feel like I am the outsider, as though I don't belong. Do you feel that way in the U.S.?"

Peter nodded wearily. "Yes. It is constant. But I keep remembering the words of Cicero, 'I am neither an Athenian nor a Corinthian; I am a citizen of the world.' That's how I have come to think of myself, and how I cope."

Jeremy laughed. "Funny. We have nostalgia for something that no longer exists. The once-storied long bar at the Strand Hotel, where some of the most important writers of the empire sipped whiskey and gin, now is but a shadow of itself. The lounge is decrepit, lit only by a bare bulb hanging from the middle of the ceiling, and the bar is stocked only with bad local beer."

"I think often of the tumultuous times through which we lived," Peter admitted. "I sit awake nights, in the dark, and wonder what would have happened if we could have retreated to the Belin River and held the line there, if the stubborn British General had allowed the Chinese to come down to defend Toungoo. If they had held the line, could we have stopped or even blunted the Japanese offensive? Could the course of history have been different?"

Peter continued, "The Japanese still could have taken Rangoon by sea, but the containment would have prevented them from occupying all of Burma. If the British had retained control of most of Burma, especially North Burma, I think the course of history would indeed have been different. There would have been no rebel ethnic armies. There would not have been such a plethora of arms."

Jeremy looked deep into Peter's eyes and said, "And our lives and those of our families would have been different. The people of Burma, like Tin Oo, would have been spared the agony and misrule of the generals."

Peter poured more whiskey. "I must tell you, Jeremy, that before I came here, I was overcome with the desire to see the hills again. I had to contend with the usual Indian bureaucracy, which is unbelievably frustrating. But after much wrangling, I visited Kohima." Jeremy's eyes looked wistful.

"Mostly it is the same," Peter related, "except for the war memorial. I visited the Kohima War cemetery. It is in what is now called Nagaland, and I spent an afternoon walking the hallowed ground to see if I could recognize any names." Out of the corner of his eye, Peter saw the young girl bringing the large river prawns to the table; the aroma wafted to tease the taste buds. He took a swig of whiskey and continued. "At the end of the day, I walked to the main gate of the cemetery to take a second look. On a large granite wall plaque was etched an epigraph, "When you have gone home, tell them that we gave our all today, so that your tomorrows may be free."

Peter turned to Jeremy and said, "Tomorrow we leave all of this behind and return to our comfortable lives. But for all the people of Burma—Burmans, Kachins, Shans, Karens, Mons, and other ethnic groups—the agony continues."

Epilogue

Prior to World War II, the Minami Kikan was a clandestine organization. Its role was to gather intelligence for the forthcoming war. Toward that end it recruited Burmese youth, sprinted them out of the country for training, and then returned them to Burma to help the Japanese Imperial Army's invasion in 1941. Training of recruits was intense and took place in jungle training camps on islands in the South China Sea. Training techniques were ruthless and would stay with the future Tatmadaw. The goal of all this was two-fold. First was to gather information and intelligence and to ease the way for the Japanese to defeat the British Army. The second was more ominous: to foster conflict between the ethnic hill people and the majority Burman people, because the Karens, Kachins, and Chins who favored the British might present a problem for the Japanese Army.

Colonel Suzuki Keiji commanded the Minami Kikan and formed the future Burma Defense Army (BDA) in Bangkok on 26 December 1941. He was a mysterious figure. His rank in the Japanese Army Intelligence (Nakano School) was that of colonel. However, as the war began, he promoted himself to Major General and became commanding general of the BDA. The future General Aung San was third in the command structure, and Ne Win was seventeenth. Colonel Suzuki promised immediate independence to Burma upon capture of Moulmein, but when his group reached Moudon (south of Moulmein), Lieutenant General Takeuchi of the 55th division refused to honor this promise. Only after the defeat of the British Army at Rangoon did the Japanese government consider the issue of independence for Burma. The Burma Area commander and the Tokyo high command invited Dr. Ba Maw to head the Burma Independence Preparatory Committee. The Committee met on 8 May 1943 in Tokyo, and on 31 May 1943, the Imperial Conference granted "independence" to Burma. That lasted until 1945.

Ironically, the first major city to fall to the Japanese Army in 1942 was Moulmein, and it was also the city where, three years later, in May of 1945, the retreating and defeated Japanese forces surrendered to allied forces. Members of the Ba Maw government retreated to Moulmein together with the Japanese commanders. Tokyo dissolved the Minami Kikan in 1944. The formal surrender in Southeast Asia was signed in Singapore, in 1945. The instrument of surrender and related papers can be seen at the Fort Canning Museum, along with a diorama of the surrender. All the Allied generals who signed the formal surrender were British, with the exception of General Carriappa of the Indian Army. No representatives from Burma were present.

Of the Japanese generals, only General H. Kimura, the last commander of the Burma Area Army, was charged with war crimes in Burma. He was tried at the Tokyo War crimes trial, convicted, and hanged.

Burma was granted independence in January of 1948. The Burma Army was now re-formed with remnants of Burma Rifle battalions and members of the Burma Independence Army. To balance the leadership between Burmans and the ethnic groups, a Karen colonel (promoted to General), Smith Dun, was appointed as Chief of Staff of the Burma Army. The Burmese general Ne Win never accepted that insult, and he eventually engineered the ouster of Dun.

Prior to independence (at the Panglong Conference), the Kayah and Shan States (princely states) had secured the right to secede from the Union after ten years. At independence, the majority Burman government promised equality and autonomy to the ethnic peoples, but these promises were not kept. In January of 1949, the Karens revolted, and the KNDO (Karen National Defense Organization) attacked and seized Insein. In response, General Ne Win purged the army of all non-Burmans, retired Smith Dun, and appointed his own cronies in high positions. The Shan rulers exercised their option to secede, but Ne Win staged a coup d'état in 1962; the Tatmadaw occupied both the Kayah and Shan states and overthrew their governments. It then instituted a brutal occupation and a process of Burmanization, deeply resented by the ethnic peoples. All ethnic groups—who make up 35 per cent of the population and in whose lands all the country's mineral wealth (excluding rice and timber) resides—were persecuted and robbed of their wealth. No investments were made to improve the lot of the ethnic peoples.

The ethnic groups rejected this policy of domination and exploitation and took to armed rebellion. Today there are seventeen armed ethnic groups who continue to wage a guerilla war against the Tatmadaw. There can be no peace unless the persecution of all the peoples ceases.

A Note from the Author

Most of the characters and stories in this book are based on oral history from senior members of my family and neighbors and friends in Burma; some incidents remain fresh in my own memory.

I have visited the sites of battles, including the "Beach of Passionate Love" in Kota Baru in the northeast Malaysian state of Kelantan, where the invasion of southeast Asia started on 8 December 1941. A lone pillbox stands on the beach as a reminder of that war. After overrunning the defenders at Kota Baru, the Japanese crossed Malaya and headed on to conquer Singapore. I have also visited Singapore and various battlefields at the Thai-Burma border and in northern Burma.

The Singapore Museum contains many documents of the war, including the document of surrender of the Japanese. The Imperial War Museum in London contains a wealth of photos, and the National Archives in Kew contain recently released and hitherto secret documents from the British government and armed forces.

References that were also helpful to me include:

Burma: The Longest War, 1941–45, by Louis Allen (New York: St. Martin's Press, 1984)

Burma and General Ne Win, by U Maung Maung (London: Asia Publishing House, 1969)

Cruel and Vicious Repression of Myanmar Peoples by Imperialists and Fascists and the True Story about the Plunder of the Royal Jewels, by the Committee for Propaganda and Agitation to Intensify Patriotism, Media Group ([S.I.]: News and Periodicals Enterprise, 1991)

Indian Armed Forces in World War Two, by B. L. Raina (Combined Inter-Services Historical Section, India & Pakistan, 1953)

The Minami Organ, by Izumiya Tatsurō (Tokyo: Tokma Shoten, 1967)

The Reconquest of Burma, by S. N. Prasad, K. D. Bhargava, and P. N. Khera (Bombay: Combined Inter-Services Historical Section, India and Pakistan, 1958)

The War Against Japan, by S. Woodburn Kirby, 5 vols. (London: H.M.S.O., 1957–69)

Thanks are due to my wife Juleen for copyediting and to Josephine Samuel for proofreading; and to illustrators Dave Fischer and John Edwards for their enthusiasm and talent.

The illustration on the front cover depicts the blowing of the Sittang Bridge in 1942.